Beyond the Center of Grief

Cindy McIntyre

Disclaimers:

The information contained in this book is not intended
as a substitute for professional, medical, or emergency
treatment. Do not use this information to diagnose
or develop a treatment plan for a health problem
or disease without consulting a qualified medical
professional. For a life-threatening mood or situation,
please seek assistance immediately.

This book is a work of realistic fiction. Names,
characters, businesses, places, events, and incidents
are either the product of the author's imagination or
used in a fictitious manner. Any resemblance to actual
persons, dead or alive, is purely coincidental.

Cindy McIntyre's books may be ordered through
booksellers or by contacting IngramSpark.

Editor: Shirley Rash

FIRST EDITION, BOOK 2 in the Summerfort Grief
series

The cover image: Thebookcoverdesigner: Beti
Interior designer: Andrea Reider

E-book: 978-1-7349228-2-0
Softcover: 978-1-7349228-3-7

DEDICATION:

A hero is an ordinary individual who finds the strength to persevere and endure in spite of over-whelming obstacles. ~ Christopher Reeves, also known as Superman

To the unsung heroes surviving grief. And to those who sit beside them. Often, you're one and the same.

Chapter One

**Summerfort High School Christmas
Vacation 2019**

Dear Mom,

Time to confess a secret: I got way too intimate with a con man.

Now, I'm worried the con man won't leave me alone. Like a shadow, what if he follows me through the Christmas holidays again this year? Because I sense lurking. Behind doors, corners turned, stockings hung, even Christmas trees decorated; sometimes, he's dormant but waiting. He searches my calendar—every column and row—finding dates, information, and events to plot against me. That's his secret method. He knows when to chase me. But, in the end, even if I attempt to outsmart him, he always seems to win.

Faulting you, Mother, may come across harshly. But WTFDD? I mean, what-in-the-flippity-do-da should I do? I hate feeling guilty blaming you. Since blaming you adds layers of regret. So, today, that's where I'm stuck.

No one acts like they suspect a thing about the con man. Probably because I'm doing well for the most part. I attend group and OCD therapies at the Summerfort Grief Center. And I earned decent grades last semester. In addition, I continue to work part-time helping Dad with the animals in our backyard at Gardener's Vet Clinic. Plus, I'm still happily dating Hayden Tucker.

My holiday to-do list: dodging the con man. At the same time, I will make room in my heart for him, Hayden, and everyone else while designing everything to fit neatly into the December and January calendar months. Even if it means staring at **"Date with Gabby,"** which Dad tacked onto the agenda with a *permanent black* marker. It's baffling to look at since I've yet to decide whether Gabby warrants such permanence on our kitchen wall so close to the words "Merry Christmas" and "Happy New Year."

Merry Christmas! Hearing or seeing this holiday phrase causes my heart to flatten. My gut plummets, and my mind runs memory relay races. "Merry Christmas" translated into a million recollections and many hopeful visuals for this year. Do you think I can unlock more of the Christmas spirit—the warmth that radiated from my childhood—even without you, Mom? I want simple things that most other kids my age have but take for granted. The first thing I'd ask for is my mother, of course. Yes, I want a mother.

As a six-year-old child, I remember watching you and Dad dancing by the Christmas tree's twinkling lights, believing you were alone. After eight years, Mom, your Christmas stocking remains in the attic accumulating dust. But, since your death, Dad will share something odd with me for the first time. Dad marked his first romantic date with Miss Gabby Garcia on our calendar. She's who I sometimes call "Miss Happenstance" or "Sweetie." I'll gladly divulge snarky details later.

Marking time causes calendars to behave as emotional baggage to a motherless child. People can overlook the power a few columns, rows, and numbers hold. Written dates on the calendar perform a grid line circus. But I see a blur of small numerical reminders. Boxes and numbers stand at attention, just waiting to send warning signals out about a particular day—then their acrobatic stunts begin—those tricks of emotional ups and downs.

Death causes target dates or what others might call trigger days: a countdown without someone, days gone by, years lost, or the new months ahead. For some, like me, darkness tends to fall around the holidays. And I allow this con man to enter my life and take over my thinking.

My heart dreams. No matter how old I get, the little girl in me always wants her mommy at

Christmastime. Finding connections to you in all my gifts, no matter how minor the present might seem to others, causes a beautiful ache. While opening every holiday gift, I miss you, Mom.

Knowing I will hurt, I still manage to slip on my new clothes, such as the fuzzy sweaters and socks I ask for. In my mind, I twirl around for you, doing a bit of a fashion show. As I read the different cocoa flavors on the envelopes, I think about sharing the tower with you, sampling every one of them. The same holds for those giant boxes of cream-filled chocolates. You devoured the milk chocolates while I savored the dark, if I recall correctly. Now, I can only imagine you eating and laughing. While writing in this journal, I often giggle and cry at the same time. Like now, I'm thinking of how I'd love to tell you a quote from Hayden's favorite movie. If only we had the chance to savor candy together again, I would say, "Life is like a box of chocolate. You never know what you're gonna get."

After spritzing Love Spell perfume from the boxed set Hayden purchased me, we'd walk through the mist. Would you bombard me with a thousand questions? Like, asking about the significance of his gift since he bought something called Love Spell? Sometimes I wonder if our talks about him would end in arguments or laughter. Yet my heart and mind always wander. Every day I want the chance to know.

No matter what, I *can* envision us figuring life out enough to watch my new rom-com movies. We would lounge across my bed into the night, gorging on various popcorn flavors: cheese, caramel, butter, and kettle corn from the cute cat-and-dog Christmas tin. Of course, we would do much of this with a Bath and Body scented candle flickering with hints of peppermint or cinnamon.

We'd add glowing green face masks to the mix while wearing matching Rudolph the Reindeer flannel PJs like Dad and I did for an early Christmas when we gathered with Hayden and Gene. Maybe we'd challenge each other. "Don't crack a smile," you might have said, pointing at me. Losing our composure, we would double over, literally cracking up as the bits of clay crumbled from our faces.

Mother, I could teach you about the new Color Street nail art by applying them to your nails and toes. Made with natural polish, they remind me of tattoo stickers. It is fun nail art. The Color Street company chooses the best names using a play on words. While reading through a list, these sounded the catchiest: Capitol Hill, Glamsterdam, Russian Around, Best of Both Swirls, and Drop & Give Me Zen. One style retiring: light purple confetti Capitol Hill.

Seeing America compromising or celebrating as a whole right now made me laugh nervously.

Without going all political on you, our democracy scares me a bit. The nation appears so divided. Combining the two main political parties, blue Democrat and red Republican, would render an independent purple hue. Still, turning the overall concept into a confetti party might be pushing it, Mom. Dad appreciated my joke and understanding of political parties when I showed him. He said, "Order one of those. Maybe it will bring better luck and some hope for a happier America."

I trim my nails short to work with Dad in the vet clinic, and after reading the brochure, I learned I keep them filed in an oval shape. So, the long stiletto style appeared too cat scratch fever and frightening for my taste. How did you keep your nails? I wish I could remember these details. In most photographs, your hands do not appear on display.

On a side note, Gabby bought me some of these press-on nails for Christmas. It's strange to write this. Knowing my love of aqua, she found a Color Street item called Long Time No Sea. In layers of sparkling blues, the colors ranged from glacier to cobalt. Once Gabby saw my fingertips shimmering, she and I wiggled our matching nails giggling. At the same time, we took a nail photo together.

Soon after, my guts flip-flopped. So, I slipped to the bathroom to cry when Gabby left. Then, I reached into the medicine cabinet and grabbed the fingernail polish remover, ridding the painful evidence—Long Time No Sea, Gabby.

Studying the beautiful glitter and its name, I cannot help but remember the last birthday I planned with you. Waves of grief hit me. Again, I miss my mother—I flashback to your absence at my "Under the Sea" seventh birthday party.

Slumped on the toilet, using the sink as a headrest, I sobbed, squeaking out a whispered "I'm so sorry, Mama. This isn't cheating on you, is it?" Trying my best to understand life and this whole situation with Dad, I told myself I thought *you* would be okay with Dad dating Gabby. Rubbing my fingers until the guilty thoughts almost faded away hurt so badly. Gritting my teeth, I wiped my cheeks with the sleeve of my hoodie. You'll never answer, but I just keep on asking anyway. Would the idea of a woman showing your daughter kindness make you happy? Why should I even care, Mom? God, Gabby cannot stop calling people "sweetie!" And I do not appreciate that part of her. There, I said it. Maybe I will just keep focusing on that. Perhaps I only need you, Mom. So, Long Time No Sea, Gabby. Long Time No Sea.

When I looked into the bathroom mirror, ignoring my throbbing red fingers, I saw bits of you in me. Touching my copper hair reminded me of another trillion things I miss: not having my mom around to brush my hair. So, dreaming about a new ritual with my new Christmas accessories, such as you trying to braid my hair or even attempting to give me a unique updo. I even thought of how you might help me create a new curly style using my straightener. Then, after a movie marathon night of food and glammed-up fun in the morning, I can just make-believe Dad finds us asleep in my bed. Also, I'll pretend to recall every detail of your hands—even your preferred nail polish.

My heart continues beating in a rhythm going against time. Like a stopwatch, ticking fast, speeding seconds pass me by. Counting down the days, I stare at the calendar, wanting to rely on upcoming events. Looking back, I long for what could've been if my mom had survived. And glancing forward, I still dream of what will become of me without a mother.

Happy New Year! For me, these words represent another year without my mother. Another year to come and go without you. Each year, I count, and as I add the years, I feel like I am leaving more and more of you behind. Seeing square calendar reminders or dragging them everywhere gets painfully heavy. But, oh, the year 2020 soon looms ahead.

Living in a world with electronics, I'm always toting a calendar. I feel my cell quivering, even on silent or hidden in my purse or pocket. Every ping nudges me. PING. Look—incoming! Another type of warning bell announces another missed opportunity for a memorable moment; with my ringer on, hearing the electronic hints slam my heart.

Valentine's Day, Spring Break, Easter, Mother's Day, and Memorial Day follow, triggering those "Missing Mom" days. Holidays and special events have phrases that include pretty words to introduce them, such as "new," "happy," "merry," and "mother." Unfortunately, these words seem to deceive, putting a calendar box on overload, even though they are meant to encourage.

Easing some of the pain, I enjoy jazzing up the rows and columns, often covering up the dates with slivers of hope. With scrolling fonts, phrases, and photos, maybe I can pretty up the days, causing a pretty outcome to follow?

PING! **Alert: New Year's Eve. Two days before the Holiday Party with Hayden Tucker.** This sound makes me want to do "Jingle Bell Rock" I think. Hayden lives with his dad, Gene, who will host the party. I'm STALLING TO ANSWER since I do not know what to say in response to Hayden's recent text.

Hayden: How do you feel about seeing your dad on a date with Gabby this Christmas? I'll have to watch Dad with Lisa.

I'm copping out with mostly an emoji reply (non Gretchen), betting Hayden might see right through this technique. Rarely do I resort to using the "I don't know" emoji or the heart eyes, but I am freaking lost at what else to do. At least in the past, Hayden has enjoyed my awkward attempts at humor, calling them "sassy." So, maybe enough funny will glaze over the truth today?

Me: IDK about our dads. Hide and save some mistletoe just for us. XO.

After I hit send, I gulped. Then a massive sigh escaped me. I hated to sound dorky. Plus, writing something is problematic when trying to keep my feeling on the down-low. If my mother were here, my father would not require a dang holly jolly date with Miss Happenstance. And dealing with Gabby's nonstop "Oh, sweetie" talk all the time. Enough already. She's sweet, but I still get sick of hearing her say *sweetie*. So, what-the-flippity-do-da—WTFDD, get a new word, Gabby.

UGH! After all of Dad's affairs, he doesn't even think of choosing the best by picking Lisa. Gene got Lisa, not Dad. There, I said it. Well, I wrote it down, at least. In some regard, I think I'm jealous of Hayden because he has Lisa. So what? I like Lisa better than Gabby. If I said anything like this aloud, I'd hurt everyone involved, everyone I love. For now, I can only share this in my grief diary with my mom. How messed up am I? How nutty would I sound if I told people I wish my dad were dating my boyfriend's dad's girlfriend?

Breathing deeply, I press on because I should. And I must. What other choices do I have? My mother's gone. Every single holiday remains difficult. I remind myself to make the best of it. Here I go again. Sorry if you feel like all I do is complain. Writing with complete honesty takes a lot of guts. Getting out what hurts seems to help me heal. Sometimes I can't stop the pain.

As I look around my room—just as achy—I find paper versions of the calendar tacked up on my walls with pushpin announcements. Downstairs, in the kitchen, some calendars have magnets stuck to the back, which Doctor Gardener, a.k.a. "Dad," put on the refrigerator. Even those cause concern. Dad ordered them to advertise the family's vet business.

This morning, with a lopsided grin, Dad slapped the calendar into place on the side of the refrigerator after it failed to stick to the front of our stainless steel fridge. "What do you think of the new 2020 calendar, Gretchen?"

As I flipped through the months, I thought, no matter how many colorful gel pens go into decorating those days' "boxes," I can't control how any of those dates unfold. But if I try my best, I might turn each day into something beautiful or at least get some good moments. So, as the weeks pass, I hope they will fall into a good month, ultimately ending in a solid year.

Pointing at a scene, I stop to look up at Dad and smile. "A cute, fuzzy baby animal every month. I love it. Look at April's baby chicks. Good choice, Dad." He high-fived me as he left. I easily catch a glimpse of Dad from the kitchen window as he held the door open for his first patient, Sunny, who requires an annual checkup. Then, the yellow lab and Dad's white lab coat disappear through the door of Gardener's Vet Clinic.

Sometimes I earn money assisting Dad with feeding, watering, walking, and cleaning when we have a whole house of animals. Dad finally finished the paperwork for the grant you started. He requested and received a grant to add on a small animal shelter, allowing us to take emergency cases of rescue dogs and cats, which we adopt out to the community. Daydreaming (a pastime), I recall when Gene saved a group of kittens from one of his construction sites. Unknown to Hayden and me, he brought them to Dad. One of the cats became part of Hayden's surprise birthday gifts. Her silly name is Miss Spicy Boots Tucker. Hayden treats her like a queen with lots of playtimes, cuddling, and cat treats.

Later, sitting in the living room relaxing, I asked Dad, "What made you write the grant for the shelter?"

His droopy-dog eyes stared at me for a long minute before answering. "Well, in all honesty, your mom's the one who started writing the grant. She had the paperwork almost filled out right before she died. For a long time, I lacked the energy to fool with it. The actual writing didn't get finished for a couple of years. I missed the deadlines. Some days I got so angry I wanted to wad up every page and throw the papers against the wall." Dad heaved a sigh of relief. "Thankfully, I didn't give up."

Pulling a throw pillow into my lap, I frowned because I understood grief's tug-of-war on the heart. Not wanting to care but the drive to care told a different story because it doesn't let you stop. "I get that, Dad," I spoke just above a whisper. My fingernails dug deep into the fabric, focusing as my tear ducts itched and ached heavily. But I kept the welling tears from spilling.

The evening news droned on in the background as I sat on the couch, half-listening. Something called coronavirus keeps spreading, causing Dad's eyebrows to rise higher every night. China sounds a million miles away, but I vaguely understand science and how diseases work because I live with Dr. John Gardener. Also, I listen to Dad grumble under his breath, catching his edgy tone. "I'm not sure why American leaders aren't showing much concern for this. Too many Americans think they're untouchable." Viewing tragic world events together is a common occurrence now that you're gone—the "new normal," as people like to say. Finally, grabbing the remote off the coffee table, Dad hit mute. He paused, freezing the channel on the people in China wearing hazmat suits while cleaning their streets with a thick mist. For once, I considered myself lucky to live in the middle of nowhere, away from sad and scary scenes. Across the globe, I'm safe in my little Midwestern town of Summerfort, Missouri, where nothing much ever happens.

Dad said, "If you remember, my six-year-old daughter and I were devastated," without lifting his gaze from the TV or his finger off the button. "As a result, I often felt too inadequate to take care of you. But as you know, I hid my pain secretly. So, instead, I went about solving my problems with drinking and womanizing, which didn't work."

At the word "womanizing," my eyes instinctively rolled before I could even stop them. Because, WTFDD, where did this speech come from, Dad?

Dad paused, gripping the remote and gawking at the ceiling as if the sky might fall on us. "Gretchen, I think you should know I never cheated on your mom. I loved her." Tilting forward, Dad moved until he was in a semi-seated position. Dad sailed the TV remote through the air, where it landed in the side chair, freeing up his fingers to pinch the bridge of his nose. "In fact, I still do love her. My behaviors—" He hesitated before going on, gazing at me long enough to see if we had an understanding. "Those activities you learned about not long ago were never meant to hurt you, kid." Dad scratched his chin and whiskers.

You mean your sexcapades with Debbie—my enemy Lilly's mom?

Even though I was a tad miffed, I still leaned toward him. "I miss Mom, and I love her too. I know you didn't mean to hurt me. You're a pretty decent dad."

"Hmm. I'm trying, Gretchen. Do you realize I let you get away with things? Like wearing certain clothing?" he asked, with a slight chuckle.

Except for the time you made me wear hideous leggings with my Halloween ensemble, Dad! I did not look very Madonna, thank you very much.

I offered a nonchalant shrug, wondering where the conversation would trail next.

"Sometimes, I let you speak certain words out loud."

Like what? WTFDD—what-the-flippity-do-da? Shittle-sticks and effing when I'm thoroughly agitated?

I repeated my hand gesture, but Dad kept right on talking.

"And I let you go places and give you tons of freedom, which means I *trust* you, GG."

Where's this all going? I plucked at loose strings on the pillow while my gut tumbled, fearful of where Dad's message will lead. Feeling as though Dad dragged the word *trust* out too long, I thought maybe I was unaware that he no longer trusts me for some reason.

I released my grip on the pillow to use air quotes. "Are you trying to say you don't 'trust' me anymore? So, what did I supposedly do?" The pillow got shoved behind my back before I crossed my arms and legs.

Smirking, Dad said, "Ah, I'm about to make a point." Then, teasing me, Dad drifted toward me to pull my big toe. He pointed at me. "You're making a solid point for me."

Lifting one of his dark bushy eyebrows, Dad continued. "Just before you interrupted me, I was about to tell you that some of your attitudes and behaviors over the years wouldn't have slipped by Gwen so easily. I believe she would've had some serious come-to-Jesus meetings with you, kid. She'd have chewed your ass big time."

"No way!" Bursting into laughter, I fell onto the couch cushion. Hearing Dr. Gardener's cursing always amuses me because it's so unlike him. It's an odd sensation to laugh and cry simultaneously because the emotions of sadness and humor get so twisted up. We both lose control for a few moments.

I've said it before, but Dad reminds me of Superman's alter ego, the good-natured Clark Kent. Especially at night when he sits around wearing his black hipster glasses while watching the news. It's bizarre for me to think of him in this new Super-MAN role with women fawning over him. He had kept this side hidden from me for so long.

As we regained our breath, Dad leaned back on the couch, clearing his throat. "Your mom could be pigheaded like another copper beauty I know." He grinned at me. "You asked me earlier why I finished writing the grant your mother started. About three years ago, I completed the first grant. That allowed us to build and open the small shelter addition. I decided the timing seemed right to honor her memory, Gretchen. I wanted to give you a piece of your mom's legacy. She loved us, this home, our vet business, and our animals. Now, everywhere we look—those things she longed for—they surround us."

For a moment, I watched as his eyes grew glassy, surveying the perimeter and secret edges of our home. Finally, the corner of his mouth turned up in a hint of a grin. I saw and felt his love for my mother in his happy-sad expression.

Dad's hands lifted, fingers splayed. "We have all of it right here at home." Dad turned to me, wiping my cheeks, as he pulled me into a full hug. The slamming in my chest reminded me of each beat: hope, sadness, and pride. Then, in silence, he let me cry against his shoulder.

"Oh, and some of the grants are renewable. It's how I help pay for some of the extras around here. Want to help me write the next one?" Dad asked, squeezing me.

I bobbed my head yes, quietly against him.

Mom, did you enjoy small-town Summerfort, Missouri, living in this two-story house and building a veterinary business right in the backyard? And with Dad always around? Didn't he drive you freaking crazy? I guess I remember him using his "wooing" magic on you. I keep writing everything down from my memory bank since a six-year-old mind might forget things. Somedays, this compact bubble known as Summerfort, with a population of 5,000, fits me perfectly, like home. But other times, I think it might implode. This tiny bubble may pop at any time.

What's going to happen next?

Dad gave me one of the 2020 vet calendars for my room. I'm happy, staring into a nest of yellow fuzz inside a chicken coop. On the calendar, I adore all the pictures. However, the numbers below the photos trouble me. Dates on a calendar look like a nagging grid of possibilities. I see it as the land of opportunities versus the land of realities. Both options whirl around in my head, worrying me all the time. Like I asked before, what's going to happen next?

Mom, how will the next trek in life begin? Asking myself these types of questions happens often. Imagine a silver-and-aqua Christmas bag sparkling with sequins spelling out hope. Soft tissue paper resembling snow peeks out at the top to hide what's inside the gift. The crumpled tissue paper protects the hope that happiness might lurk inside. A bag sounds like a good representation of me: trying to paint a stunning picture on the outside with a pretty smile as I face down fear. Even though my mother's dead, I pretend I can handle anything. Trying to feel pretty and hopeful, I prepare to confront another Christmas.

Chapter One

Grief and the holidays *do not* mix because grief comes knocking at the door. BANG! BANG! BANG! Or ding-dong, ding-dong, ding-dong. Maybe grief and holidays gel too well? For the duration of every holiday event, surprise appearances never seem to end. Store displays, commercials, and kids at school talk on and on about plans. All of this brings up some kind of reminder.

Most of the time, I hoard issues. Keeping thoughts to myself because I've heard people say many rude, insensitive comments over the years. *"Aren't you done grieving? It's been years already. At least you still have your dad. Besides, aren't you glad your mom is now in a better place? Lucky you, you don't have an annoying mother bossing you around. It's funny to think of it, you have one less gift to buy, and your family saves money."*

Let's see: No, I'll never stop missing my mom, no matter how long it's been. No price tag could set a value on her life. Perhaps my mom's in a better place, but I can think of no better place for her than with me as her child. Over time, coping mechanisms improve, but the longing never truly disappears. Yes, I'm so thankful for Dad, but that doesn't diminish my love or my sorrow for my mom.

Some days, I feel a sense of peace thinking about such a beautiful place, like heaven. I'm hoping my mom's there, happy. Then the rages come. God gets to take on some blame. Why did He take my mother when I was only six years old? How do

I stop all these mixed-up feelings of awkwardness when dealing with these low days in life? Aloneness? Dread?

I want to stop the hurt and the anger, but I can't always do that. Besides, God's supposed to be full of love, understanding, and forgiveness. I'm human, so I spend time questioning. My faith's a bit cloudy with silver linings. When I look at my life in terms of blessings, I thank God when counting the gifts granted to me. Like the people and places I love —Dad, Hayden, Gene, Lisa, the Summerfort Grief Center, and my friends. As you can tell, I'm thoroughly confused. At the core, I feel God hasn't given up on me yet. I just need more time, proof, or hope—to deal with this topic. I don't know? I'm human—like I already said—a doubter of the whole wide world.

Sure, I would sometimes get aggravated if you were alive, bossing me around, Mother. And for the chance to stand beside you in real life, comparing your copper freckles and hair against mine—I'd give anything. I'd give anything to listen to your voice yelling, "Gretchen!"—for the chance to just fight back—to have the option of one whole second to tune you out. I want so badly to take for granted the word **MOM** will appear when I open a list of contacts on my phone. To access you by sending a message via text sounds magical. But first, what would you look like if I saw you on FaceTime? Second, what advice would you give? Third, would you please at least consider more visits in dreams? Finally, I'd give anything for another embrace.

Besides getting regular hugs from moms, I know these same people haven't experienced the lack of baking Christmas cookies or not seeing their mother sitting near the tree. This child felt hollow when told "make a Mother's Day card" at school, and it gutted me. I didn't always know what to say or do. Kids in the classroom ignored me or made fun of me for lacking a mother. Or because they enjoyed pointing out the tears pooling in my eyes as I held them back while forced to create a dang nonsense card for a dead mother. Commercials and store cards taught me how to turn MOM upside down to create WOW crafts. A new tradition of "WOW, I love you, Dad" cards became the norm on Mother's Day. Or I sent one to Aunt Jolene, who loves hearing WOW thoughts from me.

Showing weakness or crying after eight years causes an uproar. Take the population of Summerfort High School as a prime example. Remember, Hayden also lost his mom? So, he shed a few tears at the sports banquet they held near Mother's Day while the other guys gifted their mom roses. It seemed like a natural emotion. But because of it, some of the guys started calling him "Hayden Queer AF."

Mom, please know I'm not a complete downer or complainer. I have many positive aspects of my life to share with you. But, of course, I wish they could be with you in person. So, hang in there with me. Be proud of me. Please try to believe in me.

Let's switch gears for some of those positives.

Before the Summerfort Grief Center closed for Christmas vacation, I had an appointment with Dr. Han. Lisa Marks caught me on the way out, plunking a rough draft of chapter one of *Love at the Center of Grief* in my palm that day. Lisa's index finger tapped the title page. "Gretchen, here's my part of our project."

"I'm so excited, Lisa."

"Gretchen, remember, it's only a first draft. Please, read through all the pages before giving me your thoughts."

Sensing what's about to happen, I watched Lisa's hand slip from the papers. At the bend of her arm, she grabbed ahold of her elbow, pausing for a second. Again, on the move, her hand traveled. Her palm finally arrived at its routine and soothing place—near her heart. *Such typical Lisa.* A twitch played at the corner of my mouth as I held back a grin. Considering how often I catch sight of Lisa in this pose, I cannot help but crack a smile. Lisa always appeared ready, like she would recite the Pledge of Allegiance with the utmost sincerity.

Lisa and I bonded quickly. During my first night at the Summerfort Grief Center, I remember barely getting the following words out: "My name's Gretchen Grace Gardener. I'm six years old. My mom had a stroke and died."

Chapter One

"Welcome, Gretchen. My mom died from stroke complications, too," Lisa had said, glancing at me with *her* gesture. All those years ago, she served as the group facilitator.

I always felt somewhat "normal" inside her little group because other kids, like me, missed loved ones too. Grief counseling with others meant learning to introduce yourself and talk about who you lost while listening to others tell stories to help you cope.

In a zippy tone, Lisa continued. "Now, I understand vulnerability from your point of view and Hayden's. After my short bits, the remaining chapters of *Love at the Center of Grief* focus on the stories of you and Hayden. Real stories are full of honest and raw emotions about losing your mothers so young. Plus, your struggles at navigating life because of Grief. Gretchen, we explored your OCD and bullying issues, plus Hayden's school bullying. So far, we have talked about addressing the question 'Can the heart accept love after loss?'"

I nodded.

Lisa took a deep breath. "Oh, and your home life with widower fathers, school, love—and grief activities you found helpful."

Hugging the papers to me, I said, "Lisa, I know Hayden's looking forward to seeing the cover ideas and interior printouts as much as I am. But first, I know we have a lot of time, research, and work ahead of us." The words leave my mouth, but I felt them so deep in my bones, causing my heart to flutter. A huge part of me wanted to do a cartwheel and squeal as my eyes misted. Working on this project with Lisa and Hayden and achieving this goal overwhelms me.

Mom, I hope you will be proud of me and how hard I have worked on this project so far.

Lisa said, "I appreciate your willingness to include journal entries for the book. Both you and Hayden offered some insightful and personal stuff. In that level of realness, I believe we will help others most. Be patient. The book may take a long time to come together, but in the end, it will be worthwhile."

Maybe Lisa holds a hand to her heart to monitor the beats? Plunk-plunk-plunk—the palpitations in my chest went to hypersonic speed. On overdrive, my soul tried to keep up with my brain. *So much of this book's about you, Mom.* Still clutching Lisa's chapter, my hands were aware of every beat, every pulse. I am alive. "All these emotions leave a person feeling very exposed."

"Gretchen, I couldn't agree more, especially since I wrote that." Lisa pointed to her work, smiling. "It includes a few personal details, plus background information about the Summerfort Grief Center." Lisa lets out a nervous-sounding sigh. "Well, Gretchen, there's my soul on paper. Did you and Hayden feel like that?"

As I nodded, Lisa pulled me into a side-hug before saying good-bye, making plans to see each other soon at Tuckers' holiday gathering.

Back home, I lounged across my bed to read the draft of Lisa's story and how we *all* began with *Love at the Center of Grief*.

Eight years ago, Hayden Oliver Tucker entered my world.

Chapter Two

December 2019

Dear Mom,

Somebody's holly jolly balls just might end up getting decked this Christmas. Winning the first-place medal on my possible jolly list belongs to your oldest son Cole, who's acting stranger by the day. Falling in love with Ariana must've caused the stick lodged up his butt so tightly to slip from the jerk's ass. Cole has decided to pop up in my life in unexpected and confusing ways. After years of near radio silence, my big brother wants to participate in Throwback Thursday's social media ritual. Cole has sent pictures in text messages for the last couple of weeks, starting with the Thursday after Thanksgiving. Each one leaves me puzzled as to the why of it all. At the same time, I hate to admit it, but I look forward to getting them.

The first caption: **Ariana suggested I get in on the whole TBT with these pics. At Christmastime, we can talk about the funny backstory.**

An array of photos of a family BBQ happening in our backyard appeared on my phone screen.

A spread of blankets littered the yard. Discarded paper plates stacked with leftovers and mini corn on the cob remnants sat nearby. Three smiling boys piled on top of Dad, tackling him in various poses as they played football. Judging by the grins on our faces, Mom, I knew you were behind the camera lens *alive* and smiling back at us that day, even if I can't remember. I blew up the snapshots using my fingers until the pixels distorted everything, hoping to catch a glimpse of you on any reflective surface. But after scrolling and searching my entire screen, you existed nowhere. Not even a hint of you resided inside the intensity of Dad's gaze as he winked in your direction. Beneath one of the trees, you must have propped yourself at an odd angle to capture the photo. Inside the crook of his arm, Dad grasped his sons, sprawled on the ground while holding up the football in a victorious gesture with the other hand.

I loved the joy I saw on everyone's faces in the photo, but I wish you had made an appearance. In a roundabout way, you were there. As I believe, you're just on the outskirts looking in. I hate this part of my life. For this exact reason, I somewhat hate these photos too. When looking back at my earlier years, I struggle to recall moments. Studying photos, I realize I'm also on the outskirts looking in, hoping to find my way back.

It's a mix of feelings—of wanting to remain connected to my family but knowing you're never again going to be our mother. Wait. That's not true. You'll never stop being Mom. You'll never get an opportunity to *physically act as our mother*. So, what's the point I'm trying to make? This family can never be the same. Nor can it ever be recreated. Whatever charade Cole has going on or whatever he thinks he's doing, I appreciate the gesture. Or at least I want to. But I also get mad at myself for my anger toward him because I don't understand his intentions or what outcome awaits.

Fear, jumbled with confusion, settles in late at night. When I should sleep, I overthink. Don't get me wrong—I like hearing from Cole. Long before now, I wish I had some of these photos and this family history and brotherly connection. But this part of me gets scared of enjoying this new feeling too much. I worry. Sometimes, I like having my big brother back in my life too much. I want to text him in the middle of the night. *Why now, Cole? What's up with this TBT? When will you bail on me again? Do you really care?*

I reread Cole's messages again and replayed the words in my mind. *What's wrong?*

Is Cole sick? Dad? Drew? I get this sense Cole knows something, but he's not talking. Are he and

Dad in on a secret I don't know anything about? Did they or will they recruit Drew? My fists ache to punch something. But, again, I am overthinking. Or am I? The "C" word comes flooding into my mind. Lumps clog my throat. I drown in sadness and worry. Has the "C" word entered our lives again? Men can't die from uterine cancer. I try soothing and reminding myself of this. My God, though, cancer's genetic.

Please, God, I can't deal with these obsessive thoughts about one of them dying as you did, Mom. If Dad's ill and things go wrong, what will happen to me? Did you two consider this scenario? And did you and Dad ever make a plan? Living with Cole makes me sound like his burden. I can't. Moving to Florida to your parent's home seems all sorts of awkward. My grandparents hardly even know me. And Drew, if you put the two of us together, all I see in my mind is an endless bachelor pad. Or a funhouse of wonky mirrors like in a house of horrors filled with loud-ass laughter, piles of clothes, and dirty dishes (literally and figuratively). Since I'm thinking of Drew's *outgoing personality* with hot girls, I don't even know if the term "dish" is derogatory, Mom. Maybe not because we call people snacks now. Dish, dime, hottie, snack, or doll—I guess they all mean about the same. Whatever anyone wants to call it, Gretchen's got them all beat.

Anyway, I'm watching. Cole and Dad keep circling me, bonding with me as if preparing me. For

God's sake, for what? I'm bracing myself, waiting for Drew's enlistment into their scam. This time, I'm older and more demanding. Cole, Dad, or Drew—one of them plans to gently break horrific news to me. I want to know what's going on. Yet I want to remain blissfully unaware and happy. Because, in a way, I'm the baby of this family again, a position that I believe went unfilled for years. For once, I feel like my life's getting better. Why can't I just have my little family reunion and let it remain intact for a while?

Pulling out my phone, I glared once more at the most recent reasons why—again, studying Cole's words. For this TBT round, he included a group text, adding Dad and Drew. Staring at the young faces in the attachment, I realized I love those people, but I don't remember them. At least not from the timeframe the photo occurred.

Cole: Ariana prodded me to share this TBT of Christmas past. Let's share more of the story at Christmas.

I see you, my mother, holding me in an embrace near the Christmas tree before my tears flowed.

Dad: What happened to my sweet, innocent little boys? Lol. What a good pic. Cole.

Drew: Dad, we turned into our father. Lol. BTW, you rocked as a photographer.

My blurry eyes scanned the scene. I recognized the house some, noticing the wallpaper I never remembered (thankfully). As Dad remodeled over the years, so much changed. Mom, I sometimes forget the timeline of events. I don't know. Did you see the new drywall and the paint colors in each room? We keep the Christmas tree in the same corner of the den. Your boys now stand so much taller than in the picture. I keep scanning for clues. Plus, we'll rest against pale gray-blue walls instead of floral-patterned paper. Again, I look over and over at another memory I shared with my mom. But sadly, the connection with my mom happens only through a photo: a pile of Christmas gifts, two boys, and a toddler hugging his mother under the tree. I was at a loss for a reply, so I simply thanked Cole.

Later, I lounged in bed, longing to ask for more information and photos. Pulling up Cole's number on the phone, I backed out like a chickenshit and never hit the call button. Why? I wanted to talk. Knowing I had to wait until Christmas to hear the stories felt torturous because I required answers to many questions. I didn't want to wait. Before Christmas, I needed to know things. Didn't I deserve to know something? Anything? The conversation I wished for went inside my head while clutching my cell.

I got left hanging since Mom died, ass-jerk. Do you think you can be bothered to speak to me about her? After all, as the oldest child, you stored or stole all of Mom's pictures and memories. Cole, you had eighteen years with Mom to build reliable memories, and Drew got a bunch too. I got a measly six. None of this is effing fair. So, why did I have to find her body? Who tried to help me remember my childhood when the only year of her life I vividly recall is that which revolves around her dying? Is this your attempt to fix the past, Mr. TBT? What's up with your change in attitude? You said Ariana nagged you to start TBT. Is she trying to be our savior? If so, why?

Who would I ask anyway if I wanted answers about what's going on behind these TBT messages? Dad's so up in my business now with his undying love for me. Some days he suffocates the crap out of me with his dad jokes and extra weirdness. Do I hold him accountable too? Is it my responsibility to ask Dad if I can see more family photos besides those hanging on the wall? Where the hell does Dad keep them hidden? For the most part, I like where Dad and I stand and don't want to fight or have something stupid get between us if this TBT turns out legit. What if there's nothing menacing backing this?

Speaking of menacing, let's chat about Dennis the Menace Drew. Get this. He claims only to love one hot girl now. LOL. Knowing this doesn't change my "dish" and bachelor pad thoughts about him. Drew settling down with one girl cracks me the hell up. Of all your boys, I'm surprised the outgoing Drew's man parts remain intact, or they haven't fallen off from disease. Sorry, Ma. That's crude to say about my brother. I'd say it to his face, and I might over Christmas vacation. "Deck the Halls" could get a new meaning. Yep, I'm just sayin'.

Have I written much about Ava before? It's challenging to keep up with the names of Drew's lovers since they change frequently. Anyway, Drew says, "Ava's 'the one,' so I'm bringing her home to Summerfort for Christmas." When he called Dad the other day, Dad put Drew on speaker, so I could say hi, and then Drew made sure to add, "Hey, please help me show Ava a good time over Christmas."

As Dad spoke, he chuckled, telling Drew, "I've been working on a plan that's going to be F-U-N for everybody." The spelling of fun made me moan. Plus, the hair on the back of my neck stood at attention. What the heck does Dad even mean? Has Dad always been this weird?

Mom, this family and this household you created turned into a mess of testosterone. Every one of them—Dad, Cole, and Drew—equals a bunch of strangeness. As a mother, I'm sure you understand what I mean. I imagine Drew shouting his threatening "I'm going to beat your ass." Or I may call someone, probably Cole, an ass-jerk. Because of this, Cole may again turn to stone and sit like a statue. Dad's reaction to us remains an F-U-N mystery.

When should I ask the questions that matter? Who do I even ask? Should I say, "Happy Holidays! Who's dying?" Maybe I will wait for the night Dad plans to bring his new lover, my old grief mom, Lisa, into the fold to start a Christmas brawl by speaking out. Do you like how I dropped this little nugget of information about Dad's love life? Seeing Dad excited about the holidays, I think, makes me happy. Lisa treats me like a son. Well, because I've heard her boss me around for years with her "Hayden this-and-that." I've grown up getting used to her. Over the years, I've written about Lisa and how caring she has become. When overwhelmed, she makes this hand-over-her-heart gesture. Life's full of weirdness and confusion, and Lisa sure goes on my list. It's a mix of love and hate, and there are so many layers I call hints of toleration in the in-between.

If my girlfriend Gretchen hadn't copped a little attitude, I'd have asked her for advice. She worries me. Sometimes Gretch seems too blah. Her new motto appears to be "Nothing matters today." This behavior doesn't apply so much toward me but at school, mostly. She's a whole lot fewer shit-tle-sticks and flippity-do-da, and I miss hearing her ramble these catchphrases. If I described her behavior, I'd say she's acting like she's in shock or something. Looking at her, I notice a scared, blank, and unanimated appearance she's never had before Thomas Sharp and his BS happened. She still brings up Lilly, and when I ask if she wants to talk about things, she shuts me down. Gretchen spouted off at me, "I don't want to talk about them. They're a waste of time."

She's right to an extent, but I don't want Gretchen to shut me out. Nor do I wish to see her shut down emotionally and have her OCD flare up again. One day, I got a bit aggravated, and I almost asked, "Gretchen, am I a waste of your time too?" She just seemed too sad, and I couldn't start a fight. I love her so much, but I miss the feisty girl who fought back with fire in her eyes. I don't think her behaviors are to the point of telling an adult. John keeps her so busy at the vet clinic. It helps him to spy on her, I think.

I know Gretch isn't a fan of Gabby, but I believe Gabby has her back and would do anything to help Gretchen or John. I guess I need to see Gabby through Gretchen's eyes as the new woman in her dad's life. Summerfort High School hired her as our counselor, making any problem Gretchen might battle at school feel even more awkward. I can relate to this since Lisa counseled me before, and now Dad's *canoodling* her. I picked this word on purpose because it has the *noodle* in it, which has some weird history we can get into another time. Not a huge issue, but I have no words for it yet.

Let's get back to Gabby. Knowing Gabby outside of school gives Gretchen an edge on the Thomas Sharp bullying front. Anytime she needs backup, Gabby, an adult ally on staff, will be there.

So, when the timing's right, I'm going to drop this bomb on Gretchen.

In contrast, I fear our grief group might crumble if I don't open up anymore around Lisa. I wonder if Gretchen gets that? Does Lisa? Dad? I love all of them, but we have such intertwined lives. It's kind of a cursed blessing. In a lot of ways, it's like having this tight-knit, annoying, loving family again—like when you were alive, Mom.

Just the other day, I had a concern, though. When we have problems, who are we supposed to "complain" to about each other? Can I still hang out with Gretchen, Miles, Kelsey, and Mia while Lisa overhears personal things at the grief center? Tag. You're it, Mom. I guess I'll blast every one of them on the pages of my grief journal. Maybe that's what I'm doing now. LOL.

Getting back to Gabby—she says "sweetie" too much when addressing almost anyone. So, on this front, I tend to agree with Gretchen. Listening to someone use the same term of endearment gets annoying. However, just because someone says a word repeatedly isn't a solid reason to dislike them. Gretchen and I agreed to see her kindness. I also pointed out Gabby's positive attitude toward animals, and we decided that equals a lot of bonus points. She brings her dog, Poco, to my games and cheers for me while sitting by Dad and the gang. Finding out Dr. John and Dad ended up in relationships with Gabby and Lisa, both counselors, seems laugh-out-loud funny.

Of all the adults (Dad, Lisa, John, and Gabby), I'd say Gabby's changed the least since joining forces with us. She's sort of the *new Lisa*. By this, I mean I recognize Gabby as goofy but kind and caring. Like Lisa *used to be*—Gabby's our latest adult mystery.

As a group, we sound like a bunch of misfits.

.

Chapter Three

Still Christmas Break

Dear Mom,

First-semester grades came out. Since Summerfort High School doesn't have a weighted GPA system, I will keep my 4.0. Mr. Wright's math class challenged me, but I ended up with a high A minus. Numbers tend to freak me out. So, why do I waste time second-guessing math formulas? It's maybe because plugging and plopping numbers next to funny-looking symbols requires trust.

I don't always know when to believe in matters involving numbers. In real life, I know mathematical methods fight against time. Maybe, I remember standing helplessly as a child at the hospital. While waiting and hoping, I watched the world fly by. At the same time, the whole world fell still.

"Doctor Gardener, we will continue trying every solution we know to try," promised the doctor behind his mask. He showed Dad a clipboard as he spoke, pointing out the scratches from every solution and the medical formulas they had tried without success.

Aren't they able to save my mommy? I wished to ask my dad, but dread hit me. I stared at Dad as he became overwhelmed, his eyes welling with so many tears he couldn't stop a couple of them from free-falling.

After handing the clipboard back to the doctor, Dad scooped my six-year-old body into his arms as he choked out, "Thank you. Gretchen and I need one of your miracles to work."

Sometimes, math battles against time. Failure occurs. Finding a solution may or may not come. Dangling problems remain. When you're too young to understand everything, you still pick up on the tiniest vibes while listening as someone's life span gets explained to you. In those minor percentages, opinions about math change. Results roll in as percentages, positives, and negatives. A positive or negative test can be a cause for celebration and, at other times, cause heartbreak. Life and death sentences happen every day.

"I'm so sorry, Doctor Gardener and Gretchen, we tried everything."

Everything can come to nothing. Living inside of nothingness, you survive as a fraction of yourself.

Until one day, piece after piece, you build enough hope to begin feeling whole.

Miss Tweed emailed about my recent English essay: "You've earned an A for finding a creative way to address the rough draft assignment. Gretchen, you describe mixed emotions with a lot of depth." Before I share my essay, let me tell you about the text I sent to Hayden.

Me: Hayden—I got way too intimate with a con man. Most people might even call him a hitman, which sounds quite fitting. But, since I'm confiding secrets, here's another: this guy should've come with a warning label.

Hayden: WTH? Me? I'm confused. I need to talk to you ASAP!

Me: Sorry, don't get mad. Essay for English—I thought you'd guess. Let's FaceTime.

Hayden: Well, Holy Crap! WTFDD. That's one hell of a freakin' hook. Okay. FaceTime. Read it to me while my heart stops pounding out of my dang chest. LOL!

I giggled at the fact Hayden used three poop emojis after texting, "Holy Crap!" Then, wasting no time, he initiated the call. After answering, I apologized. Then I asked, "Want me to start from the heart attack beginning?" with a giggle as I zoned in on his gray-blue eyes. Hayden's smile grew so toothy that both the sliver gap in his front teeth and the dimple appeared.

Pulling a Lisa, he placed a hand over his heart. "Yes, because now I'm prepared. I think I've recovered enough," he said, chuckling. "So far, it's intriguing."

"Yay! Thanks. Okay, well, here goes nothing:

I got way too intimate with a con man. Most people might even call him a hitman, which sounds quite fitting. But, since I'm confiding secrets, here's another: this guy should've come with a warning label. Like a superhero, he possesses strengths. But only his level of ability stretches into strange universal powers. Because after just one skillful visit, he can jump inside a family calendar, rearranging their universe forever."

Hayden cleared his throat. "Sorry to interrupt you. Your essay sounds great. Did this come from Tweed's English class about those journal assignments on the heroes, strength, and power series we could do in any order we chose?"

"Yeah. Remember, you read some of your rough drafts to me about your dad? I told you I loved it. So, I said I'd share mine with you when I finished the last assignment. Did you ever let Gene see what you wrote? He'd be *very* proud of you. It's touching."

Hayden rubbed the back of his neck. "Nope. Not happening. That's not Dad's thing—"

"Wrong. It is, too, Gene's thing."

He scoffed. "Well, anyway, Miss Tweed emailed today with grades, asking my permission to enter my essay into some local contest when I finish the final draft. So, thankfully, we have until after Christmas to edit them and turn in the final copy."

My hands weren't free to clap, so I tossed my head back and forth. Then, getting my face too close to the phone, I rambled, "Wow. What contest? What did you say? How exciting! I'm so happy. And I'm proud of you."

"Jeez, Gretch. Chill." He said, laughing at my enthusiasm. "Thanks. Basically, I gave her a quick hey." Hayden put a nonchalant hand in the air. "I think I mainly said okay. I thought, 'whatever' because I know I'll never win anything."

After rolling my eyes and sticking my tongue out, I told him, "Don't be so sure, Tucker. Your writing's top-notch. Plus, I think it's heartfelt. Look up the name of the dang contest, so you can tell me later."

He stuck his tongue back out at me, then smiled. "Later. Back to you. Now, read, please."

Feeling my pulse race a bit, I sipped from my glass of water. Realizing this section's not a "let's read aloud for fun," I adjusted my phone, so I was semi-hidden behind my words, but Hayden still knew I was there. Before opening my mouth, I sense myself turning into a throat-clogging mess. Blinking, I held back tears. My paper shook.

"Gretchen, you alright? Take a deep breath, okay."

Feeling like a blob, I nodded like a bobblehead.

"Good. Remember, I'm not going to hurt you. But, hey, do you want to stop reading?"

I shook my head.

"I want to listen. Start when you're ready." Then, for a long minute, Hayden just laid back on his pillow, waiting in silence.

Filling my lungs with air, I blew out negative energies, realizing that my audience had always supported me. And with a half-smile, I got enough confidence to continue. At first, the words tumbled out softly, but I quickly recovered and read with passion.

When I was only six years old, he came to me, breaking my heart, implanting fears, and robbing me of every daily security. In his wake, he left unanswered questions behind. Greed consumes him.

Growth seeps in as another of his superpowers. With this ability, he spreads like a disease, producing anticipatory dread. He wreaks havoc on the calendar, hiding inside the little boxes. Creeping into my mind, he camps for days on end in the fall, roasting marshmallows until my brain's mush and on fire. Every crisp October day, he returns to the date I said good-bye to my mother forever. She missed my seventh birthday. He comes as we relive the events of that very day—he loves twisting my heart into two shattered pieces, toying with these memories, making me smile and cry with so many thoughts of her.

On the one hand, he makes me think about things too painful to remember. But on the other hand, he's also the one to remind me I do not ever want to forget. He's the invader of my mind, heart, and every one of Mom's memories. On holidays he makes unannounced appearances, battling me for fun, sucking the joy from the room, and trying to steal the excitement from colossal moments.

I have gotten too intimate and self-absorbed by his pain. Like kryptonite, sometimes, he's too hard to shake. But deep in my bones, his strength ropes me in. Because of him, I ache to hear my mother's voice. So, everywhere I go, his whispered reminders follow me. Like when he nudged me, pointing out her favorite pecan log candy sitting on display near the checkout at the store. Or when he made my throat raw with unshed tears because I got so choked up as the radio played Christmas hymns she used to sing, and now I listen to them without her.

At home, he confuses me by transforming into an ally. Home seems the most logical place I can count on for his assistance. Here, we believe we work undercover best, hiding from the outside world. We once buried Mother's old Christmas presents in my dresser drawer, hoping no one would uncover our secrets. But our mission failed.

During school, he refuses to stop and take breaks. On alert, his ears perk up, listening and reporting too many details back to me. He yaks on about the mother-daughter stuff I miss year after year—shop-ping trips, spa days, movie outings, and cookie bakes. Or the daily basics of just simply talking, texting, even fighting—every last one of them. Some days he turns me into a lonely little girl who's jealous and shy, eavesdropping in envy.

When I harness his power, I learn about my strength from all his energy. Sometimes grief becomes an ally, capable of healing my heart when I think of him as my memory keeper who honors my mother's life. Grief does not have a hit on me. He wants me to live!

My mother, Gwen Gardener, may never again wrap me in her arms because she's gone from my physical universe. Still, I will never forget her because of an odd con man. Through stories and photographs, evidence of her love exists in this world.

Grief, the con man, will never take these things away. In fact, he likes pointing this out. As long as I permit loving memories of my mom in my heart, those belong to me. And outside or inside the calendar, she remains. Anytime I'm ready to accept it, that's the power grief grants me.

Once again, Hayden cleared his throat, his eyes glistening. "That really got to me. I can relate. It's so good. You've got to show it to Lisa and Doc Han. They're going to love it. Both will probably want a copy."

"Thanks. I plan to. What's your favorite part?"

"Hmm. Well, the first line threw me *way* off." Hayden said, growling. "Seriously, though, the chunk about grief helping you hide old Christmas presents—I knew you meant hiding the Christmas underwear your mom had given you. It made me think about your OCD—all the things you've been through." Hayden's mouth curved into a lopsided grin. His face appeared to beam with pride for me.

"Yeah. I'm still working at it, going to my OCD sessions."

"I'm glad. You're doing great. I also related to the stuff about school. You know, like being left out." Hayden shifts to sprawl across his bed, letting out a sigh. "I bet that's even harder for you with all the girly-girl outings and stuff."

"I know you get it. You just get me. Do you think the fact my former friends and their moms asked me to do things out of pity and I went along with it hurt me worse?" Waving my free hand, I exclaimed, "Forget it! Don't even answer." With my eyes closed, I lifted one shoulder and then lowered it with the energy of a sloth. I snapped open my eyes, faking a half-grin. "I mean it. Never mind. Thank goodness for you and the grief center."

"No. Hey, I don't think Darcy, Meghan, or their moms set out to hurt you intentionally. I don't know, Gretch. Sometimes, I wonder if they were caught off guard and just didn't have a clue about how to help you. You seemed to outgrow those friendships. At school, you know Jun's got your back. She makes you laugh. And at the grief center, we have our group of friends. The jury's still out on the mostly quiet Mia. We don't understand her story as well as we do Miles and Kelsey. I can't imagine losing both parents."

I nodded.

Hayden continued. "Sometimes, I think, at the core, Mia's a good person. But even though Mia is quite odd, I get this feeling she's struggling. Now, do I think Lilly's evil? I'll be more blunt than normal—she's a bitch. We both know that."

"Ugh, I *don't* want to talk about *Lilly*," I moaned. Peering into Hayden's wide gray-blue eyes felt calming—like an open door whispering, "Welcome home."

"I hear ya. I'll try changing the subject, then." Pulling a Lisa Marks, he placed his hand over his heart, saying, "I'm *beyond* thankful for you."

My mouth exploded into a smile.

Talking with an exaggerated hand gesture, Hayden kept the conversation light, asking, "*Soooo*, did you ace Mr. Wright's class? Like I'm sure you did all the others?"

I snorted. "Close enough. An A minus. Oh, hey, by the way, Dad wanted me to ask you guys—you, Gene, and Lisa—if you wanted to get together to celebrate our good grades and eat later, I guess? Dad invited Gabby, but she's not able to come."

"I'll go if they don't. Lisa's not here right now. Are you making us border-hop into Arkansas or just into Branson?"

"Stop making fun of me. On FaceTime, I *can* see your smirky face, you know?"

"I'm not—" Hayden stared wild-eyed back at me, gritting his teeth, trying not to crack up.

"Dad mentioned going back to the hibachi place."

Hayden broke his stare, roaring in laughter. "Really?"

Rearranging myself across the bed, I giggled.

"God, Gretch, I'll never forget the look of horror on all our faces when we got seated next to the old drunk guy and his fancy-pants wife last time."

My eyebrows moved up, trying to recall the people we sat beside. My expression and lack of memory seemed to amuse Hayden.

"Ah, come on, you know. As the hibachi chef placed two stacks of onions up high, lighting them on fire, the guy next to you pounded the table?" Hayden paused. When I blankly stared, he continued. "The drunk guy screamed in his slurred voice 'Dolly Parton!' repeatedly. And the guy resembled an original 1920s gangsta in his pin-striped suit. Remember?"

Still, I shook my head.

Hayden gawked at me with his head cocked, hoping I'd get as tickled as he had. Pantomiming the scene, Hayden pretended he was the hibachi chef loading food high on the grill. As the imaginary fire exploded, his mouth formed an *o* as he mouthed the word *boom*, and his fingers arced into a spirited display. Hayden waited for me to channel the memory.

Not a sound came from me. I'm grinning at him, unable to recall a single thing.

Finally, Hayden shifted his acting skills, cutting in with, "Okay, do you remember *smelling* the lady? She'd doused herself in so much perfume? I'm surprised sitting by a fire with her that we all didn't burst or vanish into flames."

The images finally registered with me, and I died laughing with tears rolling down my cheeks. Hayden's still cracking up. One more time, Hayden performs "Dolly Parton! Dolly Parton! Dolly Parton!" His impression of the man sounds so spot on now. Again, a mental image of the man's suit paints a cartoon caricature of the scene in my brain.

"S-stop-p!" I begged, grabbing my side. I'm hurting from laughing too hard.

Hayden wiggled his eyebrows. "Do you think she was the wife or mistress?"

I said, "Don't you think the strangest people tend to have the most mistresses? I'm sure Mr. Mafia has an empire of perfumed ladies, but it's hard to say."

Hayden's laugh sounded muffled.

Tossing his cell on his bed, he tilted it, so I was still visible again. On my screen, I watched as his gray T-shirt with the Summerfort Basketball Eagles #41 stitched in blue flew over his head. "I need to shower soon if we're going out."

My pulse kicks up a notch at the sight of my boyfriend standing only in his basketball shorts. *Shall I play some music for you to dance to? I'm happy to stay in.* I swallowed, saying, "Text an update for my dad about who wants to go."

"No problem. Love ya. Bye."

"Love you too. Bye."

Oh. My. Hayden stirred me up.

Mom,

Earlier, Hayden mentioned the name Lilly.

Mom, I still remember standing inside the Victoria's Secret at Branson Landing, shopping for back-to-school items. My smile faded after scoring underwear on sale as I listened to Lilly's hateful words. "Just because Gretchen's mom is dead, it doesn't give her the right to steal your mom." Lilly directed her comment to my friends, but the whole store heard, and nobody stood up for me or said anything.

Lilly's voice no longer haunts me as often, but it hurts me. And her boyfriend, Thomas Sharp, still acts like an ass-jerk. I try not to let it bother me, but I don't bother expecting much to change, either. Sadly, Summerfort loves its sports stars. So, instead, I pretend he doesn't exist as much as possible. Therapy with Doctor Han at the Summerfort Grief Center for my OCD treatment goes well when I talk about it. At least with the Thomas situation, Dad, Gene, and Hayden proved they cared about me. Dad went to the police station. When Thomas sent horrible messages, Gene went to the cemetery to check on the grave. When Thomas made sexually degrading comments about my photos pulled up on his phone, Hayden punched him. At school, Jun assured me several people silently cheered when Hayden attacked the untouchable Thomas Sharp.

Well, Summerfort Grief Center closed down for Christmas break, but I can reach Doctor Han if needed. With her eyeglasses perched on the edge of her little nose, she had said, "Gretchen, I'm just a phone call away, anytime." So, I'll manage—minus an appearance from the con man.

Like Lisa, Doctor Han has me do journal exercises to work through my pain when required. This new poem I'm working on I titled "Motherless Child." It made me think of the Lilly situation, my relationship with Lisa over the years, and how Lisa helped me grow. When I finish the work, I plan to give it to her.

I'll tuck it away for now. Maybe I'll share it with Doctor Han on my next visit. So, here's a sneak peek.

Motherless Child

"Why are you all alone, sitting in the dark?"

"Lady, turn off the light. Let me hide.
I'm a motherless child."

"Other children go outside to play and wear
    smiles."
"Lady, I try, but my frown just won't bend.
Turn off the light. Let me hide.
I'm a motherless child."

HAYDEN

Chapter Four

December 2019

Yo, Ma,

Did you have a favorite Christmas carol? Every day a new question jams up in my mind, making me wish for more wishes, so I could know more about you.

"God rest ye merry gentlemen, let nothing you dismay. . . ." played in the background, but I think "The Little Drummer Boy" ranks as my top pick for a holiday song. Every time I listen, I consider the lyrics. Today, I think I realize the intended meaning. Maybe even though we seem flawed, or others live in poverty, they can still share their talents. These talents can be gifts to the world. Most mothers seem to have a lot of natural talents and gifts. Some know how to wrap presents, tie bows, and bake snickerdoodle cookies. Some even throw a football and capture the memories for me on film. Maybe that's why you're so missed.

The only skill I know I've got so far—I'm decent at playing sports. Let's also not forget I got good at knocking Thomas Sharp in the face. I got tired of hearing him call me Hardly Speak Hayden and Momma's Boy Queer as Fuck. He pulled up a photo of Gretchen on his phone and gyrated and licked like he wanted to do some pretty nasty things to Gretchen. I lost my mind in the locker room.

Besides, from what Gretchen tells me, she thinks I'm on my way to becoming one hella hot lover in the future. We believe we are worth waiting for. My girlfriend nicknamed me Hot Boy, thanks to you. Maybe I've never told you this before. Hayden Oliver Tucker—really, Mom? You and Dad didn't sit down, talk things over, and think, Oh, our son's initials H-O-T spells out the word hot? If not, that's one of your flaws. Then Gretchen pointed out to me how wordsmithing runs in our family. Did you realize Grandpa Emerson's initials spell out WOE, as in woe is me? I did not since he went by Bill, but sexy Gretch asked, "Where did your middle name come from?" ~~So, my name descended from woe is me with a side of hotness because of my grandparents and parents.~~ Yuck, let's scratch that because there are many interpretations in that last sentence. Too much about people getting holly jolly, so moving on.

Yeah, sorry, Ma. I drifted a bit. I felt I might be too philosophical with the chat about the Jesus tunes, so I changed the subject. But, unfortunately, my mind (and other parts, too) got carried away with thoughts—*dancing around the Christmas tree*—my *mind* parties a lot. So, I got jazzed up thinking of Gretchen in those matching Rudolph PJs we share. Then there was the dress with the black leather knee boots she wore over here recently. And she created a freaking smoke show event—flaming dress and hair. Time to rein my thoughts in and behave. From saint to sinner to saint. By the way, I think a devilish Santa is wearing a crooked hat and sitting on my shoulder on standby. Just sayin'.

After scrolling through social media, I needed a break from the negativity. One person wrote they wanted the radio stations to stop "churching up" Christmas music. At first, the comment made me laugh, but then I wondered why the person might be hurting so badly. As I read the words aloud, they sounded lost or lonely. The comments also sounded like a cry for help, as if someone needed to debate long enough until they found some hope or faith again. Another person wished someone a blessed holiday. After the man deleted the person's reply, he explained the situation to everyone on his social media post. "Someone told me to go have sex with myself today after wishing them a blessed holiday."

Wow. A big eff you for wishing someone a nice day. What an ass-jerk move. Behind those words, I imagined the angry man with a broken heart, needing a Christmas blessing he just can't believe in. I'm not sure if I prayed correctly or just sent vibes out into the universe. Either way, with good intentions, I sent out positive thoughts to people I didn't know.

Even if someone isn't religious or overly spiritual but they believe, isn't there supposed to be Christmas magic or holiday cheer people find this time of year? I want to know what to do. What's the right thing to say? How am I supposed to make sure Gretchen has the best Christmas ever? She struggles so much around Christmastime with memories of her mom. I worry about her. Can someone awkward like me help give her new memories to focus on?

Speaking of giving, I want to share a story.
***

Clunk. Clunk. Clunk. Footsteps approached the front porch, followed by the doorbell's chiming, all sounds courtesy of the mail carrier.

Opened on the coffee table, my Summerfort High School planner had **CHRISTMAS BREAK** written in big, bold letters over the next couple of weeks. Gretchen had decorated the days with Christmas trees, adding heart ornaments, snowmen, and holly, which I think looks like mistletoe. Maybe my girlfriend's dropping hints with those little drawings of mistletoe? Believe it or not, even though it was December, I dressed in my blue-and-gray Summerfort Eagles #41 basketball practice shorts and T-shirt I'd slept in the night before. Today's weather felt more like spring break.

As I unlocked the door, a smirk spread across my face. Next, I scooped the package into my arms. Then, I got geared up, ready to unveil the news.

Rubbernecking, my head bobbed as I peeked around the basket I lugged. Trotting up a few steps, I waited a second before calling, "Yo, Dad." I held up the anticipated annual gift in a *Lion King* fashion. As soon as Dad leaned his head out of his bedroom, I gave the basket a little shimmy shake, announcing, "Look what we got. It's here." I couldn't even hide the upbeat tempo in my voice.

"Oh, goody. I'm sure a holiday letter might be in there for me," Dad replied as we both chuckled. "Hayden, I'll be downstairs in a minute, so we can rummage through it."

"Are you sure about this, Dad?"

From upstairs, Dad hollered down, "Of course. I've known the Emersons for about thirty years. I'll find some level of love and humor among all the insults."

At the bottom of the stairs, I yelled, "Yo, Dad, can I eat some of this candy before you read the letter?"

"Well, yeah. You don't have to ask. Dig in, buddy."

I held up a piece as Dad entered the living room. "Ding!" I stuttered with my mouth full. Then, trying to swallow, I said, "I think I found us a winner." After I inspected several items, another Anastasia coconut lime candy surfaced. "Dad, you've gotta try this." Opening the sweet treat, I tossed it.

Dad wasted no time devouring it. "Wow. That's freakin' awesome, buddy. Give me a different sample. Bet we'll need the sugar rush for strength."

We chuckled.

"Wait a minute," I mumbled, pointing at Dad. "Why are you wearing my football sweats? And my hoodie?"

Slapping his gut, laughing, Dad said, "Aww, shut it, bud. It's laundry day. Deal with the high-water pants and my little paunchy belly. You better enjoy your body and youth while you can."

"Oh, don't worry. I plan to, Dad." I wiggled my eyebrows, bursting into laughter.

Dad sauntered by, settling in the chair beside me in the den, pausing to pull on my ear playfully. "Giggle all you want, bud. But remember, you better behave. Also, take a good look because you're basically a Mini-Me."

"Yep, I hear you. Lisa says you, Cole, Drew, and I just look like we're just different ages of Paul Rudd."

Dad rubbed his hands together, staring me down. "Lisa likes that Paul Rudd an awful lot."

"Gross, Dad."

"Hayden, I didn't mean anything by that. Anyway, do we need to have a *big ole* father-son talk about your body and the stuff making your eyebrows continue to go all wiggly?" His voice sounded half-serious and half-joking. Sometimes, I still find it hard to monitor Gene Tucker's moods.

Closing my eyes, I knew I didn't want to fight with him today because we'd been getting along lately. "Jeez, Dad. No! Oh my God, you know I'm only kidding around. Right?" I held up my palms with a smile. Then, reaching back into the basket to pick out candy, I suggested one to him as a peace offering. "Just pop this original coconut flavor in your mouth."

Dad pretended to look stern for a moment, but I saw the corner of his mouth curve into his smirk. He's only joking around, I realized.

"Alrighty, I'm watching you. Nice change of subject. You and Gretchen know chocolate is my weakness."

I nodded, watching Dad's lopsided grin, pure happiness at the acceptance of sugar.

"That's pretty tasty." After a moment, Dad touched the envelope. Sucking in a deep breath, he released a groan. His finger tugged under the flap, tearing open the contents. "Grandma Suzi has a bit to say this year," Dad said, elevating the note in the air to give me a peek. He cleared his throat before reading.

"Hayden, I'm going to do my best to get through this whole dang thing without any off-the-wall commentary this year. Afterward, though . . . well, you know how I get." Dad paused, staring with a glazed expression like he might need one last minute to prepare himself.

With elbows propped on the table and my hands resting under my chin, I offered him all my attention with a bit of a pep talk. "Yep. Take it away, Dad."

He smiled, glancing at me before looking back at part of our annual gift. Gradually, his shaky fingers unfolded the fancy stationery. At first, the contents fooled me. A pale yellow legal pad turned into a tri-folded note—designed with a watermarked bowl of fruit set in the background.

Dad read:

Dear Gene & Boys,

Happy Holidays from the Sunshine State of Florida, U.S.A. Relish these fruits and treats. We shopped from the best orchard in the world. First, the fine folks at Eden's Hill allowed us to pick out the basket. Secondly, they insisted on mailing these tasty goods directly to you. Thirdly, they secured the stationery, sat me down, and told me to send you a personalized message.

Talk about customer service. Perhaps you'll feel obligated to grant them a kind review after you've eaten a few orange slices. Or after you've cut into a juicy grapefruit at breakfast.

NOTE Read your pill bottles carefully if you're on any medication because grapefruit don't mix with certain drugs.

By the way, the higher-calorie nuts and chocolates mostly pertain to Hayden and his little redheaded beauty. So, save some back to share with Cole and Drew. Keep their lady friends in mind, as well, when you go to divvy up things. But, Gene, at fifty, you better heed the warnings about laying off the sweets and stick with biting into more oranges and grapefruits.

We miss all of you and sure hope you're well. However, we don't regret leaving the insurance industry or retiring and moving from Missouri to sunny Florida right before Rose got sick. Losing Rosie was hard on you and the boys, especially after a long and loving battle. It's a shame you didn't pack up the boys and come live with us.

Work didn't have to be such a big issue. Florida offers builders year-round money, unlike temperamental Missouri weather.

Dad stopped reading and met my eyes.

Slapping the table in disbelief, I moaned out a warning. "Dad, you promised not to get off on a tangent or do your commentary during the letter this year."

Hands flew up along with the letter. "I know. I know. But you need to hear about the alligators."

I tilted my head. "Um, what alligators?"

Still gripping the letter, Dad dropped his fist to his hip before explaining. "Oh, just the ones Grandma wanted me to build enclosures for. She arranged for me to interview with a company that builds pens for alligators and crocodiles."

My eyes grew wide until I met Dad's raised brows. A staring match with smirking began, with both of us blinking too soon, falling into a fit of laughter. Then, gasping back, I heard Dad sigh before asking, "Shall I go on?"

With a hint of humor lingering in the air, I replied, "Of course."

Dad focused again on the letter and went on reading:

Constructing those gator enclosures would've been very interesting. And it wasn't the only qualified position I found for you. I set up many interviews unique to your blue-collar talents. All of which you declined.

Anyway, keep sending us Hayden's school pictures. Unfortunately, our eyes aren't working as well as they used to, so we aren't online as much, but we are always glad you send emails with a quick update now and then. Once in a while, we search the Gene Tucker Construction website, catching up with your whereabouts and work ethic. The projects seem nice.

Thank you for remembering our birthdays with cards or the occasional plant delivery to the door. This year, I tossed extra chocolate pieces in the basket to honor each person's birthday, including you,

Gene. Let everybody know that Grandma loves them (Grandpa too). Imagine all the possibilities of celebrating if everyone lived together in Florida. Unfortunately, scattered like we are, I simply can't keep track of everyone anymore. It's heartbreaking. Happy belated birthday to all, though.

Billy and I are in our mid-to-upper seventies, so topics of life and death carry a lot of weight. So, remember the importance of letting us know about exciting news or changes in the Tucker households. Of course, call anytime. When possible, please mail document information clarifying things, along with photo proof. Send notices for things like the following: Awards, new courtships, engagements, marriages, military deployments, births, graduations, job promotions, moves, and deaths.

As always, we do extend an invitation to welcome visitors who insist on living and remaining in Summerfort, Missouri.

Love and good wishes to all.

Merry Christmas & Happy New Year

Grandpa Billy & Grandma Suzi Emerson

"Dad?" *What the hell is wrong with Grandma?*

"Hayden?" Dad stood with a deadpan expression, holding the envelope with years of practice yet still having no idea what to do afterward.

"I'm not sure how to feel or react. This year's letter is extra weird with gators and guilt trips. It's somewhat sad too. I mean, I've got grandparents, but I don't really know them at all. Did she honestly try getting you a job building alligator pens?" I asked, laughing.

"Yep, Grandma stepped in trying to save us by getting me a job in Florida. She set up some nutty interviews. At first, I got mad. Then, I just shook my head and laughed so dang much after thinking about it. I will always love that goofy woman."

Popping another piece of candy, fresh from Florida, U.S.A., in our mouths, we met each other's gaze and snorted.

"By the way, happy birthday, Dad," I doubled over, trying to get the words out, but I was cracking up.

"Right back at you, buddy." Dad threw a piece of candy at me. "Happy birthday and Merry Christmas."

"Hey. I still don't understand Grandma Suzi's beef with you. She sounds kind of mean, even a little hoity-toity. Is that the right wording?"

"Yeah. I know. Crazy to think these are the same people capable of raising your mom, a person who was so thoughtful and loving, huh?" Dad held his hands up, bewildered, before delivering a big shrug, sighing.

I nodded. Dad's right because I didn't get it.

His lips seem headed toward a frown. "I loved Suzi and Bill. I even got along with them pretty well while they lived in Missouri. But it seemed like your grandmother got angry with me after your mom died. She refused to listen when I explained I had a thriving business. You boys had established activities in school. Plus, this was your home. I didn't want to uproot us and relocate. It sounds like she blames me for you boys missing out on knowing them since I wouldn't haul you off to Florida."

"I don't blame you, Dad. I'm glad we hung around here. Do Billy and Suzi not understand you *own* your company? That you earned an architectural degree? You're successful. Her blue-collar comment is such a slam. It's freaking rude."

"Ah, she realizes it, but she won't acknowledge it. So, for now, her digs serve as her roundabout way of getting back at me, I guess," Dad said with his shoulders hunching.

"Does it bother you? You know, like, hurt your feelings? Because I don't like it."

"Sometimes it gets to me. Let's see. This year, your grandma called me fat, dumb, old, and lazy, I believe."

"Dad, you know you're none of those things, right? I mean, look—you're even wearing *my* clothes."

Pulling down the hem of the too-tight hoodie, he said, "Thanks, bud." Dad beamed with a lopsided grin.

I scoffed. "Besides, it's like Grandma doesn't even know us at all."

"She used to. Deep down, I know she cares about what happens to us. But I can also read between the lines of Suzi's words. Notice how she compliments me on looking after your mom when she got sick. And she knows I'm a hard worker. Quite frankly, that's what matters. I feel bad about my boys missing out on having more family."

"Dad, how would Mom want us to deal with these letters?"

Dad paused, looking me in the eye. "I wish I had easy answers, Hayden. I suppose your mom would want us to remain cordial. We try. I want you to know your grandparents, Hayden. But, on the other hand, I don't believe you wish to spend time with relatives who send outrageous letters. Or send a once-a-year basket of gifts or make minimal attempts to reach out otherwise."

I shook my head. "No way, but I'll eat the treats and play nice." Still, I wanted to understand more. Because knowing my grandparents connected me a little more to my mother.

Dad fist-bumped me. "Let's browse through the note again. After the first reading, the shock wears off. During the second rendition of her words, humor often slides in." As Dad spoke, he gestured as if he were a referee at a baseball game, calling a player safe at home plate.

I plucked out various candies, dug in the basket, rolling him a few selections. "First, let's chow down on this 'high-calorie' dark chocolate coconut candy. Do it despite your age, Gene, as Grandma said."

Dad picked up the pina colada.

We cheered by clunking two slices of coconut patties still left in the wrapper.

Dad started singing the song about liking pina coladas. He twirled his fists while pausing the song, telling me, "This is called the hand jive." His face transformed into a smile comparable to the happy Grinch as he sampled.

Returning the expressive facial gesture, I sing-songed back something about the rain.

"Thanks, Grandma Suzi." Dad sang to the tune of our recent song, holding up a fistful of candy and dying with laughter.

"I think key lime remains my favorite so far." I shrugged. "Just saying, Dad."

With the empty candy wrappers in his hand, Dad held them with his pinky out, preparing to speak. So, Dad started talking in his over-the-top southern accent. "Perhaps, Hayden, your inclination toward those delicious limes will urge you or make you feel obligated to write a review? Don't be too hasty and forget the oranges, though."

"Oh, my God. Dad, you're so weird." It's too hard not to crack up. Dad's notorious for laughing at his own jokes, making the situation even funnier.

Dad shuffled and tossed the candies, choosing island rum covered in dark chocolate. Then, finally, he threw me a piece.

"Whew, Dad, that's too much. Way too strong."

"Well, Hayden, I say, 'Yum for rum.' Set some of those aside for our 'lady friends' to try. Tell that 'redheaded beauty' of yours it's a birthday and Christmas-worthy treat rolled into one."

Dad's excessive use of air quotes made the moment hilarious. We swiped at the tears flowing down our cheeks during our sugar high using the back of our hands.

We dug around inside the basket before locating another variety.

Reading the next label, I scrunched my nose, asking, "Split it with me, Dad? I'm not feeling this combo. Um, does dark chocolate go with orange coconut?"

"I don't know, bud. Recently, I read men should limit the number of sugary things they eat past a certain age, you know?"

"All right, just eat half of a half," I said, with a chuckle while shaking my head and getting a tiny pinch at the corner for us to nibble for our taste test.

"Dang it all. I enjoy that one too. Do you?" Dad pointed toward my cringing face.

Using my hand, I wave the gesture for so-so, passing the rest to Dad.

My fingers wiggled as I held them up for Dad. I planned to use them for numbering my preference for the five varieties of coconut candies. To show Dad, I flexed my index finger, saying, "First place, of course, goes to key lime." Repeating, I added my next finger. "Second goes to pina colada.

The third-place winner is the original. Island rum comes in fourth due to its strength. Icky orange takes the last place. What about you?"

Dad rattled off his preferences quickly, "Rum, key lime, pina colada, original, and orange, but I'm a fan of all of them."

"Want to tackle the big bag of Florida's delicious Anastasia taffy? I could blindfold you—"

"Wait! Do what?" Dad asked with a raised eyebrow. "Uh, no."

A crooked smirk stretched across my face at Dad's confused expression. "Oh, Dad. I didn't mean anything weird by it. You know, I'd just use a blindfold or scarf or something, so you could guess the flavors of taffy you ate." I can't hide my reaction to Dad's continuing look of horror.

Dad tosses up his "I surrender" hands before saying, "Hmm. No way! Thank you very much. I'm going to pass on this iffy blindfolding thingamajig. I'm not playing any such game with my son. But I suppose we can guess taffy flavors later. That work? Or do I need to defend myself with a loaf of Wonder Bread?"

Tilting my head, I start cracking up. "Jeez, Dad!"

He shook his head, walking toward the stairs leading to his room.

"Hey, Dad, you headed back upstairs?"

Dad nodded.

"Before you go, can you tell me who's coming to the house for the party?"

"Far as I know, Lisa, Gretchen, John, maybe Gabby, Cole, Drew, you, and me. A few couples will get together to enjoy snack foods and exchange small gifts. Nothing too crazy. Cole and Drew asked if they could bring their *lady friends*, Ariana and Ava, so I invited them. What do you think?"

"Works for me, I guess. Did you invite Lisa to come as your official *date*?

"Yes, I did. Does that make you uncomfortable, Hayden?"

I don't know? Yeah, I guess. "No, it's fine. I like Lisa a lot."

"I also like Lisa *a lot*. But I'm nervous, too, Hayden. Dating again, at my age and after losing your mom, feels strange. At any time, if you need to talk to me about this whole Lisa thing, you can. I know it might be strange at times. I've never brought anyone home to meet you in the eight years since your mom's death. The main reason is that I didn't go out much. But I also knew no one measured up to your mom." Dad stood at the bottom of the staircase. His glassy eyes were fixed on me.

Staring into Dad's face, I pondered questions. *So, Lisa measures up? Do you already think her love equals what you had with Mom?* My heart raced. Studying Dad, I wanted to understand what this new situation meant for all of us. I tried to form a reply. Blank. I just went blank. Drawing in a deep breath, I considered things from Dad's viewpoint. *Eight years?* He's endured *years* without any real romantic possibility. After experiencing Gretchen's hugs, kisses, and friendship, I can't imagine losing her. Going that long without any kind of romantic human connection just seemed too sad. Remembering how affectionate Mom used to be, I can't imagine Dad staying stuck in this unloving predicament.

Mom, I believe you've told Dad he shouldn't have given up on love as he did. Maybe his workaholic ways substituted for the pain? Now that Dad communicates and shows up in my life more than ever before, I feel torn. With the daily addition of Lisa to our lives, what will change? Could she get between us and pull Dad and me apart? Or will she act like glue, making our bond stronger?

Before speaking, I think, *If Mom and I aren't forgotten, Dad.* "Lisa's a good person, Dad."

He appeared to fake a grin while his eyes focused on the floor. I noticed Dad's feet shuffling until he moved toward me, letting go of the railing. Then, without saying a word, he plopped down beside me.

After a long minute, Dad asked, "This isn't easy, huh?"

I shrugged.

Struggling for words, I managed to say, "You deserve to be happy. And I do like Lisa. I told you already I'm okay with you inviting her." My throat filled with the lumpy thickness I have learned to fight and choke back.

"Change is hard, Hayden. It's scary when we don't know what's ahead. Maybe it's time to take some chances. Thanks for talking to me about Lisa. Hayden, I promise she and I will be sensitive to your feelings. She made sure to talk to me at great length about how much she cares about you. She doesn't want to hurt you."

Tugging on the left side of my lip with my teeth, I mumbled through my clenched jaw. "I'll be all right." A silent tear escaped.

Dad pulled me against his shoulder. "Do I need to cancel or postpone the party?"

Shaking my head, I whispered, "No." Then I glanced up at Dad. "I'm sorry—"

"Hey, you did nothing wrong." Dad side-squeezed me. "No apology necessary, bud."

"Dad, I think I'm just a bit nervous."

"That's understandable. You've known Lisa as part of your Summerfort Grief Center background. Of course, she's been a friend to me over the years. But now she will be coming into our home as my official girlfriend."

I nodded and gave Dad a closed-mouth grin.

Side by side, we sat quietly for a moment. Dad draped his arm around me. "Something's still bothering you, bud. What's going on? Spill it. Tell me your biggest fear about Lisa."

For a second, I debated what to say in response. How about the sound of silence as the answer? But my fingers curled into fists. What words can make anybody feel okay?

"Hey!" Dad grumbled at me, glaring at my hands, reaching to uncurl them.

Getting defensive, I spouted off, "If I say something right now, I'm going to sound so freaking stupid." *And I might hurt your feelings and ruin my relationship with you, Dad!*

"Stop it, Hayden. I've warned you before about saying you're stupid. I don't appreciate my son using that language." Dad squeezed my shoulder. "Be honest. Take your time and talk."

"F-fine. I'll try." The room felt void of air as I tried sucking in a deep breath. Finally, after a loud exhale, I said, "Lisa's a decent person. Sometimes she drives me nuts. It's like Lisa's already part of the family. Maybe because she's like—" Words failed me. I choked down the effing throat lumps, swallowing hard before stammering on. "Um, she's like the closest thing I have"—I can barely get any words out— "to a *mother*." Dad trailed his eyes around the room until his glance met mine. "But, Dad, feeling this way makes me feel freaking guilty. I can't just go and replace Mom."

"Ah, buddy." Dad sighed. "Lisa would throw her hand over her heart if she heard you saying all this. You know?"

With watery eyes, I nodded. Back and forth, my lips fought from twitching downward into a frown into curling upward into a little grin, imagining Lisa doing just that. "Duh," I admitted.

Dad nudged me, chuckling. "Listen, you're allowed any emotion you need. However, I bet Mom would tell you to quit stressing with so much guilt. 'Stop denying yourself opportunities for happiness.' I'm sorry. I'm terrible at imitating her." Dad's shoulders lightly hunch. "I try."

"Dad?" I say in a questioning tone. "You know you're weird, right?"

"Yep. I know I'm goofy."

We chuckled.

"I'm excited for you and Lisa, but I keep worrying you'll forget Mom. Then, I won't be allowed to talk about her as much."

"Unforgettable—that's always going to be your mother. She will *always* remain your mom. I trust Lisa. As a person who understands grief, she relates to us and our wants and needs to honor Rosie. We'll figure this all out." Dad shook my shoulders in a lighthearted manner.

"Oh, and Hayden, just so you know, *no* woman's coming up in this house, bossing my son around with nonsense about not being allowed to remember his mom. Or saying he's not allowed to talk about her."

Dad clears his throat. "Furthermore, if *any* woman ever tried pulling such crap, I'd show her ass where the damn door's located. Then I'd holler,

bye-bye. Only I'd say it more like this: Buh-bye."
Dad's voice reached a near-screeching level.

I held my hands over my ears. "Dad—?" A full-on smile lit up my whole face. Like a parrot, I mimicked Dad, playing up his dramatic flair. Laughing, the words I tried to use against him came out all jumbled. "'H-ollerr bye-bye'? Seriously, Dad? No. 'Buh-bye!'"

Lost in a fit of giggles, we huddled together like two kids on a playground until the bursts of silliness simmered.

Over my shoulder, I said, "Time to holler 'Buh-bye' now. See you tonight." I'm laughing again. A few paces away, the staircase became my goal. Like I was in a relay race, I sprinted. Dad leaped up in a quest to chase me. Dad's ability to skip steps and stumble up fewer of them through tearful laughter allowed him to catch up to me. He beat me to the top of the landing in a football tackle, where we landed on the rug, and he ruffled my hair.

"I surrender, Dad!" Now, on our backs, we rested, staring at the ceiling. Life felt less challenging while lying on a rug in the upstairs landing hallway.

"Hayden, your Grandma Suzi might think I'm old, but as you can see, I've still got some fight left in me."

"Yep, I see that, but I already knew it before today," I said, catching my breath and resting a finger on my neck to count my drumming pulse.

"Speaking of Grandma and her birthday-Christmas combo gift, did you know Lisa's birthday's coming up?"

"No, but now I get why you had a reason to put Lisa and Grandma in the same sentence."

"Ironic, huh?" Dad looked at me with a furrowed brow. "Ha! 'Redheaded beauty and lady friends,'" Dad repeated, reliving part of the infamous letter. The magic of those words still didn't seem to be growing old, so we cracked up.

Dad continued. "Well, after today's events, I want to run an idea by you. I thought I'd have Lisa's birthday-Christmas party during Cole and Drew's visit, close to New Year's Eve. Getting all of you boys and John onboard puts my idea in motion. It's a little something humorous—a story related to our history with the grief center. My overall goal isn't to make anyone uncomfortable. I just have this huge plan. It's a 'didn't see that comin'' moment—"

"Dad. Stop. You're making me edgy. Why the word *uncomfortable*? Are you going to ask me to do something weird?" Then, running my hands through my hair, I sighed.

"Nah, not really." Dad hears me groan. "Come on, let me complete my whole plan. It's the perfect fun and will make our lady friends, oh, and your redheaded beauty, Gretchen, swoon." Dad rubbed his palms together loudly.

I pleaded, "D-a-a-a-d," pronouncing it in a pouty tone with added syllables. Then I continued to whine, "Gretchen likes me enough already. She thinks I'm plenty swoony."

Springing to his feet, Dad announced, "Save those pouty lips for some singing and dancing, son."

Immediately, sweaty palms and nervous fingers scrubbed down my entire face. My head's shaking no. Words rattled in my brain, shouting, but they were stuck inside. *What the—?* Dad doesn't bother replying to my growl or foot-stomping. I glared at him, but he only ignored me.

Shifting his feet, Dad said, "Whew. I'll tell you more as soon as I figure out all the deets. All I can say—it's spelled like this: F-U-N but with '*different letters*.'" Dad used his hand and cupped his mouth to whisper *different letters* as a little boy who might want to provide a clue to a riddle.

To my horror, Dad expected me to *sing and dance*. WTF?

A clicking noise ricocheted. Dad had closed and locked his bedroom door, mere steps away from me. Behind closed doors, Dad's giddiness echoed. Sitting up, I glanced around the hallway, realizing I was too late to grovel. He's already scamming everyone for some F-U-N. Already, I heard him rambling to someone on the phone.

Mom, I've got a word for Dad about all this. It starts with F-U but doesn't end with the letter N. Sorry, I know it's tacky, Mom. Sometimes I think I hear your voice, a nagging whisper in my head.

Lisa does this to me too. So, now I'm haunted by *two phantom moms* telling me what to do? How am I supposed to deal with that? Well, it's not F-U-N.

Having a girlfriend as sweet as Gretchen to spend time with and spoil for the holidays appeals to me. But watching Dad with a girlfriend for the first time? Not sure how much I'll enjoy being a spectator.

Add to the fact it's Lisa, whom I know so well.

Then add another fact. I just realized Dad's F-U-N freaking song and dance. Dad only thinks he's conning me into performing!

PS Soon, I want to confess some things about *your* mom, Grandma Suzi. It's confusing about what to do concerning Gretchen and Grandma. Do secrets and love share a recipe for disaster?

Chapter Five

Still Christmas Break

Dear Mom,

One second after Hayden's TBT text arrived, my mind flooded with Gardener family memories. We had traveled to Columbia, Missouri, to pick up Aunt Jolene from her group home for the weekend. I remember how she came back home with us to spend the weekend from time to time. On one particular trip back to Summerfort, she pointed, laughing at you and Dad because he rested his hand on top of yours while he drove. Jolene repeatedly sang one of her favorite old tunes about a happy-go-lucky boy. Again, she giggled away, teasing her older brother for being so in love.

Dad watched Jolene and me, using the rearview mirror while stopping at a stoplight. Then, leaning over to kiss you, he gave her something to cackle and sing about from her seat in the back. Even inside her seatbelt's confines, she swayed, singing and dancing, from verse to verse.

I suppose I view Hayden this way in life right now: as the happy-go-lucky guy. Well, son of a gun, what do I do to handle my feelings of envy?

Staring at my phone, I reread his text.

Hayden: Gretch, look what I got from Cole today. Are you free to take a call? Or do you want to come over? Watch a movie? Bake snickerdoodle cookies? I need to hear my girlfriend's voice or see her. Xo.

Jolene's lyrics stay stuck in my head. As the earworm played on, I scrutinized the beautiful photo, seeing Hayden in his mother's arms. Honestly, my first reaction: I wished someone in my family could send me pictures. And while I was ranting, I wanted an eccentric grandma too. Even if this grandmother writes me passive-aggressive notes and ships offbeat snail mail gifts in fancy baskets once a year. At least I'd feel more connected to the world.

One day I doodled what remained of my family tree. When most leaves die, trees become so barren. My drawing turned into something reminiscent of a first grader's work. Gnarled branches poked into the sky, empty of color, reaching out as if grasping for any spring color, only finding the darkness of winter. Four stick figures appeared beneath the tree. A sad little girl sat inside a tire swing that hung from one of the long extended branches. Two other stick figures stood to the side, trying to reach for each other's hands, but one person seemed too far away. She was fading fast. Another stick figure peeked out from behind the tree. At first glance, she appeared like an adult. Glancing again, I noticed her childlike nature with eyes of wonder, and a big grin appeared.

Mom, I love and miss you. I love Dad and Jolene too. I'm the loser! My family tree makes me feel like I've lost a round of that kid's game Hangman—dangling leftover letters no one's around to claim. My whole secretive project comes off as depressing. Sometimes, I get frustrated at how lonely and alone I feel. Why? What if I continue to remain this way in the future? Envious thoughts eat away at me all the time. I long for what I see others have, hoping to acquire my fair share. Is it wrong to want a turn at average? —to desire, take a chance, live without so much fear, find the ability to escape the con man for a long time—to destroy him from attacking dates on the calendar?

Mama, I know I'm young, but do you think I'll ever have a family? And will I get to watch my family tree grow? If so, I'll be sad knowing you'll miss every seed, sprout, bud, leaf, and blossom—because you'll bypass every season of our lives.

Love scares me because it could lead to having everything I want or losing it all. Then I think of Dad too. And I worry about getting in his way with Gabby. Will I only deny him a chance for happiness again? Would you accept Gabby? She's not the worst, but she's not who reigns as the best, either. Once again, Hayden's a happy-go-lucky guy who might end up getting Lisa as a mother.

I am thrilled for Hayden and love spending time with him and at his house. But my heart just needs to learn to balance these emotions of jealousy and love. All these mixed-up parts of myself, I'm finding hard to like. Most of me would rather grab ahold of the people I care about, squeezing them tight. But the realistic part of me keeps them at a very close distance—like a batch of Silly Putty, I wish the best features could rub off. But, at the same time, the bad stuff could stay hidden inside the fragile plastic egg.

Oh, before I forget, let me share what I wrote in my text to Hayden:

Me: Let me finish helping "Dr. Dad Gardener," who says it's ok for me to come over. OMG, you were such a cute baby—still are! What a great surprise from Cole! Can't wait to see you. I'll hurry. Xo.

Miss Spicy Boots Tucker, wearing her festive jingle bell collar, greeted me when Hayden yanked open his door. In feisty, talkative form, Miss Spicy Boots pranced around us. Her tail curled almost into a question mark. She rambled on as if going over the ground rules. Stooping down, I petted her until she flopped over, signaling her acceptance of my arrival.

Hayden helped me to my feet, waved my dad on, and secured the door shut. Then, with no more than a "hello," Hayden's arms circled me before his mouth locked onto mine intensely.

"Whoa," I whispered against his neck, "you'd think I'd been MIA. That was some kiss." Before either of us could say anything, Miss Spicy Boots let out the loudest meow of disgust, sounding like she'd smoked three packs of kitty cigarettes a day. If cats can stomp, that's what she did, going in Gene's home office direction.

"I want more." Hayden hauled me against him again. Next, he planted his arms around my lower back, letting them slip lower as he walked me backward until we leaned against the banister.

Down the hallway, Gene cleared his throat. "Well, hey, Strawberry Shortcake. Miss Spicy Boots told me I better check on you two."

We pulled away, interlocking fingers, making our way into the kitchen. "Hey, Gene," I called out with an embarrassed giggle.

Gene stood in the doorway of his office, peeking out but grinning. He gestured to his eyes using his fingers and then at us, a nonverbal "I'm watching you" warning. "Bring me some cookies when you're done."

Hayden threw a thumbs-up for his dad.

Hayden tossed the aprons Gene made us onto the counter inside the kitchen. If you don't remember, mine included a caricature of me as an intelligent "Constitutional whiz" version of Strawberry Shortcake. Gene lovingly refers to me this way because of my red hair. In comparison, Hayden's design has a Huckleberry Pie sports theme. I think Gene gave us aprons because his late wife Rosie loved cooking. He still keeps her "Kiss the Cook" apron hanging in their kitchen. On a side note, I often wonder how these issues affect his relationship with Lisa. Is there room in a house for the ghost of true love and a new love?

"Ready to get cookin'?" Hayden asked, pretending to help me cinch my apron's ties around my neck and waist as his hands lingered. I listened to his breathing thicken as he stood so close behind me.

Turning around to face Hayden, I said, "Now it's time for me to fix your strings." Using the thin pieces of material, I teased him with his back to me, tickling the sensitive areas of his neck and ears, grazing him with my fingertips.

"Gretch, you're doing some bad things to me. Don't get me wrong. What you do to me is some good shit."

Raising onto my tiptoes, I laughed, repeating, "Good shit?" in a whisper.

Hayden chuckled, slowly spinning around to face me, placing his forehead against mine, and wrapping me into a hug. Hayden's apron slipped from his shoulders.

"I supposed that means the time has come for me to tie you up," I said.

"Go ahead." Hayden's lips quirk against my earlobe, his hot breath spilling out. "You're the boss."

Pulling slightly away and looking up at him, I scoffed, asking, "Did you just act like a total *dude* and take what I said as *dirty*?"

He gave me an exaggerated shrug with his palms up. "Duh," he said, then biting his lip, waiting for my response, almost bracing for the impact of my playful swat to the arm he knew to expect.

"Hayden Oliver Tucker," I whisper-shouted as I performed some nonsensical disco dance with both fingers zigzagging toward Gene's office. I'm sure my face glowed as red as my tacky Christmas sweater with the giant bulb read "Shine On."

Slapping a hand over his mouth, Hayden failed to stifle his laughter. He pulled his hand down, mocking me as he danced toward me, singing "Stayin' Alive."

"Shut up," I said, reaching for him, laughing.

"Come here." Hayden twirled me around, singing the words "Stayin' Alive" one more time.

I glared up at him, wrinkling my nose. "Hey, you know I love kidding around with you." For several minutes after, we stayed quiet as he held me. His palm stroked my hair as we leaned against the kitchen bar, but I knew how his body responded to me wasn't a joke.

My body surged as we pressed against the island while he showered me with feathery soft kisses. How did his tenderness continue getting to me just as much as the passionate side? "I don't want to, but I need to stop," Hayden mumbled into my ear.

Then don't stop, I wished I could've said. But, instead, my body tingled, on edge, unsure which way to turn.

He tore himself away until only his pinky looped with mine. Hayden balled his other hand into a fist, sighing and placing it on the bar.

Hanging his head, Hayden said in an asking tone, "So, snickerdoodles?" To ease the awkwardness, I didn't look in his direction.

"Thanks for getting this stuff ready."

"No problem," Hayden answered, stealing a superfast glance at me and then looking away at the ingredients on the bar—butter, eggs, cinnamon, and some of the extras. Plus, the cookie sheet, potholders, and recipe card appear ready for us to use. "I read over the recipe, and some things needed to be room temperature, but I had them ready."

Seeing the handwritten index-style card, I froze for a moment in awe. "Hayden, is this one of your mom's recipe cards?"

Hayden only nodded.

Hayden touched the card with a lopsided grin and glassy eyes. I recognized this as a happy-sad moment. Those of us who grieve must learn to celebrate the memories. Witnessing or experiencing something like this truly fits living inside the word *bittersweet*. "Yep. Today will be the first time I've ever baked any of her cookies. Other than making Thanksgiving stuff with you, I don't do anything like this. I guess snickerdoodles will get me as close to the flavor of her cinnamon toast."

Sensing Hayden's need to talk more about his mom, I placed a hand on his back, offering quiet support. Then, holding back tears, Hayden choked out the words, "Am I crazy because I want to trace the words and numbers because my mom's hands wrote them?"

"No, I want to do the same with you and get to know her too. Learning, or thinking about this, makes me wish my mom had a cute set of Suzy Zoo recipe cards with ducks on them in silly poses."

Hayden smiled as a silent wayward tear fell down his cheek, and I think to lighten the mood, he playfully shoulder-checked me.

Wiping away the evidence, Hayden rolled his eyes, sniffling with slight embarrassment. "God, I'm so sorry. I didn't invite you over here to watch me tear up."

"Never apologize to me for loving and missing your mom. I get it. Remember? You've let me cry with you plenty of times. We have a right to hurt and to have hearts."

So, for a long minute, Hayden wrapped his arm around me, allowing himself the time to grieve and celebrate simultaneously. Sometimes that's all we need: Permission—the chance or permission to speak or remain silent. And we need second chances—a second to touch the past and bring something with us to the future in whatever way we can. For Hayden, his happy-go-lucky moment came in the form of a recipe.

Nudging me again, Hayden said, "I think the time has come to read the card and bake these. I'm hungry."

"Wait"—I held up my index finger—"one quick thought." Then, snagging the recipe from the bar, I held the card in my hand and stared down at the handwritten words. "Do you think your grandma's the one who gifted these cards to your mom?" I leaned closer toward Hayden. "Or maybe even passed down this recipe?"

Hayden shrugged. "Anything's possible, I suppose."

I offered my theory, pointing to Suzy Zoo's name on the card. "Well, Grandma Emerson's name is Suzi. Okay, I get that this Suzy duck has a spelling with a 'Y' at the end. And Grandma Suzi uses an 'I' at the end of her name. But don't you think it's possible?"

Hayden nodded. Blowing me off, he said, "Don't know. Interesting theory."

Still, I continued. "You should break the ice sometime and ask your grandma?"

"I don't know because my grandmother isn't like other grannies, mimis, or whatever else people call them, you know?"

Grabbing a wooden spoon, I held it so tightly my nailbeds ached. I could sense the blood pounding in my brain, signaling a headache might soon rage. Instantly, my tone went to a level of snarky it shouldn't have when I said, "No, Hayden. I wouldn't know."

Hayden just stared at me with his head tilted and one hand shoved into the pocket of his gray sweatpants. I kept looking at him. *At least you've got one for the time being, ass-jerk.*

Hayden shifted, placing both his hands flat on the bar. "I'll think about it, Gretch. Maybe you can help me write her or we can call her together sometime. Try to understand. She's like a stranger to me, and I hate it. I wish I didn't feel this way. Her letters are off-the-chart weird and kind of mean, like how she throws shade at Dad for being blue-collar. It's like she blames him for stuff he can't control. He didn't cause my mom to die. There are a lot of times I think about how I wish I could know my mom's story more."

Hayden picked up a nearby stainless steel mixing bowl before clunking it back onto the counter. "Sometimes I believe the adults in my life keep on holding a lot of effing crap from me, okay?" Hayden blew out a heavy breath before hanging his head with his nostrils slightly flared.

"Care to share more about that?"

Lifting his gaze, he answered, "No. Not right now. Right now, I want to have fun making cookies." Hayden glared at me, dipping his fingers into the flour bowl. Then, without warning, he flung a bit of powdery mix at me, chuckling. Minimal amounts landed across my sweater, not covered by my apron. It looked like a dusting of snow had fallen on my "Shine On" Christmas bulb.

Reaching into the flour, I grabbed a pinch, screeching, "You brat!"

Hayden took off running around the bar. Hayden had the best moves at dodging me, swooping in, and playing this game to win. Finally, I surrendered because he was too athletic for me to keep up with his pace.

Out of breath from chasing each other, we sat on the kitchen floor. Propping our backs against the bar's cabinet, we took a moment to laugh while gaining strength. Hayden stretched his long arm up to the counter, pulling his phone down. He opened his camera with these instructions: "Lean in, smile, and shine on, flour girl."

After, Hayden helped me to my feet. As I started to dust myself off near the sink area, Hayden came at me, winking with his palms, "Need any help?"

I just shook my head, smiling.

A jingling sounded in the hallway. Miss Spicy Boots and Gene appeared minutes later to check on the non-progress. In his over-the-top southern accent, Gene whined, "Where are my cookies?"

Hayden replied, "Getting ready to mix everything now."

"Want to join us and help?" I asked.

"I've got to get back to drawing up some plans." Gene whistled a little tune as Miss Spicy Boots followed him, singing along.

"Meow."

"Your cat loves your dad as much as she does you," I said.

"You have no idea how much he spoils her. He doesn't think I know, but he hides cat treats, catnip, and toys in his office. No wonder she camps out in there with him so much."

We chuckled.

"Well, your dad did save her life." I reminded Hayden.

He nodded, smiling.

I gave Hayden a sideways glance while sampling a mixture of sugar and cinnamon from one of the smaller stainless steel bowls. Then, after dipping my finger again in the bowls, I offered Hayden a taste. "Are you ready for me to read the recipe card while you gather the goods, so we can do this?"

"Go for it—I mean the recipe, not eating the toppings, *sweetie*," Hayden teased.

With my hand on my hip, I read each of the following items from the recipe card while Hayden said, "Check."

Ingredients:

3 cups all-purpose flour

2 teaspoons cream of tartar

1 teaspoon baking soda

1 1/2 teaspoons ground cinnamon

1/2 teaspoon salt

1 cup (or 2 sticks) unsalted butter, softened to room temperature

1 1/3 cups of granulated sugar

1 large egg & 1 large egg yolk (room temperature)

2 teaspoons pure vanilla extract

Instructions:

1. Preheat the oven to 375 degrees. Line cookie sheet(s) with parchment paper or spray with oil. Set aside.

2. Make the topping: Combine the sugar and cinnamon in a small bowl.

3. Make the cookies: Whisk the flour, cream of tartar, baking soda, cinnamon, and salt together.

4. Using a mixer, beat the butter and sugar together on high speed until smooth and creamy (about 2 minutes). Next, add the egg, egg yolk, and vanilla extract. Beat on medium-high speed until combined. Scrape the sides and bottom of the bowl with a rubber spatula as needed. While the mixer runs at low speed,

slowly add the dry ingredients in 3 different parts. The dough will get thick.

5. Roll the cookie dough into balls, about 1 1/2 tablespoons (or use a small cookie scoop).

6. Roll the dough balls in the cinnamon-sugar topping.

7. Arrange 3" apart on the baking sheet(s).

8. Bake cookies for 10 minutes. The cookies will look puffy and soft. When still warm, lightly press down on them with the back of a spoon to help flatten them. Allow the cookies to cool on the baking sheet for 10 minutes before transferring them to a wire rack to cool completely.

9. The cookies will remain fresh for about seven days in an airtight container.

10. If desired, the cookie dough can be made ahead of time and frozen without topping. Then, use it within three months by thawing it at room temperature to add the topping before baking.

Quickly, I snapped a photo of the recipe card I envied. Soon after, while trying to enjoy eating cookies, the handwritten words *"From the kitchen of Rosie Tucker"* ate away at me.

HAYDEN

Chapter Six

Dear Mom,

"Hip, hip, hooray for *Christmas Vacation!*"

Dad and I laughed through this stupid funny movie again this year. Sometimes, I consider asking him about the films you used to watch together. And if you had other silly Christmas rituals as he and I do. But I worry I'll make him upset when he's having such a good time, so I don't bother bringing sad issues up.

John let Gretchen out of his veterinary clutches, so she could visit for a while, giving us enough time to bake your snickerdoodles. On our very first attempt, we succeeded. Dad sure enjoyed your cookies. After taking the first bite, he got the oddest expression. Mom, I could've sworn he teared up. But I guess I understood and didn't blame him. Dad closed his eyes, saying, "Hmm. Wow. You kids did a great job. I'm headed back to my office." Then, joking, Dad called out in his southern voice,

"Miss Spicy Boots, I'm coming back, but I'm not empty-handed." With that, Dad loaded up a saucer with cookies and grabbed a sweet tea before scampering out of the kitchen.

It would've been so easy for me to transport myself into the pantry for a bit of time traveling with my mother. When we baked your cookies, the kitchen smelled of my childhood—those platters of buttery cinnamon toast you always made for me. Then after you got so sick, I learned how to make them for you. Cinnamon still gets to me. The aroma wraps me up in a weird cocoon of warmth, happiness, sadness, longing, and remembrances— all these emotions of wants and wishes. Will these feelings ever go away? Is it wrong that I can't move on or don't always believe I should have to? These memories belong to me because of you. I need them.

For Gretchen, the experience of cooking with me seemed a bit confusing too. After I said, "You know what it's like to have a grandmother—"

She narrowed her eyes and barked, "No! I don't know what it's like to have a grandmother, Hayden."

Her poor knuckles turned pale, squeezing the wooden spoon. It made her nails look white, then bloodred and sore. For a minute, I worried, thinking Gretchen might want to beat me with that thing. How did she manage to look so freaking hot while seething? I mean, Gretch had pinched-up eyebrows plus pursed lips. Throwing some humor at her occurred to me, but I thought I better not take any risky chances asking her how she pulled off her hotness. Especially not with her red hair appearing like flames along with the Devil's glare going down.

Part of me wanted to take Gretchen's hand, get rid of the wooden spoon, and pull her away from the oven, where she kept pretending to stir something. I wanted to gift her the call to Grandma Emerson, no matter how awkward the situation turned out. Another part of me considered throwing my cell at her with a "knock yourself out" message. But I thought better of that scenario too. And let the guilt wash over me.

I can't lie. The recipe cards piqued my interest in connecting with Grandma. Did Grandma give you those dumb-looking duck cards you wrote the snickerdoodle recipe on? If you want the answers, you must ask the questions. The only person who can answer me is Grandma, but I fear she might get rude. Am I willing to take the risk? I may not like her answers. But if I don't reach out to her, will I regret not taking the chance to know her and *you* more?

Grandma's been fairly decent on those super rare occasions she's called to chat. When Dad sends my school pictures or holiday cards, she calls to thank him. Dad sometimes makes me talk for a couple of very awkward minutes. So, she can be kind. Once, Dad helped me deal with the anxiety of being on the phone with her by saying, "Remember, Grandma Suzi gave birth to your mom. She raised her. Grandma's not a bad person. She's unique. Just listen for a couple of minutes and answer her questions."

Mostly she asks me about my classes at school and what sports I like best. And I think I've talked to her once since dating Gretchen. I think it's funny she calls Gretchen my redheaded beauty. Grandma's not wrong; she makes an excellent point. Dad emailed Grandma some photos of Gretchen and me from my birthday, Halloween, and Thanksgiving. Mom, I bet you'd be proud of Dad for at least trying to keep in touch with your parents.

Grandpa Emerson makes me smile every time we call. While I'm sweating it out chatting with your mom, your dad typically yells something like "Tell that good-looking grandson of ours hello for me!" in the background. Well, that's the gist of what I know about your parents and my grandparents. Other than they live in sunny Florida, U.S.A., as Grandma always puts in her quirky letters.

I hate that your mom's such a mystery to me. She's as much a stranger to me as the old ladies in the aisles at the Summerfort grocery store. The ones who grin at me in passing as they're sniffing, thumping, and lightly squeezing the fruit, testing them for ripeness. Knowing I should thank Grandma for the candy and tell her how much

I loved the key lime coconut best, I decided to replace my standard thank you note with a call. With shaky, swampy hands, I hit the numbers connecting to Florida, U.S.A.

My finger hovered over the call button. Then, throwing my phone to the bed, I stalled.

Instead, I stomped out of my room, pacing in circles in the hallway where Dad keeps some family portraits hanging. I stared at three faces until they blurred, my eyes welling. At thirty-nine or forty years old and healthy, you stood on the front porch of our home, arm in arm, like links between your parents, smiling. Taking the frame off the wall, I realized life would deny me the chance to share a moment like this with my two parents. My heart throbbed with an unfixable ache, knowing I'll miss seeing you grow old.

Studying the photo further, I saw how much you resembled Grandma. And I wondered if Grandma offered me a vision of who you would've become. Glancing at the younger version of my grandmother, am I peeking into the future? Am I looking at my mother somewhat? Could this be what might've been for us? So, I asked, already knowing I would never have the privilege of meeting you past this age or spending a single day getting to know you in the future. But somehow, my heart still knows how to love you in the now.

Maybe I can still get to know Grandma better? But, keeping my expectations low, I won't get as hurt by the outcome if it doesn't go well. I told myself that calling Grandma felt even more important as I held the frame. Even if talking to her sounds as frightening as crossing a swinging bridge through a tornado—Grandma's knowledge could bridge us closer to you, Mom. Because I need something to count on, something just for me. Damn it.

After I hung the picture back up, I got in bed, closed my eyes, listening to the heaviness of my inhaling and exhaling. What the hell did I know about anything? Maybe she wouldn't answer. God, I felt so stupid, drenched in a pool of my sweat. Just effing do it, I repeated. I thrashed around, squeezing my phone one second, only to toss it the next. Picking it back up, I dialed again, just to slam the phone back down on the bed.

Accidentally on purpose, I let my finger slip and graze the call button. "Oh please, God, don't let her be home," I mumbled. I prayed she'd answer in the next breath, hoping she'd want to hear from her grandson. My free hand wadded up a fist full of blue comforter, waiting, listening to the ringing.

"Hello," a high-pitched female voice chirped. Pausing, I swallowed. Why did my mouth suddenly choose to fill with cotton balls? "Hello?" She repeated. The more I think about this female voice—the rhythm of a high-pitched bird—as the melody turned into soft and soothing tones, I want to believe I heard fragments of you, Mom.

"Grandma?" I said, sounding like a kid asking a question because he didn't know if he'd dialed correctly. "Surprise, it's Hayden," I added, trying to redeem myself.

"How wonderful. Did you get my basket?"

"Yeah. Thanks. That's why I called. I thought I'd call instead of writing to you this year. I wanted to tell you how much I like those key lime coconut candies. They're my favorite."

"Those are my favorites too. Grandpa Ed likes the dark chocolate rum candies best."

"So does Dad."

We laughed.

"Hayden, those two always had a lot in common."

"That's cool," I said, my back plastered to my sheets, eyes glued to the ceiling, scrambling for anything to talk about with her.

Looking back, I know now I could've said so many things. Something as simple as "Really, like what?" But the opportunity for me to learn about Grandpa and Dad's relationship floated away. As always, I acted nervous and stupid. I got worried Grandma would rant about Dad to the point I let myself down.

Grandma kept the conversation going, asking, "Do you have big holiday plans?"

"No, just a small get-together with Cole, Drew, and some friends. What about you and Grandpa?"

"Grandpa and I have plans at a nearby golf resort that offers a Christmas buffet."

"That sounds nice and sunny."

"Yes, the weather's lovely here. That's why you should talk Gene into bringing you to Florida for spring break or on your summer vacation. He keeps *claiming* he will someday." Her emphasis on the word "claiming" made me believe I heard doubt, hurt, anger, or some combo of them all in her tone. Then, finally, she scolded Dad through me: "Tell your dad someday has come."

"Okay," I whispered, hoping she'd change the subject.

"You can swim in the pool or the ocean. Take your pick. Which one would you choose?

"I like them both, but I think the ocean because I don't remember my time there," I answered, recalling the photos from childhood.

"I like the ocean too. Say, Hayden, do you also like alligators?"

Biting down on my lip, I held in my laughter. My eyes darted around my bedroom, trying to formulate some answer quickly. *Damn, Grandma, you had to go with the alligators?*

Throwing my hand in the air, I gave up trying to get clever and just said, "I don't know," through my clenched jaw.

Grandma chuckled, so I finally allowed myself to chuckle a little too.

Then, squeezing my eyes shut, I said, "I've never even met one, Grandma."

Grandma laughed so loudly. I listened as she cupped her hand over the phone to repeat what

I'd said to Grandpa. I still heard him howling in the background through the garbled phone lines. When she got back on the phone, she said, "You sound just like your wisecracking dad and Grandpa with that joke."

I smiled.

"Well, Hayden, we have an alligator sanctuary where you can learn so much about them. There's a restaurant nearby where you can eat them too. Grandpa says they taste as good as chicken, but I'll take his word for it."

I cracked up. "I've never met one or eaten one either."

"Speaking of food, are you having a big Christmas dinner?"

"Not really, a family and friends' potluck, I guess you call it."

"That sounds fun."

Fun? I considered Dad's idea of the word. "I hope so," I answered back. "Hey, Grandma?" I asked, raking my fingers through my hair. "Since we're talking about food, I should tell you that Gretchen and I baked Mom's snickerdoodle cookies. They turned out good." I yelled at myself, *Stop sounding like you're confessing a sin, ass-jerk.*

"Your mom was a gifted baker."

"I remember some of her cakes and things. I'm glad I have some of her recipes, cookbooks, and pictures of her cooking with me." Saying this hit me hard, and tears stung my eyes. I had to pause from speaking. I stumbled, asking Grandma, "I used Mom's recipe card—"

I stopped, sighing loudly.

"Hayden, what happened, honey?"

"Well, Gretchen noticed the cards had a character called Suzy Zoo—"

"Yes!" She sounded so excited. If it's possible to hear a smile over the phone, I did. "I remember giving those to Rose as a joke because of the Suzy name. I told her it would be my way of bossing her around in her kitchen when she got married. Your redheaded beauty sure picks up on things. She must be the smartest girl in your class."

"She's at the top in history for sure. She knows every Constitutional amendment by heart."

"Now that's honorable. That redhead's a keeper. Too many girls want to act dumb nowadays. Dressing and wearing makeup as if they worship evil spirits, work at a haunted house, or as if they escaped prison cells."

Jeez, Grandma. "Yeah," I said before she got any more eccentric and judgmental. Then, recognizing the letter-writing side of her and sensing we were headed in a downward spiral, I added, "Well, Grandma, I just wanted to call to say thanks for everything."

"You're welcome. Don't let Gene overindulge."

Rubbing my forehead, I prepared myself to listen to her ramble on about Dad, so I closed my eyes.

"You know, I might have a lemon bar recipe your mom enjoyed. Plus, since you love coconut, I'll also look for our coconut macaroon one."

My eyes snapped to attention. As I opened my mouth about to speak, Grandma went on.

"Your mom loved those. I'll send them to you. Take care of your dad. And talk to him about visiting. Say hello to your brothers." Her voice weakened. "Grandma loves everyone so much." Her voice cracked before whispering, "Bye."

She hung up on me without allowing me to say another word.

GRETCHEN

Chapter Seven

And Christmas Continues

Dear Mom,

No wonder envy remains one of the seven deadly sins.

Again, I'd gone to Hayden's to have a fun day. What happened? I cocked it up. I allowed moments to get swallowed up, wanting. The need to jump inside Hayden's shoes felt so powerful. I tried to take over his life: to devour every sugary sweet morsel granted to him.

Baking and eating snickerdoodle cookies *should* bring on a good mood. Instead, I left Hayden, wondering where the equivalent of my mother's recipe cards was hidden. As I climbed into the passenger seat of Dad's Nissan Rogue, I wanted to interrogate him. But I quietly handed him a cookie and nibbled at the edges of one myself, pretending to eat. Except for Dad's approving "Mmm" noises, we drove a couple of blocks home in silence. Unknowingly to Dad, I gave him side-eye glares the whole way home.

A list of questions formed in my mind, as one by one, I fired them off at him: *Where are the family heirlooms? What can you tell me about my grandparents? Can't I see more photographs? Where did Mom's cell phone go? Why did the answering machine tape recording of Mom's voice disappear? Do we still have any video recordings of her left? Do you still love Mom now that Gabby's in the picture?*

A freaking Suzy Zoo recipe card ripped me to shreds. When would the universe deem me worthy enough to deliver the equivalent of a recipe card? I'd settle for an effing half cup of luck. Heck, I'll lower the odds and accept a quarter cup. Stealing or destroying other people's property isn't something I've ever done. Still, when Hayden's back was turned, I'd even considered slipping the recipe card into my purse to pretend it belonged to me for a microsecond. Seeing Rosie Tucker's name on the card as I watched Hayden living in some fantasy—

I swear I stared at his mom's handwriting until the letters blurred, transforming **From the Kitchen of Rosie Tucker** into **From the Kitchen of Gwen Gardener**.

Somehow, I felt Hayden got another golden opportunity for a significant connection to his mother's story because Grandma Suzi offered him a pathway. She's alive. Why can't he accept this?

It hurts watching Hayden throw this chance away. Mom, does the world ever plan to give me a stab at something like this? I'll shove him out of the way and take over his opportunity if he doesn't want a grandma. Because I have no one to call—no grandparent waiting. Grandma Emerson can continue to provide him with a family history filled with stories and pictures. But, of course, Suzi's also a little bit crazy. Doesn't she have the right to be odd? My God, she lost her only child to cancer.

I lost sensibility when Hayden said something close to "I don't know, Gretch. My grandmother isn't like other people's, you know?" My wanting Hayden to reach out to her about the recipe card overwhelmed me. Maybe I wished he'd have called her right then or thought to include me somehow. Or maybe let me share his grandma with him— flaws and all.

"No, Hayden. I wouldn't know," I'd answered, making Hayden's eyes look pained because I'd raised my voice. Then, he lovingly changed the topic. Again, his words, "My grandmother isn't like other people's . . . you know?" caused my body to tingle, but this time not in a good way. This time it got rage filled. Soon, we moved on to bake and laugh, but the idea of wanting something new to learn about my mother nagged me.

When I got home, I went downstairs to our kitchen. I rifled through the cupboards, searching for answers. Dad trudged toward me. "Gretchen, why are you slamming doors?" He motioned to the adjacent room using the TV remote he grasped. "I can hear you in the living room, which means I can't hear the news. I like getting updates about that spreading virus." Dad cranked the volume up, propping a hip against the counter. He crossed his arms after placing the remote down, staring at me, his eyebrows drawn together, asking, "What's going on?"

Cupping my hand around my ear, I asked in a dramatic tone, "What? I can't hear you."

Dad huffed, picking up the remote again and hitting mute. Unfortunately, the plastic piece holding the batteries bounced open when Dad forcefully made contact with the countertop again. Next, his shoving of the fruit bowl resulted in the bananas tumbling onto the countertop. Dad picked up the wayward fruit, draping them with some force over the Granny Smith apples. Then, looking at me through his Clark Kent black reading glasses, he said, "Go sit down at the kitchen table."

Oh, what-the-flippity-do-da. The kitchen table happened to be Dad's most famous lecturing spot. "I'm sorry. I didn't mean to interrupt your nightly routine. Just watch your late-night news shows, Dad. You don't have to deal with me," I said, waving a dismissive hand in the air.

Dad sat beside me at the table and stared at me silently for the longest awkward minute, drumming his fingers near the table's edge. He finally said, "I will deal with you because you're my daughter. Being your dad is an important part of my job. It's my priority, GG. Can you understand that?"

My eyes burned. I nodded quietly, just bracing myself for more serious-toned Dr. John Gardener's lecture. Even in his Rudolph the Red-Nosed Reindeer Christmas PJs, the way he sat all ramrod straight, his eyes blazed all businesslike at me. One by one, the questions bounced around in my brain, where they remained stuck. Next to me sat the person hoarding my answers. *Where are the family heirlooms? What can you tell me about my grandparents? Can't I see more photographs? Where did Mom's cell phone go? Why did the answering machine tape recording of Mom's voice disappear? Do we still have any video recordings of her left? Do you still love Mom now that Gabby's in the picture?* Nothing fell from my mouth. Only the tears came.

"Hey, what's wrong?" Dad asked, coming down from his stone wall perch and reaching out to hug me. "Did something happen with Hayden today?"

"Not really," I managed through a sob. "I got mad at Hayden about having a grandma and him not taking advantage of talking to her more, I guess. We're okay, though. I get so jealous of stupid things. It's too embarrassing to talk about." More tears trickled down.

Using the pad of his thumb, Dad whisked a few of my tears. "You have the right to hurt and even feel some jealousy from time to time. Promise me, though, if you ever need to, you'll talk to some-one—Doctor Han, me, Hayden, Lisa, Gene, Gabby, or anyone you trust. I mean, *ever*, Gretchen."

Loosely, I crossed my fingers. Then, like a six-year-old, I said, "I promise, Dad."

"GG, please, please, let me know. Are you hiding anything or having scary thoughts?"

"No," I somewhat lied again, continuing to sniffle. "You know, only the minor jealousy issues I already told you, Dad." Again, I wanted to pull away and hide. But instead, I picked at peeling nail polish on my thumbnail.

"If it helps to know, even as an adult, I suffer from jealousy from time to time. I know it can be hard to do. But I've learned you must allow others the chance to celebrate and live their lives on their terms. Over the years, I've also learned that people who envy someone often find out later people envy them for some reason. Remember, behind the scenes of a person's life is where the whole story lives, and we can't see or feel everything that's happened."

"I hear you, Dad." Raising my hand, I used my index finger to stab the center of my chest. "But I still don't think you understand, Dad. I'm an only child with no grandpar—"

Dad cut me off, pulling my hand down, saying, "Look." He cupped my face. "Gretchen, I'm right there with you in many ways." After he released my face, my head fell to his shoulder. He continued. "I'm an adult orphan, widower, and single father. Sure, I have my sister Jolene, but was she capable of helping me through my grief? —No. What I say next stays between us. It hurts to admit this, but I resented Jolene at different times. I wanted her to be able to step it up and assist me. How messed up is that?"

My heart throbbed for Dad. In my head, I listed all the titles he juggled and served successfully: adult orphan, widower, single parent, adult caregiver, brother, Doctor Gardener, John, Dad, Clark Kent, Superman, (UGH) Mr. Happenstance, and loyal friend.

"When your mom died, followed by my parents, there were times I wished Jolene could've helped. At least stepped in to pick out the clothes, a funeral song, a casket, or sit down with the funeral director to make any decision or even write any part of the obituary. Gretchen, I got angry at innocent Jolene for not knowing what an obituary meant. Talk about living with a guilty conscience."

My heart squeezed into a painful heaviness before fluttering. Then it pounded. Being so young when Dad lost everyone, I realized I didn't or couldn't have helped him during any of those moments. So, who did he have?

Tears filled my eyes quickly. Finally, I asked, sobbing, "Did you also resent me? And regret having me?"

"Never!" Dad answered. "Hon, I don't mean to upset you." Dad patted my back. "I just wanted you to understand I get where you're coming from. Even at my age, I still look around and see happy couples and remember falling in love and being married to your mom. I see people bringing their parents in with them and their pets at the clinic every day. Or I might overhear conversations at the grocery store between siblings planning get-aways or lunches." Dad paused, moving around into a more comfortable reclining position. Then, after sucking in a deep breath, Dad exhaled and continued. "It all just sounds basic, but sometimes that's life. I wish for those kinds of moments too." He finished with a shrug, halfway smiling.

Dad's words crushed me, but by the way he described himself, he did kind of understand me. "I had no idea you felt this way. I'm so sorry, Dad."

"You have nothing to be sorry for," Dad said, pushing his glasses up. "Listen," he continued. "You're why I kept going every day. But I knew you and Jolene were not capable of handling my pain. So, I'm sorry for the ways I chose to cope. And I'm sorry for how you found out and how badly my past behaviors hurt you."

"So, you promise you're not dating anyone but Gabby, and you're not secretly drinking anymore?"

"I'm only seeing Gabby. Drinking is rare these days or in moderation only."

"Dad, do you *love* Gabby?"

Dad's chin jutted out as if surprised by my question, his hand scrubbed at his whiskers.

First, he grinned. Maybe as only one of his stall tactics. But he answered, "Wow. What a difficult question to answer with a simple yes or no."

"Explain yourself in the Doctor Gardener way or however you need to," I said.

Second, he resorted to using his light, humorous voice. "Nice, GG. You're back to picking on your dad?"

I snorted.

"Let's see." Dad went on. "I enjoy spending time with Gabby. I see the possibility of potential for something for us in the far-out future."

What, Dad? I shouted in my head. Thankfully, he didn't see the confusion seeping from every one of my facial pores while he shared his convoluted gossip. Seriously, I believe my eyes popped open wide before they almost melted out of their sockets. My cheeks sagged downward until I went slack-jawed. Mother, women fall for this Mr. Happenstance persona. Who strings together the phrase "possibility of potential" on the same day with a "far-out future"? Mother, your husband, *Doctor* John, has an advanced degree. Did going gaga over Gabby render him unintelligent? I didn't know if I should laugh, applaud, stomp, or halt him from speaking. WTFDD, I gave up counting what he was doing. My decision-making abilities flew away, so there I sat, stunned to silence, listening to my father, who I thought I once knew.

"We get along well because we share a lot in common, but she is a bit more outgoing them me, which helps keep me busy. I appreciate her humor, intelligence, and attachment to animals. Poco adores me too. She talks about my daughter with a lot of affection. When she speaks about Jolene, she seems to understand her needs. Gabby's not pressuring me to rush our relationship. We agreed to be exclusive. As a bonus, Gabby knows about going through grief."

Um, okay. "Yeah, I bet, Dad." And there's the image of Gabby tossing her beautiful black hair over her shoulder as she quoted the five stages of grief in order. My nails dug into my thigh. They were covered in Color Street polish from Gabby today. Not for long. Chelsea Ya Later, I reasoned, knowing just how to scrub her away. Yeah, I am sure Gabby knew all the facts about death and dying from her training in counseling. We can all list the five steps in order, *sweetie*: Denial, anger, bargaining, depression, and acceptance. But living the steps by falling up and down them over and over is a totally different experience than just spewing them off randomly.

Why had I conjured up the image of Gabby in a *Legally Blonde* wig—her "blonde" locks drifting in the wind, with Poco, her Boston Terrier, beside her? Maybe it's because of the Color Street nail polish Chelsea Ya Later in the shiny golden glitter.

Dad's goofy cockeyed grin made him appear quite smitten. Focusing on Dad's Rudolph sleep pants, I allowed myself a needed smile.

"Okay, is that basically all you have for me? How do you feel about Gabby and me?"

"Gabby's all right. I guess she's a *sweetie*." I said, chuckling.

Dad smiled, bopping me on the nose in a teasing fashion. "Lucky you. Every once in a while, she's got quite an edge to her. You don't want to get off her sweetie list."

"I believe you, Dad."

"What else is going on, GG? You look like you want to say something."

Oh, Dad. I have a million things I wish I could say out loud. What if I unloaded all the painful questions inside my brain? How would it change us?

When I peered into Dad's droopy-dog eyes, I exclaimed, "How will you balance loving Mom if you grow to love Gabby too? Because I think you might love her, Dad."

Suffocating silence shouted and echoed.

WTFDD were you thinking, Gretchen?

My stomach flip-flopped as Dad squeezed his eyes shut. When spoken, the word love held too much weight, but I didn't know how to gobble it back up. Under the table, I felt the vibration of Dad's leg jiggling. I watched his hands ball into fists. Then, like I'd punched him in the mouth, one of Dad's fists flew to cover his lips. When he opened his waterlogged eyes, they were not focused on me but seemed to be absently studying the wood grains on the table. Using his index finger, he traced the waves of the wood before speaking or looking at me.

His cheeks puffed out after a long exhale, reminding me of the angry purple octopus from the book he and I once read together. At that moment, he perfectly resurrected the huffing octopus I used to love. Finally, Dad managed to talk in a shaky voice. "I'll always love and miss your mom, but I want to live a full and happy life too. I care deeply about Gabby because she's willing to take our relationship slowly and help me figure out how to answer your question. I'm thankful she's understanding. I don't know what else to say."

Dad paused, pinching the bridge of his nose in a manly fashion, allowing him to wipe the corners of his eyes beneath his Superman glasses. He continued. "As my daughter, I hope you'll extend me some understanding. I'm trying hard to give us a good life. Look around. I bet a lot of people envy this."

I hid my longing for a recipe card without saying anything, choosing to put the matter on hold. Then, leaning toward Dad, I placed my head against his shoulder.

My golden glittery nails sparkled. And I stared, adoring them. My mind was overloaded with love-hate images and thoughts, some of Gabby—but mostly a disappointment in myself. *Chelsea Ya Later*, *Chelsea Ya Later*, *Chelsea Ya Later*.

Chelsea Ya Later . . . something had to give.

Chapter Eight

Dear Mom,

It's almost 2020.

Mr. TBT, Cole, showed up for our Christmas gathering to crash into the New Year together. As the doorbell rang, the holiday lights danced, but I wondered if the Tucker darkness would burn them out. I can't believe him sometimes. God, I wish I could've known about what he told me a lot sooner. Had I learned of our story before now, I could've spent less time calling him an uptight ass-jerk. Setting aside long-buried secrets mixed with every emotion, such as too much pride, proved challenging at times for us.

Before Cole arrived in Summerfort, he checked into a hotel with Ariana in Branson and called. Dad paced downstairs, walking around the bar where I sat, observing. I overheard Dad on the phone, trying not to sound too upset, saying something like, "Cole, I cleaned up your spare room with brand-new sheets. Drew's pulling this romantic getaway crap on me too. I better get some time with my sons. Get over here to learn about the fun stuff I have planned." Dad's tone seemed to rise and fall, sounding filled with hope, hurt, and humor—he's getting good at juggling those things.

After Dad hung up from Cole, he patted me on the shoulder without saying a word, stomping off toward his office, where he slammed the door. A few minutes later, while sipping my sweet tea and scrolling on my phone, I heard Dad again. I shouldn't have heard Dad on the phone from down the hall with the door closed. "Drew Alexander, I am trying to ensure my three sons will be back under this roof for the holiday activity I planned." Dad's office went silent, so I assumed he'd calmed down some.

"Here, kitty," I called out for Miss Spicy Boots, even whistling a little, thinking she might be camped out with Dad again.

Walking toward his office door to check, I heard, "Listen, Dennis the Menace—" I paused, waiting to see if I could enter his office safely. Only, I overhear more muffled arguing with Dad threatening Drew. "Whatever, Drew. I'll use your words against you. I don't care how old you are. I'll beat your ass—" At that point, I didn't know if Dad had reached the teasing mark, so I pivoted in the hallway, shaking my head, smirking, as I tiptoed back to the kitchen to bake cookies.

Drew and Dad always verbally fight the most. Sometimes I think it's their weird thing that bonds them closer. Of course, not in a romantic way, but they find stupid reasons to fight, so they will have grounds to get loud, rude, joke, and forgive each other. Deep down, I still believe Cole and Drew hurt Dad's feelings by not staying at the house. So, instead of returning to the kitchen, Dad stayed in his office quietly. At the same time, I baked an entire batch of snickerdoodles.

With a dose of courage on a platter in the form of cinnamon and sugar, I delivered Dad a redeeming treat. I knocked, turning the handle using my free hand but finding it locked.

"Just a second, bud," Dad called out. Slowly he cracked the door open, peering down, yawning. He stared at the treats I brought him with my traitorous cat cradled in his arms. Both of them had sleepy eyes.

"Taking a cat nap, Dad?"

He grinned, grabbing a cookie. Dad shoved half the thing in his mouth, motioning me to join him in the office of Gene Tucker and his sidekick, Miss Spicy Boots.

Flopping down on the oversized loveseat, I said, "No wonder Miss Spicy Boots took up residence in your man cave." My palms rubbed the dark chocolate leather, admiring the softness. Then, I added, "This little sofa's a game changer. It's pulled me in.

Maybe I'll start hanging out in here now. Just hang up a TV, and I'll be set."

"Good. You show up, I'll put you to work." Dad muttered, with his mouth full. He sat diagonally from me at his desk, swiveling his chair to face me. Miss Spicy Boots scurried behind Dad to get beneath the desk in hiding, where I assumed she liked to sleep.

"So, Cole and Drew will be coming over later?"

Dad groaned, taking a sip of sweet tea and nodding.

Detecting a pissy eye roll possibly in the making, I chose not to address the subject further due to Dad's darting glares around the room.

If someone judged Dad by his home office, they might call him a hipster. Or people might label him as freaking *GQ*, even though the rooms are only about the size of a large bedroom with one window. In spring and summer, Dad's got one of the best views in the house, sitting at his desk looking out at the backyard and seeing flowers, trees, and the pool deck. Knowing him, he designed it that way on purpose. He custom-built his desk into two parts that separate naturally by the window. One area gets used for sitting, speaking on the phone, and computer work. The other side offers a workspace for standing or sitting, which Dad uses as a drafting table with a mini fridge thrown in for fun underneath. Regarding furniture, it's all love seats, desks, and minor accent pieces.

A coffee table and two small bookshelves he put at the end of the sofa do "double duty," as he calls it. "They can hold my work manuals, portfolios, contracts, and things, but then you can plop a drink on top and call it an end table," Dad said. Behind the door, I noticed a stack of new linens in the corner. Christmas-themed Kansas City Chiefs sheets to fit the full-sized bed were semi-hidden. Those "double duty" items went with the leather office sofa Dad meant for Drew to use. Squabbling about football fit with Dad and Drew. My heart ached a little bit looking at those unused items, knowing Dad picked them out on purpose. Poor Dad, wanting and now waiting for his little boy to come home, even though Drew's in his twenties.

I hung out with Dad for a while, just nibbling on cookies and looking around his office. I asked a few questions, admiring his talent, turning my attention to the two large framed blueprints hanging above me on the wall. Squinting, I studied the fine print: 726 Lavender Lane, Summerfort, Missouri. Then, getting on my knees, I surveyed closer. My eyes scanned every dimension as I took in every dotted line. Next, I followed the angle of each swinging door and every built-in cabinet. My fingers traced the arrows pointing to raised roofs through the framed glass. In awe, I saw the island in the kitchen come into view and noticed appliances and individual pieces of furniture drawn to scale to show depth in every room. Even the subtle curve of the staircase going to the second story appeared. That's my address, all right.

Like a little kid standing in an elevator with the buttons pushed, waiting for the floor to fall beneath me in a scary, exciting, fast way, my heart and stomach surged. "Dad?" I nearly screeched.

"Yeah?" Dad replied with a nonchalant shoulder lift.

I pecked at the glass. Then still on my knees, I pointed to the address. "That's our house," I said, almost shrieking as if Dad was clueless.

After gulping down sweet tea from his glass designed to mimic a Mason jar, Dad held on to the handle of his drink in midair. He chuckled at me before he explained, "I started remodeling this house before you were born. I drew those blueprints a long time ago. They're some of my earliest work. Let's look at a few more examples if you've got a minute." When I nodded, Dad pulled a sizable three-ring binder from one of the bookshelves, turning the pages to show me some of this earliest work when the doorbell interrupted us.

My insides froze. I hated not knowing how to greet my older brother. Still, I followed Dad to the door with a fake grin on my face, wiping the sweat off my palms onto my shirt. Dad unlocked the door, pulling Cole into one of his famous back-slapping man hugs, forgetting all about their phone fight. Cole reached for me, so I extended my arm, settling for a fist bump at this stage in the visit.

"Ariana wanted to explore Branson Landing for some last-minute shopping. She and Ava might meet up later. So, it looks like it's a guy's night here," Cole said.

"Hayden and I were hanging out in my office eating Christmas cookies while talking trash about you and Drew," Dad said, laughing.

I threw my hands up. "Oh my God, Dad. I was not."

They laughed at me.

Dad said, "Duh, Hayden. Chill."

As we strolled toward his office, he kept smirking at me. My lips didn't crack a smile. Instead, the weird togetherness of this father-son banter sent my adrenaline into heart attack mode. I wanted to scream, "WTF, what is wrong with you people? *And WTH are you wearing, Mr. TBT?*" Last time Cole showed up here in his uptight khaki pants and stuff. I think Dad's F-U-N plan involves chopping wood if Cole's clothes give any hints away.

Filing into Dad's office, Cole commented, "Dad, quit teasing Hayden. Instead, let's shift our focus to Drew. If we eat all the cookies before he gets here, he's bound to throw a Dennis the Menace fit on us."

I could visualize the scene, and the corner of my mouth twitched.

Dad wheeled his chair to angle himself in front of us while we sat on the loveseat. Immediately, the room shifted from the *GQ* vibe with the cool gray walls and comfy leather into a principal's office filled with lectures, secrets, strangers, or even a hidden fraternity paddle. If I felt I could've, I'd have bolted. I feared my stomach might revolt if any initiation happened. They could keep the fucking "C" word to themselves. No one needed to die. I didn't want to hear the truth. At that moment, I hated the world. I bit down on my lip with all my force to keep from lashing out or crying.

"My gosh, Hayden, your expression right now reminds me of poor Cole when Mom and I told him she was pregnant with you."

Cole tsked. "Dad, I was around thirteen at the time, thinking how gross my parents were for not being able to keep their hands off each other. And wondering what the hell are they thinking having a baby when they're so old."

"Old?" Dad laughed. "I could still have a baby at fifty."

I bolted up, crossing my arms. "What the heck? Are you trying to tell me that you got Lisa pregnant?"

Dad looked at me with his head cocked, eyebrows raised. "Ugh, no, *Dad*—but thanks for the safe sex talk, my dear son, Hayden."

Levelheaded Cole took charge. "Okay, guys. Wasn't this conversation about *Mom's* pregnancy with Hayden?"

Dad motioned me to sit back down as he said, "Yeah. So, sue me. I loved your mom. You're right. I couldn't keep my hands to myself." Dad smiled.

I flopped down beside Cole but kept my arms crossed.

Clearing his throat, Cole pretending to act serious, popped off with "Oh, don't worry, Dad. I heard how much you loved her through our paper-thin walls before you remodeled them."

Dad laughed. "Good one, Cole, keep on roasting your poor *old* Dad."

"Ugh," I mumbled. "This conversation's weird." Blowing a raspberry, I raked my fingers through my hair. They found this hilarious.

Cole glanced over to me, "Hayden, I'm the most scarred by Mom and Dad raising me in 'those conditions.'" He said the words those conditions with animated air quotes. I smiled a toothy grin, finding this side of Cole likable. If I had closed my eyes to listen to the sound of his voice, I wouldn't have known the difference between him and Dad. I'm amazed at how similar they sound when Cole lets his guard down, allowing some humor to seep in a bit.

My cell phone buzzed in my pocket. I glanced at the message from Gretchen, grinning.

Gretchen: Did your brothers arrive safely?

Me: Cole made it. He and Dad want to torture me with sex talk. Gross! Please save me. LOL!

Gretchen: Lol! I can't wait to hear all about this. Call later.

"Are you on your phone trying to ignore me?" Cole asked.

"Yes, you pervs," I answered, slipping my phone back into my pocket.

We laughed. Dad swiveled in his chair, obliging Miss Spicy Boots a chance to prance, performing her figure eights around Dad's feet. Then, with Dad's chair at just the right angle, I caught sight of something yellow, wedged beneath his desk, way in the back corner.

As I opened my mouth about to speak, Cole stole the words from me. "D-dad, tell me I do not see a freaking cat bed in the shape of a banana?"

"Yep." Dad shrugged. "So, sue me," he deadpanned.

Cole and I exchanged looks of disbelief, getting so tickled we burst into tears.

"Oh, knock it off. It's not so funny that you two need to make my couch shake," Dad said.

I slapped my thigh, catching my breath. "You stole my cat by wooing Spicy Boots into your private lair with fancy treats and gifts, Dad," I picked up the pink mouse sitting on the small round glass-topped coffee table. Then, holding it up by the tail, I announced with pride, "Proof."

Chuckling, Cole pointed to Dad. "You're so busted."

Dad pretended to look at his imaginary watch, smiling.

"What? You're not going to say, 'So, sue me,' just one more time?" I asked, laughing. Cole high-fived me.

Dad shook his head and swatted his hands toward me, brushing off my questions. He stood up. First, he rolled his chair neatly under his desk before collecting empty Mason jar glasses by dangling them from his fingertips. "Hey, I gotta use the phone, but I'll come back in a few minutes. I'm headed upstairs. Help me listen for Drew."

At the door, the sound of jingling occurred. Miss Spicy Boots appeared ready to follow Dad anywhere.

"Don't forget to take your new favorite child, Dad," Cole said.

I snorted.

Soon, the room felt claustrophobic without Dad. Sitting stock-still, I didn't know what to say. My palms went into WTF sweat mode. Questions took over my brain. Inside my head, I shouted: *What's up with your TBT pictures? Who's sick? What the hell do you know, but you're not saying?* I worked to keep the inquiries from falling out of my mouth.

After a long, suffocating silence, Cole spoke up. "I'm glad you like the pictures I sent."

"Oh, yeah, thanks. You said you had more to show me."

"There are some at the hotel. Maybe I have screenshots on my phone. I'll look." He pulled his phone from his pocket. Then, he let out an embarrassed sigh with a side-eye glance. "I'm sorry, Hayden."

"Next time," I replied.

"No. You don't understand. I'm sorry. I'm sorry I disappeared on you when we were younger."

What? "I don't care anymore," I said, turning my body away to look out the window.

"From your curt reply, I don't think you mean it, little brother."

"Don't call me little brother. You don't even really know me, Cole."

"Hayden, I know. I've soul-searched, realizing how much grief changed me. Even hardened grown men can act like children when their hearts break. I didn't disappear on purpose." He sniffled a bit, continuing. "I was your favorite person when you were little. This relationship we have now bothers me. I want to fix it."

Refusing to look at him, I asked, "What relationship?" I wanted to scream, *But I don't remember much*. My head fell forward as I cupped my hands over my face. But, my God, I didn't want to cry.

"Hayden, I'll always be your brother. Please try to understand. I fell apart too. I lost Mom too."

My brain pounded, reliving the scene. Still, with my hands cupping my face, choking out sobs, I mumbled, "Were you the fucking six-year-old who found Mom's body?" Bile burned my throat as my shoulders shook with grief. The stranger beside me sat quietly.

In a whisper, I finally heard, "No, I wasn't the one who found her." Cole placed a hand on my shoulder. In a confused state, I didn't know if I wanted to punch or hug him. Slumped on the couch with my hands resting in a pool of tears and snot, I failed to conceal anything. Even the roots of my hair felt doused in fire, but I didn't have the strength to fight, run, or say anything.

My heart cried. *Why, Mama? Why?*

"Hayden, I grieved for my little brother with no idea what to say to him or how to help him. But, Hayden, we reacted to grief the same if you think about it. We both got quiet and hid. You played alone in the pantry with the cars Mom bought you. I locked myself in my room, listening to the CDs she had gifted me. We both wanted to get lost as a way to find Mom. That should make sense because we are more alike than different."

When you've needed reassurance for eight years, words level a person on the day of reckoning. Knowing someone didn't stop loving you guts you. Cole tried pulling me into him, but I jerked away. Sobs just kept racking my body.

Recalling the years of pent-up anguish, I blubbered, not caring anymore about sounding stupid or all the tears. Enough anger finally built up inside me. My words tasted salty on my lips and across my gritted teeth. "*You* made me feel insignificant. The world felt like too big a place to accept me." Finally, I pulled myself back up long enough to glare at Cole through blurry eyes. "Sometimes, I— I had very—very dark thoughts." I swallowed. "You know like I should have just disappeared." I barely got the words out.

Cole grabbed my arm. "Stop it, Hayden. I'd miss you. Stop thinking things about me that weren't and still aren't true."

"God quit being so rough. Want me to slug you to prove I'm strong too?" I asked, wiping the last of the tears with the back of my hand. Reaching over, I pushed Cole to the edge of the couch. "You showed up today looking like a lumberjack or the Brawny man wearing black-and-red plaid. You're not your usual ass-jerk, uptight self. Plus, you're not even clean-shaven. What the heck? Who are you?" I asked, staring him down.

Cole quirked his lip for a second before he laughed. Once I released him, he shoved me back to my end of the couch, pinning me. "Give up, Hayden. I can't believe you called me the quicker-picker-upper-dude."

Jokingly, I choked out, "Stupid! I said *Brawny man*. Not the *Bounty* man."

We both died laughing, so he let me go.

"Truce," Cole announced, holding up both hands.

In reply, I gave him a thumbs-up, smiling. I had had enough emotional nonsense for the day, but Cole just kept right on bringing more.

He even cut through the current happiness with "Before Drew or Dad get here, I want to tell you a story."

My gut dropped. I finally understood Gretchen's private saying, "I might shit myself because they're making me emotional," in the worst way. By the time this never-ending night ceased, Cole might upset me to this level. In the ten minutes or so that Dad had left me alone with the Lumberjack, Cole had made me cry, swear, laugh, and fight him. So now, he wanted a story hour too?

After I nodded my approval, Cole began.

"One day, while finishing yard work, Mom and Dad left you inside the house in my care. So, naturally, I seized the opportunity and rearranged *some* items, meaning *all* of your baby gear got pushed into my room. At first, I thought Mom and Dad's bulging-eyed expressions meant pure aggravation. Then, of course, Dad put on a theatrical show. You know, Dad—the whole throwing his hands in the air dramatics—his voice growing even more southern—when he first saw the room."

I laughed. "Oh, yeah."

Continuing the story, Cole said, "I realize now it must've all been an act. Against my doorjamb, Dad finally leaned, biting his lip. Dad shoved his hands in his pockets. He swiveled, turning his gaze away from Mom and me toward the ground. I now comprehend the look on Dad's face. The lopsided look on Dad's mouth meant he struggled to hold in the laughter by avoiding eye contact with Mom and me. Trying not to listen too carefully because it seemed one more word, one more second, or even one more look, and everything would've been game over. His smile would've cracked wide open. And you know Dad. He would've erupted."

Again, I chuckled.

"Well, Mom stood with her hands planted on her hips. Staring me down, she cocked her head. Her eyes remained unblinking as I begged and pleaded my case. 'He's a good baby. Plus, you're right next door. So, you'll hear him if he cries.' Maybe I would've won if I'd filled them in on what I'd *heard* out of them."

We both died laughing for a moment.

"Anyway, so I say something like, 'I'll bring him to you if he cries too much. I'm great with Hayden. He loves me the best in this family. Why can't he be my roommate?'"

Cole looked at me and asked, "Hayden, do you think I appreciated listening to Mother's lengthy lecture, a.k.a. the justification of breastfeeding?"

"Ugh." I shook my head.

"Oh, she went on to tell me all about why Mom needed her baby boy nearby. Oh, I recall Dad's tippy-toed, chuckle-cough performance in the hall-way. As soon as Mom finished one lecture, another began."

"Mom instructed me with swooping hand gestures." Cole tried to make his voice sound feminine. "'Cole Allen Tucker, put all this stuff back in its proper place. Today! I'm snapping pictures of this to blackmail you when you grow up. Then, I will have evidence to prove to you guys the crap you put your mother through. This little scene you've created is insanity, Cole.' Exiting the room, on her way to get her camera, she glared at Dad. 'And, Gene Allen,' she said, slapping his butt, 'jump in and lend your son a hand.'"

Cole's storytelling so far has given me a lot of visuals.

"Instead, he pressed Mom against the wall for a lingering kiss. 'Gross,' I said, 'Jeez, get a room.'"

"I can imagine I'd say just about the same," I said to Cole, smiling.

Cole chuckled before going on. "'Oh, we can't,' Dad murmured against Mom's lips. Then, teasing, Dad hitched his thumb to point out the various piles of diapers, wipes, and baby clothes I'd stacked on the floor, blocking the doorway to their bedroom. I'd started relocating things back in place. 'Look. My son has destroyed my love life because I've got no room to go to.' Dad chuckled, kissing Mom *again* partly to annoy me, I think."

"'Jeez? Can you two at least stop for like five seconds with your little freak shows?' I asked, scoffing. 'Come up for air, Dad!'

"'Cole, it's only kissing. One day you'll see how fortunate you were to have two parents in a loving marriage,' Mom had said.

"'Well, I don't feel that way today, *Mother*.' I groaned.

"'All right, Cole, I'll go get my camera.' Mom said."

I stared at Cole. "So, you brought me the pictures?"

"They're at the hotel, I think." But Cole added, "Well, I have other stories too."

Keep them to yourself. "Like what?"

"Some things might be too heavy for today. I want to talk to you more about my experiences with Mom," Cole said.

"Like what?"

Cole shrugged. "You know those moments where you get barely through a day with lumps in your throat, needing Mom?"

Again, I nodded, knowing too well.

Cole continued. "At my high school graduation, I jumped those lump-in-the-throat hurdles trying to drown out the darkness in my head. All those 'What the hell, God? Why? I want my mom' moments on a loop that never ends. I wanted to hear her voice saying, 'I'm proud of you. I love you.'"

Tears sat on the edges of my eyes. I didn't say anything, but I understood Cole.

Cole went on yakking. "At eighteen, I remember thinking, Hayden's the lucky one. He doesn't have a long history with Mom, tons of memories, all those stories, all the years of living with her to miss."

As I listened, Cole's words got harder and harder to focus on. They jumbled in my mind with Thomas Sharp's face. I was back in school, inside the locker room and halls of torture and taunting: "Momma's Boy Hayden's queer as fuck. There's Hardly Speaks Hayden." WTF! Now, my brother wanted to bully me about my mother's death as if losing out on memories with her my entire life didn't destroy me as much as it did him. At first, my legs got jittery. Then, my hands pushed into the cushions of the sofa, curling. Finally, I couldn't take any more of him.

I jumped up, turning toward Cole with a fist drawn. "That's bullshit!" I shouted.

"Hayden!" Cole reared back into the sofa with his hands up in protest. "I don't feel like that anymore. Please. Please, let me explain. I am so sorry if what I said came out all wrong. Let's not fight. There's more to say, but not this way."

"Why? Why, Cole? Why are you coming at me with all this family history like a know-it-all? Why, Cole? Why now? What's the deal?"

Cole motioned for me to sit back down, but I shook my head. I scoffed, marching toward the door, tempted to leave. But instead, I leaned against the wall facing him. I just stood there as if in line for my firing squad. My heart hammered, and my fists were ready at my hips. I refused to speak except with silent tears snaking down my cheeks again.

"Hayden, I've realized you missed out on so much because you lost her so young. Grief affected all of us. There's no right way or wrong way to grieve. We can't measure the pain because missing Mom's love hurts us differently."

It sounded as if Lisa had possessed Cole's body and she had force-fed him the correct words to say to me.

The doorbell rang.

Looking down at myself, I sighed. Cole sprang to his feet, running to the bathroom. Not long ago, Dad renovated the small walk-in closet into a tiny half-bath, adding a pedestal sink and toilet. Cole grabbed me some tissue plus a drink of water from a paper cup dispenser. And balancing the cup in one hand, he used his other hand to quickly pull me to my feet and into one of Dad's one-handed, backslapping man hugs before I could even protest. Then, hurriedly, Cole said, "Listen. I have more stories and pictures, Hayden," as he offered me the swig of water.

After chugging the water down, I looked up at Cole, halfway smiling while I wiped my face with the tissue. "Dang, you're like a freaking infomercial with your never-ending options, 'Oh, but wait, there's more,'" I said, joking.

Beneath Dad's desk, I found the small trash can, so I discarded the tissue and paper cup. Still, something felt off. I couldn't shake the feeling because Dad's weird disappearance from his office for so long seemed shady tonight too. But I wondered what else Cole had left to say. Like, what life-altering crap did he have to stew about?

We exited Dad's office together, ready to greet Drew as brothers.

As Cole held the door opening for me, he said, "For now, let's go see what *fun* stuff Dad's planned for us."

Chapter Nine

Happy Holidays!

Dear Mom,

Sitting in my room about to get dressed for the holiday party, I recall asking Dad for Huggable Hangers in the shade of deep-sea blue as an early Christmas gift. I showed him the laptop screen and explained practical reasons for needing them—space-saving, safety coating.

"Gretchen, you're nearly sixteen. Honestly, hangers? That's one of the items you want?" Dad swallowed hard. His Adam's apple bobbed. From the corner of my eye, I watched him studying me with a furrowed brow, most likely concerned my gift choice had some kind of OCD connection. Maybe his feeling equaled more than a hunch? I didn't know.

"See, watch this video, Dad." I smiled, pushing the laptop toward him. "You'll want some, too," I teased.

He smirked to appease me. As he viewed the two-minute home shopping sales pitch, I knew when Dad heard "buy one set, get one half off sale," I'd won. Besides, I got rid of hoarding the old Christmas underwear you bought me, Mom. Plus, because Dad made me get therapy, I agreed to stop keeping a record of each pair as they fell to ruin. So, arranging my whole closet with a color-coding scheme with all my hangers matching seems harmless enough. The plan both excites and calms me. So much so that I'm biting the inside of my cheek as I write this journal entry. Using a fine-tip Sharpie, I marked the shipping and arrival dates on the calendar by drawing tiny aqua stars to track my hangers. Again, my heart counts down.

My mind obsesses about things like this: life gets sorted into seasons and measurements of time. Clocks tick down seconds into minutes into hours into a day—grid lines drawn on calendars record weeks as they roll into months until the entire year drifts away. This cycle repeats as the heart clutches to the milestones, pausing to stress at meaningful times, such as birthdays. Or first moments, like walking, talking, and heading off to school for kindergarten or other events. Every month gets filled. Birthdays, anniversaries, holidays, and activities keep life busy. Is this how some people measure their success? Do we try finding purpose in the square spaces called dates set aside for celebration as we live our lives?

At birth, individuals receive only a set amount of time, labeled as milestones to live and love on earth. My mother existed as a precious timepiece. Perhaps we should all think this way about life. Time is running out.

Time ran out for my mother. She died too young. Mother, your death made me want to discover ways to arrange everything in my life so that I might find some order. Or so I might have a little control over something. I still crave this because it helps me make sense of things. How do you take something ugly and turn it into something more beautiful?

ROY-G-BIV: red, orange, yellow, green, blue, indigo, violet. With my rainbow method, I like to organize items by color, including my closet. First, clothes need to hang, starting with red, fading into pink hues, before switching to orange. After violet or purple tones, the magical design ends with white, brown, gray, and black.

Anyone who unfolds my closet doors can evaluate the effects of neatness. Just don't judge the limited wardrobe: Gardener's Vet Clinic polo work shirts, leggings, yoga pants in various prints, jeans, tunics, sweaters, a couple of dresses, and lots of hoodies with causes printed on the front. Some of my T-shirts say things like "Save Animals" or

"Be Kind to the Earth." Dad bought me a "School House Rock!" sweatshirt made to appear vintage. Lately, I practically live in the thing. I've added a smattering of Summerfort Eagles gear now that I date Hayden and learned how to have some school spirit. Wearing our school colors, blue and gray, still reminds me of the Civil War battles. That part doesn't appeal to me much, but knowing I'm supporting Hayden matters. Those T-shirts and hoodies the booster club sell at the football and basketball games get softer and mighty cozy after wearing them. My first baseball season will happen soon, so I assume more purchases will come. When I went to the Tuckers' house, I "snagged" one of Hayden's last season's shirts since I liked the three-quarter-length sleeves in bright blue, and his #41 iron-on patch on the back still had some life left in it. Hayden relinquished the shirt with a toothy grin when I inquired about it, sitting inside the clean clothes basket, waiting to go upstairs.

So, I'm looking forward to the spring. It's when T-shirts will replace those bulky hoodies.

Guess I'm a part-time sports fan now. I enjoy staring at #41 while he's running, jumping, dribbling, shooting, and all those ball game things. When I think about sports, I giggle, Mom. Isn't it funny that most sports involve getting some kind of ball into a hole, space, or goal? But, anyway, you know how I get when I digress. The tackling, violent huddles, whistle-blowing, squeaky tennis shoes, mean-spirited plays leading to fouls, and of course, the clipboard-wielding, yelling coach part of the whole deal still annoys me. And, as Hayden likes to call them, some of the ass-jerks he has as team-mates don't do much for me, either. Let's face it. I've ignored the name Thomas Sharp. Besides, I'm thankful his locker-room antics and name-calling have gone into more hibernation after Dad's F-bomb speech at the vet clinic. If possible, I want to leave well enough alone. People seem to accept the status quo, anyway—you know, "boys will be boys."

Anyway, what got to me or sold me on going to games was when Hayden told me he secretly took on his number because it's the age his mom died. For this reason, he helped me develop more of a love of sports. So, when I wear my Summerfort gear, I paint my toenails with a hidden #41. Only Hayden knows. Hearing secrets no one else knew about his mom bonded us like I know the #41 connects Hayden to his mother, Rosie.

With a blank stare inside my closet, I think I've got to stop stalling, daydreaming, and get ready.

Back in bed, I worry about what I'm supposed to wear to a holiday party at my boyfriend's home. A dress? Ugly sweater and jeans? Leggings with a dressy shirt and boots? Mom, I need you! I want a makeover. Near sobbing, I try to keep it together and text Hayden.

Gretchen: Hayden, what do I wear tonight? Dress? Jeans?

Hayden: Gretch, wear what you want. You're hot no matter what.

Gretchen: Thanks, but not helping. What are you wearing?

Hayden: Sweater and nice jeans. Better? Still think you're hot in anything.

Several flame emojis and heart eyes caused my cell to buzz and ding. Part of me wished I could chuckle. Or at least crack a smile. Instead, I tried reasoning with myself. Finally, I said, "Stop obsessing over clothing, roll out from under the aqua bedding, and quit thinking how annoying it can be to lack help to get ready."

What's new, though? Since you died, with every outing, I expect anxiety. What do I wear? How do I style my hair—up or down, straight or curly? Which shade of lipstick and eyeshade best goes with our red hair? How do I pull off looking classy and sexy like you always did, Mom? The scenario always goes the same.

Mom, imagine: Dad and I go to the Tuckers' house tonight and enter a room filled with people. See, we accepted an invitation to our first real holiday party. Can you picture this? :) A real Christmas to celebrate since you died. That's my freaking problem! My overwhelming thrill of horror and excitement. I don't want to mess this up. Ugh—what if I show up overdressed or underdressed? What's the right balance? I need to know what works.

If I listen very carefully, sometimes I imagine I hear you yelling at me. But, instead, I think you'd say, "You need to breathe. Allow yourself to relax and enjoy this year's events. The Tucker family cares about you, not your wardrobe, Gretchen."

My eyes glazed over. Picking up my phone again, I'm thankful for Hayden. Grateful for the privilege of surrendering my heart to love. I'm blessed to have a place to belong and feel welcome. It's like a second home at the Tuckers'.

After trying on a red sweater dress with black boots, I snapped a selfie, sharing it in a group text, including Gabby. Before hitting send, I studied the name Gabby. Then, I closed my eyes and hit send because I knew including her was the right thing to do.

Gretchen: Lisa/Gabby, please tell me what you think of my outfit. What are you wearing tonight?

Lisa: You always look beautiful. I like it. I'm also wearing a comfortable sweater dress with boots!

Gretchen: LISA! Did Hayden tell you to say that?

Lisa: NO! Lol. I'm still at home.

Gabby: Sweetie, I love the dress. It's perfect. If you feel comfortable, wear it. I'm coming over to catch a ride with you and your dad. Do you want me to come early to help with anything?

Gabby added sweet nail polish emoticons, hearts, and smiling faces to the end.

Gretchen: No, thanks, Gabby. I think I'll be fine. I appreciate the offer. You made me feel better about the dress.

Mom, I realize Dad likes Gabby. So do I, but I don't believe I'm prepared for her full-time. What do I do? I don't want to get rude. She offers me kindness, asking *nothing* in return. I know she's just waiting for me to need her, like her, maybe even ask for her help. I can't be effing pleasing everybody when I don't even know what I'm supposed to wear, say, or do. It freaks me out too much. On a night I needed some peace on earth, her peppy energy would probably not work.

Through texting, I test the waters. Every single time she replies, offering to come to me. In response, I turn her down. I'm too afraid or uncomfortable. Heck, I don't know. I don't understand what emotions I'm going through because of this.

Sometimes I wonder if I'm jealous of Hayden's new life. Why? Because Gene got to Lisa before Dad. If Gene and Lisa stay together, Hayden wins! He gets Lisa, who rocks. Lisa's easy to talk to about anything. Hayden and I already broke her in with years spent at the Summerfort Grief Center. Maybe it's stupid and jealous of me to think this way. I feel bad, but it's true. Dealing with it isn't a huge problem but big enough. Guilt scolds me over this issue. As I said, I can't talk about it with anyone but you,

Mom. Not yet, anyway. How can I, without hurting everyone involved, everyone I love?

Gabby presents a risk. Many requirements, like time, need to go into this new relationship. Around me, Dad and Gabby act decently. Thankfully, I don't have to watch them flaunting a new love life. Knowing Dad, I'm sure they're "doing it," just not around me. Dad uses what he calls Happenstance stuff, a.k.a. his secret slutty skills, mainly to woo her at her house.

Let's analyze Gabby with a pro-con list.

Gabby's Pro List: She's a hardworking counselor who likes animals and has her own Boston Terrier, Poco. With Dad and me, she's not overly pushy but will offer to help with an upbeat personality.

Gabby's Con List: She overuses the word *sweetie*. If I had to guess, she might be ten years younger than Dad (will she want kids)? Do I want siblings? Does Dad want another kid at *his age*? Why isn't she already married? Has she ever been engaged or even married? Or has she ever gotten a divorce? What unknown facts remain about her extended family? She never seems to hang out with her parents or any siblings—too many whys.

Well, *sweetie*, maybe the time has come to find out and answer *why*.

Grief Diary

Dear Mom,

WTFDD. Heed my warning: Dad's officially a screwball. And I think I blame my boyfriend's dad, Gene Tucker. He dragged Dad into his holiday, F-U-N fiasco. Rewarding Gene crossed my mind. Shouting obscenities at him also seemed an option. Still, I remain undecided.

An unusual sighting came out of Hayden and Gene's kitchen during a family-friendly Christmas party. First, I heard a swish. Next, black polyester pants grabbed my attention as I saw swirling coming into the living room from the corner of my eye. Without hesitation, I asked myself, *WTFDD— what-the-flippity-do-da is going on? Holy shittlesticks!* I gawked, my eyes making every effort to adjust, not believing what appeared. My mind tried registering the sight but refused.

Finally, my brain acknowledged the scene. Determining the moment in front of me, I dug in my purse, snagging my cell phone. Still, I don't believe it. Is this a dream? Or one of those freaky-funny nightmares I'll eventually blab to people about before asking them for a dream interpretation?

I alternated between blurting out fill-in-the-blank questions with my cell recording, starting with something like "What the—" Squeezing my eyes shut, they filled to the brim before I opened them, releasing a cascade. My voice drowns out over the sounds of the other women. A whistling ignited around the room. Along with crying, I joined them in cackling and cheering.

Like me, Lisa can't resist ogling the scene. After black pants flew by, Lisa's "boyfriend," Gene, skipped into the living room. In some construction worker getup, including a skimpy orange vest, tank top (wifebeater), faded tight jeans, and steel toe boots, Gene topped off his look with the hard hat he wears on the job day-to-day.

Quotation marks for "boyfriend" illustrate my lack of knowledge of their relationship status. Since they've known and liked each other for years but only recently announced wanting to take things to another level. Nothing like putting Lisa in a room full of nonsensical people. Will these *events* amp things up several notches?

My focus settled on Hayden Oliver Tucker! The HOT dude dressed as a cowboy swaggering in. Under a big black Stetson hat, he was a stallion. His hair was primarily hidden. It's an unknown wild mustang's mane—the shy boy peeking at me with gray-blue eyes, sporting a crooked smile in painted-on jeans. The buffalo plaid button-up shirt snaking around his chest has rolled-up sleeves. Inside those boots stood the guy who could throw me over his shoulder and haul me off.

According to Gene, who announced through a karaoke microphone, "This charade promises even more fun to come."

Returning to Mr. Black Polyester Pants, the first person mentioned, makes me want to scream, "Scene of the crime!" Questions flew from my mouth again, muttered, "What the fu—" but I didn't dare finish the thought. Able to take the whole thing in, I realized it was a police officer uniform, appearing way too skintight.

"Dad?" I asked, shouting. Then, behind both hands, I hide my face in a fit of appalling giggles. In a nearby chair, Gabby, Dad's "special friend," clapped, smiling and wiggling, obviously hearing her own beat, which did not match the music. Still, she let her beautiful long black hair bounce. She zoned in on Dad big time. Back and forth, I glance at them, googly-eyeing each other. This whole thing—Dad's flirting and on a date in front of me—felt weird. And even though this whole thing with

Dad and Gabby is still pretty new and it's throwing me off a bit, I managed to stay in awe of this entire performance.

Leaning over to Ariana, I rest my head on her shoulder, still laughing. She's too busy whooping for her longtime boyfriend, Cole, wearing combat boots and camouflage. Onward, soldier. Prepare for battle because this *war* prevails. He's adorned with the ribbon "Dance King" on his lapel. According to Hayden, Cole had always been pretty uptight. Who knew the most stoic man of them all could march into a room gyrating like hell? WTFDD? Where did this Cole come from?

Usually, I am a Cole and not into the social scene. However, Hayden and I enjoyed chatting with Ariana before the dancing began. She instantly made me feel at ease, so I sat by her. Nudging Ariana, I asked, "You look an awful lot like Jennifer Lopez. Are you sure you're not related to her? Did you teach Cole these moves?"

Ariana shook her head before throwing it back in laughter.

Perched on the end of the sofa near me, with her feet crossed over at her ankles, rests Miss Ava Jade Elliott. She's what most might be too quick to dub as refined elegance—a southern belle with a voice as sticky and sweet as molasses. Yet, as the newest member of our party, Ava remained timid but very civil. While observing her, I noted blonde curls with eyes of rich mahogany. Perhaps comparable features of Carrie Underwood. And Jesus, well, He better take back the wheel. Her boyfriend, Drew, brought Ava to this exhibition. For a prim and proper southern lady, I believe Miss Ava's fond of bad boys if her uncrossed ankles and laser beam stare offer any indication.

Drew, outfitted in black leather, jeans, and an artificial sleeve of tattoos, had me wondering when he got a Harley-Davidson. Did he park it close by tonight? Drew's motorcycle jacket splayed open, and a quick second peep show of abs was displayed. Then, he cracked open a wide-mouthed smile for good measure, throwing out a perfect line of gleaming white.

"Oh, Lord," I heard Ava drawl.

I wanted to know what "Oh, Lord" meant to Miss Ava. While looking at Drew, with her eyelashes dusted in Better Than Sex mascara, she seemed to buzz with holiday lust and hatred or a mixed-up variety of the two with a side of sweet tea.

Strategic planning took place for this degree of nonsense. Concocting this devious plan required the scheming mind of a freaking master. Right at that moment, call me horrified. If I could have stood up to flee, I would've. But knowing me, I'd have stumbled. And cracking up, my tears made my vision blur. Until I saw this performance all the way through, I couldn't imagine turning away. But I couldn't imagine watching either. But I was afraid

I'd miss out if I dared to move. Better to just wipe my eyes and learn to press on.

Gene clutched the karaoke microphone again once the guys finished their initial lineup, declaring openly, "Happy Birthday, Lisa Noelle Marks."

Then in Lisa Marks's signature move—she went for the hand over her heart, blushing. Then, perching on the edge of the couch, she asked, "Thank you, Gene, *I think*?" She shrugged, followed by a huge smile, one reaching her eyes.

"Okay, Ava and Ariana, for those who don't know the backstory. This little song and dance number about to go down is dedicated to Lisa. Lisa recently wrote about her impression of me from a long time ago. It's written in a secret book she's working on, *Love at the Center of Grief*. I'll explain even more later."

Lisa groaned, slapping her palms over her face. "Oh. Gene." She whisper-gasped, knowing what was ahead.

Laughing, I get carried away. My body shuddered until no sound came because I knew what was about to happen—this event—funny, sweet, and weird—so awkward and everything utterly Gene.

Dad, how did Gene talk you into this? I'm sweating with embarrassment because my dad had no business moving like that, and he looked ridiculous in that outfit. But my boyfriend stood there, appearing so hot.

Gene continued. "On the day we met, your grief center was simply an idea dating back to the summer of 2012. Recently, I got to read your first impression or opinion, well, of me. So, I thought this little ditty seemed only fitting. Like I told Hayden, think of it as **F-U-N**. You know, *fun* but spelled with different letters."

Since I'm still cracking up, Hayden throws me a sideways glance, sporting a lopsided smirk. I think he's also trying to hold it all together. He tilted his hat with his cheeks crimson and placed his hips into moderate motion. Gene launched the disco music, and the men lined up.

The "YMCA" lineup: next to Construction Man Gene stood Cowboy Hayden; Phony Police Officer Dr. John Gardener, DVM; Military Man Cole; and Leather-Clad Biker Drew. They appeared dressed as a group of friends who may have stolen costumes from a Halloween store. Some components probably come from the must-be-over-eighteen sections.

They appeared stuck between two types of magic—first, showing alluring vibes of a mini Magic Mike extravaganza with a promising start-up. It quickly fell into the cute boys' category—like *The Mickey Mouse Club*—only at the "edgy" side of Magic Kingdom.

Most of us begin shouting "YMCA!" in unison. About halfway through the song, we all performed types of fist-pumping, hand-dancing, or singing.

The guys move toward us, tugging us to our feet. At first, Ava shook her head, digging her heels into the floor until she was the last one sitting. Then, she must've felt safe joining the party. We create a makeshift dance floor in the Tuckers' living room. As an entire group, we toss our heads back, filling the room with a mix of song and laughter. At the same time, arms soar into the air before contorting into Y-M-C-A formations. Gene had a point. F-U-N could indeed be spelled with different letters.

Eight years ago, our bodies slumped with grief. Tonight, surviving souls accepted invitations, making new connections. Some found their way back home, learning to let go of guilt, if only for a moment. Or, like me, felt a purpose for togetherness—the right to celebrate life, friendship, and love. Deep within our bones, with hearts still healing, we again laughed, sang, and danced.

But gifts remained unopened.

Chapter Ten

Dear Mom,

I titled this part of the story "Under the Tuckers' Christmas Tree."

After dancing, the guys changed into their proper clothing, meeting us in the kitchen for a smorgasbord of holiday snacking. Soon, we gathered in the living room. Under the Tuckers' Christmas tree, a long, lean rectangular box nestled on top of the heap of presents. A white curling ribbon with a tiny matching bow spruced up the shiny red gift, making the whole package a real humdinger.

A word like "humdinger" works, in this case, because it reminds me of something the gift giver says. Or terms such as jim-dandy or doozy work as well. The tag reads to Lisa from Gene. I grew eager to watch Lisa's expression when she discovered how much effort Gene had put into this. If I were Lisa, I'd assume Gene was in love with me the *instant* I untied the ribbon or ripped it into the Christmas gift, even before I stole my first peek.

Playing Santa, host Gene passed out boxes and bags at each of our feet. "Let's go round-robin," Gene said to the five couples in the room, balancing the last few small items in his arms.

Gene placed the pretty red box in front of Lisa. A half-smile materialized at the corner of her mouth, pausing as if she were waiting for a safety clearance before allowing herself permission to reach a full-blown smile. Nervous about what lurked inside, Lisa glanced at Gene before giving in. Seeing his expression, she mirrored his. And her smile once again tonight went all the way to her eyes. Then, stretching out, she patted Gene's hand, asking, "Before I lift the lid in a bit, will I find more F-U-N inside but with different types of letters?"

Laughter filled the room at the recent memory of Gene's choreography skills demonstrated during the contemporary "YMCA" dance. Then, everyone joined in on the action of recalling and chuckling.

I noted Gene was stewing as he drew a gusty breath before exhaling. "To get back to your question, Lisa, yes, there are some letters, but I'm not going to dance," he offered this reply as a hint and a phony grin. Gene used a kind but quiet and subdued tone. "It's not a gag gift. I'm hoping you like it." Gene tapped a finger to his chin, looking around, ensuring everyone was ready. Deep anticipation shows in his eyes.

Swallowing, he sighed. Having finished his Santa duty, he sat down, rigid and tight-lipped—everything anti-Gene. Maybe giving a gift like this in front of others seemed overwhelming and private. Even Hayden seemed affected by all this idle sidebar chatter. His palm felt soggy, hugged against mine. I realized the need to lean closer and tighten my grip, even if my sweat added to the slickness.

Purchasing something for Lisa at this stage of their relationship might seem too intimate or emotional? Gene's friendship with Lisa had existed for years. Now, the romance portion looked ready to begin with gusto. How many years had it been since Gene had bought a woman an extraordinary gift? Probably not since the death of Rosie, his late wife. If so, then at least eight years. Hayden claims Gene never brought anyone home in all this time, but he assumes he may have been like Dr. Gardener (Dad) and did some "Happenstance" dating.

"Happenstance," according to Dad, means running into someone out of the blue, like at the post office, so you go out on a date. Or, as I call it—the uppity way Dad described his no-strings-attached casual sex charades. His man-whore companionship confessions had forced me to come clean about hoarding Christmas underwear my mother gave me, realizing I had OCD. So, heavy stuff. BOOM—nothing like dropping a bomb in the middle of a Christmas party of fun to remember a bunch of crap. Dad spending time with Gabby seems far preferable to him sexing it up with Deb-*BORE*ah, Lilly's mother.

Shifting my thoughts, they wander to Hayden and his brothers, Drew and Cole. How does catching sight of their dad buying and giving a woman a gift of this level feel? Are they happy for Gene? Do they see flashbacks to boyhood—remembering everything about their mother? Or do they try their best to forget she's gone? Maybe a big mixture of guilt for being both happy for Gene and Lisa but sad about missing their mom? Do all the Tucker guys adore and respect Lisa? Hayden mentioned worries about what might change. Gene had strong enough emotions about Lisa to bring her into his home to share his sons, traditions, and family holiday.

My heart rattled watching. Fear, love, hope, and sadness surged through me. Maybe I picked up on Hayden's vibes? I don't know. It's one of those misty-eyed happy-sad moments grief puts people through. You hang on loving the past, try living in the present, look forward to the future, hoping to take the past and present with you. It's so confusing.

For a fleeting second, I worried, pondering how I would handle dealing with Dad. And these kinds of problems in the future? What will I do or feel if Dad ever buys Gabby something as charming as

Gene has for Lisa? Of course, I don't dislike Gabby. She's okay. But right now, *sweetie*, I don't want to address the issue. So, let's not get ahead of things with speculation.

Gene says, "You're up, Gabby."

She leaned to her stash, reading "To Gabby and Poco from John and Gretchen. Aww, thank you. Look at the paper." Gabby holds up the box, showing the Boston Terrier playing in the snow. Yes, I told Dad about the gift wrap, so he'd buy it. Big hints for Gabby's gift appeared on the outside for the items awaiting her on the inside. "*Sweetie*, did you help your dad pick out everything?"

I nodded. "Dad did a lot of research, but I helped. We hope you love everything,"

Hayden pinched my hip.

Dad plastered a goofy grin on his face as he focused on her tearing the paper. A safety barrier for my father in the area of jewelry that looks like Poco, Gabby's beloved black-and-white Boston Terrier, whose vet just happens to be the good Dr. John Gardener, DVM. He ordered fancy identification tags for Poco. Dad found a website, maybe through Etsy, which allowed us to shower Gabby with a matching hoodie sweater set for her and Poco. Thank God the madness stopped there. No additional shirts for Dad and me, even though Poco's freaking cute.

"Oh, how cute!" she exclaimed, dragging out every syllable. Gabby's eyes drifted into focus on

Dad as she held up her sweater. "John, you need a matching one."

He grinned, shaking his head.

Gabby turned her gaze toward me. "Maybe you should get one, *sweetie*?"

"I don't know. I think I'll leave all that style to you and Poco," I said, laughing. "It's going to be so *sweet*." I felt Hayden's ribs expand with air as he held in a laugh. Then, he gave my thigh area another "sweetie" squeeze. I about elbowed him.

Maybe the hoodie's stylish, but I don't think I desire to dress as a twin with my high school counselor and her dog. So, Dad ordered the blue-and-gray striped pattern since these colors fit Summerfort High School. Plus, Poco acts as the unofficial mascot, waddling around, so this will look so darn adorable.

"Thank you, John and Gretchen. I do love it."

Dad patted her shoulder. "You're welcome, Gab. I can't wait to see you and Poco wearing them."

Then, *it* happened. Dad positioned himself to lean into Gabby to quickly and lightly kiss her. Dad. Kissed. Gabby. Dad kissed Gabby in front of me. Not just me but in front of *everyone*.

Hayden gave me a reassuring hand squeeze.

Gab? Oh, how freaking sweet. My face and stomach fell. *Why did that seem so awkward? I knew they were dating.* I stared at the present yet to be opened, worrying about something else.

Hayden gave me a crooked smile, releasing my hand and draping his arm around me instead. He dusted a kiss against my temple. "Jeez, what's up with this freakin' stalling? The gawking at presents? Now, we're throwing away tissue paper, taking bathroom breaks, and getting drinks? It's making me nervous. I'm stupid and awkward, right?"

Interrupting us, Gene barged in, carrying a few small gift bags. "I forgot to set these out earlier. Remind me to tell everyone to just go for it and enjoy. It's some stocking stuffer-type items," he said, looking at Hayden and me.

Peeking in my bag, I said, "I've got you covered, Gene."

He smiled, giving me a thumbs-up, and took off for the kitchen again.

"Oh, thanks for the aqua gloves," I called out, laughing.

"I'm sorry," I said, jumping back into my conversation with Hayden. "You're never stupid. I think everything's going okay, even if it's been strange at times." I offer a reassuring smile.

Hayden pulled his hand down from my shoulder, holding it up. "Um, embarrassing, Gretch. Sorry I pulled away—sweaty palm."

As Hayden wiped his palm on his jeans, I leaned close, saying, "It's only hot, humid Hayden hands, *sweetie*. I don't mind." Hayden poked me gently in the ribs with a smirk, so I assumed he understood and appreciated the joke. Hayden walked his fingers across my knee, pretending to offer a little sway as his approach began dangerously nearing my midthigh. A deep guttural sound, like a grunt, surfaced. The bodily vibrations he caused felt powerful enough to surge through me. I tingled with a need for more closeness—a type of nearness that would allow me to hear his thick black eyelashes flutter against me.

His fingers stayed posed on my leg. Hayden used them as puppets to quietly say, "You look hot tonight. You make it hard to behave. I know I should care that people are around, but I'm not sure I do. Besides, most aren't in the room right now." As I smiled, attempting to thank him, he claimed my mouth with a feathery kiss, stealing words away. Making the noise once again, he squeezed my knee before grabbing my hand. We laced fingers.

Merry Christmas!

All five couples gathered back together. The red gift sat in front of Lisa, taunting all of us. So, with Gabby's turn done and all ten of us in the room, it was back to Lisa. Aware of Lisa's gift contents, Hayden's eyes darted around the room, *appearing* uncomfortable as he bounced looks off each of his brothers. Then, his thumb caressed gently over my wrist while holding my hand again.

"Did your dad get a chance to show Drew and Cole the gift?" I asked.

Ava, Ariana, and Gabby seemed engrossed in their bag of trinkets from Gene.

"Not sure if he had time to show them, but he told them. Cole told Dad he was happy for him. And Drew said he sorta remembered Lisa from way back, and she's a good person. So, we got lucky. He let us see it. So, I'm a little more at ease."

"Yeah, I understand how knowing would take the edge off. Your dad went above and beyond. He's looking kind of freaked out, though. You think your brothers are fine?"

"Do you think Dad's worried about scaring Lisa off? Or, you think, like, there's a possibility she won't like it?"

I shook my head.

"Drew and Cole seem—"

Before Hayden could finish his thoughts, "Open it!" erupted around us.

"Open it!" The room repeated the chant with Drew as the ringleader.

Cole joined in, shouting, "Open it!"

My questions were answered about whether Drew and Cole accepted Gene and Lisa. Gene offered Lisa a go-ahead nod, smiling.

Past the red-and-white packaging, Lisa's prying eyes caused her mouth to form an "O." Shaky fingers covered her mouth. "Wow, Gene." For a moment, she stared dumbfounded. Then, moving her fingers down, she tenderly touched each piece of gold. A speechless, silent downpouring of tears occurred. Gene permitted Lisa time to read the note she found inside silently. Before the party,

Chapter Ten

Gene had let Hayden and me see the gift and letter, and the words had touched my heart so much that I memorized them:

Dear Lisa,

For literally putting up with all my grief. For all the lives you've changed, making "macaroni necklaces." Like your heart, you deserve macaroni pieces formed into gold. Even ones engraved with the same lasting reminder of a little center you opened for others. I now realize your center isn't just a building. It's your heart offering a place to heal, hope, and belong. Thank you, Lisa.

Merry Christmas

Kumbaya,

Gene

Gene slid across the floor as Lisa clutched the card, moving next to her. Both of them sat on the floor in front of the Christmas tree. He whispered something to her while they embraced. Then, with her back turned to the people in the room, Gene held her with his eyes closed.

"What do you think he said?" I asked Hayden.

"Kumbaya"? WTFDD? Another moment of strangeness to endure tonight.

Hayden tilted into me on the couch, cupping his hand for privacy, so he could whisper. "I don't know, but I'd tell you I love you. I'm not sure if Dad and Lisa are at that point?" Hayden sighed. "I just don't know."

"I love you, too." I replied as my head went on a bender. *God bless America. I want to take you to*

165

the kitchen pantry and smear cinnamon, sugar, and butter all over you, Hayden Tucker. I want to turn you into a snickerdoodle cookie to devour. But, of course, I'm not supposed to have impure thoughts in the same room with a crowd of people, I'm guessing. Still, it doesn't change the fact that I want to go make out.

I also thought, *Oh, and yeah, Gene and Lisa have reached that point, Hayden. Whether they say it or not, I see it in their eyes and how they touch. I guess they haven't gone past saying Kumbaya yet.* So, keeping my comments on the down-low, I brushed against Hayden's lips, offering a little public peck.

"I don't know about them, but I know what I'm thinking about you," I answered, grinning. Then, giving me a toothy grin, Hayden squeezed my hand tightly. Guessing the feeling might be mutual.

Overwhelmed by the sentimentality, Lisa needed a semi-private moment with Gene. Crying happy tears, she pulled herself together. Then, grabbing Gene's arm, Lisa fanned her face, taking cleansing breaths before facing us.

Gene asked, "Lisa, may I show the necklace to everyone?"

"Oh, sure. Afterward, will you put it on me?" Lisa asked.

"Sure will. Guess this means you still like me. Is it for my skilled *dancin'*? Or the necklace?"

Lisa laughed, accepting Gene's hand as he helped her off the floor. I saw Lisa's lips silently mouth "For everything." I wondered if anyone else noticed, but I decided not to ask.

Making their rounds, they showed everyone the necklace.

"Lisa, I love the necklace," Ava said.

"Thank you," Lisa said.

"Gene, tell me how you came up with this idea?" Ariana asked.

Ava nodded, grinning.

"When I first met Lisa, can you imagine me spoutin' off rude comments?" He shrugged. "First, I said something stupid about her designing the grief center as a place people could make macaroni necklaces." Gene hangs his head shamefully. And, looking up, he added, "Secondly, to make matters worse, I go and add something even dumber about her having people gather and sing 'Kumbaya.'"

Lisa cut in, encircling Gene's arm with a wide grin plastered on her face. "After eight years, let it go. I've forgiven you." She seemed ready to move the conversation to the inscription on the gold macaroni with her eyes dried. She explained, "A letter in my dad's will mentions the phrases 'heal, hope, and belong.'" As she touched the necklace, she said, "Dad believed if I found a place that brought me hope and healing, it would be where my heart belonged. And the motto of the Summerfort Grief Center states 'a place to heal, a place to hope, a place to belong.'"

Gripping Gene's arm even harder, Lisa says, "Mr. YMCA made sure he packed a punch, putting everything into one beautiful gift." Pointing out the necklace to Ava and Ariana, Lisa leans over for them to see, adding, "Read Gene's note now that you know of the backstory. You'll understand my emotional reaction."

"Oh, Lisa, it's amazing. The note's perfect. Gene, you did great," Ariana said. "I have loved learning about this story." She glanced at Cole, giving a slight hand gesture. "Your son's a super guy, but you're the one who's got game, Mr. Tucker." Ariana reached for Cole's hand, chuckling.

Cole pretended to kick toward Gene. "Dad, look at you—you better stop strutting around, wreaking havoc on everyone's love life."

A huge grin stretched across several faces. Studying the Tucker boys beginning to stand and form in this semi-circle, I'm in awe of the resemblance. Warmth beamed from their eyes and mouths. This feeling of a family of inclusion brought me a sense of happiness. Remaining quiet, studying the faces, I simply enjoyed the company.

"Cole, since I'm your dad, I'm always available for lessons. And to give out pointers." Everyone's quick to laugh at Gene's comeback.

"Well, Ava may want to take you up on those lessons, Dad," Drew said as the couple gathered closer to Lisa and Gene.

Blonde waves of hair cascade against Drew's chest. "That's unnecessary," Ava says, gazing up at Drew.

"Ava, I hope my son Drew stifles his Dennis the Menace character when he's on campus in Cape Girardeau or around you at school?"

From Gene to Drew, Ava's eyes ping-pong back and forth. Finally, she settled on Drew with fierce concentration, like she was under interrogation. I imagine meeting many family members at once might have a scrutinizing ambush feeling in a group like this. Ava acts like a wounded deer, unaware of how to answer her life questions with Drew. I consider jumping in to help her, telling her Gene's kind and everything's okay. Yet, I know very little about Drew, even less about his persona Dennis the Menace. Drew offered Ava a shoulder squeeze as if to say, "Whatever you say, I support you."

"Drew has helped my family and me so much. But I'm not sure how much of my situation he's told you."

Drew latched on to Ava, cinching her in closer at the waist. "I kept most of your story to myself, Ava, unsure what to tell."

Ava appeared on the verge of being misty-eyed. Then, focusing on Drew, she said, "Since he invited me to Summerfort, I assumed he explained some things."

Sounded curious and interesting. Then, with my fingers interlocking Hayden's, I stared up at him, sharing a WTFDD grin and secret hand scrunch. Hayden returned with an extra grasp of private acknowledgment.

"Sorry, Ava. I wanted to allow you to divulge the story on your terms," Drew said.

Gene said, "Ava, I'm sorry. We don't mean to put you on the spot. We're happy you're here. Feel free to share as much or as little as you want."

"Thanks, Gene. Earlier, you asked about Drew and his Dennis the Menace ways."

Gene nodded.

"Eavesdropping on me after class—well, that's how Drew met me."

Collectively we perked up. Somehow, I found myself part of the group, shuffling forward until we were standing shoulder to shoulder, our circle more intimate. Ava was quite a southern charmer and knew how to introduce a story.

A well-manicured hand flew up, and her polished nails in pale pink with glittery silver tips went on display as she curled her fingers into the zero symbol. "We had a teacher with zero empathy." Ava's voice raised a few notches. Rehashing the event seemed to cause her perfectly pouty lips to droop.

Hayden tugged on my arm, whispering, "You know by the look on her face, this teacher's a total ass-jerk."

I nodded, snarling my lip in disgust.

Ava leaned hard into Drew's side as she continued. Then, after she sighed, she said, "Feeling defeated, I left class crying because he wouldn't give me an extension to take my mom to chemo."

"That's so messed up," I said.

"I thought so, too, Gretchen. But I figured I'd juggle everything somehow."

Hayden and I cocked our heads, feeling appalled.

Pointing at Drew, Ava grinned. We all want to hear more—this part of the story—the upbeat portion.

"You going to tell us your part of the story, Drew?" Hayden asked.

"Oh, Ava's the pro at storytelling," he said. "I'll let her continue."

She smiled. "Well, Drew *overheard* everything because he'd been outside the door, waiting. So, when I floundered into the hall, I ran right into him. He said, 'Please, wait for me in the hallway.' Confused, I watched this guy I barely knew march through the door. Without showing any fear, he looked ready for a confrontation. In disbelief, I propped myself against the wall, listening as this guy"—Ava patted Drew's arm—"threatened to go to the Dean's office to report the professor's *unprofessional* and *unreasonable* behavior."

Our group chuckled.

Ava paused, beaming up at Drew.

"I meant it," Drew said, wrapping Ava in another tight squeeze, kissing the top of her head.

As Ava spoke, I envisioned Drew helping Ava, so I fell in love with his kindness. He's a Tucker for sure, I thought, looking at those men around my circle.

Ava continued. "I kept thinking, Who is this guy? Does he even know my name? We've only had a couple of class sessions together. So, why's he defending me? Then Drew's words touched me. I recall his rambling rant as he said, 'Let me guess—you're one of the fortunate guys—the type who takes his mother for granted. I bet she's healthy and alive. My mom died of cancer. And that girl's mom is trying to survive.' The instructor interrupted Drew. 'Drew—enough—you've made your point. Take off. Enlighten your ladylove, Ava. Tell her I am gifting her those two days. That's it. Two.' 'Oh, she's not my girlfriend *yet*.' Drew made sure he had enunciated the word *yet*. About this time, Drew appeared in the doorway. He peeked out, smiling at me, before peering back over his shoulder at the professor, saying, 'I'm not even sure this Ava will go on a date with me. But I'm curious to find out. Regardless, thanks for helping her and her family.' 'Hey, Ava,' Drew said, strolling up to me, staring straight, with every tooth in his head shining bright. After he shook my hand, he said, 'I'm in this class with you. I'm Drew, by the way.' That's when I knew I was a goner," Ava said, finishing her story.

"Aww," I said, with all the girls chiming in unison.

In the background, I heard the familiar Christmas carol, "Chestnuts Roasting on an Open Fire," which took my focus away from the party. I zoned into the past by reaching inside my Christmas stocking to open a gift from childhood. And now, I saw my favorite childhood pair of underwear. My days-of-the-week underwear with the Christmas-themed squirrels roasting marshmallows around the campfire. But they were gone. And, so was the giver—

"Hey. Did you hear me?" Hayden asked.

"No, what? Sorry, I guess I didn't hear you." I answered.

Hayden rested his chin on my shoulder. "Just wanted to remind you that a few days ago, Drew claimed Ava's the one on the phone. Do you think he might mean it? He does act differently with her."

"How so? What's different mean?" I asked.

"I don't know. Drew still jokes around some, but he pays way more attention to Ava than anybody he's ever dated. He brought her home. He's different. I can't see him wanting to ghost her or anything as he normally would. Drew used to pride himself on giving consensual 'dine and dash' a whole new meaning. If you know what I mean."

"Ew. Gross. Hayden." I said, peeking around to make sure no one heard us. We'd pulled away a few feet from the circle to chat alone.

Hayden threw up his arms. "I'm just repeating stuff. Saying some truths." He chuckled. "I'm not the one who talks like that. Blame *Dennis*. See, that's what I mean. It's all good. I think *Drew's* changed." Hayden dragged out the name Drew in a whisper-shout.

I smiled, looking at Drew with his arm around Ava's waist.

Gene said, "Ava, I'm pleased to hear my son acted on your behalf. Glad he's using his Dennis the Menace act for good reasons. Sorry about your mom's cancer diagnosis. Treatments, as we know around here, can be a stressful business. I imagine going to school at the same time is tough." Gene hesitates but asks, "H-how is your mom doing?"

"Thanks for asking about her, Gene. My mom is in remission. Her hair's growing back, and she's getting stronger every day. My family feels hopeful—"

Ava's smooth Kentucky bourbon voice faded. Unable to focus, her sweet southern words evaporated in the air until they entirely disappeared.

Ava's mom got to live. I'm thrilled for her family. I don't want anyone's mom to die. *But my mom's dead! My mom's dead! Why didn't my mom get to live? Why did she have to die? I hate myself right now for inviting DEATH to the party. The effing con man found me like I knew he would. Why do I feel like this? Is this jealousy? A regular part of grief?*

I got sucked right into a vortex.

But eff you, Ava. My mom's dead. Dead! —this startling realization slapped my face yet again.

Even my squirrel panties are gone forever. Over and over, a reality I find too painful and too hard to explain sometimes. Why? I dragged out so many whys. Was Hayden thinking similar thoughts? Feeling trapped, I gawked at the smiling faces around the room, pausing at Dad's. Something about his expressive holiday *grin* pulled me into a memory time warp.

While staring at my father, my mind conjured up a conversation from years ago.

"GG, come on, let's see Santa and look at Christmas decorations."

Bundling up in winter gear, my hands nestled inside the mittens Mom had bought me. In the passenger seat, my focus stays on my smashed fingers. The warmth urges me to remember, to feel her. I press my palms together, linking them, thinking how often she clutches my hand.

With my eyes closed, I shut down the world rolling by outside. I pretend Mom's still inside the car with Dad and me for a while. This isn't my hand holding on to me with a death grip. She's still here. It's her, and she's able to love and parent me. She's not dead. Because I'm just a little girl, she can't be gone because I need her here with me. It's Christmastime.

Restless in the silence, Dad turns the radio station to the holiday classics. "Hark the Herald Angels" he sings, along with his fingers drumming the steering wheel, begging me with his droopy-dog eyes to smile and join in. Everything shrieks, sounding too sad—lyrics about angels, good tidings, comfort and joy, a mother and child.

Dad makes an effort to find songs I might like. A wad of tinsel bounds into my throat, winding around every vital organ when the radio station plays that eff-ing song "Christmas Shoes." So, there's a tune about my ordeal with Christmas. DEATH, without a mom. Not every child receives a cookie-cutter holiday season wrapped up with a pretty ribbon. I don't want my mommy with Jesus. I want her with me.

When I'm whispering to Santa at the mall, I lean close to his ear to say, "The only thing I want, I know you can't bring—my mom—she died." I think I destroyed the holly jolly red-and-white elf with "Santa, I guess I'll just settle for a new pair of Christmas shoes, like in that terrible sad song?" Finally, I scooted off his lap, walking back toward Dad with watery eyes.

Even though Dad figured I no longer believed in Santa at ten, he only wished for me to take a photo with Mr. Ho Ho Ho for the heck of it. I know Dad tried to make my holiday as normal as possible. But after spending a couple of years of motherless holidays, I guess I'd grown as prickly as the needles on the evergreen trees. My heart ached.

Perhaps I craved the same gingerbread cookies my friend Darcy baked with her mom. Other girls in my class planned sleepovers while some went on shopping trips. A lot of mother-daughter pampering events started happening at the beauty salons. A group of girls returned to school for the Christmas program with painted fingernails. In comparison, mine were uneven and translucent next to the shiny sparkle of the Little Miss Merry Christmas crowd. But I believe I am the only one who noticed the status of the odd girl out.

Playing the odd girl out, I learned to avoid the hurt by never asking to go. Staying quiet remained the goal. Sometimes, I didn't want to face the truth. Most of the time, I didn't even get invited in the first place. People felt sorry for me or awkward around me. Mothers seemed to clam up about my mom, pretending she never existed—even her friends. It confused me as if I had done something wrong. After I lost my mom, other people drifted away. So, I lost even more people. Dad became my only true constant.

It's good that I didn't realize my father was the real Mr. Ho Ho Ho behind the scenes at this time in our lives. Dating by Happenstance: Single Father Widower *creates the best title for my father's non-fiction book. In tiny letters for a subtitle, it reads—* A Secret Persona. *(Good thing he's outgrowing this behavior). Or is he?*

In reality, I think Dad and I felt like losers back then. Playing a game already forfeited—defeated before our eyes met any tangling of colored Christmas lights flashing, blinking, or dancing in celebration. Defeat had occurred before walking out the door to sit on Santa's lap. It didn't seem to matter that we'd bundled up in mittens, gloves, scarves, and coats. We lacked her warmth. Defeated from the very first day she died.

Hayden pressed his lips to my temple, bringing me back to the present day. "You, okay?" he asked, his eyes narrowing with the tell-tale look that he knew I had gone a million miles away. Drew and Ava were still talking about how they met, passing around their first meet-cute texting he'd saved on his phone.

"Yeah. I am now"—warmth encircled me. Maybe fighting isn't as necessary anymore, but I can't stop it. So, this holiday season, sensing only slightly defeated, I stood with a hand to hold. *Mother, I miss you dearly.*

"I'm not very convinced, Gretchen," Hayden said.

Across the room, another roar of laughter mixed with holiday music. The scent of Christmas pine mingled with vanilla cookies. Gene and Hayden went overboard decorating. A personalized stocking for each of us hung from the staircase railing, our names written in gold glitter. White twinkling lights twirled around the ivy near each sock. Knowing how much went into this triggered unshed silent tears.

Hayden led me toward the kitchen, away from the crowd, where we could hide in the pantry.

More tears threatened to fall when I saw giant chocolate Santas peeking out from red-and-white felt material as we walked by. An oversized candy cane looped over the edge tucked next to *my Santa*. For some reason, this sight overwhelmed me. Seeing a glittery "Gretchen" scrolled in Gene's artsy handwriting on a Christmas stocking made me feel golden. As an open invitation, it lets me know: Gretchen, you are wanted. You fit in here. Just being myself, which I'm allowed to be, the Tuckers' home is a place I belong to. Do I deserve it, though?

Looking around, I wished I had believed it more. Laughter stirred in the air, but the con man kept bluffing me. Why did giggling seem inappropriate if my mother weren't here? Why did I want to scream, kick, cry, and punch someone under the guise of joy? See, that's how it felt when I wanted to cry and smile at the same time as I watched my father lightly and quickly kiss a woman beneath the mistletoe. He looked happy. Dizziness set in as if I had ridden a roller coaster, got stuck hanging on a loop upside down until the blood rushed to my brain, and finally just went numb.

The sweetness of gingerbread, pine, vanilla, and peppermint shook me outside the pantry door. I tasted most flavors through feathery kisses. While the scent of pine needles poked me to death with memories.

So, what was this overwhelming confusion of emotions I experienced? Part joy? Part anger? Part jealousy? Part guilt? Part hope? Dad and I had the invitation to be included somewhere. And for that, I breathed in a moment of weird happiness.

I wanted one of the stockings to spell out the letters G-W-E-N for you, Mom, in golden letters. But unfortunately, my Christmas wish and miracle will never come true. Instead, the con man wanted to kill my spirit.

Perhaps the internal fighter inside this little girl who's hell-bent on missing her mother can shift some of her determination to win. Can she ever accept the love and kindness offered? Even if it's from the *sweetest* people? If so, when? How?

HAYDEN

Chapter Eleven

Dear Ma,

Let the Christmas party hop and hop or con-tort into the "YMCA" if you're a Tucker. Things got flirty with John and Gabby under the mistle-toe. Gretchen gave them a double take but didn't act like she cared much. She's maybe been putting a slight robotic spin on things lately. Or I think Gretch might have been too busy time traveling to Christmas past, judging by her downturned mouth while scrutinizing the Christmas stockings. Dad and I wanted her to love them. Before she dove too deep into a portal, I grabbed her arm, pulling her toward my childhood sanctuary. "Let's talk away from everyone," I said, giving her a sideways glance, trying out my winking skills. One side of her mouth quirked up.

After closing the door, I unfolded two micro-mini chairs better suited for little kids. Still, they fit the center of the pantry nicely. Spinning my chair backward, I could easily sit straddled in the seat facing Gretchen, get more comfortable, and get close to her mouth.

"God, you look so hot," I said, lunging forward. I captured a few lingering candy cane kisses from Gretchen. Then, with our eyes closed, I ramped up the kisses. Sucking in her bottom lip with my teeth. Our hands were busy with our hair, and I forgot to breathe. When we inched apart, I felt a tad guilty. I knew she needed to talk, not make out. Sometimes, though, I just can't think straight around her.

She responded well to my hugs, mouth, hands, and such but remained too quiet, so I knew I better press her for information. I wanted to do the right thing to help her.

Against her lips, with a feathery caress, I asked, "Remember doing the grief center activity with me called 'The Ghost of Christmas Past, Present, and Future'?"

"Sure, of course, I remember. Why are you asking me this, Hayden?"

Damn. I noticed Gretchen's watery eyes.

"Well, we talked about if we could time travel to the past, what we would see, feel, touch, and then move on to the present and future. I learned so much about you, Gretchen." Placing my hand on her knee, I sighed. Then some courage came. So, I finally said, "I fell so in love with you for what you've been through and overcome." Pretty sure the words didn't come out smoothly at all. A few

182

silent tears ran down Gretchen's face, so I used my thumb to wipe them away.

After a few seconds, I added, "Don't forget to look at yourself and see your growth too. Tonight, at times, I kind of felt like I might've done something wrong, or I could've done something better. Maybe you didn't like my dancing?" I threw in a bit of humor because I got tongue-tied with stupidity once again.

Her head jerked up at me. She did a hiccup-giggle-cry if that's such a thing. But before she spoke, her crying grew more intense. Then, looking puzzled, both her eyes and mouth opened wide. "What?" she cried. "No, Hayden, it's not you. By the way, I loved your dancing." She forced her mouth closed and smiled. Then, she said, "I think I just put too much pressure on myself to enjoy the holidays. You know how I write things down on a calendar, then decorate the dates?"

I nodded.

"Hayden, it's to give me hope. I beg myself to get excited. I tell myself to have something to look forward to. 'Do not look back. Stop dwelling in your childhood.' But the more I fight trying to forget my mom, the more she keeps showing up."

I understood her, feeling the feels of every freaking word, and squeezed her. I held her tightly, my silent tears cascading. Then, through my sniffling, I managed to speak in a gravelly voice after a few moments. "Tell me more if you want. What triggered you?"

Gretchen let out a heavy breath. "I don't want to sound ungrateful or mean or insane. I don't want you to hate me, Hayden."

"I promise to listen without judgment, Gretchen."

"There were so many things. The minute I heard Ava's mom lived, I had to wonder why mine died." Gretchen scoffed, wiping under her eyes. "Then I punished myself with guilt."

"I get it, Gretch. I hope it helps if I tell you that I had a similar thought. Whenever I hear about someone surviving cancer, I get jealous too. I hate feeling like God chooses to save some while others still die. Especially since my mom had cancer. I'm not sure it's a healthy way to think, but I understand. I worry about others getting cancer all the time." I wanted to scream, *Even now, I'm worried.* "It's a painful and guilt-ridden shitty thing. I'm sorry you went through it tonight, though."

"I'm sorry you worry about cancer. I don't want to burden you."

I shook my head. "Talk, Gretch."

"Hayden, I loved my Christmas stocking so much. But unfortunately, my history with Christmas stockings hasn't always been a healthy one. As you know, Mom left me my days-of-the-week underwear in my stocking. I hoarded them, which led to some of my OCD behaviors. Tonight, I visualized her name on one of the stockings. The absence of her name stung. Not seeing my mom's name, Gwen, next to mine still gets to me. I guess when I saw those sparkling stockings, I wanted my mom's name Gwen written in gold so much. It's still weird. This is my first real holiday party since she died. She doesn't get to be at the party, yet she's here. Oh, my gosh, I'm rambling." Gretchen hung her head.

"Gretch, I wish I knew what to say. I'm glad you like the stocking I made. How could I help you honor your mom's memory, so it doesn't hurt so much at Christmastime?"

Lightly, I touched the tip of her hair, combing through it with my fingers. "I don't know, Hayden. I'm glad I have you. I'm so sorry if I'm a downer."

"If you think of something I can do, let me know. You're my grief hero. You've taken flowers to my mom's grave for me. I'll never forget it. I'd love to help you."

"Hayden, you painted my favorite painting from the grief center tree and wrote me poems. You're already my hero too."

Okay. So, we kissed again. And again.

Pulling apart, I hated to ask but did anyway. "So, my dad and Lisa. Give me some deets on your opinion of how the night went." Staring at Gretchen, I wanted the truth.

"I think the YMCA portion went great. A lot of memorable embarrassing times for everyone. Your dad will never live this down. Awkward and goofy. I never want my dad wearing tight cop pants again in front of me. Ew. Gross."

We died laughing.

"You were freaking hot."

Gretchen grabbed my shirt pulling me to her and biting my lip. "I didn't know I liked cowboys."

I chuckled at her enthusiasm. "Maybe I'll borrow Cole's ridiculous Brawny man shirt if it turns you on this much," I said, nibbling her ear.

She sat up, giggling at the thought. "Anyways, to answer your question. There were some mild nervous looks about the necklace, but afterward, everyone seemed to get along."

"So, what's your take on your dad with Gabby?"

Gretchen closed her eyes.

Gretchen, I know you saw the peck, but did you catch the action under the mistletoe?

Mom, Gretchen's hand went into a death squeeze on mine when John leaned down to give Gabby a light peck after opening a present. I'm not sure if it bothered Gretchen or only startled her. John and Gabby have dated mainly at Gabby's or have kept the PDA to a minimum. Tonight, they ventured into party mode with affection. But John keeps trying to reassure Gretchen he's exclusive with Gabby. It's all sorts of weird watching our dads dating—just saying.

She rambled, fluttering her eyes open, "What-the-flippity-do-da? When you asked me that, my whole body tingled?" She wiggled her fingers above her head, bringing them down slowly as if performing raindrops to the "Itsy Bitsy Spider."

"You know, starting with the prickling scalp, but then I went numb. Okay, I'm about to freak myself out," Gretchen said, scrunching up her nose.

"Gretchen?"

"I'm scared to admit this, but *sweetie*, could I be starting to see Gabby with Dad as doable? I don't know. Would things—"

Dad cut Gretchen off, barging into the pantry, announcing: "Figured I'd find you two hiding out in the pantry. Party's winding down."

I knew scenes like this happened on TV, but I never thought they'd happen in my living room, snaking their way onto my front porch. Then, in a huddle, everyone shuffled to the door in a mess of coats, gift bags, hugs, and loud good-byes.

Even Ava and Ariana left together to go back to the hotel to allow what they dubbed "Gene a night alone with his sons." A cold night air slapped my face as I stood with the door open, saying the final good-byes. Rocking back and forth, I rubbed my hands for warmth. This is it. Soon, Dad, Cole, and Drew will dump their dirty laundry or terrible news on me. Will they finally explain tonight as someone's last hurrah?

Overall, Dad's embarrassing ass-jerk plan turned into the fun he promised. Dad won. I'll never tell him his spelling words with different letters or whatever nonsense equaled anything sensible. Sometimes, I wish I could be more like Dad, maybe the outgoing side of stuff.

Drew and Dad headed off to the den to watch ESPN, so I followed when Cole crept up behind my shoulder to ask, "Hayden, can I see you a minute?"

He pointed down the hall toward Dad's office like he wanted to lecture me, with his mouth set in a straight line, way too serious-minded. As cold as I felt seconds ago, heat prickled the back of my neck. *Oh, great, another story hour fight session? My gosh, Mom, has Cole always been so stern and fatherly with everyone or just me?* My devious creative side considered throwing out, "Cole, are we about to write out all the rules for the Brotherhood of the Traveling Brawny Shirt?"

Following Cole, I kept up the pace as he led the way until we ducked back into Dad's office. I felt like I were back at the crime scene with him for a fleeting moment. "What do you need?" I asked. Until I saw a present sitting in the center of the coffee table.

Cole smiled, motioning to the couch. So, we flopped down next to each other.

Without saying a word, Cole lifted the Santa box from the center of the coffee table, placing it in my lap. He smiled broadly at me. "Hayden, I didn't want to give this to you in front of everyone." Across Santa's beard, Cole had written in black permanent marker

Merry Christmas, Hayden.
Love, Your Brother, Cole.

Silently, I fiddled with the tape on the sides of the box, biting my lip to ward off the excitement and anxiety. After I lifted the lid, my eyes clouded so fast. Parts of me felt like an ass-jerk for my Brawny shirt thoughts, and pieces of me wanted to ask him what this was about, and other parts of me wished I could shut up my effing brain. *Relax.*

Inside the box, I stared into the day Cole had told me all about. In an eight-by-ten personalized wooden frame Cole had ordered online from the Personalization Mall, I saw the photo you took of us, Mom. And now I know the story behind it, even if I couldn't remember.

I picked up the frame, touched each corner, and read the inscription: ***A brother shares childhood memories and grown-up dreams. Brothers Forever, Cole and Hayden.***

"Wow," I said, quickly giving Cole a sideways glance before looking back at the photo. "I don't know what to say. Thank you."

Cole cleared his throat. His tone seemed flat, monotoned, or nervous. How was I to know? What did I know? "I'm glad you liked it. I knew I had the gift. That's why I stalled and didn't show you the picture on my phone when you asked." Propping his feet on the coffee table, he used the toe of his boot as a signal. "There's also a card in there. I typed you a letter because I thought about using snail mail, but here we are."

Let me tell you, it takes a lot of bravery to read a personal note from someone sitting beside you. Inside the green envelope, I noticed a cute Christmas card with a few Saint Louis Blues Hockey team members on the front bundled up in their gear, smiling with missing teeth. That's where the novelty ended and my typed-up sentimental journey began.

Dear Hayden,

Mom somehow paused life, capturing a story for us that day. I hope you enjoy the photo. I know without Mom, the universe changed. Fears about love set in. Hearts broke. The pain of loss becomes too much where love resides. But, beyond grief, when hearts begin to mend, we discover love as the emotion capable of healing us. We are all reaching places where it's easier to open up, give, receive, and choose love again.

Little brother, we once had it all. We once resided in the kind of home others envied, one so jam-packed with love. No matter where you go, where you live, or who you're with, love is the element you must grasp.

I think my heart will never forget you as the little guy propped on my shoulder. Especially on that day, I shoved everything you had in your world into mine, making room for you. No matter what, I'd like to believe we can again uncover empty corners of the world together.

Love, Your Brother,
Cole

Those words measured up like gold inside my hand, but that's a hefty medal. I worried about the message being a good-bye letter of sorts if something were wrong with Cole. My hand scrubbed down my cheeks, wiping off the wetness of silent tears. *If he were sick, he wouldn't make future promises to uncover the world together. Did Dad and Drew know about this?*

"Thank you so much, Cole. But, God, I don't know what to say?" I choked out.

Awkwardly, he reached out to pull me into a side-hug, but I decided that I could turn this thing into a full-on bro hug with a slight turn of my body. I even let him slap my back, Dad style, with a chuckle.

Standing up, Cole swung his arms, stretching, then yawned. "Ready to track down Dork-ass Dennis and Dad to see what they're squabbling about?"

Yawns work like a virus. And my eyelids were salty anchors at this point. So, I slid off the couch with sloth speed. Miss Spicy Boots came trotting out from her banana bed under Dad's desk. She put on quite the show, stretching, jingling, and yawning. Cole and I cracked up. Thank God the cat gave us a second wind because it had to be past midnight.

"I can't believe she slept through the entire night of F-U-N," I said, chuckling.

Cole shook his head, smiling.

In the hallway, Cole leaned against the wall, clasping his palms over his ears before he yelled, "Hey, Dork-ass, turn the volume down."

While Drew and Dad talked over the announcers, ESPN blared in the background, debating which team might win the next big football game.

Smirking, I scooped up Miss Spicy Boots. *Did my uptight brother Cole call Drew "Dork-ass?"*

"Fight nice, kids," Dad called out. "And please bring me a refill of sweet tea on your way and come join us." Dad said "sweet tea" in his extra thick southern accent. This caused Drew to cackle so loudly.

While he grabbed the tea, Cole mumbled something under his breath. I swear an F-bomb and Dennis the Dork-ass popped out of his mouth again. I feel like a little brother who's a tattletale right now. It's weird to realize I never had or remember those moments with you. They happened with Dad a ton because of Drew. Grief sneaks up on us to remind us of those odd pieces of ordinary life we miss out on.

So. . . .

Mommy! Mommy! Cole called Drew a dork-ass more than once today. Plus, Cole said the word fuck too.

Well, Miss Spicy Boots wanted down to prance into the living room. So, she led as Cole and I followed her with the southern sweet tea.

To the best of his ability (not good), Drew pretended to kick it old-school style with some freestylin' scratching or beatboxing. I suppose you call what he tried to do rapping as we entered the room.

"Yo, yo, Miss Spicy Boots
I hear you're a feline hoot
You and Daddio live in cahoots
'Cuz he gets you lots of loot."

Mom, I wished I had known he planned to perform this stunt. I would've recorded the whole prank. Because seeing Dad's expression killed me— his lip curled up in disgust.

And he hugged the couch pillow, making accusing remarks. "So, which one of you put Dennis up to singing, or whatever the hell you want to call that?" His serious tone of voice and the way he got right on the edge of his seat, his eyes bouncing from Drew to Cole, almost made me wet my pants because I had nothing to do with it.

I fell over the arm of my chair, wheezing.

Like Velcro, Miss Spicy Boots wasted no time finding her way to Dad's lap, proving Drew's debut rap right. So, we only laughed longer and harder.

"Let's take a picture," I said. "Drew and Cole, if we stand behind Dad while holding the cat, some of the Christmas decorations will show in the background. We need to take family Christmas pictures too. Even better, Drew should perform his rap again, so we can play the video for just a few people."

"Some pictures are a great idea," Dad said, beaming. "Still, I can't believe you guys suckered three amazing girls into becoming your girlfriends. Do they know how you treat your poor old father?"

Dad asked in his goofy southern accent, but, of course, he agreed to the video's whole charade.

After a couple of takes on the video, we settled for a halfway decent photo with the lyrics instead. But, Mommy, Cole called Drew names again during filming. And Dad's not innocent, either. I heard Dad cuss back at both of them. I stepped aside, laughing at everyone, thinking, *Yep, somebody's holly jolly balls might get decked.* My favorite moment happened when Dad slapped the top of Cole's hand for trying to grab Drew's phone away from him when he didn't want him to take any more videos. I'm undecided on who held the title for the biggest baby tonight —currently, it's in this order: Cole, Dad, and Drew. That's so surprising to me. Maybe Dennis isn't our Dennis as much anymore.

Afterward, we settled down with a platter of snickerdoodle cookies to go with the tea. Drew said, "You looked happy tonight, Dad. Did the party go over the way you wanted?"

"I think everyone had fun. People got a kick out of the YMCA. Lisa liked her necklace. I hope it's okay that Lisa was here. Did you think everything went okay? Were *you* happy, Drew?"

"Yes, Dad. I liked seeing people in our home again. Having you happy makes me happy. Lisa's a good person. Seeing you dating brings out some new feelings. But they aren't painful ones, if that makes sense. Dad, you've waited a long, long time."

Dad nodded.

Cole smiled. Again, his quiet demeanor frightened me because I worried he might be waiting for the right moment to speak. Did he need to come clean with a secret? Gut feelings can eat away at the silence, making you believe everyone in the room knows something except you. Did our togetherness mean something? And was it going to last long? Could I trust us? In my limited experience, too much goodness or too much love leads to secrets, bad news, and even death. Then silence falls to aloneness.

Instead, Mom, I want to build our lives back. I'd like to learn something new instead of going backward. Sometimes, though, my brothers and Dad appear as strangers. So, one picture, one story, one holiday at a time, I'll hopefully build a trusting relationship with them.

Finally, Cole broke the thick silence. "Do you care if I get out a few photo albums?"

"No. I'd love to look at the pictures with you boys. But first, will you answer the same questions I asked Drew a minute ago?"

"Sure. For once, I agree with everything Drew said."

Drew scoffed.

Cole tossed a throw pillow at Drew. "Seriously, when I talk to you on the phone, you sound different—in a good way. Tonight, you seemed nervous but happy about the necklace. I think nervous and happy is an excellent way to explain how I feel."

"Okay," Dad said. "That's fair. What else are you thinking, Cole?"

"Lisa seems like an incredible source of friendship and strength for you and Hayden. And for that, I'm grateful. I'm glad you have other friends too. The evening went well. We all had a good time. But, please, dear God, Dad, don't ever make me dance again, though," Cole said, grinning.

Dad chuckled.

It helped me to listen to their perspective. A mixed happy-nervous combination sounded about accurate, with Dad waiting years to invite Lisa into our home.

"My twins," Dad said.

Then, I noticed Cole and me standing up to wipe our palms on our jeans in unison. I also liked knowing I wasn't the only one sweating through Dad's love life discussion.

Dad added, "Boys, since you're both standing, check the gray storage bench by the staircase for some of the photos. You'll find a few in some shoeboxes in the hall coat closet. There are probably more up in my room. Let's save them for the next visit to organize."

We gathered on the rug, flopping on our bellies with your ugly purple floral throw pillows tucked under us. There's freaking Drew, who talked Dad into opening the Kansas City Chief sheet set from his office. So, he rolled himself up in a cocoon.

Cole dumped the first batch of shoebox pictures, spreading across the floor like a blackjack dealer, tapping on them like a fortune teller when one caught his eye.

"Those were the good old days," Dad said, sporting a crooked smile with a glazed, faraway look.

"We were all so young, but I remember everything about this day when I stared at this," Cole said.

Dad got the photo next and passed it to Drew, who paused to study it, smiling.

Drew's fingers shook from gripping the corners as if reluctant to let go. But he did hand the snapshot to me.

I saw Summerfort Eagles across Cole's baseball uniform. So, I figured Cole tossed me up on his shoulders in victory after one of his games near the dugout. Leaning against the fence, copycat Drew looked to be climbing on Dad in a piggyback stance.

"Was I about four?" I asked.

Dad turned the photo toward him, flipping it over to see if you'd written a date. "Yeah. That's a good guess."

I swallowed hard, wishing my mind worked better than an amnesia patient's. Still, no matter how much I wanted to put myself inside that day, it wasn't going to happen inside that picture. "Old photos get to me. I don't remember these things." I said, my voice cracking.

"That's okay," Dad said. "You were young."

"No, you don't get it," I said, fighting for every defense against my aches. Wobbling chin, snotty lips, and teary-eyed messes unfolded. "Look," I cried, picking up random pictures. "I guess I realize Mom took most of these. And it's her, I don't know. I don't have many memories of her. None of you get that."

Everyone remained silent for a long minute. And I just sat there on my knees, sniffling while clutching a handful of confusing memories playing out like a mind game of connecting the dots.

Drew unrolled himself from his stupid sheet and squeezed my wrist. "I'm sorry, Hayden. I'm glad you finally talked about this." He sat up, helping me put things down on the rug as he said, so matter-of-factly, "I was only eleven. My memory of her gets very fuzzy at times." Then he collected me into his sheet, making sure he ended with his arm draped around my shoulder.

Dad patted my foot. "Do you want to stop looking at stuff?"

"No, tell me more about this day," I said, my index finger on myself before moving it to another picture. "What's going on? Where are we, and can you tell me who's there? What did Mom say and do that day?"

Dad frowned, touching a stack of photos. "All right, let's start talking, then, because we have a lot of catching up to do."

Cole started with two piles. He called them the brother's favorites. "Notice how Mom or Dad captured images of me constantly raising you up on my shoulders, running bases with you, or carrying you on my hip. Now, in contrast, let's look at the Drew stack. Drew's sitting on you, tackling you, or causing the pouting."

We cracked up.

"See, pictures don't lie, Hayden. I'm the nice brother." Cole said.

"Yeah, I forgot, Mr. Cool," Drew said.

"What?" I asked.

"You don't remember calling me Cool?" Cole asked.

I shook my head.

"You went through a phase when you couldn't pronounce Cole, so you'd follow me around saying, 'I want up, Cool.' 'Pick me up, Cool.' So, I carried you around everywhere. Girls thought you were cute, too, so I had chick bait."

Drew said behind a cough, "Whatever, dude. You're still an introvert."

"Mom and Dad used to let me take you guys everywhere once I got my license," Cole said.

"Duh," I said, glancing over to Dad, who shrugged, holding a hand over his mouth and stifling a yawn. And, I mouthed, "Perv."

We laughed.

Soon after, I dozed off on the floor next to Drew. Once I woke up, hearing Drew snoring and loud voices in the kitchen and drifted back to sleep. But I flinched at the shouting with adrenaline causing my eyes to pop wide open.

"We watched as our mother descended into a hole in the ground."

Pounding fists against countertops or maybe cabinet doors slamming immobilized me with fear. I trembled in a cold sweat. Blood rushed to my brain, thrumming in my ears. I hated eavesdropping when the topic could make me vomit. I curled up into a ball and covered my ears.

But Cole kept yelling. "We were so young. It ate me alive, Dad. Every day. The words, 'What the hell, God, why do you hate me?' exploded in my head." Still, even from the den, I could hear Cole's pain erupting.

Dad's words floated too quietly, trying to soothe Cole, who I realized wasn't fighting Dad or screaming at him, just venting and sobbing to him.

Drew stirred next to me, asking, "Bud, you, okay?"

"I don't know," I whispered. "How do we help?"

Drew pulled a few inches closer, answering, "Cole and Dad have battled demons for years. We give them time. Cole's got a lot of pent-up guilt about Mom."

"Why didn't I know?" I asked Drew.

"You were young. Dad did the best he could to protect you from Cole's anger. But before Mom died, you saw in pictures how much Cole loved you. How much he smiled."

Except for the few twinkling Christmas lights, the room remained dark. Dad had turned off the TV. Even in the darkness, though, I clearly heard and saw some of Cole's grief. But mostly, I felt it. First, I thought of Cole and Dad's relationship. Then I had to grow up without Dad at my school events after your death. Secondly, I considered how each of us likely experienced a different Dad because of your death. And it broke me.

"Mom wanted me to attend medical school, but I failed her, you, and this whole effing family!" Cole continued shouting.

"Cole, knock it off!" Dad yelled.

Hot, salty tears burned my eyes again for the umpteenth time today.

"No, because I walk around feeling like I betrayed her memory every day. I'm a loser, Dad. How can I possibly deal with all that's ahead?"

"A successful hospital administrator with a kind heart is hardly a loser, Cole. You found an alternative to medicine. Your mother would be proud of you. I know this."

"So, my loser's inability to cut up a cadaver in medical school would pass Mom's standards for me?"

"Harsh, kid. But considering how you feel, my God, yes. A thousand times, yes. Your mother loved you, not the fact you were going to be a doctor. She just wanted you to be happy."

"Dad, don't you think she wants that for you too?"

"What are you getting at, Cole?"

"Figure it out, Dad. Figure it out. Kumbaya and all that bullshit. Because my mind's too scattered with Ariana. Every day, I'm this stupid little kid at heart, wishing my mom was here telling me what to do next. It's so damn frustrating."

"Cole, I want to stop arguing. Dang, I made three babies with your mom. But then, think about it, I didn't have her help raising them. I used to share a bed with the love of my life, then I suffered night after night, learning to sleep alone. I worked hard, doing the best I could. Believe me, son, I know what it's like to feel like a loser. We all hurt, Cole. But I see us getting better too."

Mom, their conversation grew quiet, becoming a murmur of undetected voices.

Finally, in the darkness, Drew whispered, "Sleep, Hayden. Dad's got our backs. Remember, give them time."

GRETCHEN

Chapter Twelve

Rose Elizabeth-Anne Tucker
December 8, 1969–November 21, 2011
An Angel on Earth "Our Rosie"
Beloved Wife & Mother

I hope you don't mind if I call you Rosie today. It's me again, Gretchen Gardener. Gene and Hayden crammed my stocking full of goodies for Christmas, including this striped aqua scarf and glove set I'm wearing. Even though it's New Year's Eve Eve, the weather's pretty sunny, so I even rode my bike today. Since there's a basket on the front of my bike, I stopped at Martin's Memorial Shop to create holiday-inspired wreaths for you and my mom, knowing I could bring them. Later, I'll explain my choices for the design. Sorry, I'm a little late this Christmas season.

When Summerfort Grief Center closed for Christmas break, so did Summerfort High School.

Soon after, my dad and I hosted our first-ever Rudolph the Red-Nosed Reindeer pajama party to get things kicked off with Gene and Hayden. I'm grateful for these new memories. We had so much fun. So, as I marked off the squares on the December calendar as they inched closer and closer to more holiday events, I thought I could outcon the con man, Rosie.

Ugh. When I visit, I always promise not to cry. But I just can't help it. I feel like I've also failed at keeping it together over most of Christmas vacation. With every present wrapped, twinkling light watched, stocking hung, or cookie baked, even every song I listened to, they left this aching hole where my mom once belonged to me. I know it's not wrong to miss her. But I'm so jealous of other people who have moms. And now I'm angry at myself for feeling this way. So, instead, I know I should focus on some positives. By the way, visiting you and talking helps calm me down.

Let me tell you a funny story. Gene, your crazy husband, made my dad and your sons dance to "YMCA." The reasoning was because of Lisa Marks's birthday, which seems odd to talk to you about. How would you react to this news?

My dad's dating too. But Gabby's not as polished as Lisa because she goes around calling me *sweetie* all the time. She had the nerve to bring her dog Poco to my dad's vet clinic to start things with him. Her dog's super cute. WTFDD. Wait. I think the flirty communication began with me starting my period at school. Now, how weird and awkward is that, right? I want to trust her, but I don't know her like I do Lisa. So, I can tell you, Rosie, that Hayden, Gene, Cole, and Drew will be in good hands with Lisa. She won't disrespect your memory. See, I can't honestly answer that about Miss Happenstance, Gabby. I'll save more Gabby talk for another day, though.

Since Hayden struggles to come to the cemetery, I'm here on his behalf to surprise him. I didn't tell anyone about coming today. I just said, "Hey, Dad, I'm taking a quick bike ride." Can I make a confession? You know I already love your son so much. But can I also say I'm kind of mad at him? It's hard to love somebody so much when you wish they'd do something you think would benefit them. I have such jumbled-up emotions over all of this.

Maybe I'm jealous of him too? He's got Lisa. I'm sorry. Is that inappropriate? Or is that weird for me to talk about, Rosie? Somehow, I'm not feeling any negative vibes from you. When it comes to Lisa, there's just a history already built in, like she's our surrogate mother. We've known her for eight years at the grief center. Maybe you'd appreciate her looking out for Hayden? I don't know. I keep thinking how lucky Hayden got with her. Plus, Hayden's getting text messages from Cole. Two brothers! Sometimes, I want a sibling. Easy to say, I guess, when you're an only child. An issue happened with

Grandma Suzi, plus a Suzy Zoo recipe card. I'll try to make my long story short: we had a fun day baking your snickerdoodle cookies. Still, he froze when I suggested he contact your mom to track down the Suzy Zoo recipe card history.

Let's face it. Your son has this chance to talk to a grandma once in a while, but he hardly ever does because she's eccentric. Sometimes the weirdest people turn out to be the best for us. Maybe they're just the most misunderstood. My gut keeps urging me to believe in your mom. After all, she lost her only daughter. I imagine she misses you. Well, I'll take your weird mom off Hayden's hands. And I'll eat her basket of strange coconut orange clusters to experience having a living grandmother for a while.

Upstairs, old pictures of your mom hang in the hallway. Rosie, with her mother Suzi, I've seen the two of you inside frames together. In photographs, smiles radiating all the way into someone's eyes don't lie. That's a lot of happiness. When it comes to Grandma Suzi, I'm hoping for something new for Hayden. I don't care if I only get to live vicariously through him. Maybe one of my New Year's resolutions will revolve around understanding my jealousy while continuing to help others connect to the happiness I want.

On the topic of happiness, let me say how much warmth I feel in your home. Gene remodeled the house, but elements of Rosie Tucker remain everywhere. So, even though you're not there, I absorb your spirit.

Then, when I visit you here, I always tell you I wish I knew you or remembered you from childhood. But when I'm lounging in the living room, I notice your throw pillows remain. In the kitchen, your "Kiss the Cook" apron still hangs on a hook. Gene continues to keep your picture on his nightstand. I use the stories of love Hayden shares with me when we hide in the pantry to understand such a beautiful soul.

Anyway, I know you love purple. So, this time, I'm calling my wreath theme "Christmas Glitz and Glam." Using a purple, white, and gold color scheme, I found my supplies again at Martin's Memorial Shop. Artificial flowers, trimmed in glitter gold, could be the real deal. With their help, I designed a bow using a gold ribbon, placing it at the bottom of the wreath's center. Also, battery-operated twinkle lights wrap around the wreath. Martin's jazzes up almost everything around the holidays.

I've turned on the lights now since it's nearing twilight. But before it gets too dark and cold, I'm going to say hello to my momma. The wreath I made for my mom looks almost identical to yours, except her flowers are aqua, the color she and I always loved.

Wow. This looks so pretty. It reminds me of your house at Christmastime. Ivy traveled up the banister with white lights where the stockings hung with gold letters for our names. In some way, I wanted to try recreating that for you and my mom. And, of course, for Hayden, Gene, Cole, and Drew.

Thank you, Rosie, for listening to me. Next time, I won't be so jealous and sad. I don't know if it's weird to ask you to say a prayer for me. I don't know what all those things mean. But I know, in some sense, there's a spiritual world more significant than me.

So, if you can help, remember my goal—stay healthy, talk things out in secret with Doctor Han, and keep journaling. I love your family, especially Hayden. And I will still treat them well, even when I get mad or don't understand everything.

Happy New Year, Rosie. Bye-bye.

Gwendolyn Margo Parker-Gardener
November 15, 1970–October 13, 2011
Beloved Wife & Mother

Oh, Momma. I want to believe you heard every word I said to Rosie. Right now, I wish you could hold me because crying this hard always hurts so much. I hope you love your sparkling wreath. Hayden and Gene decorated their home with such pretty stockings. I wanted you to have something similar with white lights and gold glitter. Since I can only stay a few more minutes, can I just catch my breath, close my eyes, and sit here quietly while remembering all I can of you?

Chapter Thirteen

Dear Ma,

Instead of yelling, I woke to the laughter of Cole and Dad drifting from the kitchen. It caused Miss Spicy Boots to be curious. Enough so, she danced on my head, demanding answers. Who had the nerve to laugh in her kitchen? And who dared to snore loudly in his Kansas City cocoon of sheets on the floor?

After crawling off the couch, I stumbled over Drew.

"Jesus, Hayden," he grumbled, re-covering his head like a mummy. Miss Spicy Boots pounced into action. "Oh. My. God." In an archaeological dig, Miss Spicy Boots swung her paw under the sheet and found Drew's feet. As I bent to scoop up the cat, I laughed because Drew said, "I better not get cat scratch fever from her." I tossed Miss Spicy Boots over my shoulder, where she purred, nudging me with love and meowing to fill me in on her recent "kill."

A Tiffany blue (a color I learned from Gretchen) box rested on the kitchen bar where Dad and Cole were sitting. I quickly recognized the Summerfort Bakery packaging. Dad and I keep them in business. Miss Spicy Boots saw Dad and pranced around him. I washed my hands and flipped open the lid. Inside the oversized boxes were one dozen treats minus two. I looked over at Dad and shook my head. Next, I grinned and pulled my phone out.

Dad said, "They were still selling their holiday-themed items. I thought my kids needed them. So, sue me."

Cole and I exchanged quick glances before bursting into laughter.

"Dad, stop saying that phrase," Cole said as he grabbed a reindeer doughnut by the pretzel antler.

"Dude." I slapped his hand. "Can't you see I'm trying to photograph these for Gretchen?"

Jokingly, Dad asked, "Good God. Do I need to put everybody in time out?" Then, he told me I could take Gretchen and John some doughnuts.

About this time, Drew stomped into the kitchen wearing his Kansas City Chiefs sheets like a toga. So, I got sidetracked taking his picture. I threatened to send it to Ava, and Drew didn't believe me. Anytime Drew dares me not to do something, I get this surge of energy to prove something. It's like I can't give in. So, I took him up on such an easy dare. Dad and Cole didn't even jump in to come to his rescue. They just sat there with their arms crossed, laughing. Not even when Drew chased me around the kitchen as I sent the text to Ava did they intervene. Dad and Cole blocked him and cheered me on.

Me: Are you sure you want him?

Ava: Lol. Yes. Isn't he a loving adventure?

Until then, they were unaware of how much they looked like twins. So, I took a snapshot of Dad and Cole wearing semi-matching Brawny shirts again today.

"While I'm at it, Cole, I sent Ariana a text, too, Brawny Man." Then I pointed out to Drew how he and Dad have dressed alike again today.

Me: The Brawny Men

Ariana: How funny! Thanks for sharing this gem. I'll call it my quicker-picker-upper picture.

Dad and Cole looked down at themselves, still oblivious. Until it finally hits them, and we howl. Dad laughed until tears snaked down his face. Then, he playfully pushed Cole off his bar stool. For the first time in a long while, I experienced the phrase ROFLMAO (rolling on the floor laughing my ass off).

For a second, I recalled our house once filled with these stupid teasing moments and all these minor fights. Then, I looked over, noticing Dad's shoulders again shaking due to laughter. His face met mine, and it filled with a toothy grin. Through my teary giggling, I heard his nonsensical loving banter.

Sometimes, I suppose, this family was fun.

Would you have loved us in these moments, Mom? I bet we would have driven you crazy.

Okay, let me get back to the doughnuts, Dad, Drew, and Cole. After breakfast, we said our good-byes to them midmorning with plans to meet up for a late dinner with everyone in Branson before they officially left Summerfort. Their visit took me on a white-knuckle amusement park ride. One minute I wanted to scream. Next, I sat glued to my seat, wishing it were over. Then in the next second, I found myself laughing. By the end, I felt thankful I had found the courage to take the ride. Knowing what I know now, maybe I'd buy a season pass. If I find out, they aren't still keeping nasty secrets from me.

Once Dad and I were alone, I told him about my plan to surprise Gretchen with a late holiday gift. Even though he and Miss Spicy Boots yawned through my entire presentation about my idea, Dad helped me gather the supplies I needed to show support. At one point, Miss Spicy Boot let out one of her "purr-rawls," which I can only describe as a loud, demanding purr-meow combo as she flopped onto my project.

Dad cradled her. "Dang, I need a catnap too, Miss Spicy Boots." Dad yawned again, eyeing first the mountain of dirty dishes we failed to tackle after dinner last night, then the pile of Christmas explosions down the hall. Thank God Dad couldn't see the mound of dirty clothes in my room upstairs. We needed an intervention from all this F-U-N.

Using a Boy Scout salute, I said, "I promise I'll help with everything later, Dad."

We chuckled.

Dad gratefully nodded. Miss Spicy Boots followed him up the stairs for their much-needed nap. While my masterpiece dried, I got a head start on cleaning by loading the dishwasher and showering.

It felt more like a crisp fall day than a winter day in late December. The Christmas bag I wrapped Gretchen's present in rustled in the breeze as I walked to Gretchen's in the chilly afternoon. So, of course, I chose aqua tissue paper today to stuff inside Gretchen's whimsical Christmas gift bag with llamas wearing ice skates. As I jumped over the cracks in the sidewalk, I thought of that dumb kid saying. "Jump over the cracks, or you'll break your mother's back." Then, balancing my doughnut box and llama bag, I thought about how weird it was to believe it was almost 2020—another year without a mom.

Also, while making my way to Gardener's Vet Clinic, I realized Gretchen and I spend most of our time at our house, so I thought I'd switch things up. But as I neared, I grew more nervous. John works so hard in his backyard, so I don't want to interrupt his daily routine. But sometimes, Gretchen and John's life seemed so charmed. I mean, for real, imagine owning a mini animal shelter.

Before I had too much time to breathe and process, John saw me gawking outside. Through the
transparent door and the big black letters **Gardener's Veterinary Clinic**, I couldn't hide. I know he
still saw me standing there like a dork. Gretchen's
llama bag dangled from my wrist. And the box of
doughnuts stayed hoisted to my hip, but they were
one second from being crushed by my stupidity.
John motioned for me to come in, but my eyes
went wide and dry. *Get a grip, ass-jerk*, I warned
myself. I blamed the wind, fumbling with the stuff
in my arms.

John trotted to the door and smiled. "Does Miss
Spicy Boots have an appointment I forgot to pencil
in my planner?"

"No, I'm sorry I stopped by uninvited. I wanted
to surprise Gretchen with a treat and gift." I sat
the proof on the counter, flipping open the pastry
box. "There's one for you too." I glanced at John,
grinning.

"You're always welcome to visit, Hayden.
Thanks for bringing treats."

After inspecting them, John laughed. "That's
got Gene written all over it. Did he pick those out?"

I nodded. My body relaxed. So, I leaned against
the front counter, where my eyes darted around
the building. Cute little whimpering yelps and
meows circulated. Occasionally, I caught whiffs of
bleach water they used for mopping, which mixed
with something medicinal on John's lab coat. I'm

214

sure an animal with a stomach virus had also used the bathroom because I caught that in the air. Animals were so unpredictable.

"Oh, I'll wait to eat one when Gretchen gets back. She took off on her bike to run a quick errand." John looked down at his watch. "She promised she would be back before it got dark, and that's pretty early in winter. So, I expect her about anytime. I'm working on closing up. Want to walk around with me and double-check on things, meet some of the newest crew?"

"Yeah, of course," I said.

John locked the front door and turned out the overhead light for the small waiting area. Down the narrow corridor, I followed John into the dog room, where he introduced me to a new breed of dog I'd never seen in person before. John and I crouched down where this blond puppy with a happy tail came running to say hello. "This cutie is a cross between a pug and a beagle. They call this hybrid a puggle." The puppy hopped like a rabbit on my lap, trying to kiss my face.

"It's so loving and energetic," I said, laughing but careful to turn my mouth, so I didn't get French-kissed.

"Would you believe that's why they got rid of him? He's too loving."

John and I both shook our heads.

Next, I got to hold a sphynx in the cat room. I had always dreamed of touching one of these creepy-cool cats. To me, they look like hairless aliens. Most of what I know about them comes from comedy movies. But this one had soulful blue eyes. Apparently, she had a story to share because she stayed vocal.

"Sadly, this beauty arrived because the former owner paraded her around at cat shows. Then claimed she wasn't winning enough of them," John said, rubbing beneath her chin while she concurred with him. I helped John gather clean food, water, and litter for her enclosure.

"Dad, where are you?"

My palms grew sweaty at the sound of Gretchen's voice.

"Is this llama bag for me? What's in the box? Hello?"

Down the hallway, I peeked my head around the corner. "Hey. Don't you dare touch those doughnuts without me."

Gretchen startled, then laughed. "Hayden?"

I walked toward her and hugged her so tightly.

Dr. Gardener (it's harder for me to just call him John when he's wearing that lab coat) joined us at the front. "I'm headed home for the day. Thanks, Hayden."

"No problem. I appreciate you showing me around. Take a doughnut."

Dr. Gardener flipped the aqua lid. Gretchen glanced inside.

"Aww. How cute. They're so glitz and glam. Sometimes Christmas can be so much fun. But wait. Can we really eat those? They're edible?"

I nodded.

Gretchen grinned, pulling her phone out and snapping a picture before Dr. Gardener chose the Santa with the coconut flakes for his designer beard. "Wait. Hey, before you leave, Dad, I want a group photo. Let's each pick one."

Confessions about how many I had already eaten that morning seemed unnecessary, so I picked the polar bear with jellybean accents stuffed with Bavarian cream. And just like I predicted, and—rightfully so—Gretchen picked the angel. Frosted pretzels formed into wings and a halo. The bakery had stuffed her full of the fluffy cream horn goodness.

After John left, Gretchen kissed me. Then she pointed to the llama bag, bouncing from foot to foot. "So, what's in the bag?" she asked.

In the very short hallway to the main lobby, we almost knocked one of the framed copies of Dr. Gardener's grants off the wall. We'd been kissing while attempting to also walk down the hallway. We paused, laughing as we adjusted the photograph.

"Where have I seen this name before?" I asked, underlining and saying the name G. Santos G.

"I don't know? Doesn't Santos mean something like a saint in Spanish? Maybe that's all it is. They chose the name based on helping animals—the Saints?" She shrugged.

So, I nodded in agreement because I liked her straightforward logic.

Once we sat in the lobby, I snatched the llamas and closed my eyes, gathering courage, hoping Gretchen would love her gift.

I passed the bag over. "Dig in."

With a huge smile, Gretchen tore through the tissue paper. But when she saw the stocking, she held it in her lap, staring at her mom's name, tracing the letters as the tears slipped. "I don't deserve you, Hayden," she finally said.

My face fell. *What does that mean?* Seconds ticked while I waited for her to speak again. I had no clue what to say as sweat beads formed everywhere. And blood pounded in my ears. My legs jiggled. In a splintered voice, I asked, "Gretchen, are you okay?"

Instead of answering, she jumped up from her club chair, sprinted into the bathroom behind the counter for vet visitors, and slammed the door.

"Gretchen!" I ran to stop her. To beg her to talk to me. I jiggled the door, but she'd locked the damn thing. I heard her sobbing and making a racket in the small medicine cabinet above the sink. "Gretchen!" *Fuck. What's in there?* I banged on the door. "Please, let me in. Talk to me. I just need to know that you're all right."

"Go, Hayden. I'm fine." But she continued crying as she slammed doors or dropped items onto the sink.

I stood on my tiptoes with my shaky fingers fumbling across the top of the doorjamb, searching for a hidden key. That's one place Dad keeps keys hidden at home. Nothing. Damn it. With my hands on the top of my head, I twirled in a circle, lost. Then, I sprinted to the front reception desk. Bingo. I found an effing paper clip and untangled it to use as an emergency key.

"Hayden, go home. I'm fine," Gretchen cried the closer I got to her.

My hand shook severely. I felt as bent out of shape as the paper clip. But I didn't give up until I heard the pin inside the lock finally click. "Gretchen, please let me come in and check on you," I said, with my head leaning against the door, a migraine already forming. I twisted the knob a crack. I wanted to kick my way in, yell, cry, and get angry.

"Why do you even want me?"

"Because I love you, Gretchen."

"Why?" She sobbed.

She didn't need to be left alone any longer. So, I barged in. I found Gretchen coiled on the floor with piles of discarded tissue doused with fingernail polish remover next to her. Nail tips in colorful patterns inside envelope packages were thrown around the room.

I picked one set of Color Street nails in a glittery pattern off the floor and read the package, Long Time No Sea. And I scooped up another, Chelsea Ya Later. Slowly, I made room for myself and quietly sat beside her, noticing the damage she'd done to her fingernails. Thankfully, I didn't see broken skin or blood. On some fingers, the top layer had dry layers of flakes peeling off. And what I think is called the cuticle appeared inflamed. Finally, I asked, "How can I help?"

Gretchen turned her head away. "I feel beyond help," she whispered.

"I'm sorry if I triggered you by bringing the stocking."

"No. I love the stocking. It's perfect, but I'm not. I don't deserve it. I'm too jealous-hearted of a person. For a while now, all I have wanted is your life. That's all I've thought about. How much I wanted an odd grandma who would send me weird candy. I want my mom to have recipe cards. And, please, don't get mad, but I wish my dad would've picked Lisa instead of Gabby—" Gretchen paused, wiping her eyes.

"Wow. I'm a tad hurt, but not totally surprised. I have always known you were a Lisa fan. But it doesn't mean you're not entitled to my gift. I'm not mad at you for a feeling I thought you might be harboring. Because sometimes, I've thought Gabby would've been a hell of a lot easier pick for my dad."

Gretchen glared at me. "Why would you say such a cruel thing right now, Hayden?"

"It's not mean. It's just honesty since Gabby's not so much a part of my life already. I would like a more private life. I don't like having my grief center world and my private world so confusing. If things become permanent, Lisa may take away my chance to vent at the center. It's not so bad so far. Overall, maybe we're making things harder on ourselves than they should be. Our dads have been a lot cooler about this dating shit than I thought they'd ever be."

Gretchen didn't speak to me for several seconds. Then, finally, she held her head on her knees, silently crying.

"Are you mad?" I asked.

Still, without looking up, she said, "I don't know. Life and love confuse me. Our parents shouldn't be allowed to date. It's just too weird."

She raised her head, a few tears still flowing, staining her cheeks. Then, after she realized what she had said, we glanced at each other, chuckling.

"Hayden, I'm sorry I ran off. And I'm sorry I didn't take more time to think about how much of an impact the grief center world and your home life would collide. I know I see Gabby at school, but it's not on such an intimate level. Plus, I know our work on *Love at the Center of Grief* is slow and steady. But that also puts you and Lisa on a whole new level. I didn't think about that. Gabby and I don't have that yet." Gretchen held her hands up. "We have fingernail polish. And look how much that scares me. I care too much."

I reached for her and pulled her in close. "We better run some cool water over your hands, Gretchen."

Again, she tilted away slightly. "I'm so embarrassed. I keep having obsessive thoughts. Gabby is so good to me. She bought me so many nice things for Christmas. But, growing up, I missed out on so much with my mom, like doing our nails." Gretchen reached for one of the discarded items on the floor. "These nail applications are called Color Street. I hid them out here. I freaked out about them being in the house. I love them too much. I want to use them. But then, after I applied this stuff, I felt so guilty. Like I should've only experienced this with my mom. But I can't. Do you understand?" Gretchen asked, sobbing.

I nodded.

In a cracked voice, Gretchen added, "I feel robbed. It should be me and my mom, Hayden." She pointed to her chest, crying, and repeated. "Me and my mom."

"Of course, I understand. But I think you have the right to accept Gabby's love and to be happy, Gretchen. Please, talk to Dr. Han, your dad, Gabby, Lisa, or someone about it, so you don't hurt yourself." I sighed. "Gabby would never gift you something if she knew it hurt you. I think she just wanted to give you a normal present."

"I-I know. It's a per-perfect present. I'm trying. I'm trying. I'm trying to trust. And I'm trying to accept love, Hayden. And I agree we have the right to accept love. I will ask Dr. Han to help me *if* I keep doing this. I've only done this a couple of times. It hurts so much—the remover stings and burns. I'm sorry you had to witness this. I hate this."

"I'm sorry, Gretchen. I'm glad I'm here to help. Do you want me to get your dad?"

"No. I'm embarrassed. I'm fine. I just let the entire holiday season grief 'jellys' get to me too much without talking before I exploded. When you showed up, I felt unworthy. Will you help me clean up?"

I nodded, pulling Gretchen to her feet. I gathered little pieces of the colorful nail tips and tossed discarded tissues soaked in polish remover.

"Gretchen, you're more than worthy. You know that, right?" I waited to say this for a moment that wasn't so intense to ease her burden.

A smile appeared along with a half-nod, half-shrug.

What the hell?

Gretchen stood beside me, smiling again, this time with more truth in her eyes, before asking, "After we're done, will you take a walk to help clear our heads?"

"That sounds great." Then I read my nail envelope, "Drop & Give me Zen," and laughed out loud. "No wonder you love these. You should. Do you want me to entertain you and 'drop and give you *Zen*'?" I asked, smiling to lighten the mood.

She grinned with mascara tears staining her cheeks.

So, I asked, "What do some of the others say?"

"Well, you might think this one's funny, Good Girls Gone Plaid."

We both giggled.

"Just do your best to enjoy them, Gretchen."

Gretchen stepped closer. She shifted the mood of the room again. "I can't thank you enough for my stocking. I am so, so sorry about my weird reaction. After our walk, maybe things will make more sense." She said as she buried her hands over her face. My gaze studied her fingertips again. I turned on some cool water.

I thought about telling her about my calls to Grandma for a second, but the timing seemed off. At the moment, I didn't know if she might be more hurt if I shared or kept the secret. We were dealing with enough. So, instead, I said, "I am so glad you liked it. Our moms will always be our moms, even with Gabby and Lisa coming into the picture. Maybe we need to help each other remember that more. It might even help you to know that I had a meltdown with Dad about Lisa coming to the house for the holiday party. I don't remember what I said exactly. But I remember thinking, if Dad loves Lisa, will his memories of Mom disappear? And will I be expected to act differently? Or will I have to pretend my mom didn't exist to save Lisa's feelings? Because even though Lisa's all about grief, now that she's at my house, I don't want to put my mom's stuff away, like her apron or photo. So, I know your stocking holds a lot of meaning."

We hugged for a long time.

"I'm so thankful for my mom's stocking. You're the king of thoughtful gifts. Thank you for telling me how it feels to see your dad dating Lisa too, Hayden," she whispered into my shoulder. "I'm so-so-sor—"

I cut her off, squeezing her close. "No, Gretch. Everyone gets jealous. You didn't mean to hurt anyone by acting on your jealous feelings. I understand how it gets when too much love, hurt, and grief mix together. But grief does not mean you're a bad person." I paused to think if I should say anything about her hands, but I had to address them. Carefully, I inspected her swollen index finger. "I think the person you're hurting most is yourself."

We embraced for a long time in silence before we finally held her red, tender fingers under the water again and patted them dry.

She pulled cream from the medicine cabinet. "This works great."

As we left, I wondered how often she had done this before. How long could I carry her secret?

GRETCHEN

Chapter Fourteen

Dear Mom,

Hayden and I bundled up in our winter gear to walk around Summerfort in January. Luckily, the mild weather made it possible.

"Wear layers, Gretchen," Dad said as we checked in with him before leaving.

I rolled my eyes, smiling at Hayden as I twirled the aqua scarf Gene had bought me around my neck. Already, I'd slid on the matching gloves. "Dad, my phone's on me in case you need me."

As Hayden and I walked, he brought up the jealousy thing again. "When I headed over here earlier today, I thought about how cool it must be to have a small animal shelter in your backyard. I'd love that, Gretchen."

"I do enjoy it most days. Do you want me to share the pros and cons?"

"Sure," Hayden answered, trying to hold my hand.

I pulled away.

Instead, he draped an arm around my shoulder.

"I think it goes along with why I snapped today. Dad needed to euthanize someone's beloved dog today. I know sometimes it's the best decision to put an animal down, but every time it happens, it's still so painful. Sometimes it's a grief trigger for me."

Hayden stopped walking. "I bet. I'm so sorry." He kissed my forehead before we moved forward again.

"Remember how we've used the term 'snowball effect' at the grief center?"

"Yeah, it happens a lot to me. What's going on, Gretch?"

"Well, I think I let my jealousy of Lisa, your grandma, Ava's mom, Gabby, the death of animals, Gabby and Dad dating, and so many other silly little things at school, too, build and build. Then, finally, the angry side of grief got in. I'm really sorry I ruined your holidays, Hayden."

Hayden stopped walking again. He grabbed me gently by the shoulders, turning me to face him. "You ruined nothing. I'm happy I have you. I had a lot of jealousy issues happen too. I just haven't had a chance to tell you yet. There were so many ups and downs with my brothers. Finally, I got them to understand my point of view, like how it felt as a six-year-old to lose Mom. And what it's like to lack memories, even if pictures exist, because I can't remember our family history as they can. But thankfully, they went through some pictures, and I have more history now."

I slipped off my glove to rub my watery eye. "I love that so much for you."

We picked up our pace again.

"So, tell more of the pros. Or what do you like about living with the vet clinic and animal shelter in your backyard? Since you won't tell me where you're dragging me off to in the dark," Hayden said, teasing me.

"Saving an animal's life that's on the brink makes my day. Or helping to find them loving homes, so they can be adopted feels good, *mostly*."

"Why do you say *mostly* like you're not sure?"

"The adoptions offer those happy-sad moments. I hate taking babies from their mamas. Or breaking up little sibling pairs. I see the animals as families drifting away from one another forever. Some days if I think about it too much, I hide in the bathroom and cry. As much as I try to keep from falling in love with every kitten or puppy, I fail. Even if I tell myself, we are a business. Because I miss them when they leave. And I worry when the smiling people leave if they'll be as warm and caring if the puppy gets skittish and makes a mess on the carpet. Or if the cat scratches the leather couch or throws up in the middle of the night."

"Wow. You're so loving. But I had no idea you spent that much time worrying." Hayden squeezed me in a side-hug as we strolled.

"Dad attempts to tell me we are making way for fresh faces needing us. So, I photograph every one of the animals and keep a scrapbook. It soothes my OCD—my thoughts."

"That's a great idea. I'd love to look at it."

I smiled.

"Is there even a picture of Miss Spicy Boots as a kitten? I bet she's so tiny compared to now?"

"Oh my gosh, yes. I love knowing Miss Spicy Boots is beyond happy with two loving dads," I said, laughing.

Hayden threw his head back, chuckling. "That's so accurate. She does have two dads. What a cute idea for a children's book." We stood on the side of the quiet road, holding each other, dying laughing. We threw ideas around about Miss Spicy Boots: the cat architect who sleeps in a banana bed but loves cheering on Dad at his Summerfort sporting events.

Once we topped the hill, Hayden finally asked, "Are you taking me on a date to where I think you're taking me?"

I nodded.

"Gretchen," Hayden moaned, "I'm not a fan of this place."

Afterward, Hayden pulled away from me and grew silent. I didn't know what else to say. So, I cupped my gloved hand into his and pulled him along.

"Please, trust me, Hayden."

Then, in the darkness, she came into view.

Hayden gasped. He wrapped his arm around my waist. "Wow, Angel. My mom's angel is glowing. She looks like dancing lights because of you. I don't want to go any closer. Okay?"

"Whatever you need. I came earlier, using the stocking design as my inspiration. With the wreath around your mom's angel, you can really see her. It's dazzling. I loved the white lights so much." Then, not too far away, I pointed to your wreath, Mom. "My mom also has one."

Near us, Hayden motioned for me to sit on a bench beside him, still with a view. "See, now this is what makes me jealous of you," Hayden said, tearing up. "Your ability to come here in the face of sadness, anger, jealousy, whatever, and still give love to others. Earlier, you asked why I loved you. I don't think I ever addressed the question. Why you deserved my gift? It's not because you're perfect. It's because you're you." Hayden kissed me lightly. Then a bit more intensely.

Pulling away, I said, "Whoa, I feel somewhat awkward doing things here."

We laughed.

"I'm just saying thank you."

I playfully swatted his arm. "Thank me some more later."

So, we sat silently for a long time, staring at the twinkling lights. With every blink, a question: *Can one lost soul help another? What if I'm too jealous-hearted and not good enough for him?* A calm breeze took over.

"Now, let me get back to why I love you. It's for so many reasons. One of them for your ability to show empathy for others. You get the difference between sympathy and empathy. You don't just say, 'I feel so sorry for you.' Or 'I'm sorry for your loss.' Instead, I watch you sit and listen in our group, absorbing the pain of others—I know you tuck shit inside your heart. Then you carry it around, thinking about how to help everyone. Because for years, you've sat and stood by me. And here you still are."

The palms of my hands covered my eyes, swiping my face. My voice cracked. "That's one of the sweetest things anyone has ever said to me. Thank you for seeing me." For a few moments, we embraced.

Once again, Hayden glanced at his mother's angel. "This is so cool. Of course, it helps knowing I have you to bring flowers to my mom. It's like you don't just stop at simple flowers, though. You go all out, Gretch. Every single item has meaning, I know. Even from here, I can see a little purple in the roses—my mom's favorite color. And then there's the shimmer of the gold ribbon. So, thank you. In a picture, will you go over things with me?"

"Yeah, I uploaded the photos to the Find a Grave website. Remember, I told you anytime you want to visit your mom's grave, but you don't want to physically, you still can."

An arm snaked around me as Hayden cuddled closer. He whispered, "I was thinking, I bet my mom loves knowing I have someone who bakes her cookies with me, and she's this remarkable 'redheaded lady friend—.'"

I fell forward, chuckling at the mention of Grandma Suzi's nickname for me.

We were a mix of smiles and glassy eyes. Hayden continued. "My mom would also be so thankful you bring her specialty wreaths even when it's hard for you because you lost your mom too. So, in our relationship, don't forget, you have the right to hurt too."

Every light blurred into a night of granite angels.

Chapter Fifteen

Dear Mom,
Happy New Year
January 2020

The Summerfort Grief Center closed during the Christmas holidays. But as soon as school opened, Lisa wanted to have the teens get together for a small session on setting goals for the New Year. We would have some snacks while talking about how we survived the holidays.

Tuesday, January 2, 2020
5:30-7:30 p.m.
Summerfort Grief Center Teen Activity

As the New Year begins, people often think about the positive changes they can make to improve their lives.

Activity: Write a Grief Goal or Resolution in a Six-Word Sentence.

- How would you like to address grief this year?
- What areas or needs require focus?

I studied the words on the paper. Then I looked around the room to size up the crowd. The usuals had gathered.

"Welcome back." Lisa smiled as we greeted her in the Blue Room, my favorite spot. Hayden and I snagged spots next to each other on the semi-circled couch. Mia sat across from me in the abstract patterned chair. Since the abstract chairs are so broad, Miles and Kelsey squeezed together in one, treating it like a love seat while doing their best to remain proper. Each hugging their side of the chair. I wanted to laugh at times at how awkward Miles acted—

trying to decide whether he should wrap his arm around the chair or Kelsey. Yet I liked them together because I saw Hayden and myself in them.

"Since everyone knows each other, we don't have to go into much detail, but I still find it important to honor your person by sharing how they died. Then, if you wish, you can share how old they were. And you might share how old you were if that information might be helpful for the group in understanding your journey."

Miles sat closest to Lisa, so she pointed to him.

"Will you get us started?"

Miles touched his Def Leppard T-shirt holding his sticker name tag. Then, with a crooked smile, he said, "Hello, I'm Miles, as you can read." Suddenly he dropped the silly tone. "Anyway, my dad died by suicide. He chose to shoot himself in his home office. He'd been suffering from major depression, and I'm learning to accept that it was not my fault. It's been a little over a year now. He was around forty-eight, I believe."

"Thank you, Miles. Okay, Kelsey," Lisa said.

Kelsey rubbed her palms over her jeans as she spoke. "I'm Kelsey. My mom and I were in a car accident after she picked me up from band practice." Miles reached over and grabbed Kelsey's hand. "She died last year in her forties. My dad works lots of hours in a factory. And since I have younger brothers and sisters, I feel a lot of obligation to help care for them. But I was able to stay in the band." Kelsey pointed to her band sweatshirt. She swallowed. "Um, I'm also overcoming my fear of driving," Kelsey said, taking a big breath.

Lisa held her hand over her heart for Kelsey as she silently motioned to Hayden.

"I'm Hayden. I feel like I've been coming here forever for different events. But my mom died of cancer when I was just six. I don't know if I've ever said it out loud to all of you here, but I am the one who found her." My eyes filled with tears as I locked my pinky with Hayden's and squeezed. He continued. "I hope it's okay if I tell those of you who are

235

newer—uh, coming here can help. Grief changes as you age, but you can learn ways to cope."

Next, I had to speak. A hand rested over Lisa's heart again as she tried not to fall apart. For too many years, she had gotten used to Hayden's "I'll pass" attitude. Or his simple explanations. Lisa and Hayden had their bantering phrase of "I'm sorry you feel that way" down so well. Now, she's finally seeing so much growth. I see it too. We loved Hayden. "We love you, Hayden!" I wanted to shout. But I had to pull myself together in time to talk.

I cleared my throat, stalling. "I'm Gretchen. My mom died of a stroke when I was six. She collapsed in our dining room but later died at the hospital. My memories of the event feel vivid some days. Then, sketchy the next. I let some unresolved grief get to me last year. It caused me to have obsessive behaviors and thoughts about my mother. So, I get help for OCD in addition to this group. But, like Hayden, I've been coming here for years. I am thankful for my friends here." Hayden held my hand.

"Thank you, Gretchen. Each of you has shared so much tonight. I can tell how close-knit you're becoming. Mia, we want to hear from you too."

Thankfully, Mia sat up a little straighter. Since she sat across from me, slumped and sprawled, I almost saw lacy panties beneath her pleather

236

miniskirt. Never mind, I did see them. I just pretended not to and looked away.

"Not much to say. I'm Mia. Both my parents smoked too much dope. So, now, I have to pay the price for it. Or maybe it's my grandma paying the price for living with a granddaughter like me."

WTFDD. Where were the endless tears this girl once had? When I looked around, Kelsey's eyes met mine. Hayden squeezed my hand harder.

"Oh, Mia, I am sorry to hear you feel this way. Your grandmother seems to cherish you. How can we help?" Lisa asked.

Mia shrugged.

"We are so glad you came tonight, Mia," Lisa said.

Each of us threw out an awkward chorus of "yeah" or "of course."

Thankfully, Lisa changed the subject. "Let's jump into tonight's activity." She reread the instructions.

"Kelsey, you look ready. Do you want to share with the group?" Lisa asked, pulling random colored markers from the ledge of her whiteboard to represent each of us. Kelsey held up both her hands to mark off the six words.

Kelsey: Continue visualizing positive mom memories. Lisa wrote Kelsey's words in bright hazard cone orange. And I envisioned poor Kelsey inside the car wreckage with her mom. This activity was supposed to be positive, I thought. Well, if nothing else, it made me see how grief affected my friends.

"That's an excellent way to get us started. I know you continue to struggle with the visuals of the accident."

As do I, Lisa.

"Still, you say you've been improving with the A-to-Z technique at bedtime?" Lisa asked.

Kelsey nodded, picking off a loose thread at the hem of her red-and-black Branson band hoodie. Something about the aggressive mascot resting against the gentle Kelsey made the corner of my mouth twitch, holding in my giggle. This topic in no way was laughable.

"What kind of psychobabble activity is that?" Mia asked.

As I glanced at the judgmental pirate's crossed arms staring at Mia, I wanted to blurt out, "Arrgh, matey. Shut the eff up, Mia. What's wrong with you?"

Lisa rescued me from venturing into a sinking ship of thoughts. "What a good question. I prefer to call it a technique to help others. Of course, there are different ways to explain it. But the easiest way is to think positive thoughts of your mom and dad. Or look at happy photos. Or you can even write down your favorite memories in your grief journal. It's the moments of joy that made you laugh, smile, or embarrass you most that you'll want to remember. These help to relax a lot of people before bedtime, and for some, these techniques ease nightmares."

Mia laughed. "Why are you calling it A to Z?"

"Good point, Mia. Sometimes you can think of places you've been from A to Z, or as you look at photos, you can organize them in some A-to-Z fashion. Remember, everyone has a different story and is comforted by different things, so this technique stays wide open for interpretation. Feel free to use it as you wish."

"Okay. Gotcha," Mia said, slumping back in her chair and fiddling in her purse until she pulled out gum. From my vantage point, the gum box appeared to say Nicorette on it, but if she's a smoker and wants to quit, I'm not stopping her. Thank God her notebook covered her lap when she got done being fidgety. She scribbled and doodled.

Lisa moved on. "Miles, can I hear from you?"

Miles: Stop the what-if self-doubts. "Wait. Do compound words count as one word or two?"

"Oh, Miles, your sentence speaks an impressive statement for *you*. I think it should count as six words today. It works for *you*," Lisa said.

Miles grinned, raking shaky fingers through his thick hair. I agreed so much with Lisa. This wasn't English class but a place to heal Miles's heart. His words nearly gutted me. I never wanted to imagine Dad with a gunshot wound.

With her back turned, Lisa randomly picked the red marker. *No, Lisa.* But the others in the group didn't have OCD. And they didn't see colors, grief, and pain and how I make connections in weird ways. So, now the "pain" of Miles's dad would be written across the board. Now it gave me what-if self-doubts. How does Miles do this day after day?

"How about you, Mia?" Lisa's eyes darted around the room. She seemed to be asking, "Who saves me if Mia doesn't want a turn? Or if she acts out again?"

Not bothering to sit up much, Mia told us her sad six words in the most monotoned voice possible. **Mia: Stay happy, healthy, and alive, Grandma.**

Lisa wrote Mia's words in blue. "There's a lot of love for Grandma in those words, Mia. What other emotions would you say are going on?"

"What do you want me to say? I'm pissed. I'm angry. I'm afraid. I hate living with her. School sucks. She's old. There. I'm done."

"Thank you, Mia, for your honesty. We appreciate where you're at on your grief journey. But remember, the group wants to help you."

Mia snorted.

"Hayden or Gretchen? Who's up?"

Hayden looked at me, but I pointed to him to go first. I needed a breather after Mia's sad anger—she had created too big a bubble of darkness. I'd give anything to have a grandmother, but when I looked at Mia, it seemed to her that's *all* she had.

Since I was thigh to thigh on the couch with Hayden, I had already peeked at his six words.

Then, Lisa grabbed the purple marker off the ledge of the whiteboard. So, immediately I'm zoned in on Rosie's throw pillows back at Hayden's house. I'm so touched by them—Rosie's favorite color.

"Tell me what you have, Hayden?" Lisa said.

Hayden: Be unapologetically honest through grief journaling. "I picked it because it's been the most helpful thing for me so far. I know. I hated it when you suggested I focus on it over a year ago. We used to fight so hard. It's not so bad now."

Everyone laughed. Lisa chuckled and said, "Well, that's good to hear. Keep writing."

And, of course, Lisa gripped the green-with-envy Expo marker just in time for me. "You're the last one, Gretchen."

Gretchen: Find constructive ways to release jealousy.

Before I could say another word, Mia rolled her body upward like a girl possessed and snorted. "What do you have to be jealous of, Rich Girl?"

Tears scorched my eyelids, but I held them back. "Mia, money has nothing to do with grief. It can't buy back my mother's life," I tried reasoning.

Lisa stepped forward with the green marker still in her hand, about to intervene. But she realized I had it under control. So, she let me keep talking.

"Besides, my dad and I are hardly rich. We scoop animal turds daily for extra spending cash."

Everyone giggled.

Mia stuck her gum out at me before sucking it in loudly with her head cocked. "Whatevs."

WTFDD? My blurry eyes scanned the room, wondering if anyone else thought her behavior came off as way beyond weird. Kelsey and her pirate met me with wide-eyed confusion. Hayden pushed his hand into the side of my thigh on the couch cushion as a silent signal.

Lisa cleared her throat. "Gretchen, perhaps you might share an example of your jealousy for Mia to help her understand you better?"

I pinched my toes, hoping not to cry. "Let me tell you, Mia, I'm jealous of so many things. Like you, for example."

"What? Why me?" Mia leaned forward, mouth agape, her freaking gum on display. She smugly glared at me as if quietly calling me a liar.

"Well, for one, you have a grandmother." I bit into my thumbnail, wearing down the edges of my Color Street pattern of Wrap it Up. The alternating diamonds, stripes, and faux glitter in red were staring at me like a red light. Yet my heart wanted me to act like a green light and go. To talk and solve. Quite literally, to wrap it up.

Mia chomped her gum, giggling.

One tear escaped. I swiped it away.

Hayden handed me a Kleenex. "I don't think it's funny." Then, raising his voice, he added, "I have a grandmother too." Finally, he pointed and asked, "Kelsey, Miles, do you have grandparents?"

"Yes," they said in unison.

I said, "Mia, I don't remember my grandparents. So, I get jealous of that and of people who have siblings sometimes. And, of course, the never-ending mom stuff."

Mia blew a bubble. Once it popped, she said, "Oh. Gotcha."

Lisa jumped in. "Gretchen, you have a right to feel a sense of loss. Thank you for sharing your thoughts on grief and jealousy. It's a common theme that affects each of us differently."

"Lisa, can I ask a question about jealousy?" Miles asked.

"Of course."

"Am I wrong to feel jealous of others who have more closure? My father chose to die. Sometimes I can't get past my anger. I keep asking myself: why wasn't I enough to live for? I guess I still need more help to realize my dad had a mental health issue. He died from a sickness too."

"Miles, you have the right to be angry or jealous about your father's suicide. But try to see your growth. You were correct when you said you did nothing wrong because suicide stems from a mental illness. I loved your goal tonight. Listen to just how mighty you are, Miles." Then Lisa repeated his goal. **"Stop the what-if self-doubts."**

Lisa walked to Miles with one hand on her heart, and with the other, she gave him a fist bump.

Lisa brought the night to a close. Miles had a great night. But overall, I felt uneasy about Mia. Her comments seemed stranger than usual. Instead of the quiet teary version of her we had gotten used to, we met edgy and bold. But grief gets unpredictable. So, I didn't want to be too judgy. Maybe the honest Mia showed up tonight? A tearless, gum-chewing girl who likes wearing lacy black bras beneath pale sweaters, along with lacy panties under pleather skirts. This Mia caught me off guard. But I wanted *my Mia* back. The one who learned to crochet. And the one who baked with her grandma. I liked the girl who still cried when telling the story of her parents better.

I felt thankful for what Lisa said: "Thank you all for such a good conversation tonight. Gretchen, I loved your insight about wealth and grief. It's so true that we can't buy away the pain. Just a little reminder, I also don't want anyone else to belittle another person's belief or situation in the group. Please come to me if you need anything. Remember, we come here to support one another. Grief enables us to catch a glimpse of each other's stories. It's important to write in your journals as needed." Lisa pointed to the whiteboard with our words. She pulled her phone out of her pocket to capture a picture.

"May I keep your six-word sentence responses for the ongoing project I'm working on?" *Love at the Center of Grief.*

Everyone agreed. Thankfully, I saw Lisa walking Mia to the parking lot to meet Grandma.

Hauling home six little words multiplied by five people equaled a ton of baggage to process after leaving the Summerfort Grief Center.

If someone's boyfriend used words such as "unapologetically honest," should it cause concern? It's on a loop inside my head.

So, Mother, I'm going to "wrap it up now" (Color Street style) or in my own way.

Chapter Sixteen

Dear Mom,
Early January 2020

Listening to Gretchen would've served me well. Because she tried warning me to share the information with Dad. Stupid me. I refused, thinking Dad would not want to deal with my stuff. Never in any of my *wildest* dreams did I believe anything would happen. Instead, Dad got blindsided by my omission of silence. And then Miss Tweed's emails with added attachments caught up to Dad the same day as an important phone call.

Dad approached me in the kitchen without saying a word, which was out of the ordinary, so I sensed another lecture coming. I stood leaning over the bar, popping white grapes into my mouth, squirreling them away, one right after the other. Purple-and-gold wrappers called to me next. So, I reached for a couple of Dad's Godiva dark chocolates from the candy dish. Nervously, I waited. I dreaded hearing another one of Gene Tucker's goofy digital lessons or an update about his Cozi app. Instead, he sauntered by me, shaking his head. He turned his ball cap backward, which usually meant, in weatherman's terms, a shitstorm was brewin' at the Tucker house.

With a death grip, Dad held on to a handful of paperwork. He rolled them up as if they were secret blueprints but only the size of notebook paper. Then, he rubbed his forehead with his free hand, adjusting his Gene Tucker Construction cap forward and backward, sighing.

My eyes followed him as he came closer. "What's up with you, Dad?" Then, I didn't mean to use the taste of chocolate for the support, but I asked with my mouth full, "Why are you acting so weird? Am I in trouble or something?"

Dad just shrugged. He paused, staring at me in silence like I was supposed to know something.

Looking at Dad with my head cocked in confusion, I sincerely tried to figure out what the hell I might've done. Did liar ass-jerk Thomas Sharp come out of his winter hibernation to say I said or did something? There's nothing I'm failing. Gretchen and I aren't doing anything too terrible— even if I were a father, it's barely on the edge of lecture-worthy. Nobody's pregnant or caught an STD from me. I don't smoke, drink, or do drugs. Okay. I covered the big shit list. *What's up?*

Dad sidled up to me at the bar. So close Dad's work boots rubbed against my foot. Too close because I could smell a day's work of sawdust, sweat, and aftershave on Dad. "Hmm. Well, let's give something a listen together," Dad said, pulling his phone out of the pocket of his jeans. Using my mind as a calendar, I ran through recent days and events. I tried to remember anything as a checklist again, but I came up with nothing. Finally, opening his voicemail, he hit the speaker button, cranking the volume to an extreme level.

"Hello, Mr. Gene Tucker. Summerfort Chamber of Commerce, here. How does all this feel—?"

My stomach dropped. For several seconds, I squeezed my eyes shut. Gasps of air rushed through my teeth, creating a hiss. Then, slowly, I opened my eyes, greeted with an unreadable poker face. Still, I looked, taking a mental guess at what Dad felt. *Hurt? Anger? Disappointment?* I mumbled, "Guess I should've told you about all this, huh? I'm sorry, Dad."

Dad had hit play for a second time around but pushed pause. I looked down, not sure what to say. Slowly, I glanced back in Dad's direction, meeting a half-grin. Blankly, I stared. Confused, I waited for him to say something because I didn't know what to say. In a gotcha style, Dad chuckled. He pulled the wadded papers from beside him, holding them in his hand again. Then catching me off guard, he used them, playfully swatting at me.

"Hey!" I jumped back from the bar, giggling.

Still laughing, Dad gave me some advice, "Yes, you should've told me about all of this, bud," he said, thumbing through the papers he'd spread out across the bar. Those typed-up words I knew very well.

"Hayden, get your phone out and program this event into Cozi."

As I rolled my eyes, the corner of my lip twitched at the corner. I knew Dad's already begun to forgive me for keeping my silence about this secret.

After Christmas break, I had new material to add to my final essay drafts for Miss Tweed's English class. Once she read them, she bossed me around about entering two Chamber of Commerce essay contests. When Gretchen overheard, she joined in the fight to coerce me. Finally, I got brave enough to enter. Gretchen's essay about the con man missed some minor requirements on word count, so she missed the deadline on reentering. In my opinion, she's a winner.

Chapter Seventeen

Dear Mom,
The Secret Event
January 2020
Summerfort Sage Manor

The Chamber of Commerce went all out. Cream-colored linens were draped over ten round banquet tables inside this large room. In the lobby of this fancy barn structure, I noted the banquet area from a distance. I saw that each table would host up to ten guests. Doing the math—meaning I counted the chairs—generated pride. Still, it also triggered my nerves into a heart-thumping, leg-jumping realization. More than one hundred people would mill around. Standing in the middle of this Missouri barn or manor, or whatever they wished to call it, felt like a night at a fancy movie premiere.

Inside the doors, a red carpet awaited with ropes on each side leading from the main entrance to the opened double doors into the venue's ballroom. Before entering the room, the TV media, radio, and some press from the local Branson paper greeted attendees with camera flashes.

Once inside the banquet room, a sweet older man wearing the nametag "Mr. Carson" ushered our group. He said, "This way to table number two, the reserved 'Tucker Table,'" with his palm turned out. It seemed like the warmest and most welcoming motion, especially when accompanied by his bright white Hollywood dentures—not one tooth seemed misaligned. Every gray hair lay in place, combed to the side. Pausing, he stood closest to Lisa's chair, so he waited for her, pulling her chair out and offering a gentlemanly bow when finished.

Lisa smiled and said, "Thank you." Our group loudly added the same sentiment in unison as we took our seats.

Inside a glass vase, white and pale yellow flowers, maybe carnations, acted as the centerpiece. "I love the battery-operated candles on each side of the flowers. Look. They're sitting on the silver tray. It makes everything sparkle," Gretchen said as her eyes roamed the décor of the twinkle lights above us, straight ahead and all the way up to the stage. Watching her excitement made me happy. I shared an approving grin with her.

My eyes played Duck, Duck, Goose as I looked around the big round table. Gretchen, me, Dad, Lisa, Drew's girlfriend (drawing a blank—too overwhelmed to recall her name. Drew's not talked much about her since Christmas, but they still looked cozy together). I played Gretchen's A-to-Z game until it returned to me—his girlfriend's name starts with the letter *a*. Let's see. Amy? No. April. No. Oh, yeah, Ava. Then, of course, Drew sat beside *Ava*. Cole with Ariana beside him, Gabby—otherwise known as Miss Happenstance, and (last but not least) Gretchen's dad, Dr. John.

Stunning—this word explains how everyone looked tonight. I guess the term black-tie affair applies. I leaned over and whispered, "You look like a movie star, Gretchen. You kind of remind me of Emma Stone with your award-winning red hair—you're flaming hot wearing that little black ball gown. Where did you get it?"

"Why, thank you." Gretchen squeezed my arm with a smile. "You're hella hot boy, too," she giggled. Then she added, "I'm so proud of you. Would you believe Gabby texted me pictures of dresses from a high-end thrift shop in Branson? It's a new store she heard about. So, Dad took me to try on a few."

"Well, that was super nice of Gabby," I said, my fingertips grazing the silky material, not believing it wasn't brand-new.

Gretchen smiled. "Gabby's got some great ideas sometimes."

Even though I know she gets upset over stupid things like the word *sweetie*, I liked hearing some more hope from Gretchen on the Gabby front. "Did Gabby get the nails for you too?"

"Yes." Gretchen wiggled her zigzag chevron fingers. "They're called Drop the Ball and reminded me of a black-tie look, so I wore them."

Gretchen didn't hide her hands. I felt reassured. "Hmm, perfect like you," I whispered. Resisting urges, I just settled for a couple of feathery kisses on her forehead because I wanted to lunge for her mouth or drag her onto my lap. Sweat didn't pour out of me when she touched my arm, which surprised me. Part of me wanted to retreat to the bathroom, to pull what I call "a Gretchen." My nerves were too much. But I thought a cold splash of water to my face, with some self-talk in the mirror, might simmer down my jitters. But I couldn't risk missing a single minute of Dad's expressions—his face must've ached from laughing so much and grinning so wide. If he wasn't careful, his lips might've cracked open. Still, my mind raced with issues.

All the guys at the table went together to rent the tuxes. Shouldn't we have been a united front? Why the heck didn't at least one of them bother informing me I'd have smoldered all night? Or tell me I'd sit trapped in a puddle of sweat? Damn every one of 'em! If Drew were next to me, I'd kick him under the table.

Dad twisted his body from Lisa's side, asking, "Hey, what's up with you, bud?" following up with more of his chuckling. Like his whole freaking world ranked as one tee-hee-hee hilarious moment after another.

Yanking at my collar a bit, I did everything to take my mind off the heat. Finally, I grabbed the agenda off the table, using it as a makeshift fan for my face. "Ugh, I'm burning up. Dad, aren't you hot?"

"No, I'm fine. Take a deep breath, Hayden. Remember, tonight's a celebration. Please, try and relax." Dad rubbed my back. "Look." Dad pulled the paper from my hand, placing it in front of my place setting on the table. Next, pointing his finger, he went into southern accent mode, saying, "Even though you didn't think you'd win—and you tried to keep it from everyone—you made a whole lot of this happen."

He nudged me. Tapping the paper, he wanted me to glance down and read the bold words. Looking down, I saw black ink against off-white parchment paper.

~ Celebrating Community ~
Saturday, January 11, 2020
A Night of Local Heroes
Dinner & Awards Ceremony:

Many residents of Summerfort, Missouri, go above and beyond, providing services to others. All nominees and winners display the following characteristics: They demonstrate a courageous spirit through determination and a continuous commitment to worthy causes. They are positive role models who willingly sacrifice personal gain to achieve noble goals. Some seek ways to improve our community through their unselfish hard work and efforts or volunteerism.

> *Categories:*
> *Volunteer Veteran*
> *Emergency Responder*
> *Literacy Mentors (Educational)*
> *Volunteer Senior Services*
> *Faith-Based Volunteer*
> *Small Business Leader*
>
> *Chamber of Commerce Scholarship Awards:*
> *Youth Essay Contest*
> *Nonprofit Award*

*Nominees are chosen from essay entries for each of the categories.
*Local area high school students were encouraged to enter the youth essay contest with the topic: "Capturing Time" or "Preserving History" under 1,250 words.

Servers wheeled out dinner on carts to the edges of the room. Hiding under those giant stainless steel lids, I detected the smell of southern goodness. Leaning around Gretchen's back, I called out to Dr. John, "Y'all ready for some good eats down there?"

He laughed, stretching to give me a fist bump. John recently treated Gretchen and me to Paula Deen's restaurant in Branson, and we enjoyed it.

We had hoped for Paula when we learned the Summerfort Chamber of Commerce arranged for catering from a Branson restaurant tonight. We dreamed about her fried chicken, ribs, mac and cheese, and ooey-gooey butter cake.

"I'm sort of questioning the whole gnawing on some barbeque while wearing a tuxedo"—I threw up my hands—"but I'm gonna say, 'Worth it,'" I said to Gretchen.

"I agree," she replied.

Dad overheard, so we laughed.

A noise on stage diverted our attention. The emcee pulled the microphone down in an attempt to reach his mouth. "Good evening, ladies and gentlemen," he said, through a bit of screeching feedback.

Gretchen met my gaze because we both knew what the other was probably thinking since we'd said it before. He seemed designed for that job. It was Summerfort High School's Principal Marshall.

We heard Gabby attempting to whisper to John, "Oh, Mr. Marshall, that man's such a sweetie." Gretchen dug her nails into my thigh at the word *sweetie*. *Go easy, girl*.

Dad nudged me with his elbow and dragged his body closer to Gretchen to poke the beautiful redheaded bear a little further. "Don't you agree,

Gretchen —your principal's a real *sweetie*?" Dad stifled a laugh.

"Gene," Gretchen mumbled through gritted teeth before smirking. Dad appeared to always get away with anything when teasing Gretchen, his little Strawberry Shortcake buddy. Dad wanted a daughter, didn't he, Mom?

"Do you think Marshall volunteered to be master of ceremonies?" I whispered toward Gretchen and Dad, who both nodded.

"Summerfort is a special community filled with heroes. Don't you all agree?" Principal Marshall waited for the applause to end. "Tonight, right here in Summerfort, don't you feel like a shining star attending the Oscars?"

Again, more clapping.

"Tonight, it is a great honor to celebrate with you. Please enjoy your dinner catered from Paula Deen's restaurant in Branson. Let's give each staff member of the Summerfort Sage Manor a hardy round of applause before eating. After dinner, our community heroes from each category will be announced and presented with their awards on stage. So, please, enjoy the music while you dine."

A clattering of bowls and platters, with oversized serving spoons and forks, landed on our table. We gasped, excited to see the fried chicken, spare ribs, and catfish. Mr. Carson lifted each item's lid, announcing the side's name and sliding them onto the table. "Tonight, we brought you baked mac and cheese, creamed potatoes, poppy seed tossed salad, and green beans. Paula added one extra side tonight to go with her ribs"—he tilted the bowl before adding—"her famous coleslaw." Mr. Carson and his assistant server wheeled away with the empty cart. Still, they twirled around, reminding us, "Don't forget to save room for Paula's dessert. Tonight's specialty is an ooey-gooey butter cake."

Dr. John high-fived me.

"I'm going to eat till I puke," Gretchen said.

Overhearing her, Dad cleared his throat. We glanced toward him.

Dad's eyebrows raised. "Don't put me through another ordeal like that," Dad muttered. We giggled, remembering the night Gretchen and I had shown up at the house covered in vomity hot chocolate. An impromptu spinning session in the park after throwing Gretchen over my shoulder had led to misfortune.

"Dad, how was I supposed to know what Gretchen meant by her little *message*?" Touching my cheeks, I felt the transformation of my face as the shades turned pink into red. Then, recalling how Gretchen had dangled down my back and slapped my butt, trying to get me to stop the spinning, I had *assumed* she *liked* it, so I only went faster.

"Stop gossiping about me, you two," Gretchen said, her cheeks matching a hue similar to mine.

From across the table, Drew piped up with a request, looking directly at me with a smirk and wink, saying, "Brat, pass the chicken platter, *please*."

Biting my lip to stop cracking up, I shook Dad's arm and said, "Daddy, Drew's calling me names again. Tell him to quit. Make him stop. He's so mean to me. Daddy." I shook Dad's arm again.

Drew jumped in. "Dad, Hayden's such a tattle-tale. Besides, I said *please* to him."

Raising his eyebrow, Dad asked, "Really?" He glared at me first. Then turned to stare down at Drew. "You two are doing this *thing* again? So, you're not *ever* going to outgrow this routine?"

The table chuckled.

Drew and I loved aggravating Dad like this when we were together. Of course, Cole went back into his uptight and quiet self on us tonight. Where's Mr. Throwback Thursday, Cole? I wish Christmas "Cool" were in attendance or the more laid-back version of him, but tonight Cole reemerged as his more recent ass-jerk persona. Maybe he and Ariana had a fight or something. She looked tense too. What's up with them? I noticed he'd been clingy with Ariana all night. A lot of weird whispering went on between them with these nervous smiles—I guess maybe the kind that means "I'm sorry, and I still love you." Cole kept giving her sideways glances, back rubs, and constantly topping off her water glass. She responded to him with a reassuring grin. At times I wanted to say, *Screw it, Cole, get a room, brother. And take the freaking water with you if it makes you two smile that much.*

Unfortunately, Cole retreated from all of us after you died. At least with Ariana, Cole stands a chance—she's bringing Cole back to life for us, thankfully. And at Christmas, I learned so much.

So, I switched to Drew.

"Well, Daddy, aren't you making Drew mind his manners at the table?" I asked, pressing on, tugging on the sleeve of his shirt. "Why are you letting Drew get away with being mean?"

"I'm about to get mean with both of you," Dad said, pointing his fork at Drew.

"Classic, Dad," Drew said, letting out a roar, his head thrown back, which cracked us all up. Dad's lopsided smirk of embarrassment and everyone's laughter made our antics so worth it.

"Grow up, Dennis the Menace Drew," Dad said. Then, turning to me, he added, "I'll deal with you later—you still live at home, you know?"

I pulled my hands off his shirt and said, "I surrender," which brought even more chuckling from everyone.

Getting in a little more private jab at Dad, I pushed my roll toward him, saying, "How about a little more *bread*, Daddy."

In a low voice, Dad said, "Hmm, Drew's right, bud, you just might be a brat," but he squeezed my shoulder. Our inside joke about bread isn't funny because it involved Dad going bonkers, swinging at me with a loaf of dang Wonder Bread. Thank God we've moved past the incident. Since I'm writing about this moment, I forgot to mention I bought Dad a private gag gift at Christmas—a Wonder Bread cyclist jersey. I got one with those famous yellow, blue, and red dots. It says "America's Favorite Bread" across the chest. In my head, it read "weird but apparently suitable for busting somebody's ass." Dad and I laughed when I'd given it to him and bro-hugged it out.

By the time the servers cleared the tables, everyone had talked about how full they felt. The Tucker table grew quiet, listening to the music selections, all of them hero-themed.

Gretchen asked me, "What did you like best about the meal?"

The corners of my mouth pulled, turning into a toothy smile. Then, I went for the best answer of all time. Nuzzling close to Gretchen's ear, I muttered, "The company." I placed my hand on her thigh, going as high as legally possible in front of our fathers. She tilted her body toward me until she got close enough to steal a kiss. I adjusted in my seat before combusting into another fit of sweat. Transferring our hands to the safety of the tabletop, I kept my pinky looped with hers.

The sound of a drum roll occurred as the lights dimmed. Mr. Marshall graced the stage. A projector lit up with the words "Celebrating Community:

A Night of Local Heroes" flashing onto the screen. "Ladies and gentlemen, we hope you enjoyed dinner," Mr. Marshall paused for applause. He continued. "Let's begin the awards portion of the ceremony."

A photo of a young soldier propping against a sign in Vietnam captured our attention. The song "Hero of War" played in the background. The lyrics wrestled with my emotions in multiple layers. First, it explained what a veteran might sacrifice during combat while defending our freedoms, facing death, and hoping to return home alive. Then, snapshots flashed on the screen of this young soldier as he grew up. Only, coming home, he faced adversity in the forms of hate, loneliness, and alcoholism, as seen through this veteran's heart-wrenching real-life photographs.

After seeking help, he regained his life by becoming a volunteer. One of the last photos showed him placing wreaths on the graves of veterans at Christmastime. This tugged at my heart, reminding me of Gretchen's wreaths of kindness. But who was this man? Finally, I recognized the older clean-cut version of this face in the last photo. It was our very own Mr. Carson, sporting his Hollywood smile.

In a choked-up voice, Mr. Marshall spoke into the microphone, "Folks, prepare for tonight. We have a house full of special moments. Please, help me welcome Vietnam veteran Joseph Carson to the stage." Mr. Carson received a standing ovation from the audience, many with tears in their eyes (yes, mine too). Around his neck, Mr. Marshall placed a medal, like the ones they put around an Olympic winner. Mr. Marshall also handed him a framed award. Every story after Mr. Carson's is full of the feels.

As soon as Andra Day belted out the first note of her inspirational tune "Rise Up," my heart lurched into my throat. Because I also saw the words of one of my essays begin to scroll across the jumbo-sized screen. Due to time constraints, the Chamber of Commerce didn't require every award winner to read their essay or give an acceptance speech. Instead, someone trained with a deep, emotionally charged voice did an excellent audio version of me. And thank God, or else I don't think I would have survived participating. Instead, I would have suffered from a panic attack of gargantuan sweaty proportions. Just thinking about going up on stage threw me into heart palpitations. *What if everyone hates what I wrote? Please, God, don't let everyone think I'm stupid.* My stomach gurgled. As pictures on the screen began telling my story, the desire to divert my attention away from the display and squeeze my eyes shut heightened. To look away would mean forfeiting the emotions from seeing and remembering.

"Photograph"
By Hayden Tucker

The pain of losing Mom remains monumental. Often, I wonder what a family of five had been like and looked like. Recalling is difficult since my perspective comes from a six-year-old boy's shattered heart.

Grief steals family histories. In the uncomfortable aftermath of a death, some people tend to hide memories. High on the shelves of hall closets, pictures slip into shoeboxes, where they stay for nearly a decade. Still, no amount of visual removal takes the pain away. Sorrow remains.

The longing to see my mother's face and hear her voice lingers. I agree with Sally Mann, "Photographs open doors into the past, but they also allow a look into the future." Snapshots piece together times, places, and, most importantly, people. Pictures answer questions. They evoke a lot of emotions.

Despite the ache, I stepped through grief's door. Looking inside shoeboxes, I visited my mother. I wanted to see her, talk to her, and write about her.

Once again, I smiled, staring down at memories. Even through tears, I saw three boys with two parents beaming. As Mom sat beside each son, she doted on him. She had an expression on her face as if each son were an only child.

Due to cancer, some images depicted vulnerability. However, in the same picture, Mom's face revealed determination with a smile full of character.

Holding each son by her side, her husband took endless photos of mundane moments—cooking, picnicking, and playing outside as a family. Now, I understand—these times symbolize life's most precious happenings. My parents preserved these days in the pages of a family album.

My father led this mission, recording daily life to declare his undying love. Assuring her and swearing to her she would be unforgettable. Dad understood capturing seconds mattered. So, inside moments shared with Mom, he granted us a lifetime warranty.

Dad peered through a camera lens for his sons, trying to see or steal time from the future as he fought the pain of the present. In bittersweet final photographs, we still wore smiles because Dad shared his brand of humor, generating laughter during junctures in life unimaginable. Until the end, he stayed by her side, documenting. He withstood the responsibility of acquiring special moments and favorite pastimes on film with her.

I learned to prepare toast in an over-the-top outfit consisting of Mom's "Kiss the Cook" apron and chef's hat. Nose-to-nose with me, my mom smiled while wrapping me in her arms. This pose she called our buttery cinnamon toast kiss. But, of course, for a six-year-old boy, it was never about just the toast.

From viewing one photograph, I witnessed the adoration in her eyes as they shone. Mom and I ate a platter of buttery cinnamon toast, her last meal on earth. Without knowing, Dad preserved this in a snapshot. He fought bravely to take this final picture, freezing time.

Death may rob us of time, but it does not have the power to change or steal love from us. This lasting image reminds me how much my mother and father love me.

Music played as memories of my whole family continued to unfold in photographs along with my writing. My mother was healthy and alive—my father supported her through her illness. A dad with three boys attempting to live without her, smiling a half-smile, playing games, teaching them, laughing, despite the agony.

Before and after snapshots continued to flash on the screen of construction sites and ended with the location of the Summerfort Grief Center. A picture of Dad and me before one of my football games while I'm in my uniform. This one created a smile for me. At this point, hope had reentered my life. The screen stops with an image of Dad standing against his truck in his hard hat. Gretchen's arm stays curled around mine. Dad moved closer to me and patted my back. At his touch, the first tears cascaded down my face. I glanced around the table, surprised by how emotional my brothers seemed.

Others at the table seemed moved by the words and images. Glassy, watery eyes met me. Perhaps they understood more about my version of loss and grief. Or they've learned even more about Dad through my lens.

"Heroes"
By Hayden Tucker

Believing in a hero is difficult if you think no one believes in you. A year ago, I would have glared at a blank page if asked to write about a hero. Luckily, time and life lessons changed that. Hearing about my hero's positive attributes through others allowed me to study my hero from a new vantage point. Soon, I realized many people in life deserve praise. I had family and friends, many heroes, putting themselves out there to help me in some way or another.

I released the unrealistic ideal of perfection, letting them go. Learning a new fact—no one, not even heroes, reach perfection. Taking the time to listen and understand my hero's flaws, I came face-to-face with what made him more human, loveable, and real. In the end, I found we shared a whole lot more in common than I initially thought. My love started to rebuild.

I started to look around and to feel. The handiwork of builders comes into play while driving through Summerfort. The visual reminders are dotted everywhere. Starting from the earth, they rise into the sky. Assumptions get made that homes, businesses, and buildings will always remain. Like the heroes that build them, it's easy to take them for granted. Architects begin with simple ideas and mold them into realities. Often starting with only paper and pencil. Many times, I watched as my hero sketched visions for others. A modern farmhouse designed from scratch into a family home. Or the repurposing of a rundown church into a local grief center.

Because of him, several Summerfort residents live inside their dream houses, built on tree-lined streets. Children use safe playground equipment he installed in the city park. Downtown, he built many of the brick-and-mortar government buildings still standing strong. He renovated and preserved Summerfort's history. My hero does not wear a cape. But he is the builder of neighborhood dreams, the fixer of problems, and a future renovator.

Beyond his job, my hero faced raising three boys alone when his wife died from cancer. Blueprints offer no assistance on how to build a life. How does a man construct dreams for others when the foundation of his own home crumbles down to rubble with sorrow? Or especially on how to draw your way out of grief.

My hero's answer was to donate his time and supplies and use the phone to call people on behalf of others. He asked other businesses to help him create miracles with a fast renovation of a little rundown church on the town's outskirts. As the motto states, this place allowed me and many others a place to heal, hope, and belong.

My time at the Summerfort Grief Center began at the age of six because my mother died. Until recently, I did not know my hero's handiwork created this building so quickly. He worked hard, so another of my heroes might enroll me as one of her first participants.

Growing up, my hero and I suffered through years of grief. As he buried himself in overtime, I buried myself in silence, too afraid or too angry to speak. The event earned me a nickname at school, "Hardly Speaks Hayden." After finding out I was the victim of long-term school bullying and sports hazing, he surprised me as the first person to show up in my defense. The remodeling of our relationship began, and the emotional walls I built against him started to tumble. From here, we agreed it was time to rebuild.

Grief affects people in several ways. His battles with grief crossed into absences in some aspects of my life. His absences at my school and sports events never meant he stopped loving or believing in me, though. Without my mother sitting by his side, the emptiness he felt broke his heart. My hero taught me how communicating and apologizing for these shortcomings can put healthy changes in motion. Now, we both know how to tear down barriers standing in the way, repairing what's broken.

Envisioning a calmer life allows me to open my heart, communicate, and remember. It seems more natural to positively recall the past when the steps leading to my future include more guidance from a hero.

Scenes from my childhood now replay in my mind. Tossing football in the backyard with my father, watching movies huddled together, using his tools, and learning as he showed me how to construct items. And his sense of humor constantly caused me laughter. My mother seems to come back to me through his stories as I reminisce.

The human heart complicates everything. Exploring the background of my hero's heart, I see, feel, and know what he has had to overcome. As he helped others, I learned about the sacrifices he made. I understand him more. The meaning behind my mother's childhood nickname, "Gentle Giant Contractor," makes more sense now. Standing tall and strong, the "Gentle Giant Contractor" mixes generosity, kindness, and lovability.

As my mother dreamed of marriage and children, my father agreed to design and build the start of a lifetime. As she dreamed of becoming a registered nurse, he encouraged her. Working extra hours, he still shared household duties. I recall overhearing him once saying to her, "Our home, our children, our dreams." He stayed by her side through cancer, where he remained with love even after hospice came into our home until she died. I know he still loves her today.

Heroes never seem to stop working. Even after his wife's death, he took zero days off because his three sons required care. My hero tried every way he knew how to absorb their pain. For one little boy, he camped out inside a pantry playing with the cars his mother bought him until they both fell asleep. For the other boys, he pushed them to live life and get college educations. Then knowing his wife's last wishes, he watched his older children leave home, become adults, and carry out their dreams.

Step by step or brick by brick, Gene Tucker continues to rise up as a hero. In place of a cape, he sports a hard hat. Behind the scenes, he remains, designing structures for the town of Summerfort, Missouri. Or, more importantly, he may be in the business of building up the spirits of people like me. Because I get the honor of calling my hero Mr. Gene Tucker by the most crucial title: Dad.

Across the bottom of Dad's picture, in bold black letters, the message read:

Congratulations,
~ Gene Tucker Construction,
Summerfort's Small Business Leader ~

In a shaky voice, Mr. Marshall said, "Gene Tucker, please join me on stage to receive your award. On a personal note, as your son's principal, it's a privilege to learn more about your story."

Everyone in the room stood again, giving Dad a standing ovation. Before Dad walked away, he reached for me, his eyes glassy but crinkled at the edges from smiling. Inside his embrace, I nearly bawled my eyes out. Surrounded by the noise, I could still hear my heart drumming inside my ears. I didn't want Dad to release me because I struggled to get a grip. Feeling wobbly, I couldn't enjoy the moment. I felt too overwhelmed.

Dad brought me back to earth. "I love you. Do you know that?—you little *brat*—I believe all this hoopla and clapping is really about *you*. It's for the essays *you* wrote?" He tugged on my hair with just the right amount of humor, finding a way to help me celebrate. Finally, I grinned. He slipped away after giving me a hefty slug to the back—his bro hug.

Gretchen held on to my sweaty hand without complaint.

"Gene," Mr. Marshall said in a coy voice, "stay at the edge of the stage wearing your medal as we announce the next winner." Then, Mr. Marshall's voice returned to a level I'm used to, sounding loud and proud and drawing out the words on a game show. "For the youth essay contest, nominees came from local high school students. So, the Chamber of Commerce reached out to English teachers encouraging them to have students enter.

"This year's topic, 'Capturing Time' or 'Preserving History,' had to be under 1,250 words. Hayden

Tucker's essay 'Photographs' captured the hearts of the Chamber of Commerce. He is this year's $1,000 scholarship winner. So, please, Hayden, join your dad on stage. Folks, you are looking at the writer of two award-winning essays tonight. Mr. Hayden Tucker wrote both 'Photographs' and 'Heroes' about his dad, Gene Tucker. After the Chamber of Commerce poured over Hayden's words, we knew he, his dad Gene Tucker, and the Summerfort Grief Center deserved recognition."

Gretchen wiggled my hand free, throwing her arms around me for a hug. Lisa gave me her quick side-hug. As I walked by them, my brothers gave me a high five. I felt odd moving forward to go up in front of people. My lips went all twitchy, caught between half-smiling and half-crying. I hated not knowing how to get a freaking grip, but I couldn't stop thinking about how far I'd come in a year. Seeing Dad waiting up there, grinning at me, almost had me undone. Seeing Dad—period! That's a great start from over a year ago. With every seat taken, people sitting at a table behind me clapped to support *me*? Local businesses considered the words I wrote as something *worthwhile*? My life mattered?

Mom, the picture of you and I nose-to-nose stuck in my mind. At the moment, I felt like a child, wanting my mom so badly. But then, I thought about your absence from the crowd. *God, what would you say to me right now, Mom?* Dad and I did the bro hug thing again on stage before posing for photos.

Mr. Marshall said, "Now, you guys stay to the side of the stage until I call the last name of the night." My mind kept drifting, losing myself in conversations, talking to you—my mom, asking questions—*Mom, are you proud of me? I miss you. Did you like my essays? Are you happy since Dad and I get along better these days? Oh, my God, I won $1,000! I'd give anything to celebrate with your buttery cinnamon toast and one of your hugs. But, somehow, someway, I wish like hell you'd be able to just freaking tell me what you think of me.*

The projector screen lit up with photos of inside the Summerfort Grief Center. Pictures of Gretchen and me as children were in so many of them.

"As I mentioned moments ago, this is the year of the Summerfort Grief Center. It's hard to say who among them is the biggest hero. Perhaps Gene for his construction of the building? Or Hayden for writing about his heroes, Gene and Lisa? Or Lisa for coming up with the vision? When I asked Lisa, she told me the heroes are the children who work hard in her programs to honor the lives of those they have lost. The Chamber of Commerce would like to announce Lisa Marks of the Summerfort Grief Center as the winner of the nonprofit scholarship award."

Of course, Lisa also received a well-deserved standing ovation.

A reporter placed me in the middle of Dad and Lisa. The three of us linked together, arm in arm. This connection seemed so normal. But is it? *Should I feel this way?* I liked it. Should I? It's been so long. To be able to touch two parents. Can I even explain? I got caught up in the thrill. Inside all these emotions, I pretended Lisa was my mom. It just sort of happened. All of it seemed to fall into place. We smiled at the flashing cameras.

Tilting my head toward Lisa's while pressing the side of my body close to her hip, we created that typical family pose. Mom, it reminded me of the picture of you with your parents that hangs in the hallway.

I'm sorry, but the movements fell comfortably into place. Too easy. Until I scanned the crowd and spotted Drew and Cole at the table. Then, remembering you, our mother, Rosie Tucker, will never occupy a seat next to us ever again.

Standing, I had plastered myself against this woman named Lisa because of my *birth* mother's death. Repositioning my feet, I squirmed a bit, pulling away. Weird, twisted, shameful, and confusing emotions caused me to back off Lisa. My heart cracked in two. I wanted someone else to take the $1,000 because maybe I didn't deserve it anymore.

Yet gaining Lisa with Dad—two parents— equaled a freaking dream. But Lisa's not my mom. On the other hand, I would get to experience normal again. Do you want that for me, Mom? Lisa shared her smiles, and she said she was proud of me. I hear her cheering me on at football, basketball, and baseball games. If you were here, I know you'd do the same. But then, she gets under my skin, nagging me about so many things like Gretchen, grief journals, school, and Dad. Lisa yaks about everything and nothing, talking to me about life. Also, she gives side-hugs till we fall into full-on squeezes. Like a kid, sometimes, I feel like I might slip up around Lisa and say, "Shut up, and just be my mom already."

Images of a mother I already have burst into my mind. And along with the pictures, guilt tags along, with the words ungrateful and disrespectful. I have a mother. A mother whom I love and dearly miss. You can't be replaced with someone else, *right?* Even if this someone else values me like a son? Even if I handed over my soul to this someone else, knowing how trustworthy she would be with my very life? No. I don't suppose "even-ifs" make any of this right?

So, putting a cork on my stupid imagination, I bottled up my ass-jerk thoughts about make-believe families. Pressure and guilt lessened. If I go further away from Lisa, the better I'll probably feel. Lisa is *not* my mom. Again and again, I said it in my mind and wrote it in this journal. I force myself to remember this as another type of guilt lesson, utilizing it as a warning. If I don't, I'll risk too much ache.

Once again, I must tell myself: Lisa's *not* my mom.

Chapter Eighteen

January 2020
Dear Mom,

Mr. Wright jotted down numbers on his whiteboard in the following order: 8, 5, 9, 1, 7, 6, 2, 0. After the tardy bell rang, he performed his daily routine. He cleared his throat loudly. "Students, please cooperate with those around you to problem solve. Assignment: Explain why these numbers form a sequence. Brainstorm. Listen to each other. *Write* everything out." Using the black Expo marker in his hand, he pretended to use it as a laser pointer.

He said the word *write* with such an emphasis. But he expected us to show our work all the time. As he paced through the desk, he reminded us, "I'll be roaming to seek out slackers."

Mr. Wright made three thick lines under the series of numbered gibberish using his black dry-erase marker. Numbers did not look trustworthy when out of order. No wonder I preferred to write papers in English.

My math buddy, Jun, pleaded from a couple of seats away, "Gretchen, WTFDD? Will you please move closer to me, so we can work together?" A quiet little crew surrounded me, so I asked the two girls to join us.

I scribbled the figures down again for good measure, throwing addition and subtraction in the mix: 8-3 = 5 + 4 =9-1=8? Finally, I push the paper to Jun, "Notice any patterns yet?"

She scanned the page. "Nope. Where's the 2, 6, and 7?"

I laughed, shrugging. "I don't know where that two ran off to. Get it?"

The other girls darted their eyes and shook their heads without saying anything. Then, they copied a portion of my incorrect argument onto their papers.

We both laughed.

"And look, you used the number 8 twice," Jun said, tapping her pencil at the problem.

Strolling again, Mr. Wright said, "A suggestion— it does help to *write* it all out as you work."

His skinny-style khakis and untucked button-down shirt reminded me of something Hayden would wear. Like if he had a reason to dress up. Coach Ryan won't allow jeans when he has an away game. I don't think Mr. Wright even wore socks with his tan leather Sperrys. Although he's a teacher, he has this halfway-hot-but-you'll-miss-it-if-you-don't-gawk-twice look. Because it's glazed over with a hint of geek appeal. He's virtually a taller Leonard with darker hair from *The Big Bang Theory*. It's a sitcom, Mom. Yet you can't help yourself from appreciating his smiling face, intelligence, and his attempts at wit.

"Duh, that's what we're doing," Jun said under her breath, handing back my paper.

I smirked. Trying to involve the others, I asked a couple of questions. "Hey, aren't you Ari Patel's sister? He's a senior, but Hayden, my boyfriend, likes him a lot. They play basketball together."

The adorable girl with mocha-colored eyes nodded.

"That means you're Kera?"

"Keri, with an i." The corners of her mouth turned up into the slightest smile. She's glancing at me, her eyes open in wide-eyed surprise because I *almost* knew her name.

Despite this steamy classroom, the coat girl still hasn't spoken or shed her cloak. Pointing to Jun and Keri, I asked, "You two wanna try multiplying while we divide over here?"

My brain felt overloaded with more questions than answers. I asked the girl who had joined the class during the semester because some schedules get shifted after Christmas, "Any thoughts?"

She refused to make eye contact, only giving me a half-hearted shake. I scared her to death, I suppose.

Inquiring "What's your name?" doesn't seem possible then. Hmmm. I considered another tactic with a different question. "I like your brass buttons—are those owl faces centered on them?" Keeping the problem-solving to myself, I zoned in on hoot owls staring back at me.

A chuckle almost slipped out, realizing I had just killed two birds with one stone and had perfect timing for using this phrase.

After another failed attempt, Jun said, "Came up with zilch, Gretchen."

"Even and odd with a total of eight numbers— think it's something to do with averages?" I asked in reply.

The two girls looked down, pretending to add the numbers.

At the side of the classroom, Mr. Wright tossed his whiteboard eraser into the air. "Time's almost up. O-N-E."

That's the problem with time. It's always flying by until it's humanly impossible to stay—time's up—my brain sizzled with this thought.

He rushed through the spelling of the number one by doing the individual letters. After spouting off every single letter, we heard his clap following. So, it was like "O"—CLAP—"N"—CLAP—"E"—CLAP.

"I think I did that maneuver in under one second," he said with a lopsided grin. Then, holding the eraser above his head, he marched back through a cluster of cluttered desks. I watched a *Big Bang Theory* moment play out with Sheldon looking like Leonard.

What does he act like at home? As I get my weird thoughts, I think of asking my questions to Jun. Just random things she might think about Mr. Wright.

Jun's not what you'd expect at first. She has a petite frame and a feisty attitude. However, I adore her intelligence and ability to be an open-minded cheerleader without any of the mean girl antics.

Her brow is raised in approval when she sees what I'm doodling in the margins. Hayden and I trust and like her. I know I can get silly around her without worrying about gossip and judgment— just an opportunity to enjoy a minute of fun. My fingers walked my paper to the edge of the desk. She read my questions but answered them on her page.

1.) "Only sleeps in his underwear?" I scribbled in my notebook.

Anticipating Jun's comment, I held my breath. Only she wrote, "Nope. I get a nude vibe."

I held back a snort.

2.) "The old boxer/brief debate?" Jun grabbed my pencil even though she had her own on her desk.

She wrote back: "Both the boxer-brief, filling them out well. Wright's old but a savory thirtyish." We shared crooked smiles as I snatched my pencil back.

3.) "Snores?"

"No to the snoring, but I imagine him loud in other ways."

My mouth gaped open. "Jun!" I meant to whisper, but it came out too loud. The coat girl overheard us, so she grinned. Her real name is Stella, I believe. Jun gave me her usual shrug, one of her you-know-I'm-probably-right moves.

4.) "Good-looking?"

"I think when younger. Glimmers of hope if we dyed that bit of gray away," Jun wrote.

5.) "Fun husband?"

"See #1 and #3 for a 'Mr. Right' pattern! Lol! :) " Jun's grin widened as *her* pencil finished scribbling the last word.

I bit my lip, stifling the laughter. Mr. Wright's husky voice ripped through the air. "One last hint, *write* it out."

Using my foot, I nudged Jun. "Does he mean we need to *spell* out the numbers? His circus juggling earlier was to prove a point. We ignored the fact that numbers are also words. Look, when I write them out: Eight, Five, Nine, One, Seven, Six, Two, Zero. Freakazoid, this whole time those numbers were in alphabetical order!"

From the front of the classroom, Mr. Wright gestured to me using his marker. Then he put a hand up near his ear. "Gretchen, did I hear you correctly? You think you've solved the problem?"

From our pod in the back, I nodded before answering. "Maybe? The sequence is in alphabetical order, I think."

"Well done, Gretchen and team. Everyone, turn in your scratch paper for your daily participation grade as you leave class today."

"Well, crap! I guess we can quickly rewrite some random figures. We can't turn in something that says all this." My hand scrubbed over info about what does or doesn't cover my teacher's butt.

Jun and I took off work on notes in a frenzy as she giggled.

"Numbers and math equal the Devil some days. There's never been a real excuse for Dear Aunt Sally," I said.

We both cracked up. Even the hoot owl coat girl, Stella, cracked a smile.

***

Too often, the trouble with numbers is that there's too much or too little associated with them. Two thousand twenty! This number appeared futuristic, massive, and advanced when written out as a spelling word. So, I assigned 2020 a numerical value to bring you a year in review. Oh. My. God. Mother.

As 2020 began, I got conned into all the believable hype: those oohs, ahhs, and promising new gadgets. But then, the aha moments advertisers expand upon, vowing to make everything in life better, more comfortable, or extra profitable as long as we acquire this or that.

Even I expected a number like 2020 to live up to the vision.

I don't know? Human beings stretched out, kicking back, with 2020 expectations. Remember the flying cars in *Back to the Future* when the character goes back in time? Well, nix floating vehicles. In place of them, some own electric cars or hybrid types. Dad drives a hybrid Nissan Rogue. I teased him about not knowing the meaning of going rogue. Then I learned he hid secrets about his slutty "Happenstance" post office moves, which were so rogue-like. Ugh. I am moving back to the original topic of discussion.

By 2020, I thought a cleaner environment would've been created by harnessing new energy sources—utilizing the sun's natural resources and wind on the planet. Instead, our fantastic world continues to rotate. Oh, but I'm hanging on because it's necessary for survival.

At first, January delivered a dose of goodness.

Of course, I'll make a New Year's resolution to never see Dad wearing his too-tight cop costume while shaking his butt to the disco tune "YMCA" again. Okay, I admit, a bunch of laughs occurred. I swear we gave off a look in pictures as if we were all in the middle of Times Square with confetti raining down on us. Even if the dance went down kind of haphazardly, with arms thrown into the air into letters of the alphabet, we celebrated among friends. Mom, isn't that such a beautiful image and thought? Dad and I weren't sitting home alone, just watching more news. Maybe we won't spend another lonely holiday together anymore?

Many people honestly believe you know what I'm doing from heaven. They like to tell me you can look down and see all the wonderful things happening to me. And I want to imagine you did catch a glimpse of us smiling. And I want to believe you listen. So, did you hear us laughing that night? But again, I wish there were definite answers, signs, and proof.

To surprise Lisa, Gene orchestrated a birthday party for her. A birthday, Christmas, and New Year's gathering rolled into one giant gifting experience.

Life at the Tucker house seems cozy these days. Hayden and I haven't had much time to discuss Gene and Lisa and whether or not he believes he sees a long-term deal between them. I think his outlook on the situation comes off as mostly positive. The friendship had eight years to grow. I wonder how many of those years were wasted with Lisa and Gene loving each other without saying a word.

I don't want to listen to the doctor's voice in the background of my mind. "I'm so sorry, Doctor Gardener and Gretchen. We did everything to save Gwen."

When people talk about their moms, sometimes I can't shut off my emotions. Often, the reminders hit me that you're gone. The unfairness floors me. Even on those days when I perceive my whole life as a bit of nothingness, I stay upright, allowing my body to accept living. I remember Dad's words: "Aren't we lucky we had her? Aren't we lucky she loved us?" Yes!

Cole, Hayden's oldest brother, reached out to Hayden through a thoughtful note with his girlfriend Ariana's urging. Again, I felt thrilled for Hayden but experienced another ping of jealousy whack me. Hayden wrote two heart-wrenching essays about his mom and one about Gene. One caused Gene to win the Chamber of Commerce award for a small business leader, and Hayden won $1,000 for his youth essay. In addition, the themes in his writings prompted them to look closely at the Summerfort Grief Center, causing Lisa to win an award for her nonprofit. I'm so proud of Hayden, Gene, and Lisa, but again those minor parts of me wonder why I can't have a special letter sent to me. Or when will I win some kind of award? I feel like I'm failing you and Dad and at life.

Every day I present my designer nails to the world. But underneath the hidden layers of gloves and glitter: what's wrong with me?

Welcome 2020: The year of Gretchen's death envy.

I. Am. Not. Proud.

Chapter Nineteen

Dear Ma,

Lisa came to the house because she needed Gretch and me to discuss some things. At first, it felt strange—maybe claustrophobic is the best word I can muster. Again, why do I sweat so much under pressure? I figured we'd go to the Summerfort Grief Center to work. Thankfully, once Lisa arrived, she and Dad didn't turn the meeting into a gross love session. Or make me feel uncomfortable in my own home. Instead, Dad simply hugged her, got us some drinks, and left us alone to work in the den. Miss Spicy Boots retreated with Dad, jingling and prancing to his office—Dad and *his* cat.

My heart fluttered as Lisa leaned back against the floral purple throw pillows. *She means no harm,* I told myself, but I had to worry. *Would it hurt your feelings?* Dad assured me you talked about him moving on after your death. Dad waited, I reminded myself, sucking in a breath to listen.

"Years ago, you two did a version of a heart tree when you were only six years old," Lisa said. "Do you think it's possible to rework it for our teen group? And then, I want to use all the materials in *Love at the Center of Grief*. So, our hard work now will pay off twofold."

Tapping her lips, Gretchen asked, "So, Hayden could use the story 'Gretchen's Grief: Sharing Her Heart' to help write a lesson?"

"That's a good idea. But what if we gear it with a positive spin?" I asked.

Gretchen smiled. "Since it's for the teen group, we probably need to lose the tree aspect. We wouldn't need as many materials. Mainly laminated hearts or even just colored papers?"

"I agree," I said. "What do you think about calling it 'Color Your Heart a Little Bit Happy'? Then, we could ask everyone to write down a funny or happy memory related to their heart's color."

Lisa sat on the edge of her seat, clapping. "Would you both be in agreement?"

Gretchen and I high-fived, smiling. To my relief, when our hands smacked, Gretchen's shiny gold and Valentine's heart-patterned fingernails didn't flinch in pain. So, we drafted the activity using elements from Lisa's manuals and our ideas.

Color Your Heart a Little Bit Happy
Summerfort Grief Center
February Activity

Activity Idea/Introduction:

We know grief is heartbreaking. However, talking with others about your grief story might help. Having a group of like-minded people who understand and listen to you can be healing.

Think about some of your favorite memories of your loved one. Consider the places you traveled to together. Maybe the movies you watched. Or even favorites, like foods, hobbies, and stores. When we remember (especially the fun times), it might color our hearts a little bit happy.

So Many Different Options:

Depending on the size of the group and the ages:

- ✓ The hearts can be laminated. It makes them reusable for teens and adults. If colored paper/laminating is possible, the suggested colors are red, orange, yellow, green, blue, purple, white, black, gray, brown, and pink (would need several of each for a group setting—every participant needs access to each color).
- ✓ The hearts can be created as a handout for participants to color in. Provide space for writing a short memory.

✓ Just limit the activity to one to three bigger-sized hearts for young children or large groups.

Additional Direction Ideas:

Choose a laminated/colored heart. Then briefly write a memory relating to that color. Explain a fun time or share a personality trait your loved one was known for that matches the heart's colorful spirit.

For example, **WHITE:**

My father always wore white tennis shoes. People who knew him well remember him by those shoes. Only he called them "tenner shoes," not tennis shoes. He made us laugh about those shoes.

For example, **BLUE:**

My mom loved the ocean. So, our whole family traveled to Florida to swim before she got sick. We even saw dolphins. Mom thought the blue water looked so pretty.

For example, **PINK:**

My brother put more pieces of pink Bazooka bubble gum in his mouth all at once. I still smile, remembering his chipmunk cheeks. He was such a class clown.

Chapter Twenty

Dear Mom
Summerfort Grief Center
Valentine Teen Night
Color Your Heart a Little Bit Happy

"So, after reading the activity we planned for the grief center tonight, I want to thank Hayden and Gretchen for helping me. Now, a drum roll, please, because I am so proud of Hayden. Some of you might remember seeing his childhood story 'Gretchen's Grief' hanging in the hallway about us building a tree of hearts when they were just six years old. Here's a cute trip down memory lane too." Lisa pointed to the photo hanging above our heads of colorful hearts. "I used to want to laugh whenever Hayden and Gretchen called me Mrs. Marks instead of Lisa, assuming I was married."

Everyone chuckled but me. I looked at the floor. Instead, this doting behavior made me cringe. I wanted to scream, "Pass."

"Another copy of the tree of hearts photo is in my dining room. It's a gift from Hayden. He knew I loved the photo," Gretchen said. "Thanks for letting us help you jazz this up all these years later, Lisa. This group will love it."

Gretchen's OCD situation causes her to associate specific colors with emotions. I'm unsure if all OCD cases are like this, but she sees order and patterns in things. This activity helped her pair colors and memories together. We thought the others in our group might relate in some way too.

Ma, since you know Gretchen, Kelsey, Miles, and Mia's introduction stories of loss, I'll leave those parts out of my story.

"It's almost Valentine's Day, so we are introducing a heart activity. I know holidays and grief typically bring up a lot of memories. And tonight, I thought we might try focusing on funny, easygoing stories that might color your heart a little bit happy. So, Hayden, get us started since you're a veteran," Lisa said.

In both my hands, I displayed my heart with a closed-mouth smile. "As you can see, I went with yellow, but I mean for it to be gold, like in *The Golden Girls*. Because I remember my mom coming to my room to watch the show when I couldn't sleep. Sometimes, she'd sing the opening song, 'Thank you for being a friend,' And, sometimes, I still watch."

"Aww," Kelsey and Gretchen said in unison.

I added, "And I know every word of the song. Dorothy, Rose, Blanche, and Sophia feel like friends my mom left behind for me. It's comforting. The show calms me. It usually makes me smile."

"What a lovely way to get us started, Hayden. Thanks for sharing," Lisa said before she glanced at Gretchen. "I noticed you chose green. Tell us about it."

"When I looked at the green heart today, I had a sweet memory come to me about my parents and me at the park playing on the swings. The green came into play when we walked back to the car, and I spotted a penny at the edge of the sidewalk in the grass. My dad picked it up, calling Mom and me 'copper beauties,' just like finding lucky pennies from heaven."

"Aww, I don't know if I can handle this much happiness. That is so sweet," Kelsey said.

Lisa smiled. "I agree, Kelsey. Why don't you go next?"

"Well, I hope picking something band-related isn't a problem. I talk about it a lot. The red heart immediately took me back to a sea of red cheering Branson Pirates." Kelsey waved her hands as she talked. "You know, my family. And for a moment, my heart pounded with the memory of the drums. My whole family took up a big portion in the stands, with my mom sitting in the middle, smiling and clapping." Kelsey wiped her eyes. "I'm supposed to be happy."

"Some of us call those tears and those moments the happy-sad times. I was there in my heart cheering you on when you told your story, Kelsey." Lisa reached out and patted Kelsey on the arm. "Do you feel ready, Miles?"

With his fingers, Miles crinkled the edges of his heart. He held up the heart with a crooked grin. But then sat it down on his knee. For a second time, he held it up again. Then, he huffed out a big breath. "Okay. Now I'm ready. I picked orange. This funny Halloween memory came to me about my dad. Hence orange." He waved the orange heart for the third time in the air. "But my memory is also somewhat band-related, like Kelsey. Because my uncreative dad wanted to embarrass me, he dressed up in my band uniform—"

We laughed as Miles tried to finish his story. "Okay, so here's my dad passing out candy. People would come to the door. My dad's all like, 'Arrgh, trick or treat!' And I tried to tell him, 'Dad, the kids are supposed to say "trick or treat." Not you, Dad.'"

We died laughing. Each of us had tears rolling now, even Mia. After the humor subsided, Miles still wanted to talk more.

"I thought my dad acted strange and out of touch, but I realized he wanted to just have fun. I didn't like him very much that Halloween night. I remember even getting a little mad about him not asking me for permission to borrow my uniform.

Some things I wish I could take back. Grief has put me in my place and taught me to chill. Because now, this is one of my favorite memories. I like remembering my Halloween happy dad."

"Miles, I like when you said, 'Grief put me in my place and taught me to chill.' I am noticing this is a common theme for some of you. Can anyone else relate to Miles?"

Everyone nodded. Everyone but Mia.

Mia then belted out a monologue. "I know this activity is supposed to be about happy memories. But I think a lot of what Miles feels with this guilt and jealousy issues. You know, about his dad's suicide—it's maybe close to how I feel about my parents' overdoses. Because how do I know they didn't mean to do it? Last time, in our group, Miles said something like, 'Why wasn't I enough to live for?' And I thought, yeah? Why? I have those thoughts too."

Mia paused, biting her lip instead of chomping her gum. "But I'm nowhere near as chill as Miles. I live in the middle of nowhere. Imagine living in a town called Buckingham. But it ain't no palace. It's almost like not a place at all. Buck-ing-ham—that's where my parents died inside a car. The cops found me in the backseat—barely alive. Now imagine how kids at school treat someone from a tweaker family. And think about how the churches act like vultures trying to save me. Save me for what? Some think I'm a miracle, needing constant prayers. And others think I'm a waste of time. Don't get me wrong—some of those people are nice and mean well, but I'm too angry to *only* listen to faith-based things. I'm not there yet. I want to believe in the afterlife and stuff and those sorts of things, but it's just too much for me right now. It's why I begged my grandma to let me come here, even though it's a bit of a drive for us." Then she put up her hand. "Well, enough sadness."

My heart plummeted. After I grabbed a Kleenex for Gretchen, I handed one to Kelsey. Miles and I hung on, running fingers through our hair, staring at random threads on the couch cushions, or counting the number of ceiling tiles or times Mia chewed her gum.

Then Mia slapped her thighs with her two hearts. "I guess it's okay if I go now?"

Only the left side of Lisa's mouth upturned into a recovery smile. "Of course."

"How lucky am I? Look, I have two hearts. I'll start with the lovely gray. Both my mom and dad enjoyed the outdoors—camping, hiking, and fishing. So, the gray came to me from my memory of Ha Ha Tonka State Park. We roamed down a trail to an old castle ruin. Apparently, it got torched. Still, I recall seeing a lot of the outer stones. I think I have a black-and-white photograph of my mom and me sitting on the windowsill of the castle."

"I want to see your photo," I said.

"Me too. I'd love to see your photos," Kelsey said.

Gretchen jumped in. "We all would."

"I've heard of Ha Ha Tonka. It sounds like a lot of fun," Miles said. "It's not too far from Lake of the Ozarks. Isn't that right?"

Mia nodded, smiling.

Next, she grasped the blue heart so tightly her hands shook. "My blue heart represents times I remember camping with my mom and dad. We spent a lot of our summers on the river. Sometimes in the canoe or fishing."

"Mia, thank you for sharing so much of your story with us. We appreciate you being here. We understand your grandma willingly drives you here for over an hour to specifically attend here. That's awesome. And don't worry. It's okay if you're not as chill as Miles *yet*."

We chuckled.

Then she added, "Grief has no timeline, Mia."

Later Lisa brought the night to a close. "Grief seemed to be a teacher to us—helping us through guilt and jealousy when we honor or value our loved one's memories. Especially when we learn to welcome their humanity. We sometimes must forgive them and ourselves. Then we seem to love their faults as much as their strengths. And the memories flood back to us. Grief is hauntingly beautiful that way. Look around you. Shared grief even allows laughter."

Even though I helped redesign the program for tonight, our topics went in so many directions. Sometimes when that happens, it's needed. So, that's the lesson tonight. What a lot of heavy statements—Forgiveness. Guilt. Jealousy—the humanity of grief.

Chapter Twenty-One

Dear Mom,
Happy Valentine's Day

My first official Valentine's Day with a boy-friend arrived.

After the teens met at the Summerfort Grief Center, where we did an activity called "Color Your Heart a Little Bit Happy," I came up with some gift ideas for Hayden. Let me remind you once again, Mom, how your former husband makes me want to scream sometimes. He questions everything asked for, said, worn, or planned. Where's the trust? Take buying a few essential gifts for Hayden online as an example.

"Dad, can I use your debit card online to buy something for Valentine's Day? Can you just take the money I spend out of my check at the vet clinic? Seems like a fair trade."

Still wearing those godforsaken Christmas sleep pants, Dad rambled off his checklist. "Let's establish boundaries. No overspending. Appropriate items." He picked up his wallet from the table, unfolded it, pulling out his card.

With a Cheshire grin, I reached for the card. "Dad, you better clarify."

He grabbed his card away from me.

Laughing, I snatched it back. "I'm kidding." Dr. John walked away from me, sauntering into the living room. To his back, I yelled, "I'm ordering you different PJs. Those look almost threadbare and ridiculous."

"Please do. Adhere to the rules, though." He chuckled.

And just like that, he went back to his news programming. I worry about how entranced by the virus he's becoming. Most people around Summerfort just go on with life as if nothing is happening in the world. Dad and Mr. Porter seem to be the two adults in my life that know the most about it. I've overheard Gene talking to Dad in passing. They share the same hope for the future about it not spreading into a pandemic in America. It's hard to think about things like that in a world with so much medical advancement and technology. Mr. Porter, my social studies teacher, showed us on the world map where it's spreading most and killing the most people. It's sad to see those other countries suffering. International travel transmitting the disease—Dad and Mr. Porter have mentioned this could be the catalyst, bringing this scary virus into America. I guess pockets of cases are happening on our West Coast. Let's hope our government contains this, Mom. For now, I'll think about less sad things.

Valentine's Day and our upcoming trip to see Jolene help with my happiness factor.

Anyway, I wanted to tell you about the gifts. A general search when option number one appeared. When palm trees danced across the screen with the words "This is as sexy as it gets," I clicked the button for buy now.

On my second search, Google offered so many more things when I typed. But then I spotted the perfect item when I selected images. Thank you, Amazon Prime. Option number two fits with my whole Valentine's Day theme. It held the key to showing Hayden how much I valued our relationship.

Item number three made me giggle out loud. Tiny things can often carry a double meaning. What an ideal gift coming from me.

On Etsy, a lady creates the sweetest cards, so I ordered one for Hayden. It's where giving him some roses comes into the mix. For some people, the sentiment might be too cheesy. But it's Valentine's Day. So, anyway, when Hayden goes to open the card, it's going to play a song.

Later, I arrived at Hayden's. Before I could even knock, Hayden creaked open the door. A cute aqua vase was sitting on the bench with a rose for me in the entryway. Hayden gestured to the present and held his hand in a "shh" symbol to let me know Miss Spicy Boots and Gene were napping in the den.

"So, do you want to start with your card?" I whispered. I bounced quietly from heel to toe as I handed him the card.

"All right, if you insist on me going."

I followed Hayden into Gene's study. Somehow this had become Hayden's latest hangout spot.

My hands wanted to take over and rip the envelope quicker. Slowly, Hayden slipped his finger under the flap, gliding so gracefully. He removed the dozen "Roses," which were the cartoon faces of Betty White, with the caption "I love you a bunch." Opening the flap, he recognized the tune "Thank You For Being a Friend." He smiled while reading my simple words: *I am beyond blessed to love my best friend. Happy Valentine's Day*. After he closed the card, he hugged me. Then, he turned up the heat with a few kisses. My back hit the arm of the couch as I raked my fingers through his hair at one point.

When we pulled apart, Hayden teased me by asking, "Do you smooch all your friends like this?"

"Very seldom." I giggled, adjusting to a sitting position. I reached for his bag from the coffee table. "Don't look. Reach in and pick one."

Tissue paper with foil red lips came out first. Hayden gaped a second at the lips before throwing me a hopeful grin. Still, he took his sweet time unwrapping the tape.

So, I jokingly chanted, "Take it off!"

Hayden laughed. At this, he tore it free. It took him a couple of seconds to take it all in and examine the front and back of the gift.

"This is so cool, Gretchen. I'll use it soon when I drive."

It's a fun key chain to the Shady Pines Retirement Home. So much of *The Golden Girls*'stuff wasn't masculine, but the key chain was an exception, with the emerald green and the pine trees. And, of course, the saying on the back in small font size, "Thank You for Being a Friend," worked perfectly. Plus, the vintage diamond shape looked so cool. It's kind of like something you'd see in an old motel.

"I love it." Hayden hugged me again.

"I'm glad you like it. I worried but took a chance."

"I'm looking forward to driving us places someday soon." Hayden looped his arms around me, peppering my forehead with kisses. I leaned into him, deepening our kissing.

Hayden nipped at my neck, working his way to my ear. Then, finally, he whispered, "Do you want to open one of your gifts now?"

Now? I'm dealing with goosebumps and bodily issues. "Sure." I croaked, "if you like taking turns." But the hot boy kept moaning and worshipping me with feathery kisses.

Hayden pulled me into his lap and set a shiny copper bag with teal tissue paper in front of me.

"Wow, that's a fetching color combo. It almost gives me a fancy steampunk vibe. Who knew I would dig that? Hot Boy Hayden, that's who." I giggled.

Hayden pretended as if he might push me off his lap before he squeezed me tight.

Hayden jiggled the bag. "Grab the small item on top first." I pulled out a small white box with a tiny aqua bow. When I opened the lid, it surprised me. My guess that the contents would be a necklace turned out wrong. Instead, I owned a new custom key chain made from a copper penny.

"In celebration of our first Valentine's Day together, it's engraved with a heart surrounding 2020." Hayden showed me.

"Hayden, you always pick the perfect gifts." My eyes melted into puddles.

"Why don't you keep going since I already got a card and gift?"

"But you met me at the door with an aqua vase and a rose, Hayden."

"We don't have to worry about keeping score. We are both winning. Open."

I yanked out what appeared to be an assortment of chocolate candies. "Yum." I shook the Valentine's Day staple.

"No, really, take a look under the big red bow closely."

Instead of an assortment box of candy or a heart-shaped box, I'd opened a giant-sized dark chocolate Lincoln penny in copper foil. My eyes filled again, reflecting on the significance of this gesture.

Hayden reached for my hand, squeezing. "Copper pennies from heaven, like in your story."

"Thank you, Hayden. You're as thoughtful and sweet as always. It's funny how we bought each other key chains." We grabbed them, jingling them even though they were keyless.

We laughed. "We are so weird."

"Weird looks pretty on you," Hayden said.

After a few moments, he gathered his bag. "I'm anxious to see what's going on in there."

Again, Hayden pulled out the foiled lips. This time he tore open the tiny package at lightning speed. "Judgments or rather 'judgemints'—these are hilarious, Gretchen. I love that the tin has the character Sophia on it. I can't believe the candies are shaped like little pieces of cheesecake."

Sophia's face reminded me of the whole Grandma situation with the recipe card. *I hope I'm not too much of a Sophia.* But Sophia's face kept reminding me what a jealous-hearted person I am. My nails dug into my palms.

"I'm happy you like it, Hayden. One more silly item to go."

He rubbed his hands together and riffled through the bag. And he balled up and threw the last remaining red-lipped tissue into the trash. "He shoots and scores." Then, as he held the gift in his hand, he stared at me. "Should I play Twenty Questions for my safety with this one?"

We laughed.

I shook my head, but then I shrugged a bit.

"That's not very convincing." Hayden plucked off a corner of the tape.

"Ask a question."

"Is it something I can eat?" Another chunk of paper came out of the package.

"No."

"Is it something I can wear?" Hayden squeezed and shook the contents.

"Yes. Now, open it, you man-child." I laughed.

Hayden exposed enough of the gift to view "This is as sexy as it gets." He kicked off his shoes and died laughing. Once he ripped the tags off the item, he sported his new yellow "golden" Dorothy socks with the palm trees in the background. Dorothy's smirk said it all at the top.

"I'm going to go see if Dad's awake. I'll be right back."

The next thing I knew, I heard Gene screaming, "Does Dr. John know Gretchen bought you marijuana socks?"

Marijuana socks? This had to be a joke.

"Dad? Listen—"

"Get them off. Tell Gretchen you can't wear or accept drug gifts."

"It's palm trees. And it's *The Golden Girls*." Hayden said.

"Do not raise your voice at me."

"You wouldn't listen to me, Dad. So, why would I show you druggie stuff? Gretchen and I have never been into that. Once, you accused us of drinking. Now you are accusing us of being potheads. Stop jumping to conclusions. My God, I came in here to have fun with you. I'll just go back to your office."

"Get back here, Hayden. From my point of view, the socks looked like leaves. But I'm your dad, and I'm looking out for you. So, sue me."

Hayden groaned.

"Buddy, come closer, so I can see your socks. Hayden Oliver Tucker, I did not mean for you to take them off and pitch them at me."

More squabbling happened. I assumed I heard a couch scraping against the floor in anger. Or Gene's feet hitting the ground.

My sweaty hands circled the doorknob, trying to leave. But I felt trapped inside Gene's office. I knew I needed to rescue Hayden, but I didn't know how. I'd been warned about Gene's dark, gruff past with Hayden. But Gene and Hayden weren't getting physical today. Not over a silly gift I bought. So, I left Gene's office, making sniffling noises on my way into the hall bathroom. That's when I burst into tears. On my way, I peeked at them. They stood face-to-face, but I noticed nothing beyond verbal nonsense. If I had, I would've run into the den to create a scene.

Hayden came to the door first. "Gretchen. Is everything okay? No one is mad at you. I love my socks. Please come out."

With enough force, I scraped away a layer of nail polish off one thumbnail by using the other thumbnail.

Next, at the door, Gene knocked. "Shortcake. I'm sorry. I want to apologize to you and to Hayden. I jumped to conclusions. From a distance, I couldn't tell they were palm trees. Hayden loved watching *The Golden Girls* with his mom. Shortcake, you did good, hon."

Behind the door, I teared up but smiled at the same time. Then, after several seconds, I composed myself. A huge part of me wanted to see what remedies might be in the medicine cabinet to remove the pain. Not even anything for a headache—no need for men's cologne—well, I enjoyed inhaling it while pressed against Hayden. Still, I knew they likely didn't have what I needed to redo my nails. So, instead, I cracked open the door.

Hayden stood close, combing his fingers through his hair, disheveling his style into a fauxhawk while wearing the new socks. Gene's slumped against the doorjamb with dark circles under his eyes, even though Hayden had complained about Gene napping on the couch all day. Their apologies sounded sincere, even if they looked ridiculous and maybe a little pitiful. My tears dried.

"Gene, I can't believe you'd think I'd buy your son marijuana socks with my dad's credit card. Dude, I think you're the one trippin'," I said with a half-hearted smile. My nails stayed balled up and bit into my palm. "But I think it's best to go home now."

Chapter Twenty-Two

Dear Mom,
Happy Valentine's Day!

Let's just jump right to conclusions. Dad must be trippin'. He moped all day long without any real reason that I know about. Dad didn't bother getting off the couch when I got excited about Valentine's Day. So, he couldn't get close enough to investigate before shouting, "Hayden Oliver Tucker—this, that, this." And then he added, "Get those druggy socks off. I can't believe you and Gretchen smoke marijuana." He even had the freaking nerve to say something about Gretchen using John's money. Nope. That's her paycheck. She works hard at the vet clinic. What an ass-jerk. He wouldn't stop and listen, no matter how much I tried to interrupt his yelling.

So, instead of hollering, "Shut up, Dad!" I wadded the socks when he told me to take them off. Then I hurled them at him while trying to reason with him about the socks.

Good Ole Gene Tucker, the Wonder Bread Beater, caught my gifts in his fists. This provoked him to rise off the sofa and quickly stomp toward me. And I earned his glacier stare down before the possibility of a shakedown. Don't get me wrong. Maybe Dad didn't plan to hit me. But he sure stood in my face for a stern lecture.

"Look," I wanted to plead with Dad but didn't dare. "It's only *The Golden Girls*. It reminds me of Mom."

Gretchen couldn't ignore the fight. She must've heard her name being drug (full pun intended) into the whole thing. I caught a glimpse of her darting through the hallway on her tiptoes as if needing a getaway. Then, after a brief sniffling, she sailed into the bathroom, maybe hoping we wouldn't detect crying.

Thank God for Gretchen. Dad instantly relaxed because his attention averted from me to her.

After a big sigh, I glanced up at Dad, who stood nearly toe to toe with me. I swallowed, taking a step back. Dad unwadded the socks, and the slightest smile appeared as he finally read the silly caption, "This is as sexy as it gets."

"See. I kept telling you the symbols were palm trees, not marijuana. It's *The Golden Girls* because I used to watch it with Mom." I snagged them back from Dad, sitting down to put them on. "I need to hurry to check on Gretch."

"Hey, buddy. I'm sorry I overreacted. Let me talk to her too."

My hands flew up. Plus, I rolled my eyes.

As we walked to the door, I whispered, "Dad, please, don't you dare hurt her feelings today." I'm worried she will get triggered to mess with her fingernails again. They've been looking healthy and well-maintained. But maybe the polishes and gloves can hide more secrets than I thought. So, I'm watching more closely.

Of course, Dad tapped on the bathroom door, calling her Shortcake, acting charming, like using a nickname and crap. Thank God for Dad.

As we waited for Gretchen to come out, Dad reached for me, catching me in one of his bro hugs. Thankfully, he apologized for his ass-jerk moves, making jokes about it to smooth things. When Dad said to Gretchen, "You did good, hon. Hayden and his mom loved to watch that show," I got kind of misty-eyed because I could visualize us laughing as Dorothy might say, "This is as sexy as it gets, Ma."

As a child, I didn't understand why Dorothy's sexy line created so much humor for my mommy. I only knew I loved laughing and grabbing happiness with her when we watched late nights until I fell asleep.

So, I wanted you to know what a special girlfriend I have. To say she tries to find meaningful gifts for me is an understatement. So often, she finds a way to include you in everything. And I love her for that. She gets me.

After I opened the "Thank you for being a friend" card she brought me on Valentine's Day, I remembered what a stupid mistake I had created for myself. I had bought her the aqua vase with a rose, the giant penny candy, and the key chain. But I had forgotten to buy or make a card. So, instead of simply letting it go, I asked her if it counted since I jotted in cursive on the tag's gift bag: "To Gretchen, Love forever, Hayden."

She chuckled and said, "Yes."

Isn't it so funny we thought to buy each other a key chain?

Mom, do you think Dad is going to be patient while I drive? Learning to drive and getting a license are milestones. But my mom won't be there. Damn. My gut just took yet another hit.

How about some different Valentine's Day talk?

I'm going to meet Gretchen's Aunt Jolene soon. I'm excited but nervous. The tales Gretchen and John tell me about her make her a legend. Gretchen giggled when she told John he couldn't wear his Rudolph sleep pants for the trip to Jolene's group home in Columbia. Gretchen found a website selling men's sleep pants. Since she loves calling him Clark Kent, she ordered a pair with Superman. With his black reading glasses, I understand why now. I'm dying laughing writing this. Is this why he had so much sex appeal with women? Weird. Life is just freaking weird. Gretchen's dad goes and dates a counselor. Dad goes and dates a counselor. Yet I think we're all still nuts, Ma—even those counselors.

Anyway, let me tell you about more of my gifts. When I opened the cheesecake-shaped mint candies Gretchen bought me, I thought of your mom, Grandma Suzi. The "Judgemints" made me uncertain. What or how much do I reveal where Gretchen is concerned about Grandma? It's a very touchy, jealous subject for her. For now, I'm leaving it alone. Sometimes I maintain happiness. I'm not asking for trouble if the timing isn't right. It's supposed to be about Valentine's Day, so Grandma can wait.

And as for Dad trippin'—those were the famous words of Gretchen. Dad howled, grabbing her into a hug. He should've been a girl dad. So, after Dad's sock freakout, I called Cole and Drew. These days, I like having brothers. Even Gretchen said having some faux bros seemed hilarious at times.

Yo, dawg. Welcome back, Dennis. Mom, we have an F-U-N plan spelled in different letters for Dad that he never dreamed about.

Chapter Twenty-Three

Dear Mom,
Saturday, February 15, 2020
Happy Valentine's Day (continued)

Hurling the door open, Aunt Jolene greeted Dad, Hayden, and me in the lobby of Cottage Lane Group Home.

"Step on it, Johnny! Get in here, so I can meet Hayden. And you can see my groupies."

Dad patted her on the head. I hugged her, mumbling into her shoulder, "Aunt Jolene, meet Hayden."

He reached out to shake her hand. "Nice to meet you, Jolene. Gretchen and John told me lots of great things about you. Thanks for inviting me today. Happy Birthday and Happy Valentine's Day too."

Jolene stared up at Hayden before saying, "Hayden, thanks for coming to celebrate. I'm glad you're here." Next, Jolene shifted her glance to me, throwing a thumbs-up high in the air. "Gretchen, what a hunk."

Embarrassed, Dad huffed. Tumbling into his big brother role, he exclaimed, "Jolene! You shouldn't say everything you think out loud."

Hayden and I exchanged a smile.

Holding her by the arm, swaying gently, I sing-songed, "Jo-leeeeeene . . . please don't steal my Hayden even if you think you can." Jolene's beaming and giggling. Dad's plowing his fingers through his hair, worrying about what might come next. Hayden grinned, getting a kick out of the adventure. Then, channeling Dolly Parton, I continued serenading Aunt Jolene. I know I'll never come close to achieving any musical success, not even one tiny note. But performances like this make Aunt Jolene cheerful. Inventing ways to recreate the lyrics amused her, making me happy.

Inspiration for Jolene's name came from Dolly's famous song. I love that Dad told me this story. In 1974, the song's chorus hit the airways just as Aunt Jolene scheduled her entry into the world.

"Ready to party and meet my groupies?" Jolene asked.

Hayden and I nodded as Dad shrugged. Groupies—the label Jolene awarded all the individuals who live in the assisted living facility. *Her* group home, so her groupies.

She steered us through the small room. Each round table held a black tablecloth covered with confetti in the shape of hearts sprinkled across the tabletops in pink, white, and red shades. Some burlap material placed in the table's center displays a tic-tac-toe pattern.

"Look," Jolene demanded, gripping an X and an O that resemble stuffed animals. "We sew these as part of our workshop time."

Touching them, I said, "That's awesome." So, Dad and Hayden launched into playing a game with the pieces.

"Jolene, does the OATS bus still provide transportation?" Dad asked.

Jolene let out a sigh as an annoyed kid might. "We go to Walmart, Johnny. We also go to the Aldi grocery store. I like going there except for all that extra effort of bringing your own quarter and sacks. And dang it all, they still want you to bag it yourself too." She paused before adding, "I fetch rides to the doctor too."

"Fetch?" Dad cocked his head. "You're not a dog, Jolene. Nobody tells you to fetch a ride, do they?"

"No, foolish boy, I say 'fetch.'"

"Jolene, don't forget you shouldn't call your brother names or anyone else."

Jolene snorted. "I'm like the queen around here. I ride on all the floats in the parades waving and throwing candy. Look, I wave like this." She demonstrated this by twirling her wrist in front of Dad's face as he politely pulled her hand back to the table.

"I understand how important you are. But you still can't be rude to people. Not even to me, your only brother."

Sassy Jolene only expanded the argument. "I'm independently living. My apartment has a welcome mat. So, I don't see why I can't tell people to get lost and unwelcome them. They're unwelcome if I don't like what they do or say."

"What?" Dad asked. "Jolene, some of what you just said sounds bossy. Are you sure you're kind to everyone?"

"From what I remember, I'm pretty much a nice person. I don't like people who steal from me, though."

"Who steals—" Dad struggled to address the issue, but Jolene cut him off.

Standing next to Dad, she fluttered her arms like wings. She flapped, pushing herself to the limit to get the attention of those seated across the room. Jolene likes arriving first to capture the best seats. This afternoon, she preferred the location closest to the stage, where the DJ would set up his music.

Oh no. Under the table, I tapped my foot against Hayden's as he and I shared a quiet bug-eyed moment.

"Hello, groupies!" Jolene shouted, still going with her arms.

Dad tugged on the bottom of Jolene's red tunic blouse. Then, through gritted teeth, he groaned, "Jolene, please, sit down."

Jolene swatted Dad's hand. "Hank, hey, Hank, Julie, Charles"—her voice dropped the peppiness before adding—"oh, *and Judy.*" Then, with her voice on an uptake again, she said, "This is my older brother Johnny, my beautiful niece Gretchen, and her handsome beau Hayden. See you later on the dance floor, Hank and Charles."

Hayden and I stretched our arms, giving a big wave and smile. Then, feeling baffled, I suppose, Dad offered a peace sign of all things.

WTFDD, Dad?

Jolene looked at us. "Listen, see Judy over there? She likes stealing."

With a brow raised, Dad leaned in, questioning Jolene. "What did Judy take?"

Growling, Jolene said, "After watching *The Wizard of Oz*, Judy Wannabe Garland snagged my costume idea for Halloween."

"So, I guess you both wanted to be Dorothy?" I asked.

Jolene frowned, pointing at me. "You got it, Gretchen."

"As friends, couldn't you and Judy dress alike and still have fun?" Dad asked.

Jolene crossed her arms. Glaring at Dad, she said, "That's what you think, Johnny?" She huffed, leaning closer to Dad. "Judy stole my first-place ribbon in the Halloween costume party. And now she's over there"—Jolene hitched her thumb over her head in a theatrical motion—"stealing all the attention for herself with Hank and Charles. Hank used to be my most favorite and special groupie."

Hayden cleared his throat, hiding a chuckle while I went with nibbling my bottom lip. If I focused on her expression and zeroed in on *her* reality, I understood her pain. *Quiet, Hayden. Let's hold it together.* Tapping his foot again, I hoped to rein us in from laughter. Instead, I did not dare look in his direction.

Dad rubbed his face before speaking, maybe killing time, hoping he wouldn't use his lecturing tone, but he failed. "What do you mean she stole your ribbon? Did she take it away from you?"

Jolene covered her face with her hands before communicating to Dad with her if-looks-could-kill stare. "No!" Jolene slapped the tabletop. "Much worse, Johnny. We both wore the Dorothy costume, but Judy shook around dancing with her skirt so dang short and tight. Mine at least fit me."

Dad drummed his fingers on the table, nodding.

Jolene continued ranting. Her voice switched to mimic Judy's. "She kept saying, 'I'm Judy, like Judy Garland, the real Dorothy.' You should've seen the men and the way they acted, all slobbery. That's how she ripped off all my votes." Signaling to the front of the room by the dancing stage, Jolene continued. "Right there, in front of everyone, I put up with winning the second-place ugly *red* ribbon." Jolene stared at Dad. "Blue's still my favorite color, Johnny. Oh, and Hank said he voted for me, but

I think he fibbed like a danged old liar. I about kicked Hank's ass that night."

Shifting in his chair, Hayden whispered, "Wow," masking his perpetual grin with his fingers.

"Jolene!" Dad clasped both her hands. "You can't hurt people or talk to people in public with curse words and still live independently."

"I know, Johnny. I know. That's why I got me a new plan to win Hank back."

Dad tilted his head, asking, "Jolene, is Hank, like, a boyfriend-boyfriend?"

What? Dad, I can't believe you skipped over Jolene's "new plan to win Hank back."

At first, Jolene creased her forehead, not answering Dad. Finally, after thinking about Dad's question, Jolene stated her truth. "No, Johnny, Hank's only one boy that's a friend. Not some double boyfriend-boyfriend."

"Jolene, if you're ever unhappy here, you can come and stay with Gretchen and me, okay?"

Raising her voice a notch, Jolene let Dad know how she felt about his idea. "I'm living in my private cottage because I'm handicap-able. A-B-L-E. See, I can even spell the word able. So, I'm *able* to take care of my adult day-to-day life skills."

"Fine, Jolene. I'd create a little apartment space for you too."

She guided her index finger to her chest. "'Miss Independent,' like the *American Idol* lady, Kelly Clarkson. So, I'm claiming it as my theme song.

Don't go telling Judy, though. She'll just rip that off too. But I've got myself a musical plan with old Judy in mind."

"Jolene, you keep talking about some plan or idea. What's going on?" Dad asked, with his legs shaking up and down.

"My forty-sixth birthday and this Valentine's bash," Jolene said as she smirked at Dad. "Don't you love surprises, Johnny?"

"No, I don't often like Jolene surprises."

She laughed back at him. "Ha ha."

Dad closed his eyes for a second—I'm guessing to clear out the visual effects of Jolene perching on the edge of her chair, where her sights appeared fixed on Hank and Judy (Garland). Hayden walked his fingers through the ends of my hair as we played a game of tic-tac-toe, listening to the sibling bickering between Jolene and Dad.

The minute the DJ arrived, Jolene leaped off her chair, eager to share her requests with him. Back at the table, she cackled, struggling to ask us, "So, y'all think Judy's going to enjoy strutting to 'You Ain't Woman Enough to Take my Man?'"

Hayden pulled his body close, whispering, "Gretchen, seriously? That's a real song?"

I opened my eyes wide, barely nodding.

"Oh, my God."

Playfully, I elbowed him.

"Today's better than any high school dance," he added, chuckling, but his body began to shake with tears of laughter as he held his hand into a fist in front of his face.

"Jolene, you can't overreact like this," Dad pleaded.

"Oh, I'm dancing, Johnny, watch and see. I'll be having a good time." Jolene shoved her chair back. "Get up. Look"—she looked at each of us, nodding to the back of the room—"drinks and snacks got put out. Let's eat cake." She wandered ahead of us to stand in the refreshment line.

I turned to Dad and Hayden. "Let them eat cake . . . and heads rolling. That's all I could think about when she said, 'Let's eat cake.'"

Dad and Hayden grinned.

"Dad, she's a bit unruly today."

"She's always been a handful, GG. Now that you're older, you'll notice it more. It can stress me out. I just try to find the right tone, so she remembers our visits as something positive."

Still grinning, Hayden wiped his eyes with a knuckle. "John, I think you guys do a great job with Jolene. This place looks very nice. She seems to like it here too. Her spunky personality cracks me up, but I don't think I'd want to be Judy."

Dad and I smiled and nodded in agreement.

Mom, the Cottage Lane Group Home residents can now reside in one of the twenty-five apartments. Dad said when you two found the place, it had fifteen apartments. The lobby acts as a commons area and a foyer, where Jolene can find library books, movies, and snacks. Dad said they've painted it since you last saw it, and they updated it from carpet to hardwoods throughout the lobby. The exterior still resembles a small country lodge with yellow siding and white shutters. For people who appreciate nature, many outdoor lounging areas are available. From the moment you step up on the wraparound front porch, a feeling of cleanliness, safety, and comfort comes to you. Sitting on the edge of the Columbia city limits, it's far enough away from the racket of downtown traffic but near everything. But Dad said that's what you both loved about the location. I wish I had more memories of all of us visiting Jolene here.

Thankfully, the Cottages lack institutional gloom. Instead, the Cottages furnished homes to people who learned to live with minor assistance. Faculty members have expanded to include a security guard at the entrance gate, a nurse, and a custodian. And there's a receptionist around the clock. Dad said they used to be only there during the day. But now, social workers, doctors, and activity directors circulate during business hours or special occasions.

On the road trip from Summerfort, Dad explained to Hayden how you and he found the Cottages. During your time as vet students at the University of Missouri in Columbia, Dad stumbled upon the location. Unfortunately, Dad grinned too much talking about the setting (I sensed this little man-whore vibe). So, I think he skipped over your make-out scenes and instead told us about horses, cows, trees, and a pond on the nearby property.

Declaring Jolene as a person with an intellectual disability sounds awkward or strange because of her high level of expression. An assortment of stuff might tumble out of her mouth at any moment. But, like a kid, she needs a filter sometimes. That's why I love visiting. She a living, breathing reminder of the saying "Seize the day."

The Cottages organized a few desserts on a buffet table, such as cupcakes, mini pies, cookies, and finger foods. When we gathered our snacks, I noticed a cozy gazebo with a bench at the back of the clubhouse. Sometimes, I wish I knew if you'd sat in the same seats and looked out from this exact location. I hoped so.

After settling down at the table, I pointed over my shoulder, asking Jolene, "Do you like going out to the deck area?"

"I do if Hank's there and Judy's not."

"Oh. I understand. Guys can make things awkward," I pretended to whisper just to her.

"Hayden looks easy," Jolene said.

Everyone smiled.

"Look." She motioned to the closeness of our chairs. "Hayden's willing to show how much he likes you."

Jolene pointed to the way our hands meshed. In Jolene's simple terms, we gazed at the world through her eyes, and the view astounded me. She saw life and love illustrated through handholding and two chairs. In her own way, Jolene lived a straightforward life. I admired her bravery. She's not afraid to stand up, speak her mind, and love the best way she knows how—on Jolene's terms—every maneuver emerging in an outward declaration.

Through the intercom came the DJ's voice. "We have a birthday in the house." As he played the chorus of "Jolene," she fist-pumped the air, wiggling in her chair. Then, as the melody continued, he jumped off the stage, plopping a tiara on Jolene's head.

Hello, Diva (Queen) Jolene.

With a quick look around, I noticed staff, residents, and visiting family members made up the thirty or so people in attendance. Enthusiasm poured from the DJ as he fired up the small crew, saying, "If you occupy a cottage at the Commons, get on the dance floor and show us what you've got."

Dad, Hayden, and I watched as Jolene joined a dozen friends to perform the Bunny Hop. Jolene situated herself behind Hank, grabbing his waistband. The Hokey Pokey, Chicken Dance, and different line dances followed.

Spotting the nurse on staff, Dad wandered off to discuss Jolene, leaving Hayden and me alone. Hayden angled his whole body toward me, sneaking in a few kisses. "Hey, according to Jolene, I'm easy," Hayden said, offering a toothy grin.

A soft love ballad began.

"This song is the lady's choice. Pick a partner. We invite all of you to join us on the dance floor today," the DJ crooned.

Jolene stomped toward Hayden and me, slamming into her chair.

"Judy jerked Hank by the arm before I could. He's out there twitching around with her. Did you see that tacky sweater she's wearing?"

We shook our heads. Quickly, I dug my toe into Hayden's foot, hoping to suppress our laughter as Jolene continued.

"A chunky cupid's floating around on it."

We nodded, once again trying not to burst into laughter.

"Judy's a couple of years younger than me, but my dark hair has less gray than hers. So, I think I look younger and better than her."

Considering Jolene's physical features, my mind's eye turns to *Forrest Gump*, Hayden's favorite movie. I examined Jolene's stature, face, and hair and determined that Jolene reminded me of Forrest Gump's mom during middle age. After watching the film *multiple* times, I can make this assessment. No one, however, comes close to Jolene, a true original.

"You do look nice today, Jolene," Hayden said.

Jolene adjusted her tiara, smoothed her blouse down, and sat ramrod straight. Slivers of Dad shone through Jolene when she sat prim and proper. In these rare moments, it intrigued me to see family resemblances and mannerisms.

"Glad you like it, Hayden."

"Are all your friends about the same age?" I asked.

Jolene put her elbows on the table with her palms splaying. "I already told you enough about Judy. Everyone's about the thirties to fifties. Hank is fifty years old."

"Men, don't be shy" blared from the DJ's microphone. Then, he announced, "The time has come for you to pick a partner. Dance!"

The quiet Hayden pushed his chair back from the table in an unusual fashion. "Jolene, will you dance with me? We better hustle before the other men get to you. I know Gretchen won't mind if I steal you for one song."

Bending down, he planted a small peck on the side of my mouth before reaching out to a grinning Jolene.

If possible, I fell even deeper in love. Hayden gazed at me as he held Jolene in his arms, wobbling to the music. Jolene's shining tiara slipped, slumping cockeyed on her head. Still, God did her crown sparkle as her cheek rested on Hayden's shoulder. He winked at me as they moved to Elvis Presley's "I Can't Help Falling in Love with You."

Yanking my phone from my purse, I captured a short video and a few photos. Witnessing this scene touched my heart so profoundly that my mascara smudged. Bittersweet emotions heightened. Even though Jolene's my adult aunt, I reminded myself she's only a child on the inside. That realization slammed my heart. And I suppose the visual of their dancing hit me more like a futuristic daddy-daughter dance.

Because of unexpected times like these, I wanted to pick up the phone and talk to my mother more than anything else. I wished I could tell her about the kindness Hayden showed Aunt Jolene. I needed to send my mother a text message, show her pictures, or play the video in her presence to relive the moments as I listened to her thoughts. I needed something.

I wanted to tell her I fell in love with Hayden even more today. And I needed to ask her if it was normal to feel this way. Knowing my mom will never meet Hayden produced a bruising pain that surged through my heart again today. I yearned to hear my mother's laughter as I shared the story of Jolene and Hayden. Would her eyes light up at the sight of their dancing, just like mine? A bundle of strength and tenderheartedness sums me up, but I wonder if it also describes my mother. Are we alike? If so, in what ways? Especially now that I'm getting older, I keep thinking about how I have changed. Does she remember me? I also asked myself what my mother would look like today.

My thoughts continued. If my mother viewed my pink dress, what would she think of me? Would she approve of how I applied my makeup? Would my mother be proud that I taught myself how to get a smoky eye? Or would she like how I used my straightener to curl my hair? Or would she be amazed at me for learning beauty tricks by only reading or watching videos? And would she approve of my pink-toned Color Street Mount Crushmore nail polish? Or would she see the mountain crush more of me? The polish covered the new layers of flaky skin, but my cuticles weren't so red. Still, I hate how much a secret makes a person feel unworthy and ugly. I've realized I'd probably be prettier and do just about everything better if my mom still guided me. So often, I spend time hoping my mother still loves me. But, all the time, I wonder, does she know how much I miss her?

I sent a text message to Lisa, Gene, and Gabby to lighten my mood. A short video of Hayden and Jolene with a tiny note.

Gretchen: Hayden offered to dance with Aunt Jolene. We are having a good time.

Jolene took off toward Dad after the Elvis song ended, while Hayden joined me to check out the video and photos once he sat back down at the table.

Studying my face, Hayden reached up with his thumb, wiping under my eye. "Hey, what's wrong?"

"I'm fine. It's silly. Got overwhelmed thinking about how cute you were dancing with Jolene." I tilted the phone in his direction.

His lips turned slightly upward. "Okay," Hayden said, squeezing my shoulders. "Made you feel *happy* emotionally, you mean?"

"Yeah. But you know what it's like when a 'Mom moment' hits? I just wished I could talk to her."

Hayden wrapped his arms around me. "Of course, I understand. I love you, Gretchen."

"I love you too. Thanks for coming today. You were so amazing with Jolene."

Hayden's lips curled at the corners before he crashed them into mine.

Pulling away from our kiss, he said against my mouth, "I think we need more cake and more of this—" as he hauled me into a hug. "Plus, I hope you'll cling tight to me for a slow dance, and I'll gladly watch you wiggle and jiggle to a fast song."

We cracked up.

"Hayden, you sound like you've been hanging out with Jolene too long."

At my buzzing phone, we glanced a peek to read the replies.

Gabby: Sweetie, that brightened my day.

Gene: Glad you're having fun. Great video!

Lisa: Hand over my heart, perfection.

A lopsided grin stretched across Hayden's mouth as he glanced at me. "*Sweetie,* do you want anything from the snack bar?"

I let out a teasing groan. "You know I hate that term of endearment. It's like nails-on-a-chalkboard annoying. Gabby says it is enough for the whole freaking planet. When people say crap like *sweetie* repeatedly, it starts sounding phony, even when I know it's probably not meant to."

Hayden leaned over my shoulder. "I'm only kidding." He squeezed each shoulder. "Want anything?"

Holding up my glass, I gave the ice cubes coated with fruit punch a big shake.

Hayden planted a kiss on the top of my head. "Drink refill coming right up, *angel*."

"Thanks, *HOT boy*."

Hayden whirled around, glancing at me until his eyes narrowed into slits, and he just shook his head.

I giggled. It had been a while since I'd called him Hayden Oliver Tucker. Hot boy fit him in his outfit today. Black jeans, a button-down shirt with the sleeves rolled up, and his black Converse. The caramel-colored curl hidden among his dark strands—that unruly piece near his ear—poked out, looking like a tiny devil's horn, begging for a touch.

Dad and Jolene returned to the table without feuding. Jolene must be holding up her end of this independent living stuff. I understood Dad's concerns about her since he couldn't move Columbia closer to us. But a three-hour separation causes us to miss out on her daily life.

Maybe I should say I'll go to college in Columbia, Missouri? If my relocation to school helps everyone feel more comfortable and at ease. Is leaving Summerfort the same as me deserting Dad? Unless someone like Sweetie/Happenstance infiltrated Dad's life permanently by then. I don't know. That situation is weird to think about. Do I hate the idea? Did I like the idea? Dad deserves love. I know this. Yet these questions still creep into my head.

Hayden returned with the food. He teased me, feeding me samples of buttercream-frosted hearts from the top of his cake. Instead of fingers, we used forks because we were not alone. Hayden had a glazed look, which I adore, making me wonder what was going on in his mind. Hayden urged me to dip my fingertips into the icing, which rendered me weak. I desired to turn his body into an artist's canvas with frosting in my midst, and I'm not even a painter. Yet his hint of a smile led to quiet eyes that expressed a million unspoken words. I desired unchaperoned moments with Hayden. Time with our eyes closed and mouths opened as our fingers painted, linked, and spoke for us.

"Romance time, so grab a friend or a Valentine and head to the floor," the DJ barked and ended my fantasy.

Jolene craned her neck, realizing Judy wasn't sitting next to Hank. Then, getting to the point, in true Jolene fashion, she strutted over to Hank and gestured "come on." Hank appeared an expert at reading Jolene's attitude and signals and followed after her.

"All of Me," the Legend, known as the singer John, hummed through the DJ's equipment.

"Ready?" Hayden asked, extending my hand and pulling me from my chair onto the floor. Outside, the sun sighed as the evening rays flirted their way inside, brushing the surface of the disco ball hanging from in the dance floor's hub. A smattering of color swirled around, resembling warm apricot. The warmth seemed to embrace everything.

Hayden's hands gripped my hips like anchors, guiding them like waves back and forth. I hear Hayden singing portions of the lyrics as we pivoted our feet, floating across the dance floor.

The light appeared to bounce off the disco ball and waltz, giving the room a playful quality. Across the dance floor, it seemed like a bottle of glitter was shaken and spilled. My arms circled Hayden's neck. With my fingertips, I caressed his shoulders. Warmth seeped through the cotton fabric of his blue shirt. Body heat soared, nudging at my palms. One glance into Hayden's eyes, and I dove straight in. Without a doubt, I plunged deeper into love without even holding my breath.

We swayed in a slow, smooth rhythm, maintaining time with the beat. Then, toe to toe, we stood to keep up the pace. In black ballet flats, my feet felt light. But the tighter Hayden clutched me or cinched me at the waist, hauling me close to his chest—internally, my heart couldn't match the tempo—quickening and thunderous.

Everyone and everything faded, slipping away from the moment. Hayden positions his hands near my lower back, tightening his command again, pressing me as close to him as humanly possible. Inhaling, I captured mingling scents—his woodsy cologne against masculine, warm skin and the sweetness of vanilla cupcake on his breath.

A few loose strands of hair fell as Hayden wrapped them around his index finger before placing them behind my ear. Ed Sheeran's romantic song "Perfect" streamed through the speakers. Hayden hummed along with the ballad. His head veered to my shoulder as the music continued, his lips brushing against my ear. Breathy air drifted in the form of musical notes as Hayden mouthed against my earlobe, teasing as well as charming me with specific words from the song.

A rippling effect ignited, rushing throughout my whole body in the aftermath. Hayden perfectly orchestrated our evening. He whisper-sang another portion of the lyrics in a thoughtful tone, especially using my nickname, Angel. Near the end of the final note, his upper lip grazed mine, planting a timely kiss tasting of Valentine's Day—pure sweetness topped with heart-shaped sprinkles.

Before the next song began, I said, "Maybe this will sound cheesy, but thanks for giving me a 'perfect' moment carried out so *perfectly*."

"You're welcome, but, hey, I like your corndog cheesiness any—"

Hayden's words got halted by background noise. We hear praise coming from a small group. In Hank, Charles, Julie, and Judy's direction, their clapping helps bring me back to the real world. Glancing, I noticed Jolene had reemerged with her groupies. She has overcome the tension with her men, I guess. Hayden and I looked at each other, then at the secluded dance floor. With wide eyes, we stood alone—the only couple left beneath the glitz of the disco ball.

A near shout came from Jolene's voice as she unleashed "Keep dancing, Hot Pants Hayden. Gretchen, you and Hayden look quite sexy out there." A cacophony of snickering enveloped the room. I'm pink all over. I become the shade I'm wearing.

"Jeez, Gretch," Hayden said, rubbing my back with a light laugh.

I glanced at Dad, ducking behind his hands and shaking his head.

In a booming voice, the DJ announced, "Ah, please stay right where you are, Hot Pants Hayden and Gretchen. I'm playing another tune for your fans. Music's for *love*." Was the DJ fulfilling his duty of amusement or retaining the atmosphere? Or maybe even toying with Jolene, Hayden, and me?

I threw myself into Hayden's arms and plastered my hot cheek next to his. Then, trying to bury my embarrassment, I noted the feeling of his match-ing heat. "Ugh, the way he pronounced *love* made it sound almost pornographic."

"I agree," Hayden said, chuckling.

"Should we make a run for it or stay and provide entertainment?" I felt like a creepy ventriloquist dummy talking through gritted teeth.

Before Hayden answered, a strumming of music began. A soft, almost lullaby-like tune. Hayden's raised eyebrow led me to believe he had already recognized the melody.

Seldom do perfect moments come along with-out setting the stage or putting in a ton of effort to make them happen. Especially not following an embarrassing one. Sometimes, though, a DJ can simply make a musical choice. Ballads speak what heartbeats leave unspoken as people dance, phrases of a song whirl and take flight, guiding a muted conversation to a place as loud as a thou-sand trumpets. Pulses quicken as torsos press together. And hands turn clammy with achy greed. The remainder of the world floats away. Faces flush with warmth as eye messages linger in the air, telling stories through the magic of song. Are the dancers making future promises? Hoping for understanding? Or searching for hidden meaning inside these specific looks? Each of them moves, staring, on the verge of giving in, conjuring up the nerve to speak and act on an impulse. And to find a way to put as much skin against skin as possible.

My face moved closer to his mouth and then his ear. I wondered what to do—hum notes, breathe him in, kiss his ear lobes, or scrape my teeth across his neck. But, of course, I wanted to do all the above.

Hayden gently pulled away, holding my hands, never stopping his admiring look or smile. At arm's length, he kept his stance steady. His eyes zeroed in on me. Slowly, he released one hand, pulling me out by the one hand until he held on to me by only a fingertip. Hayden led me through some fancy twirl with swaying hips, shuffling feet, and tenderness. Quickly but with grace, Hayden drew me back into an embrace. We undulated to the pulse of the music, which brought on some hooting and hollering from the crowd. Hayden's forehead rested against mine. At the end of the song "Marry Me" by Train, Hayden rewarded me with a kiss. Our fans went wild.

Where did he learn all that?

"Time's running out. I encourage everyone to get out on the dance floor and join them." The DJ's voice drifted from a million miles away.

Soon, I caught Jolene moving by with Hank.

"Your dad must want to help Jolene maintain some peace. He's dancing with Judy." Hayden turned me, so I could acknowledge Dad and wave at Jolene. "What's funny?"

I plopped my head on Hayden's shoulder. "Jolene just mouthed, 'See, Hank's mine, again.'" Trying to suppress a laugh, I ended up snorting.

"God, I love you and Jolene," Hayden said.

"I love you too," I said, hugging Hayden.

A slight moan escaped from within him, making my insides flip.

As the song ended, I tugged his hand. "Ready to take a break?"

He nodded.

"This oldie but goodie is a fun one. Jump around and enjoy it!" The DJ fired up Jolene's request, "You Ain't Woman Enough to Take My Man." Dad passed Judy off to Charles with a handshake.

Lip-syncing and cackling, Hank, Jolene, Charles, and Judy slammed each other around inside their 1970s mosh pit. They rotated in circles, skirting around each other due to Jolene's insane moves.

Hayden piped up, "Well, that hip bump Jolene just gave Judy looked pretty foul-worthy."

"You and your sports references," I replied, smiling. "Judy and Jolene—frenemies, you think?"

"Yeah, kinda looks that way."

Jolene appeared to grab and jerk Hank around through parts of the song. I think the term manhandled fits. Like guns, she pointed her trigger-happy fingers. She repeatedly propelled her feet forward and backward, making every attempt at her fancy actions.

Tickled, Hayden and I turned our gaze away.

"Maybe that's supposed to be the eighties dance, the Running Man?" I asked.

Hayden hunched his shoulders. "Jolene's better at the Running Man than me."

Walking toward us, Dad's grinning wide, carrying drink refills. As he sat down to join us, he said, "Poor Hank," lightheartedly. We watched as Hank's face lit up, enjoying every stomp, shuffle, and circle. When the chorus hit, Jolene's eyes bug out, transferring all her might to Judy. Then, again, her shooting eye daggers went toward Judy during the song's part about something over someone's dead body. Hayden slapped his thigh at this, and his smile fractured into an open-mouthed silent convulsion of laughter. Dad and I couldn't help but catch his infectious giggles.

Wiping his eyes while taking a breath, Hayden began, "Oh, this song. You told me earlier this is Loretta Lynn?"

Dad nodded.

"I'm downloading this on my phone right now. John, I wish I had a sister like Jolene."

Those proverbial butterflies took flight in my stomach as I fell more in love *again*. I looked at my fingernails. *Sometimes love was like climbing Mount Crushmore.*

"Hayden, she's wonderful until all her spunkiness gets aimed at you," Dad warned him. "I imagine you understand. It's probably similar to the practical jokes you've experienced with your brothers, especially Drew."

"Oh yeah. You see how my dad calls Drew Dennis the Menace. So, I get it."

Dad smiled so wide it crinkled his eyes. Then, before sipping his soda, Dad even laughed.

As the last note of Lynn's song plays, the DJ cuts in. "Let's end tonight with a bit of fun. I bet everyone knows this last one. I invite and challenge everyone to get out here," he said as he motioned to the dance floor.

Immediately, I bent over, grabbing my stomach in a fit of giggles as I heard the opening words to "YMCA." Up and down, Jolene's bounced from foot to foot, already in Y formation. Her groupies have formed a line in a follow-the-leader pattern.

Jolene cupped her hands around her mouth. "Yeah, get out here!" Her hands slid into fists before she set off with guns blazin' in her trigger finger to signal us. Hayden, Dad, and I stood.

Under his breath, Dad mumbled, "Ah, you're shitting me. GG, did you put Jolene up to request this?"

"No, Dad."

A loud sigh poured out of Hayden in my direction.

I felt eager to show Jolene a few photos of her brother dressed as a cop performing to this exact number before we said good-bye. But shuffling toward Jolene, I knew, at least for now, there was no need to be unhappy.

GRETCHEN

Chapter Twenty-Four

February 2020
Dear Mom,

By the age of six, I established a working method with you. First, yelling "Mom" caused you to appear. Right now, I'd like to take for granted the right to shout "Mom" just to see your face again. And then, I'd stop time to notice little pieces of you. For example, you sometimes piled your copper hair into a bun on the top of your head. Then, listening closely to your voice, I'd memorize your different tones. I would hang on to every word; my heart would listen and hoard everything said. Even the most basic question ("What do you need, Gretchen?"), I'd treat everything like gold. Because today, I know what a question from my mother is worth—priceless.

Wishing every mother-child memory came with a recording device to capture the hidden motherly teaching advice. When problems flare up or oddball questions arise randomly, I'd love to scream "Mom" or push play for help. Life at five and six, with a mother, seemed less complicated. We spent hours together watching movies, stretched across my bed, playing board games on the couch, or lounging at the dining room table crafting.

Sometimes I observe the world clearer when my eyes remain shut, but my heart remains wide open. Imagining a life in which my mother hasn't died always happens. Sometimes, starting first thing in the morning. Signals awaken me, though, with a threatening reminder. After hitting snooze on my alarm, I lie there in my bed. Then, I lie to myself. But the biggest lie starts in my head, with me saying, "I'm fine."

It takes a short time before I pay attention to the mouthpieces in my brain. I listen. They're like broken fragments making weird remarks, plus acknowledging too many damn truths. They offer a little pep talk each day. "I survived another night without a mom in my world." Then, in daylight, I meet them with the truth: my mom's dead. Many gut-wrenching mornings begin the same. Just a bunch of yesterdays put on repeat.

The emptiness of my mom not being at home follows me to school. Phone call options no longer exist. This realization stings. It's one of the hardest lately. I ache for you. Kids always text at school, and I watch as they get aggravated about their mom's messages. They're over-the-top rude about food, grades, clothes, and curfews. Sure, I get snotty with Dad sometimes, but I don't think I act this way—okay, I'm just going to put the words out there—unreasonably bitchy and ass-jerky.

Writing shorthand with emojis to you sounds like perfection. I'd give anything for this privilege. Unfortunately, some days I have to fight my urges to snatch phones away from brats. Daydreaming while sitting in class, I get wild visuals going. In one, I see myself tossing an effing cell into the air as I use Hayden's baseball bat, smacking it out of a school window.

Suppose my quirky fantasy occurred in Mr. Porter's history class. In that case, I hear him asking, "Gretchen, how do you think these students have limited freedom of speech?"

At which point, Dad pops into my head to play his game One to Twenty-Seven, asking, "So, which number amendment are we debating?"

Ugh, move to the side. You're blocking my meanness, Dad and Mr. Porter! Let me hurl a freaking phone. Arguing the First Amendment and how it's not absolute, even though misinformed Americans may think so, isn't on my daydreaming agenda.

Should my thoughts happen in Miss Tweed's English class, I feel I have an ally in Hayden. My daydreams don't involve the destruction of property, except for teasing Hayden. I still sit behind him. If I lean up, I *accidentally* touch his neck and hair with my books and fingertips while reading or writing. In return, he likes pestering me. Since I put my feet in his desk basket, he enjoys reaching down to slip his pencil into the side of my shoe to tickle me.

My thoughts go to the evil side only when I see or hear fake-face Lilly in there. How many layers of god-awful piglet pink lipstick does she need to apply while hammering on and on, "Hum, ah," twisting at her desk, ogling herself in the mirror?

Mother, you and Dad taught me to love, not to hate. Miss Lilly P puts me to the test. Summerfort had cold weather the other day. Miss Lilly came bee-bopping into English with a summer dress on, her cardigan draped over her shoulder. She paused at the front of the class right before the bell rang. She looked down at her chest, feigning horror. "Oops. Didn't know it was that cold out." Of course, people looked around to see what was going on. Giggling, she stumbled around, pretending to care. Slowly, she pulled at the cardigan in a half-ass manner to cover her perky nipples.

Lilly knew, seeming proud of a few claps and cheers earned. A smile stayed glued to her made-up mouth the entire period. The incident went unnoticed by Miss Tweed, who stands in the hall to monitor kids walking between classes before the bell rings, so she didn't witness it. Dating someone like Thomas Sharp, who bullies and sexually harasses people, angers me. Isn't this sexual harassment too?

"I'm very aware Lilly shops at Victoria's Secret, where they carry a wide selection of 'bulletproof' bras," I said to Hayden. First, he sighed, then chuckled. Finally, Hayden related to my painful history with Lilly and Victoria's Secret.

In dealing with new images of Lilly's sexually charged boobs on display for all to see, I wanted to bail before I screamed, slapped her, or cried.

Thankfully, Hayden turned sideways. "Hey, you, okay?"

I shrugged, faking a smile.

Only he noticed my glassy eyes. "Want me to grab two passes? Go in the hall a minute?"

Feeling like my head can't create any sudden movements, I finally manage to shake it.

Concentrating on anything other than Lilly was difficult because of past hurts. Miss Tweed's lesson drifted, her words evaporating and turning into "Just because Gretchen's mom's dead doesn't give her the right to try and steal yours." I hated myself. I thought I'd come so far in therapy only to allow her to trigger me back to a dark place. Instead of sticking pencil lead in my shoe, Hayden grabbed a fistful of jeans at my hem, hanging on with a death grip.

After class, Lilly met up with Thomas. They glanced back at Hayden and me from the end of the hall as they were rounding a corner.

"I think Thomas flipped us off," I said.

Hayden shrugged. "He's an ass-jerk. So, you see, Sharp isn't so sharp because he thinks he's supposed to act like an ass-jerk in front of other ass-jerks. It seems this is the ass-jerk way. That's how you know when someone's a true ass-jerk."

Staring at Hayden's lopsided grin as he rants sends me into laughter. It reminds me of Dad's "Screw Thomas Sharp" comment during Thanksgiving.

In mumblings shrouded by loud squawks and coughs, we hear Thomas Sharp go for Hayden, delivering his infamous and tacky tagline "queer as fuck" down the hall. Then, we believe we hear Thomas awarding me the new title "little prude bitch." A bully like Sharp always throws shade outside the sight of authority.

As Hayden walked me to math, he raised a silent eyebrow. Then, glancing at each other, we repeat my nickname, laughing, focusing on the "prude" aspect.

"Wonder what has stirred them into awakening?" Hayden asked.

Pursing my lips, I said, "Hard to say. Let's keep trying to steer clear, I guess."

Hayden squeezed my hand. "Um, you know, I'm happy ignoring them. Besides, I'd rather spend time kissing this *hot little prude*." The giggles keep escaping as he plants a peck on me outside Mr. Wright's classroom door.

Remember, I'm jumping on a writing trampoline. Whee! I'm ready to bounce back to my journaling and English.

Should a meltdown occur in English, with cell phones flying, do you think those thick arm hairs Miss Tweed's sporting might tumble to the ground out of fear? It could help her—she's intelligent and pretty otherwise. Remember, I told you she had bushy "arm whiskers," even puffier than Dad's? Thankfully, he didn't attend *other* parent-teacher conferences or do the "Happenstance" with her. Oh. My. God. I never thought to ask him if she made his slut list. Why did my mother die, leaving me stuck with a sneaky horndog hottie for a dad? Then, across a screen of my twisted mind, a headline flashes. "Look-alike Clark Kent Vet & English Educator Miss Tweed." A special episode, "Finding Bigfoot: Happenstance ~ Love Story."

Mother, what the heck's wrong with my brain? How do I get around to thinking straight or appropriate thoughts about anything? A trampoline of nonsense, I guess I'm going to bounce from one topic to another today.

Ranting about other people who send parents rude texts caused my mind to snap. But, yeah, isn't there a quote, "If you can't beat 'em, join 'em?"

Me: Hey, Dad. Texting between classes. I can't talk to ask you this IMPORTANT question, but it's bugging me. Is my English teacher, Bigfoot Tweed, one of your "Happenstance" issues?

Dad: Put your mind at ease. Get to class, GG. I love you, but I do NOT appreciate the attitude. *Bigfoot*? Let's chat about that tonight. I'm sorry the word happenstance still upsets you.

Hiding in the bathroom stall, biting on my nails, and peeling off half the polish, leaves me saying to myself, WTFDD, why did I do that? Someone needs to create an insta-erase app. Where's the new generation of Bill Gates or Steve Jobs? My guess is probably wasting time. Too busy texting dumb effing shittle-sticks stuff like this to their parents.

When stuck in the bathroom with whiny girls (like me), I imagine a plop-and-flush maneuver for cell phones. Tempting, even for myself, on those Bigfoot beast-like days. Shattering them into tiny slivers against concrete seems the best option in school hallways.

I know most of the kids don't mean me any harm. Nor do they understand it kills me when they curse, call their mother's names, or say things like "I just wish my mom were dead." Guess they love their moms too. I'm just overly sensitive to their communication styles.

Grief heightens my awareness, making me jealous, though. Why do I feel like I should apologize? Suppressing sorrow and writing about the pain isn't a weakness or crime. I miss my mother. Some days the hurt inside of me bubbles into thoughts of destroying telephones. On other days, I feel cheated, lost, and alone. I don't want to see or talk to a soul. On rare occasions, I celebrate, knowing how lucky I was to have had a great mom. Smiling, I speak to her spirit because I feel her all around me. I see so much of her—the same copper hair and blue-green eyes when I look at myself. And remember the lessons she taught me—her voice echoes. There's a knowing, a peace that she left behind pieces of herself. Days like these require no phones.

On my best and worst days, I want to chat about everything. First, I want to show you my school-work and the books I read. Then, ask you if you know the characters from my favorite stories. Next, talk to you about love and ask if I'm an attentive-enough girlfriend without coming on too strong. Then, ask you general things about love. Finally, laugh while complaining at the same time. Am I correct about my discovery? Life's so ironic this way—a blend of every emotion most days. Every happy moment plummets a little, knowing I can't tell you. Every sad moment compounds, realizing I can't share it with you.

I don't know how much Dad ever knew. Using Gardener's Vet phone, I'd call the house or vice versa while you remained on voice mail.

Listening to my mother's voice recording was like drinking in the sound of life. Sometimes, I'd even leave you a message. I exchanged chitchat, guessing what my mother would say.

"Hi, Mommy. How are you? I'm hiding behind the desk of the vet clinic while Dad's busy helping a cat. By the way, I love you."

At times, I'd just ramble, going on about mundane things, the day-to-day stuff that seems to matter when the routines of daily life disappear. Some pieces of information I shared brought a smile or chuckle. "You won't believe what Dad did. I made him read a book about a deep-sea creature."

Slowly, as I admitted to myself what had happened, sobs would clog my throat. Soon, my eyes couldn't hold the hefty weight of tears. With no idea how to handle them, they would spill down my face. In these delicate moments of fooling myself, I'd decided I would have to stop someone. Myself? Dad? Fear of getting caught by Dad had me running, scared. Hoping I had enough time to run into our house's kitchen to erase the evidence before he saw me. But, in doing so, I felt like I had abolished my mom from the world all over again.

With fingertips shaking, I'd always dial, craving to hear your voice. *"Hello, you've reached the Gardeners. If you're trying to contact us for emergency vet service, please call Doctors John and Gwen—"* Over and over, I'd play this sound, but it still seemed like I hadn't heard from you in years. The urge to listen to you felt so fierce my heart hurt. For a while, I tried to appease myself.

"Hello, you've reached the Gardeners. If you're trying to contact us for emergency vet service, please

call Doctors John and Gwen—" I remember how the phone would ring on one end. No one accepted, but a name came through the recording. I closed my eyes in anticipation, trying to *see* words that could only be *felt* and *heard*. I wanted to talk but didn't know if chatting this way was appropriate for grief. This hiding and hurting bothered me. Was it wrong that I hid my talks with you from Dad? For me, these conversations preserved the hearing of my mother's name. I ensured my mother breathed.

After several months, Dad changed the greeting. But with my fingertips shaking, I still want to dial. Even after all these years, I crave to hear my mom's voice. My mother once read me to sleep, talked me through sadness, and helped me with schoolwork. The urge to listen to her remains so intense. I ache. I want my recordings back. I wish for more time to hit the rewind and play buttons over and over—this time ignoring delete.

Father, where did you put the old-fashioned answering machine? And the tapes? Why did you erase her?

Progress in the digital world robbed me of my mom. Time flew by, but I was never ready to leave my mom behind.

Do other motherless daughters feel this way?

HAYDEN

Chapter Twenty-Five

Dear Mom
February

"Yo, Dad, you got a package. Since the card attached was addressed to me also, I opened and read it. The card is from Drew and Cole. They said we should FaceTime or Skype them as soon as this arrives. When I texted, everyone was ready. Do you need to program it in your Cozi app before we can move forward?" I asked, shaking my cell phone at Dad in a teasing tone.

"Yep." He finished programming his ridiculous dots on the app. At a quick glance, I saw he'd written "**A Talk with All My Boys**" in red. "Let's go chat."

My whole body ached, not from the playfulness of Dad but from wanting to leap with joy. And from holding back from wanting to shout out loud, "It's here, it's here!" Then, in robotic mode, I pretended to act normal while Dad and I grabbed laptops. Since Gretchen needed to be a part of this, I set up my phone. After arranging the calls, thankfully, everybody answered.

"Well, Dad, think of this as a token of our appreciation for being you," Drew said.

"Dad, lately, we can always count on you to bring F-U-N to the table. So, now, we wanted to give something back to you," Cole chimed in.

My gut cinched, wanting to burst into laughter.

"Go ahead. Open it, Gene," Gretchen added.

"How did they involve you, Shortcake?" Dad asked.

Gretchen only smiled and shrugged.

Slowly, I used my fingertips, pushing the box to Dad. He glanced at me as if looking for clues.

Looking me up and down, Dad finally said, "All right. Your lips are sealed. But your face is red, bud. Is this something entertaining to get back at your poor old dad? It is, isn't it?"

I just kept ignoring his pleading questions. Everyone chuckled, so I nearly lost it. Before Dad even opened his box, my shoulders shook. I tried hiding my face in my hands and not looking at anyone.

Drew's probing "What do you think it is, Dad?" didn't help.

Dad shrugged.

All the new beard growth Cole sported, along with his ramblings about unrelated weather topics, made me want to snap apart even more.

My mind kept saying, "I can't believe we did this. Dad's going to flip out." On the inside, I certainly was. I could hear my heart swooshing in my ears.

The box snapped open as Dad's hands reached inside. He pulled the contents out, studying them. Then, for a long moment, he just dangled the product in front of him in disgust, his lip curling.

Drew flung his head back, barking in his guffawing way that's always contagious.

"What in the actual fu—world?" Dad asked, twirling his present. And, continuing his disdain, Dad read "Drop it Like it's Socks" on the top of the surprise box.

My feet took over like a reflex, stomping the floor. I cracked wide open. After several swipes to my eyes, I was finally able to speak. "They are your very own Snoop Dogg inspired Plant Daddy socks. Now, there's no trippin' or jumping to conclusions about the leaf on them. That's not an F-U-N palm tree. It's the real deal."

"Hayden Oliver Tucker, did Dennis put you up to this?" Dad asked.

I jokingly slapped the counter. "No, I organized this prank. We threw this together in a matter of days. Dad, Gretchen, and I have no desire to do drugs. Love is our drug."

Gretchen grinned and blushed. Of course, after I said it in a room full of guys, everyone pretended to gag before laughing.

"Besides, I freaking watch *The Golden Girls*."

Dad shoved the socks back into the box, shaking his head. I wondered if my words may have stung too much. Because Dad sidled up to me at the bar for a quick side-hug. Soon after, the unsuspecting Cole cranked the song "Drop it Like it's Hot." At this point, Dad tossed his hands in defeat, cackling. Then, he dug the socks out of the box and put them on. While Dad lifted his feet in the air to model the socks for us, Miss Spicy Boots joined the party, taking over the empty box.

Afterward, I poured two sweet teas into our Mason jar mugs, sliding one to Dad while we finished the conversation in laughter.

So, maybe no more jumping to conclusions or trippin' will occur. Or is that wishful thinking?

HAYDEN

Chapter Twenty-Six

February 20, 2020
Hey, Mom.

This morning, I forgot to tell Dad I owed lunch money at school. He'd already left for work, so he texted me back, explaining he had a small stash of cash inside his nightstand. So, outside the cemetery, chatting with you, I sit on the bench instead. Still, I can't seem to come any closer. Standing by your grave remains out of the question since I'm a total fuckup chickenshit. God, I'm so sorry. A cemetery isn't the place to act like an ass-jerk. Please know that I love you, Mom.

Don't think of me as a complete loser and disappointment. I feel bad enough already. Every day or whenever I do something, I want you to be proud of me. It's weird growing up without knowing what you think of me, Ma. I feel like someone's lost little boy, waiting to be claimed, wondering where you are and what would you look like now. Do I even still technically qualify as your son? I'll send my girlfriend Gretchen to bring flowers—she's the brave one about coming to this dang place. She's my grief hero.

I hate the cemetery because it makes me miss you so much more. Other kids talk about putting flowers on graves at the grief center all the time like it's no big deal. Having that much courage to walk up to a gravestone, stare at the engraving, and then talk about it so openly makes me so freaking jealous. Just being here brings all these hurts back up. It makes me sick in the pit of my gut. Because of freaking Dad, I'm dry-heaving.

If I hadn't found what I did next to the cash, I would've eaten breakfast, then gone to school like any other typical day. But instead, I skipped both to come running to *my mommy,* puking and bawling. Who gives a shit if I'm a baby? I didn't know what else to do or how to feel about what had happened. I'm sorry for cussing again.

But why? Why, Mom? Why did you have to die? From this bench, I can see the tips of your headstone. The angel wings let me know you're nearby. Maybe you can see me and hear me. So, for today, I believe you will listen while I read you this letter I found. Plus, I'll tell you what else I found in the drawer.

Dad's been seeing Lisa Marks, who runs the Summerfort Grief Center. It sounds like he's in love with her. Mom, is that okay? You'd want him to find happiness again, right? I like Lisa too. She loves me, Mom. But I don't want you to think I'm willing to replace you. After reading this letter, I'm guessing Lisa loves Dad a lot too. Some *very personal* things were written, which I doubt they wanted anyone to read. Well, I found out the truth. That's why I needed to talk to you. So, that's too damn bad for them if their privacy is violated.

I'm so pissed about all these secrets. I can't keep my anger to myself any longer, so I will read the freaking letter from the bench.

Dear Lisa,

After losing Rosie, I didn't have a clue about how to raise three boys all by myself. My life felt like something I had to survive for my kids' sake. I tried to do the best I could, which wasn't always that great. Then I met Lisa Marks—we all did.

While working on the grief center and projects at your house, I didn't want to come across as constantly needy. Or become a burden to you. I hated bombarding you with questions about what I was supposed to do to get over a broken heart. Just having an adult to talk to made a world of difference. At the time, I didn't realize what a blessing you were. That's why it took me eight years to get some sense and start seeing our friendship as much more.

And I want to thank God for Lisa and her grief center. She designs the best damn macaroni necklaces and sings "Kumbaya" better than anyone I know. Plus, the lady has the most forgiving and fun-loving heart. I even like her grouchy pushy side when she knows she's right and you're wrong, and she's not afraid to tell me all about it. By the way, she's sorry you feel that way about it too.

People don't realize she's equipped at home with superpowers to quickly step out of her counselor mode to yell like a sailor when she's good and mad at me. It's funny, in a way. I get a kick out of the fact that she saves this side of herself just for me. I like knowing all of her—having secrets together—sharing inside jokes.

Beyond the center of grief, there's humor!

Lisa has almost been a surrogate mother for my youngest son Hayden. I believe Lisa's a better role model and parent for Hayden than me most of the time. It was with Lisa's help that Hayden and I rebuilt our relationship. She taught me how to show up and communicate again. I often argued with her about my work and the appropriate closing time.

One night, while building storage for her darkroom, Lisa got pissed at me, packed my tools, and tossed them into my truck, saying, "Leave now, or you're fired. Hayden's got a football game later, and he needs you there."

I stomped toward her, waving my hands and yelling, "What the hell, crazy lady! I've told you I don't like goin' to games and sitting alone. It's a freaking grief trigger. We've talked and talked about it."

"Fine. Dumbass. Guess I'll meet you there. Save me a seat."

"Why the hell are you calling me names now?"

"Because!" She screamed, hands glued to her hips. "You've had me as a friend all this time, but you've never asked me to sit by you? I go to those games to support Hayden. Dumbass."

As she spoke her next round of words, she clapped her hands and enunciated everything one by one, making sure I got her message. "Helping—people—is—my—job." Tears began to flow as she continued in a weak voice. "Why do you not let me at least try to help you?"

Sobbing ended the conversation with Dumbass consoling Crazy Lady inside her utility/dark room. While leaning my back against her stackable washer and dryer, her chest pressed into mine, I learned the power of friendship. Plus, the potential for more on a late September evening in 2019.

I'd forgotten what real intimacy between a man and a woman felt like—holding you awakened life in me. I remember pulling you closer, inhaling your clean floral scent. A longing took over me instantly as the touch of your arms wrapped around me. Breathing you in made it seem like I had a new set of lungs on fire.

A rush of emotions hit me like I was some teenage boy again. My body began reacting in ways it had no business doing. Guilt and confusion shook me into reality. My heart shredded. Because I loved my wife, Rosie, I still felt married to her with so much passion. Fraud, Cheater—those words crossed my mind. It hurt to think this way about myself.

And as we stood there, I wiped away a few silent tears battling all the inner demons I had buried for too long. Rosie's been gone for eight years, I reminded myself.

Lisa, you brought back the spirit of F-U-N. I had missed too much with my son, Hayden. I love the relationship he and I have built since you sat beside me in the bleachers at the football game. You've turned me into a "Kumbaya" macaroni necklace believer, Crazy Lady Lisa. A simple act of kindness, such as sitting beside someone, can snowball into great things. Maybe even heal an entire family.

Sure, I'm a dumbass brute sometimes, but I wanted you to see how special I think what you've written to me for years in some emails means to me. I saved so many of them.

Mom, before I move on, how am I supposed to feel? Dad obviously loves Lisa. From the sounds of it, she's why I have a decent relationship with Dad now. So, why does this confuse me? It's hard to let go, trust in the future, and believe things will work out. I think Lisa loves Dad and me, too, but how will this change our everyday lives if she's always there? I wish someone had answers for me.

Let me continue. So, I'm flipping through eight years with secrets, lies, and bullshit to bring you some old, printed email information. Lisa and Dad shared some tidbits about Gretchen and me long ago.

I see Hayden connecting with other kids, especially Gretchen. I'm not supposed to have favorites, but I can't help myself when I watch those two together.

. . . . We live in a small community, which makes what I do difficult. Indeed, death, relationships, and people's painful lives get very personal. Speaking of John, have you considered some male bonding? Maybe you need guy friends? The two of you have so much in common.

I'm hosting Parent Night at the center. So what? You're not into noodle necklaces and "Kumbaya." That's not on my agenda. Just shut up about it and eat a hot dog for one night.

Gene, sometimes listening to everyone else's hurts makes me lonely. In high school, you said you had my parents as teachers. If you ever have time while working at the center, maybe a couple of minutes of your lunch break, I'd like to talk to you—it would be great to chat with someone who knew them.

Lisa

Dang, Ma, I had no idea my grief mom had tried charming the pants off Dad clear back in the day when we thought she was still Mrs. Marks. Lisa's right. He was a real dumbass if he couldn't read between those lines. Like, duh, Dad. But wait until I read Dad's stupid reply.

Dear Lisa,

Shut up and eat a hot dog? That's your sales pitch to get me to sing "Kumbaya" and do some "male bonding" with Doctor John? When I had your mom's chorus class in HS, she took more pity on me than you. I think I got away with lip-syncing everything.

Gene

Ma, the pile looks to go on forever. I don't know how to react. Lisa helped me and Dad and our whole family, but what does that mean for you? It's confusing to move forward.

This one is the hardest to read.

Lisa,

As I read over this, I realize you're a Miracle Worker Saint for putting up with some of the crap I say and sometimes do. My boys and I are smiling, laughing, and talking to each other again. I'm back as part of my family that I had disappeared from. The man in the mirror recognizes himself.

You're my hero for helping me fix my life: someone's crying Lord, kumbaya. I'm grateful for all the times you listened to a grown man in tears without judgment. Someone's praying Lord, kumbaya. I acted angrily for all those times you said you'd say a prayer for me when I thought God was too cruel. I now thank God for you.

In my research, I learned the meaning of "Kumbaya" might also be Lord, come by here. I can't think of a more fitting or touching song for two people like us.

Looking forward to happiness and exploring so many more moments with you. Please tell me you're going to love the keepsake present that goes along with this letter.

Kumbaya,
Gene

Mom? I wish you could say something. Guessing you already imagined what the keepsake present might be? Maybe I shouldn't have, but I stuffed the little box into my pocket—it's beautiful. I like and want Lisa and Dad to be together, but holding a golden band meant for the two of them? —this feels way too soon. Dad promised he'd talk to me about things. God, this is some blindsided BS.

My cell phone keeps buzzing. I freaking don't want to talk to anyone. Why can't everyone just leave me the hell alone? I don't feel like anyone gives an absolute crap about me today, anyway. So, what am I supposed to say? You're an effing liar, Dad. So, after saying he'd take his time with Lisa and talk me through everything with their relationship, he decided to do all this? He's apparently running off to marry Lisa. Secretly, she's some crazy lady who cares more about cussing and getting laid in her utility room than she does about people's feelings. It's like sitting by a stack of loaded FYI, TMI, and BS rolled into one day. Let's add WTF while we are at it. We won't add Gretchen's cute little do-da to it.

Does finding this letter and ring mean I'm supposed to magically accept Lisa as my new *mom*? For now, a phantom mom's enough; it's all I can handle. Ugh. Like I'm supposed to go along with whatever the hell people do or want—? Will she be moving into our house? Do we have to move into hers? We just got freaking happy. Why should

Dad and I have to get so mixed up again? Dad and I were getting along, except for bickering over his obsessive Cozi app for scheduling, which he uses until he's insane.

Buzz. Buzz. Buzz. Mom, this constant noise of my phone is bothering me. I'm not answering or looking.

Maybe a person can get upset with people, even to the point of being really angry, and still love them? Is it because we love them that it hurts so much? Today, that's how I feel. I hate the confusion.

Buzz. Buzz. Buzz. I'm sick of hearing this phone. Oh. My. God. They're not giving up texting or calling. Should I read them and see what I have to deal with to get myself out of this? Gretchen might break up with me for leaving her hanging at school. I meet her every morning. Dad will threaten to beat my ass or take away my right to see Gretchen or ground me for eternity and make me mark it on his effing Cozi app. Who knows who else will bark orders at me? For skipping school, the coach will bench me at my next game.

Fine. I'll face it.

Flipping my phone over, I read:

Gretchen: Hayden, I've been looking for you at school. Are you okay? Sick? Oversleep? I'll try Gene's business landline, just in case.

Gretchen: Hayden, this isn't like you not to show up or reply. I'm so worried. PLEASE text. If I don't hear from you, I'm texting Gene. Love you.

Dad: Bud, the school called, saying you're absent. Gretchen's saying the same. Why won't you answer? Are you ok? I'm worried. Please text or call me ASAP.

Dad: I came home, but you're not here. HAYDEN. COME ON! I love you and need to know you're ok. Whatever the situation, we can work it out.

Dad: If you don't respond w/in 10 minutes, I'm calling the police.

Cole: Hayden, what's going on? Are you hurt? Where are you? Please let Dad know you're okay. He's a mess. You're worrying us. We love you, bud.

John: Hayden, please let someone know you're alright. We all care very deeply about you. Come to the clinic if you're nearby. I'll help you.

Lisa: Hayden, we're frantic. Please, honey, tell us you're okay. I'll come to you if you need me.

Miles: Hey, man. The g/f says you skipped school. Thought I might know something. Guess she figured we planned a Branson-bro day. Lol! She's worried and a little pissed. She's texting Kelsey too.

Kelsey: Gretchen said you're not at school. Are you okay? I told her you're not with Miles. You better contact her.

Drew: Hayden, what the heck, kid? You're scaring the shit out of us. If you're okay, you better tell someone.

Gretchen: Hayden, I don't know what to do. I've tried to reach out to you without an answer. I've gone to Gene, but you won't answer him either. I'm sad. I don't know if I'm supposed to be mad. Is this disappearance about me? Don't hide from people. You're scaring me. I'd rather lose you knowing you're safe. But, God, let's at least talk this out!

Gabby: Hayden, Gretchen is in my office, and she's beyond concerned for you, and so am I. You've got to contact one of us so we can help.

Drew: I'm about ready to head to Summerfort to beat your ass if you don't tell someone where you are.

Dad: Bud, times about up. I'll be calling the authorities for backup SOON. You turned off the Cozi locator. Where are you?

Am I overreacting? Did I go overboard about this situation? School seemed out of the question today. I was just too upset to go. Now, I'm kind of embarrassed. Am I stupid for coming to the cemetery today? Jeez, Ma, I better tell Dad what's up before he sics Sheriff Lowell and the Summerfort police on me. How ridiculous.

Hayden: At the cemetery.

Dad: Thank God. On my way.

For now, I'm avoiding Drew—I don't want to get my ass beat. Comments like this shouldn't make me smile, but I'm actually getting the feels with that one. Drew behaves and says stuff like Dad when he's under pressure. I've come to understand and accept them as two mouthy teddy bears who mostly trash talk when they're emotional. Dad has beat my butt once with a freaking loaf of Wonder Bread in my fifteen-and-a-half years. I remember writing and telling you about that weird nightmare of a day.

Overall, Dad's pretty loving and stable. I'm not going to lie, though. I'm scared to see him. I don't know what to say. Or how I'll react. When I talk about things, I hold in my feelings and let things build up until I explode, getting too sensitive. I don't want him to think I dislike Lisa, but I need him to understand why I'm so hurt by this strange secret.

Gretchen also deserves an explanation. I better at least send a simple text for now.

Hayden: Gretch, I love you. I'm sorry I worried you. I had a last-minute issue at home. Give me time to go over it with Dad. Later tonight, I'll talk. Do me a favor, and please tell John and Gabby I'm ok.

Gretchen: Glad you're safe. But are you really okay? Let me know if you need anything. I'll give you time with Gene. PLEASE text or call when you're ready. I'll let Dad and Gabby know. Love you.

Hayden: Yes, I'm okay. I promise to explain later. But, again, I'm sorry.

Maybe I should've called Gretchen this morning when I located the note and ring. I figured the timing seemed wrong with her on her way to school. My horrible mood would've upset her and just dragged her down with me. Or I might've said something rude in anger and hurt her feelings. Skipping school to rescue me would've been a temptation for her. My angry tears would've just burdened Gretchen. Besides, she's too much of a Lisa-Gene fan. I knew I needed some space from people to think about what I'd read. And what I felt without too much interference or influence.

If reversed—if Gretchen had put me in this situation—I'd have freaked out. Disappearing for a couple of hours, then refusing to answer the phone? But, of course, knowing me, I'd pull a Drew when texting and say or do something stupid. I don't know, though.

When I recap this day, I will try to understand this from Gretchen's perspective, talking to her later. She's kind and understanding, but I imagine she's upset that I didn't text or call a lot sooner. I guess she's got a right to be. But I hope she'll get it when I explain I didn't want to pull her into my drama.

I hate myself for making everyone worry. Ma, I'm trying to live a good life. For the most part, I act decent. Let's add up some of my negatives: my one ass-jerk fight with Thomas, my funny but dirty-minded thoughts, my occasional foul mouth, my secrets from Dad, and I skipped school (once).

Dad can tell me his side of this bizarre story when he gets here.

Um, diesel gas—I *hear* and smell the faint odor of the truck coming—my gut aches. Ma, I think I might throw up. But, oh, God, my throat's on fire. Acids churn as the roar in the distance gets closer. I can almost see the Gene Tucker Construction logo plastered to the side of the truck. My head's pounding so badly. Even my heart might burst from thumping too out of whack.

Dad's door slams, and it's not long before his steel toe work boots scrunch against the rocks. As he jogs to reach me in a hurry, I hear his feet stir up the smooth pea-sized gravel along the walkway. Before he gets to me, he sees me hunching on the bench, arms folded, hugging my stomach. I couldn't scream before he yelled, "Hayden, what's the matter? Do you need a doctor?"

Reaching me, he crouched down in front of me. "Do you need a doctor?" he repeated. At the same time, shaking my head, my gut knotted up again. Burning acids rose again in my throat, but my body won against me. I was powerless. Lurching forward, Dad jerked his head out of the way just in time as I vomited next to his feet.

Dad plopped beside me, and I failed to turn away as he rubbed my arm. Finally, Dad asked softly, "Bud, I've got water in the truck. Think you can sip and talk to me?"

Through watery eyes and with shaky limbs, I nodded weakly.

When he returned with the drink, I maneuvered into an upright position. And, again, he sat beside me. Again, I wanted to shove him into the gravel, but I grabbed the water without saying a word.

"Just get whatever's bothering you all out. It's okay. I hope you know you're safe with me. Whatever is going on, I'm here, Hayden."

I bolted upright. Stalling. Guzzling the liquid fast and loud, I hoped the right words would come. The more I waited, the worse my mind raced. *Unbelievable. Are you freaking kidding me?*

Finally, staring at rows of tombstones, I said, "I can't believe you're such a freaking liar, Dad? What's with all the sneaking around? Acting like a dumbass with Lisa and stuff?"

Dad leaned slightly forward, glaring at me, his hands squeezing his kneecaps. "Hey, I don't know what you're talking about. But I sure don't appreciate you coming at me with that attitude and tone. So, please explain where this is coming from, buddy."

With the back of my hand, I wiped the corners of my eyes, then my mouth. I'm sure Dad saw the papers folded in half, sticking out of the back pocket of my jeans. *So, why wasn't Dad wondering, what the heck? What's up with the secret agent documents? Why's my son at the cemetery?* But I crossed my arms and zipped my mouth shut, refusing to play show-and-tell with someone who lies and knows precisely what I had in my dang pockets.

Dad mirrored my gestures, staying silent for a few seconds until he let out a huge huff. "Enough, Hayden. Start talking."

Sitting ramrod straight, staring at the side of Dad's head, my jaw ached to grind out this gut-wrenching question. "Why don't you care enough about me to ask me *why*?"

Dad tossed his hands up before they landed back on his lap. Then, shifting his body, he looked me straight in the eye. "Why what? Why did you run to the cemetery? Or why you skipped school? Why are your pockets stuffed with *my* papers? Which of those whys do you need from me?" He kicked rocks with the tip of his boot.

Instead of answering, I yanked the ring and his proposal letter from the wad of papers in my pocket, slamming them down on the bench. Then, picking them up, Dad gave me a narrow-eyed glance that I can only describe as—oh, dang! I'm caught.

For a few seconds, Dad suffered from jiggly leg syndrome. Dad peeked to verify the papers before quickly turning them over on the bench beside him with a heavy sigh. And after toying with the ring box, Dad looked at me with sad, bloodshot eyes. They appeared swollen as if he'd been on some kind of binge or hadn't slept for days. Or he'd bawled like a baby for hours looking for a missing person.

Finally, after what seemed like forever, Dad spoke without eye contact. He held the ring. "This isn't for Lisa. I understand why you assumed that, though. Life lesson: never 'assume' because it will make an ass of 'u' and me. Sorry, I 'assume' this is not the right time for a joke." Dad kept on going with dumb air quotes while his legs wobbled.

Still confused, I scrunched my nose and butted into Dad's nonsense. "Dad, stop. I don't get it. Why's the ring inside your nightstand with a love letter? I didn't mean to snoop, by the way. You told me to get lunch money."

Biting his lip, almost like he held something back, Dad's eyes shifted toward the sky. The shaky legs came back full force before he told me, "I didn't accuse you of doing anything wrong by finding these things. However, I'm not thrilled you read my *very personal* property."

A sound between a grunt and a snort escaped me. "Eeew, yeah, *Dumbass*, I didn't need to know you and the"—I used revenge air quotes—"'*crazy lady*' got it on in her darkroom your first time." I shuffled through the papers looking for the proof. "Shall I read the passage?"

Dad shook his head, turning it downcast. Then, finally, he chuckled and said, "Sorry. But if you think about most of the notes, I hope what you read makes you realize the positives." Then, pointing to the letter, Dad continued. "Those events changed our lives."

"Fine." I brushed my hand through the air, waving off the issue for now. "Still, it doesn't explain the ring, though."

Picking up the box, Dad twirled the ring around and around like a magical dice he was about to toss as words fell from his mouth. "Hayden, I'm torn." Studying the ring, Dad opened the hinge, inhaling. After closing the box, he exhaled sharply. "Under the unusual circumstances, I think Cole and Ariana would understand."

My stomach dropped. "Cole?!" *Mr. TBT, Cole?*

"Yeah, Cole and Ariana. They picked it out over the holidays, over in Branson. They're waiting to make things official. The ring needed sizing. So, I picked it up and only stored it for them."

"Wow."

"Wow, that is about right." Then, clearing his throat, Dad asked, "Want in on another big—or I guess it's a *little*—secret?"

Finally smiling, I replied, "Of course, I want to hear. About Cole with Ariana?"

Dad nodded.

"I like them together."

"Me too. Ariana's good people." Dad grinned until his eyes crinkled. "They told me she's pregnant. Of course, they weren't expecting this to happen. But with their degrees, they can afford a baby and a home, so they're excited. Cole planned his proposal before he even found out about the baby."

"Wow! He'll be a good dad. Do you think that's why he acted nervously and got uptight at the hero dinner? Did you see how clingy he got around Ariana?"

Dad shifted and smiled.

"That will be one cute, smart kid with their genes. We talked a lot at Christmas. In his messages and the pictures he's sent me lately, I could tell how much he liked me as a baby."

"Yeah," Dad said, scrubbing his hands down his face. Next, he grinned, adding, "Cole acted freaking ridiculous hauling you around all the time. I'm glad he told you about when he stole all your stuff and put it in his room."

"I really like my picture."

"Your mom got such a kick out of Cole that day. I'm glad she took a lot of pictures. I remember trying not to laugh in the hall, but I couldn't hold it together. Your mom gave me so much hell for that."

I smiled up at Dad. "That's one of the stories Cole told me with lots of details."

Dad motioned to the gravesites over his shoulder. "Did you visit with your mom today?"

Rubbing my palms over the edge of the wooden bench, I mumbled, "Only from here. I got sick. Thinking about everything still makes me too upset. It's so embarrassing." My throat filled, choking back the pain yet again. "I miss her so much.

And, when I got mad at you, Dad, I didn't know what else to do. I couldn't face school."

Dad pulled me into him. Most of the confusing anger lifted some, but the new emotions of change were in their place. I thought of the new things you'd miss, Mom. Cole's wedding and a grandchild. And I thought of the changes Lisa brought into our life—mostly positives. Still, in the future, it will be many unknowns. My heart both ached and cheered for all of us—for the hope of it all. Dad clutched onto me, rubbing my back. Once I completely soaked and snotted the shoulder and collar of his Gene Tucker Construction shirt, my body stopped shuddering.

"I'm glad you're okay now," Dad said, slouching against the back of the bench, not looking in my direction. He had stretched his feet out to cross them at the ankles.

"Sorry about blowing chunks at your feet, but I'm glad you turned your face away in time. And I didn't mean to get snot on your shirt again. You've had to wash so many shirts with my blood, tears, and snot on them," I said with a half-hearted chortle.

"No worries." Then, Dad repeated very deadpan, "I'm just glad you're okay."

Glad, but now that I'm okay, you're probably also mad, right?

"While I'm here with you, if you want to go to your mom's grave, I'll walk with you or even carry you piggyback."

My head shook as the tears welled. "Not today," I barely whispered.

"Okay, I'll let you visit with your mom on your bench. But if you don't mind waiting, I'll say a quick hello. Then, when I come back, let's finish talking."

"Sure," I muttered. While Dad was gone, I shut out the world, keeping my eyes closed in a daze.

A few minutes later, I heard Dad approaching the bench. I opened my eyes. When he sat down, I asked, "When you talk to Mom, what do you say?"

"Discussions about our boys mainly."

"Do you tell her about Lisa?"

"That's a good question. I certainly do. It's hard for me, though. Lisa knows I'm still working through the process." With the toe of his boot, Dad fiddled again with the grass and gravel. "Facing my first Valentine's Day with a girlfriend filled me with guilt. Memories of your mom got to me. Even though I knew I wasn't doing anything wrong in buying Lisa a present, I felt like a cheater. Same thing at Christmas. So, dating after losing the love of your life is so difficult. And telling Rosie I've developed deeper feelings for Lisa these past few months has worn me down. I'm only human and don't have all the answers." Dad shrugged. "I've never juggled two women in my life. But I am learning that only one of them is alive, Hayden."

"So, please be honest with me. Do you love Lisa and want to marry her?"

"Well, as I wrote the letter you found today, I realized I'd fallen in love with Lisa, but I've not told her *yet*. I think there's potential for marriage in the future. Not right away."

Slapping a hand over my mouth, I tried to stifle a laugh without success. "Jeez, Dad," I stuttered as I dropped my hand. Then, with a giggle in my voice, I added, "Don't get mad or anything, but do you think maybe Lisa's right? You really are a bit of a *dumbass*?"

Dad propped himself up to the edge of the bench, swiveling his body until he frowned directly at me. "Well, where's this coming from?"

Even though he scowled, the corner of his lip jerked upward.

"You wrote all this mushy stuff but never thought to say the words 'I love you'?" I laughed again.

Drastically, Dad's shoulders and hands danced as he slumped back onto the bench.

I shook my head, still laughing. "Dad, this isn't a movie like *The Princess Bride*—when 'as you wish' can substitute for love. So, when you say your special 'Kumbaya' phrase, it isn't a code for I love you. Oh, but it might as well be. So, I'll give you that," I said with a sarcastic tone. And after a quick pause, I asked, "Don't you think you better tell her?" I threw it in for good measure, still chuckling. "And soon, Dad."

Dad's eyes closed while he rested his neck on the back ledge of the bench. Then, finally, he whined, "Quit picking on me. I've not dated in years, bud."

I think, *God, Dad, I didn't know even older people freaked out this much when they fell in love. But loving after loss must be even harder.* I couldn't imagine how devastated I'd be to lose Gretchen and have to trust love to start all over again. And that's not even marriage.

"Dad, are you at least happy?"

"More than I have been in a long, long time. My boys are healthy, have homes, and plenty to eat. I'm glad you guys seem to be doing well. We now have good friends who love us. That's a pretty successful and full life. I'm not sure about this new grandpa thing, though. But God, I suppose it's pretty awesome."

I saw Dad wiggling his boots back and forth before he told me, "It breaks my heart a little because your mom's not the one I'll share the experience with since Cole's our firstborn child."

Dad's lip quivered a tad while his eyes remained closed. Still, without falling apart, he continued. "It may not make sense to anybody."

"Makes perfect sense."

"I'm focusing on the people who love us and will shower the baby with as much love as your mom would've."

Scooting closer to Dad, I placed my head on his shoulder. I closed my eyes too. Dad sloped his body with mine until we were reclining head-to-head. "Dad, that's a good idea for us to think like that. I know Lisa will be one of the best people to have around. I keep believing Mom would like her. Maybe she's okay with us having her around. Or maybe Mom even likes us having Lisa around if we're all happy?"

"Yeah," Dad whispered, but it was hard to tell if it was a statement or a question.

Is he asking for himself or for you, Mom? Did he ask you today? Can you answer for either of us?

"Sorry about freaking out and running here to Mom today. I thought you didn't want to include me in the decision to get married."

"I'm sorry you went through all this confusion. I see how you could've mistaken things. But I made a promise to you and meant it, bud. I'll always keep you in the loop of important things with Lisa. I'm not considering marriage too soon, so when I'm ready, I'll talk to you."

"I know. Then, I guess I lost my cool thinking about how drastically my life would change. First, you'd said you'd take things slow and talk. Then, I find an engagement ring with a lengthy proposal letter and all these old printouts of emails and messages."

Sensing Dad staring, I opened my eyes to look at pinched eyebrows.

"It reads like a *proposal*?" Dad asked, shifting slightly on the bench.

Springing upward, my palms flailed out. "Duh! You shared highlights from your eight-year history together. God, Dad, that's proposal territory. In the end, you wrote something about loving the gift that comes with it. Of course, the girl thinks there's a ring."

I threw my hands up again, looking at Dad with wide eyes. "Duh! Look at me. What do you think brought me here?"

"Well. Crap. I thought I'd gone all out for Lisa. She sure didn't act disappointed."

Stop! Thanks for sharing hints about your sex life with me, Dad. Mom is buried nearby, so everything in my whole freaking world is 1,000 percent awkward right now. I swallowed hard, hoping I didn't regret asking, "What did you get her? And why didn't you give her the letter with the gift?" Finally, I flopped down, giving up.

"I did give her the letter with the gift. That's just my copy of the letter I kept. I'll show you what I gave her, but you better not make fun of it."

No matter what, do not laugh.

After scrolling to find the photo, Dad handed off his phone.

I studied it. "Lisa loves photography, and it fits your history. The 'Kumbaya' watermark and lyrics make the piece *oddly romantic*."

Teasing me back, Dad pulled my ear.

Pointing out the features, he explained the gift. "Thought a collage of the grief center with before and after pictures seemed fitting. Lisa went to church there as a girl, so I got an early print to represent how the building used to look. Then, I decided to focus on the sign to honor her dad's motto with the Summerfort Grief Center for the modern-day side. 'Kumbaya' is for me. Lisa responded nicely to everything."

"We're at the cemetery. Stop being weird, Dad. You sound innuendo-ish."

Dad chuckles before replying, "Sorry, bud. I forget I have such a smart son." Dad patted my knee. "I'm gonna call the school and tell them you're sick—you did barf next to my boots. I'll have them round up your schoolwork. Text Gretchen and see if she'll bring it by later." Standing up, he plastered a hand on his hip and tried imitating Gretchen. "Unless she's too flippity-do-da mad at you?"

Grinning, I said, "I think Gretchen's okay. We've texted." And then I pushed myself off the bench, dusting my jeans.

As we began walking to Dad's Dodge, he explained his morning. "I called your brothers while I was on my way here. Calming Drew down took a minute."

"Dad, I'm glad Drew's not the one having the baby. He's way too overprotective, but in this kind of a hostile loving way." *Sort of a bit like you, Dad. After all, that's who he gets it from.*

"Yep. Dennis loves you. I don't think he means he will perform any real bodily harm. He gets emotional and spouts off. It's all talk, no action. Oh, hey, did you eat *anything* today?"

"No, I'm starving."

"If you're nice, I'll take you to some out-of-the-way café for lunch. If you're not too embarrassed to be seen with me," Dad said.

"Why would I be?"

Dad stopped to pull up his pant leg revealing his Snoop Dogg Plant Daddy socks. My mouth opened, trying to form words. Then Dad unzipped his jacket to show me the neon yellow Wonder Bread hoodie with floating red-and-blue polka dots I had bought him. "I bundled up in things my missing son bought me because I didn't know if I'd ever see him again."

At that second, I loved Dad's over-the-top southern voice and melodramatic ways. My mouth twitched from a smile to a frown and back again. And it occurred to me just how much my body fights through waves of sadness and joy. Finally, I said, "Dad, you're so weird sometimes."

We both chuckled.

"So, Dennis the Menace Drew says he tore into you?"

I shrugged. "I guess. No biggie. Same old mouth-piece Drew."

"Well, just so you know, when we get home, I'll want to, but I won't beat your ass for running away today."'

I burst into laughter. "Deal," I said as we strolled toward the truck.

"That comment's Drew inspired," Dad told me with a gleam in his eye and an evil grin, draping an arm around my shoulder.

Nearing the truck, he hauled me next to his side. Tilting his head, he got close to my ear. "Please don't *ever* take off on me again."

Recognizing the matter-of-fact Dad tone of voice, I knew to brace myself for all the emotional turmoil I'd put him through—

"You scared the hell out of me and everyone today—" Raising his voice, the words cracked. "I worried you were dead, Hayden. I'm not kidding."

I believe you, Dad. It's in your pain-filled red eyes, making my heart compress.

"And, Hayden, if you're able, you better pick up your phone, even if you want to tell me you hate me. I don't care if you say, 'Screw you, Dad. I hate you,' at least I'll know my son's alive." He paused our walking. Leaning against my ear again, a massive gust of breaths escaped. "Got it?"

Gulping, I nodded as unshed tears swam, clouding my vision. Then, resuming the pace, Dad kept his arm attached. Finally, he said, "And if you find something questionable in our home, please just ask me before jumping to any conclusions. See how everyone can make a mistake, though, Hayden? Jumping to conclusions?"

I nodded.

In a tight lecture side-hug, Dad escorted me to the passenger door. Next, he slowly released me and pointed his finger in the middle of my chest, meeting me eye to eye. "Are we clear on everything?"

"Yes," I answered, giving him a thumbs-up. Then, of course, he threw his backslap bro hug into the mix, ensuring the slate's clean. To him, I knew these symbols meant forgiveness and love at the end of a tough day.

Hey, Ma, those earlier copies of Dad's emails mentioned a bunch of stuff about me. Over the years, it seemed like Dad and Lisa showed they loved me. Lisa put a lot of effort into helping me. I didn't realize how much she did for Dad too. I mean, Lisa talked to Dad about you, Cole, Drew, and all his painful issues with grief. She seems to know us and our story. I guess she's trying to get Dad to do journaling too. Maybe even get him in on the *Love at the Center of Grief* writings. Perhaps some things should stay secret (or hidden in dark rooms). Maybe all this time, it's been Lisa I have to thank for pushing Dad into becoming a better parent?

As Dad drove away over the hill of Summerfort Cemetery, I glanced at your stone angel from the passenger's seat in the rearview mirror. I kept my blurry eyes steady, glued to her the whole way until we arrived at the iron gates. She's always supportive, whether in my mind, my grief journal, or—sometimes—even in person. Leaving—and then watching her stay behind—this part stings the most—every time.

Maybe it's why I hate the cemetery so much. It's the same again and again reminder. Furthermore, realizing I'm without my mom physically, I have to see myself growing up without her. And after every visit, it all starts with going home to too many unknowns.

Mom, before the tips of your granite wings vanished, I spoke to you once more. From my heart, I said, "Thanks for listening today. Try to help us. Maybe send us a sign or something—let us know how you feel. Bye, again, Ma. I love and miss you."

GRETCHEN

Chapter Twenty-Seven

February 20, 2020
Dear Mom,

WTFDD! Hayden stood me up this morning. After texting him, I received no reply. I called but only got voice mail. At first, my reaction was anger, but worry took over because this wasn't like Hayden. He's the type of guy who shows up to school on time to meet me in the mornings. My heartbeat slammed because I didn't want to cause any trouble, but I called Gene anyway to see if something had happened.

"Hi, Gene. Hayden didn't make it to school this morning. When I texted and called, I didn't hear back from him either. Is he sick?"

"What do you mean he's not at school?" I could tell he seemed pretty freaked out by his surprised tone. I heard him huffing deep breaths before saying, "Shortcake, let me call Hayden. Then I'll get back to you. Thanks for letting me know, so we can track him down. I had to leave for work early today. Maybe he's sick. I'll run home and see."

Gene just hung up without even saying good-bye. Figuring Gene had the right idea, I tried focusing on schoolwork. Unfortunately, Hayden probably got sick and physically couldn't get to the phone. So, I checked my phone between my first- and second-class periods to see that Hayden still hadn't replied, but Gene had.

Gene: Shortcake, Hayden's not home. Let me know if he's made it to school. He might be running late since he's walking. I'm on the case to find him.

Gretchen: I've not seen him at school, Gene. I don't see him in the hall like I usually do between classes. Please update.

Gene: Will do.

Fighting fears and tears, I strolled to the bathroom to send Hayden another text.

Gretchen: Hayden, I don't know what to do. I've tried to reach out to you without an answer. I've gone to Gene, but you won't answer him either. I'm sad. I don't know if I'm supposed to be mad. Is this disappearance about me? Don't hide from people. You're scaring me. I'd rather lose you knowing you're safe. But, God, let's at least talk this out!

Still, effing nothing. I'm so over today. I can't sit and concentrate in class, so I'm going to freaking go and bang down Gabby's door. Gabby!

In Gabby's office doorway, I yelled, "Hey, you probably don't want to deal with me, but I don't know where else to go, and I'm not dealing with stupid people today in class."

With a wave of her hand, she motioned for me to sit down. "Nice greeting, by the way."

I shrugged. "Well, blame Hayden. He put me in a nasty mood."

Gabby stood, closing the door with the tip of her black boot, shutting us off from the main office to give us more privacy. As she walked back to her desk, she said, "Gretchen, I know how hard it can be not to allow others to take over your mind with negativity and rob you of an entire day. Try to remember. You deserve happiness."

"Ugh, believe me, I want to be happy. But I think Hayden's trying to dump me. He's going to do it by ghosting all of us," I said, holding up my phone over my head, hoping that would explain everything.

She got comfortable, wheeling her chair until she sat at the edge of her desk. Then, with her elbows on her desk, she cocked her head. "Sweetie, please tell me what gives you this ghosting idea."

My body cinched with the cringy word *sweetie*. For a long second, I consider jumping out of my chair and running away like Hayden, the ass-jerk. But instead, I sucked in calming breaths. Then, showing her my unanswered texts, I bit my cheek to keep from crying.

Pointing to the last message, I told Gabby, "After I sent this final text, he still wouldn't answer, so I came to talk to you and ask for help."

Gabby looked sincere as she handed me my phone. "Let me call Gene to see if there are updates, Gretchen."

Sitting on my hands kept the temptation of frequently checking my phone at bay. Instead, my body rocked back and forth as I listened with cloudy eyes.

As Gabby talked to Gene, her eyes widened. She yanked a pencil out of her blinged-out cup holder. Using the pencil, she scribbled down names: Gretchen, school, Lisa, Drew, Cole, and John.

Gabby pushed the landline into her ear to stifle Gene, but I could still clearly hear the demanding fear. "Please. Just a simple yes or no, Gabby. Is that punk-ass bully kid, Thomas Sharp, at school, so I don't have to worry he's the one who has my kid somewhere?"

Stuffed with worry, I pretended to look at my phone again. My heart went out to Gene, and at the same time, I snuck a glance at Gabby closing her eyes and with her free hand touching her reddening cheeks.

Then, pulling the phone away from her ear, she cupped a hand over the mouthpiece, looked at me, and asked, "Sweetie, did you contact any of Hayden's friends to ask if they knew about him?"

In the background, Gene's voice was garbled, yelling "Yes or No?" It sounded like he repeated himself a few times with a "Come on, Gabby" thrown in too.

"I texted, asking Kelsey and Miles if he and Hayden went somewhere, but they haven't heard from him."

Flustered, Gabby squeezed the phone. "Yes, Gene." She rubbed her forehead. A willingness to share a secret to save a friend meant something. But, of course, Gabby probably broke some confidentiality rules. So, it's no wonder she got so flabbergasted. But in the case of a missing student, I imagine more information becomes warranted. My heart ached for Gene and Gabby, who battled delicate personal and professional issues. It made me pinch my fingertips.

Gabby also repeated my information to Gene, adding Kelsey and Miles to the names on her list. The final question she asked Gene surprised me: "May I try texting or calling him?" She smiled slightly, so I assumed Gene agreed. "Maybe if Hayden knows he's not going to be in trouble, we care, and we're all looking, it might ease things. I bet he will feel more comfortable. And even a little pressured to contact someone."

Gabby sounded more counselor-ish than I've ever heard before. The conversation ended with her twirling her long black hair and saying, "Great."

I wanted to scream. *No, sweetie, nothing's great. By the way, Gabby, nothing's sweet either.*

Shifting, I stared from Gabby to her office supplies. My gaze fell on her pencil holder. I don't know if someone made the little storage container for her or if she bought that thing. Then I wondered if Dad selected it as a gift after a Happenstance moment. I think it's supposed to look like Poco's black Boston Terrier body. The cup reminds me of a makeshift Yahtzee dice shaker. At the rim, it's a look-alike diamond dog collar. The canine's face and ears appear made from some type of felt material. I can't decide if I want to label the item as a gem or an atrocity. For a whole two seconds, I'm thankful for her weird office trinkets, taking my mind off losing Hayden Oliver Tucker.

Then, my phone vibrated and pinged. Now, I'm trying to decipher the replies Hayden finally sent. In my busy mind, I semi-argued with Gabby. *You're too upbeat with your sweetie talk. You won't understand.*

"So, tell me what's going on with you, Gretchen."

"It's nothing. Just what I said earlier. Hayden ran off. He finally texted back. But you won't understand," I whined.

Gabby's voice startled me. "Try me, Gretchen." Her tone held more attitude than usual. *Was she reading my freaking mind?*

"Talk to me more about what's going on now that he's written you back."

"As I said, Hayden didn't want to text me back or return calls." Pushing my phone across the desk to Gabby, I swallowed hard. "But, then, he sent these texts in the last couple of minutes."

Hayden: Gretch, I love you. I'm sorry I worried you. I had a last-minute issue at home. Give me time to go over it with Dad. Later tonight, I'll talk. Do me a favor, and please tell John and Gabby I'm ok.

Gretchen: Glad you're safe. But are you really okay? Let me know if you need anything. I'll give you time with Gene. PLEASE text or call when you're ready. I'll let Dad and Gabby know. Love you.

Hayden: Angel, yes, I'm okay. I promise to explain later. But, again, I'm so sorry.

"It's like Hayden's saying, 'I'm okay, but I'm not interested in talking to you right now.' I still don't know what I did wrong."

"I know it's confusing, but it doesn't sound like *you* did anything wrong. From what Hayden said, he had something happen at home. That appeared to be an issue between Gene and Hayden. And he's going to need time to work through it. Men sometimes process away from others, needing more space and quiet."

"That doesn't sound very Hayden-like to me."

"Sweetie, he's growing up. He may not want anyone to save him. Or maybe he wanted to solve this particular problem on his own. Sometimes it's about fear or embarrassment. Showing up at school upset is hard. He's been through a ton of that over the years."

"Yeah, tell me about it. Look at me. I'm camped out here with you. Hiding in the counselor's office."

"Yikes, Gretchen, am I that terrible to be around?" Actual discomfort covered Gabby's face. She even went slack-jawed.

"I'm sorry, Gabby. I didn't mean it like that."

Although we all knew I probably did mean some of those words. Gabby. Me. And even you, Mom. But, of course, this might make me an ass-jerk.

Gabby sighed. Leaning forward with her hands clasped in front of her, she looked me straight in the eye. "Sweetie, I'm also sorry if I'm doing anything to make you uncomfortable here at school and outside—well, you know what I mean."

"You're kind to me, Dad, and Hayden. We have a lot of fun. I like Poco too." I smiled.

"I've moved slowly with John because I don't want you to feel invaded with me inside your home. I respect you and your family, Gretchen." Gabby paused, just waiting for me to speak again. The awkward silence gagged me.

"Okay, I understand. There are no issues." I shrugged.

A faint smile pulled at the corners of Gabby's mouth, but she kept her eyes cast downward, studying her pink-and-silver nail polishes.

"I think you and I both know that's not the whole truth, Gretchen. Or, should I say, *sweetie*?" She said it with an edgy, angry smirk on her face.

WTFDD? I worried. So, trying to hide my flinch, I sat up straight. "What are you talking about?" Now, more than ever, I wanted to flee from this grumpier Gabby who Dad had barely warned me about.

"Gretchen, you're not as secretive as you think you are. I see when you're in pain. I know when I annoy you. Because you physically cringe every time I use the word *sweetie*."

Caught! A little mouse in the clutches of a trap—this summed up me sitting across from Miss Gabby Garcia staring at me. Not sure what to say to smooth things over, I felt my face burning. Embarrassed, scared, and angry, I covered the emotions I experienced with relief.

Finally, I squeaked out "I'm sorry."

"Sorry I annoy you? Or sorry I confronted you with some truths?"

"Both," I whispered honestly.

"Please, Gretchen, tell me what I can do better." Gabby's voice started to waver.

It hurt to answer her. Tears leaked from the corner of my eyes. "I like you, Gabby, but you say *sweetie* so, so much."

"I know." Gabby's voice cracked. She paused before saying, "Gretchen, you should be aware that my backstory isn't so different from yours, except my loss happened at ten years old. My parents and sister died in a car accident. And I barely survived. In fact, I was the only one who did. Someday, I'd love to talk to you about all the issues I went through due to survivor's guilt."

Instinctively a new batch of tears fell at the shock of hearing Gabby's words. Heat pricked my entire body as my heart skipped a beat before racing. My gut felt punched. I hurt so badly for her losses, of not knowing what to say or do. Finally, I managed to whisper shakily, "I'm so, so sorry. But, Gabby, I didn't know."

"Thank you, sweetie. For some reason, I thought you already knew. But I don't talk about it very often. Summerfort's a small town. But since I told your dad, I thought the two of you might've spoken about me."

Dumbfounded, I shook my head.

Gabby watched me, and I knew she saw me biting my lip, fighting back the demons in my head, trying not to cry even more. But of course, this tiny broom closet meant as an office made it impossible to misinterpret any gestures.

So much raced through my mind. *Oh God, I need out of here. This sadness is too much, Gabby. HOT boy, you are in so much trouble with me now. Next time, you better answer your effing phone. Dad, why didn't you tell me about Gabby? Was I supposed to interpret "Gabby gets grief" to mean this, Doctor Gardener? Why don't people communicate better?*

I needed and wanted to blame someone, or maybe everyone else, for my dislike of Gabby and her use of "sweetie" as my number-one reason for not liking her. But I want to forget about the time I sat in her office after I started my period and hid. That day I overheard her make up a story about some fund. So, a girl whose family didn't qualify for a free and reduced lunch card received one via Gabby Garcia. She secretly helped people.

If it weren't for my dying mom, I wouldn't be stuck in this godforsaken broom closet. Or if my dad hadn't chosen to become such a Happenstance man-whore. Or maybe if my boyfriend cared enough about me not to run away. And I've no effing understanding of why Hayden's fleeing from me, but I assumed I've done something stupid.

I tried opening my eyes wide, chewing on a nail, and staring at my blank phone screen.

"And, Gretchen, I'm sorry if I use the word *sweetie* too much. But it's what my mama called me. So, when I say the word, it sometimes helps—it's soothing. I say it because I care about people. Dumb, huh?"

Before I could even answer Gabby, more tears flowed. I couldn't hide them. Using the back of my hand, I dabbed at the corner of my eyes. "No. It's not dumb at all, Gabby." *So, you're a motherless daughter who's broken too?*

"Oh, sweetie, I didn't mean to make you cry."

At the word *sweetie*, a fresh batch of tears poured from me.

Gabby handed me a Kleenex, placing an arm around my shoulder for a moment. "After the accident, I got so lucky. My aunt and uncle adopted me. So, living with my mom's extended family, I had access to cousins who played and fought with me like brothers and sisters," Gabby said, chuckling. Gabby reared back in her rolling desk chair, placing a hand on her hip. "Even to this day, the sibling-cousin rivalry continues."

I smiled.

Tossing her dark hair over her shoulders, she asked, "May I show you a few photos of my family?"

"Of course," I replied, meaning every word.

I learned a lot as we browsed through the pictures on Gabby's phone.

"Oh no," Gabby said, wanting to scroll past them.

"Please, go back. I think I saw a quick glimpse of the young you."

Gabby glared at me, pretending to slip her phone into her pocket.

"No. Oh. My. God." I squeaked. "I knew I saw it. I think you had that famous perfect Rachel hairstyle everyone wanted from *Friends*."

Gabby swallowed hard. Then she smirked, asking, "Is this so you can make fun of me?"

"No! I like going through your pictures."

"Okay, I'll give you a quick peek." Gabby flipped the phone around and then back to her chest.

"Not fair."

Then Gabby allowed me to study the faces of her past.

"Who are these people?"

"I honestly don't recall their names. Just friends of the family, I suppose."

I drew the phone closer to investigate. "I'm guessing the baby you're holding is a boy since he's wrapped in a blue-and-brown-patterned train blanket. Do you remember his name?"

"I sure don't." Gabby hovered over me as if my time was up. But I found the photo so interesting.

"Why aren't you smiling?"

With a smirk, Gabby snagged her phone. "My aunt probably forced me to take a picture with these people at nineteen years old."

"Gabby, why do you save pictures of people you don't know on your phone?"

"My aunt remembers. She helps me when my memories fail. So, in some ways, I suppose, they're part of my history. Sometimes images tend to comfort us. Besides, I'm in the photo, so it provides a timeline of me."

Then Gabby returned to more of herself with a hair flip off her shoulder. As I learned more about Gabby, I realized that counselors carry not only the weight of everything they lose but also the heft of what others tell them.

Gabby's phone rang, and she told me she had an appointment in a different location, and I had to head back to class, so she wrote me a hall pass. A part of me wanted to crunch the pink slip and pitch it in the trash because I still needed to chat.

When I swung my backpack over my shoulder, it knocked one of Gabby's framed degrees cockeyed. I didn't have much time to adjust it, but I swear I saw the name G Santos G at the bottom. A faint remembrance fluttered back to me of Hayden and me at the vet clinic, talking about where we had seen this name before. Oh well. Life produced strange coincidences. But I'd mention it to him.

Afterward, I swore to myself when I heard Gabby mention the word *sweetie*, I would see a little girl much like me who just misses her mom. I'd give her a break. Maybe let her in my life a little more. I'd love to have a mother-like figure around. But feeling this way does not mean I've forgotten about you, Mom, or I miss you any less.

Mom, remember my poem "Motherless Child?" I think I have more of the rough draft done.

"Motherless Child"
"Why are you all alone, sitting in the dark?"

"Lady, turn off the light. Let me hide."
I'm a motherless child."
"Other children go outside to play and wear smiles."
"Lady, I try, but my frown just won't bend.
Turn off the light. Let me hide.
I'm a motherless child."

"Maybe other mothers will let you tuck near
     their side?"
"Lady, I try, but no one likes sharing a mother.
Not a single friend's willing.
Turn off the light. Let me hide.
I'm a motherless child."

"Maybe God or your mother sent someone like
     me?
May I try to shed some comfort, light, or hope
     in your life?"

"Go away, Lady! Let me be! Can't you see my
     heart breaking?
Besides, there's no hope for someone like me.
You can't stop this ache. So let me cry in peace.
I stopped mattering to a world that doesn't see
     me.
Inside dark spaces, no one hears, and no one sees.
Most of the time, I'm not sure God cares that I'm
     aching.
Now, turn off the light! Let me hide.
I'm a motherless child."

"May I join you in silence?
Or just hold your hand?
When you're ready to talk, I'll gladly listen.
For now, I'll turn off the light.
But I believe I might understand.

Because you see, just like you,
I, too, am a motherless child."

"Lady, you can stay. Please, sit by me.
Here, in the dark, will you squeeze my hand tight?
Lady, I know you can't promise me any
*   guarantees.*
But, still, do you wish to stay and help me?
If so, please, try to answer one big question for
*   me:*
Am I ever again going to feel all right?"

GRETCHEN

Twenty-Eight

Dear Mom,

My invitation to attend arrived via snail mail. Inside the purple envelope, the triangular flap revealed a shiny golden hue. A masquerade mask covered the letter's center with standard Mardi Gras colors in a silhouetted pattern. Lisa chose a green font, completing the look.

Mardi Gras Teen Event
Summerfort Grief Center
(Fat) Tuesday, February 25, 2020
Food & Group, 6:00–9:00 p.m.

As Dad entered the kitchen, yawning, I asked, "Did you know Lisa wanted to plan a party at the center for Mardi Gras?"

Shaking his head and stretching, he accepted the invitation as I handed it to him. With his back against the countertop, Dad adjusted his black-rimmed reading glasses. "Sounds fun, Gretchen. Are you going?" He twisted his body, placing the invite on our necessary paperwork tray near the refrigerator.

Glancing at Dad with a grin, I said, "I think so." The more I stared at him, the more I remembered. Finally, I can't stifle my laughter any longer.

"Hey!" Dad rubbed his palms down his sleep T-shirt. "Are you making fun of me?" He performed a short modeling walk, twirled, and rested one of his hands on his hip.

"You look ridiculous," I stammered through tears. Then, laughing, I continued to talk. "I love those Rudolph PJs you refuse to quit wearing because you claim the flannel's so warm. Plus, the pants provide you with pockets."

"All my claims are valid. If you recall, you have a matching pair, Gretchen."

"Oh, I will never forget, Dad. I still have the photo of you, Hayden, and Gene with your matching gear and the red noses."

We smiled.

"We had a lot of fun at our relaxing Christmas PJs pizza party," Dad said, picking up the Mardi Gras invitation to scan it. Then, he looked over at me. "Good, it's not another one of Lisa's creative costume party ideas."

"Dad, is that a slam on my Madonna outfit I wore for Halloween?"

Raising a brow, Dad said, "Let me just say I don't want to deal with any more of your fishnet pantyhose stunts."

"Ew, Dad, nobody wears 'pantyhose' anymore. Well, maybe old people do." Then, holding up the strings of my hoodie, I asked, "How about I wear something like this sweatshirt with jeans to Lisa's purple-gold-and-green-themed party?"

Dad fist-bumped me as he delivered bagels and cream cheese to the table.

February 25 arrived.

At the Summerfort Grief Center, Hayden, Kelsey, Miles, Mia, Lisa, and I made up the Mardi Gras party attendees. Once assembled in the Blue Room for a short group session, Lisa said, "Mardi Gras means 'Fat Tuesday' in French. Do any of you take French? Or have you learned some facts about this holiday?"

Miles pointed toward Kelsey. "Kelsey and I take the same French class right now, and we studied the history of Mardi Gras last week."

Much more animated than usual, Mia scoffed. So much so that I elbowed Hayden in the ribs with a WTFDD sideways glance.

Lisa watched Mia but continued to listen attentively to the conversation underway with Miles and Kelsey.

"Yeah," Kelsey jumped in, "we talked about the religious significance of celebrating before Lent." Kelsey's eyes darted from me to Mia to Lisa.

"Great, thanks for sharing." Lisa paused, clearing her throat as if waiting, so she could study the faces in the room. "I saw a link when comparing Mardi Gras and grief. We tend to search for ways to celebrate our loved ones who've died, but in doing so, we face the life we have given up. There's Fat Tuesday and then Lent. A celebration and then the sacrifice. I hope this makes sense. Does it?"

"Lisa, it makes perfect sense to me," Hayden said. "Before you helped us put it into words, I never would've combined Mardi Gras and grief. I understand how this holiday celebrates, and then it's about learning ways to let go, which is just like grief."

"I like that, Hayden," I said, squeezing his hand.

Lisa grinned. "I'm glad my thoughts weren't too far out there."

"Nope," Kelsey said. "I put grief with everything somedays."

I nodded.

"You would," Mia sarcastically mumbled under her breath. Her attitude confused and hurt me. This excessively verbal, dry-eyed girl tonight seemed nothing like the Mia I used to know.

Lisa fixed her eyes on Mia. "How do you feel about the idea of Mardi Gras and grief, Mia?"

"No comment, really. It doesn't really matter to me tonight. I just read the word *party* on the invite and came," Mia answered, shrugging.

"Well, Mia. I'm sorry you feel it doesn't matter. You matter to us, and I'm glad you're here. Thanks for coming. You decided to be here even if tonight was not a good night. I'm happy about that. I'm guessing we all are." She looked at us.

We nodded uncomfortably.

Lisa continued. "As you start to age, stresses in life grow. You will need to balance your life concerning many things, such as dating, schoolwork, college choices, work, marriage, and family, and the list might feel endless. Grief will sneak in from time to time, and I just want you to remember to tap into positive coping resources. Let's chat about this as we eat our Mardi Gras-themed foods."

Lisa handed us a small menu to pass around as she told us some of the offerings: "Shrimp and grits, Cajun mac and cheese, hushpuppies, and for dessert, there's pecan praline ice cream or King cake. Or why not try both?" Lisa mentioned, laughing as she read things off to us.

Going through the food line, Mia held up a strand of plastic gold beads, rubbing them across the back of Hayden's neck. Startled, he jerked away.

Mia chuckled. "Hey, if you'll ditch Red, I'll earn these beads with you—know what I mean?" she tried whispering to Hayden, pulling up the hem of her sweater, showing him her midriff.

"God, Mia, you're acting like you're stoned." Hayden stepped back from her.

"Mia!" I pleaded. Unsure what to say or do, I touched her arm, angered by her actions but even more concerned about what caused her behavior.

410

"Fuckin' do-gooders," Mia replied, laughing. "You people and your dumbass parties."

I wanted to grab her and yell, "Well, get the hell out of here then!" but I knew something appeared off with Mia.

"Hayden, what should we do?" I asked.

He pursed his lips, motioning with his head toward Lisa. She looked busy giggling with Miles and Kelsey across the table. Sitting, they were fanning their faces with napkins adorned with masks while sampling Cajun food. Wishing I could read Hayden's mind but betting correctly, I just wanted to ask Hayden out loud, *Do you mean let's get Lisa's attention*?

Fear held me back, worrying about Mia and the various strands of beads in all three Mardi Gras colors she had draped around her neck. Mia picked a few food items out while quietly humming a song unknown to me. Then, looking at Hayden, she touched her cheesy macaroni, licking the remnants from her fingers seductively. "It's hot. Wanna little lick?" she asked Hayden, swirling her finger back onto her paper plate.

"Please, Mia. Stop it," Hayden said in a kind but firm tone.

Mia just stood there blankly, staring.

Finally, Hayden asked, "Mia, are you okay? Do you need help? Should I call Lisa over?"

Finally, Mia came somewhat out of her trance, tossing her plate on the very edge of the table.

Rushing in, I pushed the paper plate back, so it didn't fall to the floor. Mia glared at me first and then gave Hayden a much longer look.

"Hayden, do you think you might eventually have a new mommy?" Mia asked, with her hand over her bead-strewn heart to mock Lisa, chuckling.

I noticed Hayden's eyes swimming with tears. Mia had swooped in like a vulture, and nothing she said after seemed to hurt him quite like this.

"Mia," I tried pleading, "please, let's sit down by the others."

"No way, Red!" she said, laughing at me. "I'm not about to listen to any more bitching tonight. I'm sick of all of you. Look around," she stated as she held up her palm. "You have Hayden." She pointed to the others. "And the band dorks look like they want to or are probably banging cymbals together. If you know what I mean."

"I'm glad you're a part of this group," I told Mia, hoping to make her quit ranting. "I think Hayden is glad too."

He nodded somberly.

"Poor little rich girl. Red, you live with Doctor Daddy. Boo-hoo. We know from our group that your mommy died. I hear you whispering to Kelsey and Hayden, complaining about your dad. Well, get over it. Everyone knows your dad's hot and fucks everyone in town, even Lilly's mom. Isn't that your sad-ass story you hint about in group?"

As her words tumbled out, my eyes watered, bracing for what was possibly next. My heart jolted until the blood caused ringing in my ears. I joined Hayden, standing side by side to face Mia head-on, trapping her against the table to fight through everything.

The corner of her mouth quirked up, and she held up a shaky finger. "One more thing, Red." Mia acted like she wanted to punch me with her index finger to my chest but stopped midway and dropped the idea. "Tell me about your underwear tonight—are they from Victoria's Secr—?"

"That's enough!" Hayden shouted, cutting Mia off, his voice loud enough that it startled even me.

Lisa jumped from her chair, storming toward us as Mia flipped her plate onto the floor. Some of the creamiest contents landed on me before she flew into the bathroom without apologizing.

"Mia, I will allow you to cool down, but I need to speak with you soon," Lisa told her as Mia stormed past Lisa, ignoring her.

To my knowledge, this is the first time in a group that something this wild has happened. So, naturally, I felt bad for Lisa. But I also felt terrible for Kelsey and Miles eating alone across the room, looking like they didn't know what else to do.

"I'm so sorry, Hayden and Gretchen," Lisa told us as she led us into the kitchen to quickly get our side of the story, so she could check on Mia. We shared with Lisa the odd exchanges with Mia at the food table, explaining how she seemed a little angry and more out of it than usual. Hayden left out the "mommy" story, but I understood.

"Lisa, do you think I could try talking to Mia first? I need to use the bathroom, anyway. The soap and the air dryer in there might work better," I said, motioning to the hem of my dark-washed denim jeans and aqua Converse shoes dotted with grits and Cajun mac and cheese.

Biting her lip as if in thought, Lisa finally nodded, but I wondered if she ever got on board with the idea.

I question myself a lot about this portion of the night. What do I remember seeing first? Mia's vaping pipe rested near her body as her fingers curled out for it, but it was just out of reach. Or her legs and arms splayed across the cold tile of the Summerfort Grief Center's bathroom? Her midriff showed again. This time, though, it was spotty with blood from a fresh cut or scratch of some kind covered up with a strand of golden Mardi Gras plastic beads.

What do I remember hearing first? Was it the sound of my voice screaming? Or maybe Mia's crying and slurring, "I hate all of you bitches. You losers all have someone. I only have Grandma. She's old. I'll be alone if she dies because no one loves me or wants me, Red."

Lisa stood in the doorway, calling 911 as I dropped to Mia's side. "I love you, Mia. We all do. We understand you more than you know."

Mia squeaked out the pain she'd bottled inside her soul, rambling and repeating herself at times. "I hate myself, Red. Sometimes I just want to die like my parents, but I can't leave my grandma. Are you a narc, Red? Why didn't you just let me die? I don't think I'm worth saving. Why did I start doing the things my parents did? Why? I want to be happy. But I don't know how to be. Somedays, I just want to die. I don't wanna live anymore, but I don't wanna die either. But I am just surviving, and it hurts. Is there a happy place in between?" Mia asked her broken questions weakly as silent tears streaked her cheeks.

I repeated "I am here for you" over and over. But Mia didn't want to listen.

Instead of saying much, I held my thoughts inside. *I don't know, Mia. I wish I had answers for you.* Finally, I said, "I only wanted to help you, Mia. One day, I hope you'll understand. And forgive me." Then I ran to Lisa. I planted my head on her shoulder, sobbing.

Lisa led me out of the bathroom, propping the door open for the paramedics. She'd already told Hayden, Kelsey, and Miles to wait in the Blue Room. I imagined them huddled together, peering through the blinds, very concerned.

"Gretchen, you were amazing with Mia," Lisa said. "I'm sorry you went through that, though. Do you want to call your dad and go home?"

I shook my head. "Is Mia going to make it?"

"I understand she looked scary because her eyes rolled back, but she's pretty coherent, honey. I don't know what she's taken, but paramedics will get on it immediately. Her grandma will listen to the doctors and get her help." Lisa escorted me to the Blue Room with the others.

Hayden grabbed me into a tight hug. Soon, Miles and Kelsey joined the hug, turning it into a group one. We chatted about the night's events. Red lights bounced off the walls, illuminating the Blue Room. Every one of us is painfully familiar with the sights and sounds of emergency workers. Lounging across the two oversized ottomans facing each other, we listened in silence. As Hayden has done many times here, he reached for my hand, squeezing. A few silent tears slipped as I heard the gurney snap into place. The noise took me back to my family's dining room as my mother slumped on the floor, much like Mia tonight, only my mother's stroke wasn't self-inflicted.

Hayden's legs bobbed, and I wondered if his heart listened to the noises as I did, conjuring up the past. I remember Hayden telling me, "I'm the one who found my mom. I watched as the paramedics covered her up and wheeled her out of our home."

Miles wrapped his arm around Kelsey, and she leaned in closer to him. A tear escaped. He wiped a few wayward tears of his own. As they listened, I thought about Kelsey with her mom and all she must have heard the night of their accident. Her eyes stared at the red walls from the emergency lights, and she cried harder. Finally, she closed her eyes and fell into Miles. Once, Kelsey said something in our group like this, "After my car accident, my eyes couldn't see anything, but I couldn't stop looking at every flashing light."

Miles held Kelsey as she cried, rocking her in his arms. Miles's dad had died by suicide. And the family found his body in their home. So, while we are in our group meetings, often, Miles asks, "What do I do about the guilt? What could I have done to prevent it?"

Miles deals with a lot of guilt.

I hope Miles does not feel like he must add Mia to his grief and guilt load too.

Like Mia's situation, no one can provide a clear answer for Miles.

Mental health takes on so many layers with different types and needs. But we can offer to get help for those we love. And we can begin to treat mental illnesses as physical ones affecting the brain. I remember Lisa sharing a statistic: Nearly one in five Americans (or about 53 million people) live with a mental illness. Mother, I suppose I am one of them since I have mild OCD—I need to stop being ashamed of myself. Mia's words frightened me. That "happy place in between" Mia talked about made me think it was like Mia read my mind. Because I understood every word. I don't want to live as a jealous disappointment to others. But I also don't want to die and leave behind those I love. I just wish I were normal and didn't obsess about everyone else's lives being better than mine. Mia opened my eyes to a few things, however.

"Mia said she wanted to be happy but didn't know how to be," I tell the others. Instead of using Mia's words, I paraphrased. "She rambled some, but maybe she felt mad at herself and worried about her grandmother's health. There's a lot of fear that she might be left alone if something happens to her grandmother. Of course, I'm angry about how she flirted with Hayden and the things she yelled at us, but that's the drug talking, not Mia. She seemed out of it, but I guess she's sad and open to getting help." I shrugged.

I hoped I wasn't violating Mia's trust or anything. But still, I think they all needed to know more and understand how much she was hurting and how much she wanted to get better. Besides, they were aware of most of what I said anyway. And I could see the pain in their eyes. So, I tried to help them too. But what the eff did I know anyway? WTFDD was I supposed to do?

Hayden sat stoic, his legs still shaky and clinging to my sweaty hand.

Finally, Kelsey said, "Thanks, Gretchen. That gives me some hope for Mia."

Miles offered a silent shrug and a sad half-smile.

Finally, we heard Lisa's footsteps outside the door. "I'm so sorry about tonight," Lisa announced, stepping inside the door with her cell phone plastered to her chest. "I called your parents, and if you want to stay to finish the night, that's fine. Or we can call it a night."

"I'm up to staying," I whispered to Hayden.

"You sure?" He rubbed my back.

I nodded.

Hayden shrugged, looking up at Lisa in the doorway. "I guess we're staying."

Lisa's tone turned lighthearted. "I'm glad you want to stay. Oh, and, Miles, I hear you drove tonight. Kelsey's dad allowed you to bring her for the very first time." Lisa added, "Whoo-hoo!" and grinned.

"Yeah!" Miles said, doing a little fist pump. We all laughed. God, it felt good to release some tension.

Lisa had us spread out to the couches to chat.

"As I said, I'm sorry we experienced his situation tonight. However, I'm thankful Mia came tonight because we got to help her. I imagine some of her words might have hurt you deeply. In time, I hope she will come to appreciate us and our help. Unfortunately, today is not that day, and the day may never come. I don't have an answer. Only Mia does. Please know this is hard for me too." Lisa paused. "Any questions or concerns?"

"Will you be able to tell us if Mia is going to be okay? And how is her grandma doing?" Kelsey asked.

"Great questions, Kelsey. I spoke with Grandma only briefly. I plan to call her back soon. When I do, I'll ask her what she's comfortable sharing and get back to each of you."

Hayden said, "I'm sorry, but I'm still pretty angry. She put Gretchen through hell. And a lot of her insults were aimed at Gretchen and me. I want her to get well, but I need some time to burn off this anger. Sorry, guys."

"You have the right to be angry, even at Mia. Do you have an idea or a healthy way to deal with your emotions tonight?" Lisa asked.

"Do you have time to do the plate-smashing activity with us?" Hayden asked.

Lisa tilted her head in her thinking stance, tapping at her chin. "I'm trying to recall where we stored those few extras." She snapped her fingers. "Under the kitchen sink." Lisa smiled at Hayden.

Hayden chimed in again, "Please, give me back some of my fun tonight, Lisa."

"On one condition," Lisa said.

"*What* condition?" Hayden whined, dragging the word "what" into several syllables and slapping his knee with his free hand.

Oh my gosh, Hayden. Playfully, I swatted his arm, giggling. For a moment, he'd drifted back into the cute little boy with needy big eyes, like the ones I first met in this room.

"I want you to complete the whole activity—writing and all," Lisa replied.

"You mean 'Bittersweet Busters'? Where we write down grief thoughts or goals before we smash the plate, right?" Hayden asked.

Lisa nodded.

Groaning, Hayden stood up while throwing Lisa an eye roll.

"Well?" Lisa asked.

After throwing his hands in the air, surrendering, he said, "Fine." Then, bringing those same semi-angry hands down, he rubbed his palms together with a grin plastered on his face. "Let's go slam dishes then, everyone." Hayden's words and behaviors reminded me of a cross between his father, Gene, and my Aunt Jolene. He had us all chuckling.

Lisa motioned for us to go by pointing to the door. With her hand on Hayden's shoulder, she reminded him, "Remember, part of the process is writing down what you want to release. Or a goal you wish to achieve regarding your grief before tossing the dish. You're committed?"

"Yes, I'm committed, and I know the rules, *Lisa*," Hayden replied in a sassy tone with an eye roll. How he enunciated Lisa made me wonder if he nearly slipped and called her something else.

Part of me wanted to scream the words trapped in my head. *Just get it over with, you two! Call her Mom already! And, yes, Lisa, it's okay that you boss Hayden around a bit extra like you might your own son!*

After Lisa passed out the plain white dinner plates and Sharpie markers, we spread out to write down a bulleted listing of goals or issues.

"Do one with us, Lisa," Hayden said, taking her the last plate. Then, out of the corner of my eye, I caught their little side-hug.

Hayden returned to my side, placing a kiss on my cheek. I pivoted, leaning into him for a hug and a quick kiss. "Is it okay if I read what you're writing, or do you need privacy?" Hayden asked.

"I'll share if you will."

Standing with his chin on my shoulder, Hayden replied, "Deal."

We worked for a few more minutes. Then, we agreed to share a few highlights about what we wrote before putting on the safety eyewear and throwing the plates. While we'd written our items, Lisa had hurried to set up the large storage bin on the back porch stoop for us to aim at. If we missed, no one would get hurt before it could get cleaned up in the daylight.

"Gretchen or Hayden, do one of you want to go first and show Miles and Kelsey how we do this?" Lisa asked.

Hayden held his plate with a death grip, bouncing from foot to foot. "I'm anxious to go, but I'll let Gretchen step up to the porch first."

I smiled. "Thanks, Hayden. I can see your excitement."

Everyone giggled.

Here's what I wrote:

Gretchen's Plate:

- ✓ Be more thankful for my peaceful life with Dad.
- ✓ Realize the word "Sweetie" isn't such a bad thing.
- ✓ Find positive ways to overcome jealous rages toward people who have two parents.
- ✓ Accept help and love.
- ✓ Connect with people with less anxiety and without fear of rejection.
- ✓ I love and miss you, Mom.

My plate erupted like lava, and everyone cheered. Ironically, after exclaiming what bothered me and listening to the sounds of hundreds of jagged pieces as they fell away made, I felt less broken.

Hayden's Plate:

- ✓ Learn from mistakes.
- ✓ Resist jumping into physical fights as a reaction to bullying.

- ✓ Continue learning ways to release pain and anger in positive ways.
- ✓ Don't shut people out without a chance.
- ✓ Communicate with Dad and others better.
- ✓ Lessen my fear of loving my brothers and reconnect.
- ✓ Love those who love me.
- ✓ Keep trying to visit Mom's grave (ask her for signs).
- ✓ Love & Miss ya, Ma.

After Hayden's toss, the grief center sounded like a mini sports stadium as Hayden and Miles whooped, clapped, and did some weird chest bumps. I loved every minute of seeing Hayden's full-on smile. Lisa had her camera aimed and ready. She captured Miles and Hayden in a moment of glory, feet off the ground and their shiny teeth glowing.

After Kelsey put on the eye protection and began telling us about her plate, I wondered if our moms or dads had survived, would our lives be different? Would each of us have a slightly different take on the world? For instance, might Hayden have acted more outgoing, like this version of himself tonight? Or me—would I have just fit in as a regular girl at school? Would Kelsey still fear flashing red lights and driving? And Miles and Mia—would the world have offered them something a little easier, artsier, and kinder without layers of guilt?

But the reality is that we still deserve extraordinary lives as surviving children. We continue fighting to live decent lives despite the circumstances of grief. Thankfully, we appeared to be the right fit to help each other. And we owed no one an apology for this.

Kelsey's Plate:
- ✓ Help Dad, but understand I'm not my sibling's mother.
- ✓ Continue to remember the car accident wasn't my fault.
- ✓ Find positive ways to release the guilt.
- ✓ Let go of my fears of driving.
- ✓ Asking for assistance for my family is okay.
- ✓ I should be allowed hobbies like marching band without fear and guilt.
- ✓ Loving and laughing are acceptable after a loss.
- ✓ I love you, Mom, and I miss you every single day.

After Kelsey smashed her grief plate filled with the grievances of fear and guilt into pieces, we high-fived her. Then, as four sets of hands flew in the air to meet one another in victory, Lisa caught the very second on film.

Miles held his plate with white knuckles as his hands shook. Sharing such an emotionally charged moment choked him up, and he scoffed.

Hayden said, "Amen, buddy!" making Miles grin after his fourth bullet point.

After that, Miles still read each of his items with all the emotional ups and downs he needed while relaxing his grip.

Miles's Plate:
- ✓ I need to be patient with myself.
- ✓ Dad's suicide wasn't my fault—but I must learn to believe it.
- ✓ I can't control other people or save the world.
- ✓ I'm allowed to be happy sometimes without feeling guilty about it.
- ✓ I deserve to keep my musical talents going, so I'll play on!
- ✓ Friendships and love matter and I deserve them.
- ✓ It's okay to get help; it doesn't make me weak.
- ✓ I'm angry at you, Dad, but I do love and miss you.

Oh my gosh! Once Miles's sadness blasted into the storage bin into slivers, he turned around, colliding his mouth with Kelsey's.

Happily, I gasped.

"I knew it," Hayden shouted before laughing.

Miles shrugged with a smirk.

"Remember, this is not the Dating Game," Lisa said, smiling and pointing with her hand on her hip.

While Lisa asked for help finding her marker, she chatted with Kelsey and me, so Hayden thought no one could hear him. Then, he whispered to Miles, "Mia told Gretchen and me earlier that she thought you and Kelsey were banging cymbals."

Miles died laughing. "That poor girl seemed so messed up tonight. She even dressed a *little less Mia*." Glancing over, I noticed Miles talking with his hands; his rounded palms in front of his chest gave a lot away. Then, if I'm not mistaken, he said, "I mean, we all got a nice view of some cleavage, but I didn't need to know she had on a black lace bra under her cream-colored sweater."

"Yep," Hayden said. "She kept offering to show me more or give me a peek at her stomach. Very awkward."

Miles chuckled lightly, trying to talk in a hushed tone that still carried. "Dude, she desired to show you more than her stomach. She'd have given you a look at anything tonight."

From a slight distance, I hear a scoff. "Shh. Yeah, probably, but I'm not interested in that, man. Let's just hope Mia's okay." Hayden turned in my direction.

Clearing my throat, I gave Hayden a wide-eyed smirk.

He shrugged. "I love you," he mouthed.

Retrieving her plate, Lisa walked with Kelsey and me back to the guys. "Okay, I'm ready to hurl this piece of china. Considering the events encountered earlier tonight, you made the night a success for my first Mardi Gras party. I'm proud of each of you. We found a way to turn the night around." Lisa swallowed hard. "You know, the words on your plates aren't much different than mine."

Lisa's Plate:

- ✓ I can't fix every heart, even if I want to.
- ✓ It's not my fault if someone refuses help.
- ✓ Grief feels like an everlasting good-bye. So, I find new ways to bid farewell to Mom and Dad. Because I miss you that much.
- ✓ Love appears to be worth the risk of loss, but I still get scared.
- ✓ I need to allow myself to let go of some current roadblocks and face new adventures.

We had a quick ending group session before we cleaned up and left for the night.

"What common themes did you notice tonight with the activity?" Lisa asked.

"I think almost all of us used the words fault, guilt, and fear," Miles answered first.

We nodded.

"What else?" Lisa asked.

"We cheered for each other?" Hayden said in an unsure tone.

"Yes, that's an excellent answer," Lisa replied.

I jumped in. "I think we also all used the word love."

Lisa's hand went to her signature place—over her heart. Kelsey's hands also mirrored Lisa, and she smiled.

Lisa pulled her hand down, saying, "As a final comment, since we are talking about love, I want to send you home with all the sweet and spicy leftovers for your families to try. Also, please keep Mia and her grandmother in your thoughts."

A valuable lesson came from Mia too. Humans deny themselves many things. Sometimes they spend too much time worrying or wasting too much time living in fear. Rejecting love when offered can sometimes lead to the point of self-hatred and harm, but as the saying goes, do humans practice what they preach or think?

Dear Mom,

I have a quick PS to share about the Mardi Gras party story. We salvaged the night with the plate activity. So, I wrote a short poem to show Lisa and Doctor Han about the experience. If I thought Kelsey or Miles wouldn't think I was too silly, I'd ask them to put the words to music and see what we come up with. But unfortunately, asking for help isn't my specialty. So, maybe I'll start with Hayden and see what he thinks. When I read it, I heard the words as a song—something a tad slower but similar to the tune of "Wake Me Up" by Avicii comes to mind. But then, it dawned on me you have no idea who that artist is. Gosh, anyway, I wish I had some musical abilities.

Standing alone, feeling broken.
Our lives and dreams were shattered.
So, to the world, we shouted words left unspoken.
And love pieced back together what mattered . . .
    most.

GRETCHEN

Chapter Twenty-Nine

Dear Mom,
Monday, Early March Madness,

Blasting over the Summerfort High School loudspeaker spewed the rah-rah voice of Gabby. "Gretchen Gardener, please report to the counselor's office."

My name echoed off the walls in Mr. Porter's history class. A few desks behind me, Thomas Sharp, with some posse members, muttered crap about me. But all I heard was "Ah, Little Red Riding Hood, your new mommy wants you," which made me want to shit myself. Did Gabby think conducting official business with a freaking megaphone would make us less of a target? Why didn't she privately come to get me? No, scratch that. I understood. The look of favoritism. I thought about screaming, "Fuck off, Thomas!" before thinking better of it. Because even to me, it sounded like my new mommy calling me out for a lecture.

Mr. Porter stood at the front of the room with a wide-eyed look, gripping his laser pointer, almost like pleading with me to heed Gabby's warning to go.

Instead of completing the task of cursing at Thomas, I threw him and his posse a few evil glares. I tossed my book into my backpack. A part of me still dreamed of running back to flip Sharp's desk. But, then, I'd finish my tirade against him while Thomas lay piled on the concrete. *By the way, you might tell your fake-ass girlfriend that she needs to cover her tits in English.* But there I stood, my heart racing, with naked fingers shaky and gnarled, too dazed to say anything. *WTFDD, Gabby? What could you possibly want from me during school hours? Humiliation? Now I understood Hayden's issues with Gene and Lisa dating. Gabby and Lisa—the new FBI agents, are spying on us now—and have access to us everywhere we go.*

Next, Mr. Porter waved me on with his laser point as we shared another wide-eyed look of desperation as I slinked out of his classroom. Finally, I escaped just as Mr. Porter raised his voice, redirecting the class to the world map as the Thomas Sharp wannabes continued to snigger at my expense. A daily count of the COVID-19 cases added up on the board and to Mr. Porter's United States map. Those numbers also made kids laugh at him. But not me. If this virus found its way into the United States, what would stop it from finding Summerfort?

"Stop trying to scare us, Mr. Porter" were the last words to funnel through my ringing ears.

On the way to Gabby's office, I wanted to text Hayden but knew he had PE and probably couldn't answer. Dad may not know, either. Plus, if I'm in trouble, I'm not interested in involving Mr. Happenstance with his lover. Ew, the awkwardness of it all. This could be minor. I wished I'd worn gloves to bury my hands. Before even knocking at Gabby's office door, my fingers automatically throbbed. After a quick assessment, I believed they only looked cold. Or maybe windburned like someone who'd spent time creating a snowman or had performed heavy-duty battling in a snowball fight. The trouble with those stories—the town of Summerfort hasn't seen much more than a few flurries. So, no significant winter weather as a way to blame my problems away. Perhaps too much cleaner at the vet clinic.

Gabby swung open her door. Did she catch me staring at my unpolished, puffy fingertips? I needed more time.

"Gretchen, there you are."

I smiled, tucking my hands into my pockets, slipping by her to go inside her tiny office.

"Grab a chair by my desk. I'll gather the paperwork I want to tell you about. I seem to forget to bring it to your house, so I put it on my to-do list."

My heart took off out of whack, whooshing in my ears. This paperwork business sounded like a setup. Gabby leaned over her desk, riffling and riffling through stacks of shittle-stick nonsense.

"I can come back another time, Gabby."

"Oh, no. It's here. I promise."

Promises make me uneasy. They get broken and sometimes bend to lies. A sweat bead trickled down my back. The more I tried to consider anything else except my hands, the more they ached. Every fingertip contained a pounding heartbeat. Forced against the heaviness of my denim jeans, my hands altered into detainees.

Finally, yet too soon, Gabby waved a stack of documents in front of us as she sat across from me.

"What are those?" I hoped I didn't appear sweaty-faced and red since my face burned. I thought I might hurl.

"Your dad authorized me to share the **G Santos Animal Grant** forms with you. He told me you expressed an interest in learning more about them."

G Santos? The frame Hayden and I had knocked down at the vet clinic. Before I knew what I was doing, I pointed. "You're G Santos? My mother, Gwen Gardener, wanted to earn money from you. But now you're with her husband?" I said, shaking my head as I blinked away confusion as my eyes ping-ponged from point A to point B. First, from the name G Santos G (Gabrielle Santos Garcia) at the top of the page. Second, down to the fill-in-the-blank sections on the bottom. Gabby chose to ignore my Happenstance slam against her and Dad.

Instead, she said, "It's from my mom and dad's trust. Every year, I set aside a small portion for animal rights in their honor. It's only a coincidence that I came to know your father. The grant has nothing to do with our relationship."

Gabby pushed the papers for me to read. "Please, look over them. These will just be a guide to help you fill out the forms for his upcoming grants. I thought I'd show you how it works."

It's like Gabby rolled out a sticky fly trap. I'm trapped with nowhere for my hands or me to buzz off. So, I hauled my shaky hands over the papers and glanced.

"If you're in a relationship, does it make it a conflict of interest for my dad to win?" After I asked, holding the papers seemed cringy. *My dad's Happenstance girlfriend would help carry on my mother's legacy. Was that honorable or tacky?*

"What a great question, Gretchen. My grant is small in comparison to most. And it's limited to our area. Over the years, my funds have declined. So, I'm not offering one this year. I only wanted to offer the forms as a guideline to teach you. If you let me, I can help you carry out your mom's legacy with animals. Maybe I could show you how to conduct research for new grant opportunities."

In an awkward silence, we looked at one another for what seemed like forever. Then, accidentally, I slid my thumb over my sore fingertips. Okay. Maybe I even winced. Gabby carefully brushed my arm, gesturing to my swollen hands.

Gabby swallowed. "Please tell me how I should help you, Gretchen. Because I can't continue buying fingernail polish kits if it leads to issues. I only wanted them to make you happy. But I can't condone you hurting yourself."

My vision blurred. *Oh, freaking Hayden.* "Who told you?" I crammed my hands back into my jeans.

"You just did, sweetie. I saw it for myself. You confirmed my worries at the door. I admitted to myself that you changed out the Color Street polishes too often. It concerned me. At first, I assumed you didn't like them. But then I looked closer, realizing that didn't quite make sense, but I didn't understand that until I saw your hands up closer."

Gabby paused, scooting her chair closer to me. "Talk to me. Let it all out because I need to understand."

For a moment, I hung my head. Tears floated on the edge of my eyelids. Too many thoughts rattled in my brain. *Why can't I be normal? Is this what it feels like to have a mother? To sit under investigation. To embarrass her? To break her heart? But I knew what it felt like to have people care—a boyfriend willing to risk our relationship to help me tell the one person I needed to.* My hands sprang from my pockets, swaying then wringing into fists. Emotionally my hands facilitated me by spilling the tea.

"Fine." I cried, placing my wiggling fingers on the desk for display. "I love them too much, okay? But I hate them too. Because I end up obsessing over and over with words and images. Things like not remembering what color polish *my mom* wore. One minute I admired all the sparkle. Then, my urge to eliminate the color took over the next minute. It's all from guilt, I guess." I leaned back in my chair, taking a calming breath. "I wanted to experience these kinds of things with *my mom*." A hot, fat tear stung as it rolled down my face.

"I'm sorry you went through those roller-coaster emotions. So, Gretchen, what I hear you saying is that the nail polish triggered some intrusive OCD thoughts and actions?"

I nodded with more hot tears streaming.

"I can relate to grief and how it guilts us at times. For example, we deny ourselves the right to celebrate life. Or the privilege to love. Because grief puts us in these confrontations between happiness and sadness. And I understand that everyone goes through pain in different ways."

"Yeah, but look at you. You're polished. Now, look at me. You've never made a mental fool of yourself because you missed your mom. You didn't hoard days-of-the-week underwear your mom bought you or scrub your nails raw."

Gabby puffed out a breath as if keeping her secrets sacred. "I've struggled plenty, sweetie. You only know the adult version of Gabby. I still have sad days. But, Gretchen, I am looking at you. And you're not a mental fool. You have the right to miss your mom. But if you have questions about her, it's acceptable to ask your dad. Explore that love. Remember, your OCD is manageable. From what you're telling me, you're willing to share this information with your dad and Dr. Han?"

Again, I only nodded.

Gabby's mouth turned up on one side. "Let's table my grief woes for another day. But just know, I harbor plenty," she said on a promising note. She shuffled the grant papers into a neat pile, smiling. "Oops." She pulled the blank page back from the stack. At the top, it read *Seeking Adoption or Foster Care Families.* "It goes into another pile," Gabby said, turning the paper face down. "Principal Marshall asked me to rearrange some things recently. As a result, some of my files are messier than usual. Sorry about that."

"That's okay. Anyway, do you swear to tell me more about your past and share more pictures?"

Gabby crossed her heart. "Say, Gretchen, do you think your dad might be able to help us answer some of *your* questions? For example, he may know what color polish your mom liked. Or he may know of photographs showing her hands to help you remember that part of her. And, if so, do you think you'd enjoy the nails again in the future?"

My chin quivered at the possibility and at how simple Gabby made my solution sound. "Yeah, maybe. But I'm so embarrassed about this." I held my hands up. "I wish my OCD would disappear. I hate it." With throbbing fingers, I covered my wrinkled-up chin and foolish face.

"Your dad loves you. He's proud of you for agreeing to talk about the situation. Do you want me to get additional help from Dr. Han right now?"

I wiped the corners of my eyes. "No, I'll ask Dr. Han what else I should do. It made a big difference already to get it out in the open with you."

"I'm so glad, Gretchen. Are you willing to go along with my recommendation to your dad that he monitor your access to the fingernail polish remover?"

"Are you kidding?"

Gabby's head cocked, and she had the nerve to just stare.

My voice cracked. "Why does being motherless make me feel like a loser?"

"Maybe it's not you who's the loser, Gretchen. Tell me what you're thinking—sweetie. Think beyond your grief. What's holding you back? You're not a loser. What are you so *afraid of losing*?"

"I don't know." I rested my elbows on her desk, glaring.

"Sure, you do." She said, so matter a fact. But then, this time, she had the nerve to ask, "Are you scared of me?"

"Yes." I fixed my gaze downward.

"Why?"

I shrugged.

Gabby rolled her chair next to me. Beneath her satiny blouse, I swear I inhaled and exhaled the scent of Baby Powder Secret deodorant. Now, that's how close she sat before the interrogation/mini-lecture techniques got underway and under my skin.

"Have I done something wrong to make you believe I'm unkind or untrustworthy? Or do I have any big red flags?" She leaned into me in what came across as a side-hug-ready stance. But then she withheld by straightening.

Again, I shook my head.

Gabby dragged her hair into a makeshift ponytail before flipping it free over her shoulder.

"What, Gretchen? Since we're at school, forgive my language. But why is your nose scrunched in anger as if you've just smelled a pile of shit?"

First, I committed not to bug my eyes, but I chuckled at Gabby's cursing. But she didn't laugh with me.

Okay, I supposed we were squabbling now.

So, I cleared my throat. "Gabby, don't you agree that taking away my fingernail stash seems *un-nec-es-sa-ry*." I made sure I pronounced every syllable of unnecessary for clarity. My eyes bugged out, I'm afraid.

Gabby twisted in her seat before flipping her hair (again) over her shoulder. "Not. When. You. Care. About. Someone. Gretchen." Gabby played dirty and planned to beat me in this game. Every word said was pointed at me word by word. Each one slammed into me.

Then we sat huffing, arms crossed, staring at the wall. Both of us were on mute for several seconds.

Finally, I asked, "Gabby, do you think I'll ever get over some of my fears? Like the ones I have about letting people care about me?"

Gabby slanted her head, studying me. One side of her mouth bent into a grin. "May I use myself as an example, Gretchen?"

"Sure," I replied, blowing out a raspberry. We scooted our chairs until we sat face-to-face again.

"Gretchen, my aunt can never take the place of my mom. But, sweetie, I wasted too much time throwing that in my aunt's face. I regret a lot of things I did and said years ago. Still, she stood by me. Forgiveness put us back together, and I'm thankful for that. My aunt evolved into my best friend. Finally, I realized the universe gifted me a daily phone call that I'd been missing. Finally, I had someone willing to show up for me on holidays, at school events, or just to go shopping. But it took time. Gretchen, I often felt guilty because I was too scared to trust love. Plus, I worried. What if she might die on me too? I wasn't sure if love was worth my time. But slowly, I started to take risks. And I listened. That's when I learned my aunt missed my mom too. She craved friendships as much as I did."

Inside, I sensed some kind of creepy *déjà vu*. My stomach dropped with a pins-and-needles vibe. I nearly blurted out, "Stop reading my mind, Gabby."

My fingers were all but forgotten now because my guts churned. I needed to jump out of this *Freaky Friday* moment, the Gabby roller coaster. Otherwise, I saw my future self standing in line with a lifetime supply of tokens. And every time I needed Gabby, I would reach into my overstuffed pockets, giving one token away in exchange for advice. Would this function like a *Freaky Friday* Friendship Ride? If so, I bet I'd hang upside down through loopy emotions.

A single tear slid down my face. "Gabby, are you saying you'd like to be my friend?"

Gabby playfully patted my wrist, carefully avoiding my painful hand. Then, with a smirk, she said, "Sweetie, I'm going to use a famous Hayden line . . . well, duh."

HAYDEN

Chapter Thirty

Dear Mom,
March Madness

Thomas Sharp reappeared, instigating freaking chaos. During baseball practice, he hurled insults nonstop about one of Mr. Porter's current lesson plans. The ass-jerk mocked Mr. Porter and his girl-friend, Lilly, at the same time. On the pitcher's mound, he pretended to cheer: "N-I-M-B-Y, not in my backyard," with his glove slung on his hip. He kicked up dirt, twirling. It won him some laughs. Hidden in my glove, my middle finger saluted him.

Later, in the locker room, I overheard Sharp alerting a few of the guys in a hushed tone, "Mr. P's shit talk about viruses is moving towards extinc-tion too." The guys chuckled. So, I glared. Sharp hitched his thumb at me to get out, saying, "This don't concern you, Tucker." My blood boiled as always around him, but I left before I punched him in the face again.

At first, I wanted to tell Gretchen, but I didn't want to burden her with something she couldn't fix. However, Mr. Porter deserved respect. His lessons deal with honesty about caring for what happens worldwide. Because we are interdependent—we need others for food. We share our air and oceans. Now, we must deal collectively with this healthcare crisis.

My fingers wound so tightly into a fist. It took so much strength not to pop Thomas. In my head, I repeated, "Fuck it—he's not worth it," half my mantra and half Gretchen's.

So, an idea to help came to me after remembering Gabby's announcement calling Gretchen to her office this morning. First, I'd ask Gabby if my sports physical on file needed updating. Then maybe I could get results on this Sharp and Porter situation. And other stuff. Unfortunately, the school day had ended, but I got lucky to still find Gabby in her office, packing up before heading home.

"Hayden, come on in. What's up with the frown? You okay?"

I waved my hand in a so-so motion.

"Tell me what brings you in," Gabby said, easing the door almost closed for more privacy.

After flopping down in the chair, I bypassed my story about my sports form. Instead, I surprised myself by speaking right out about things. "That ass-jerk Thomas Sharp made fun of Mr. Porter and

Lilly today at practice." I shook my head. "Wow, I can't believe I'm defending Lilly."

Gabby gave me a closed-mouth smile. "Go on, Hayden"

"Well, Sharp pretended to cheer in Lilly's voice, spelling out some things from our current lessons about global society."

"Can you demonstrate what Thomas said and did to the best of your ability?"

"Listen, Gabby, I'm not a cheerleader. Well, duh. You know that."

Gabby threw her hair over her shoulder and smiled.

In horror, I found my hands drawn in the air. "Gabby, this feels like the YMCA, but Thomas went N-I-M-B-Y, not in my backyard." I performed the cheer with very little vim or vigor.

"Thank you, Hayden." Gabby bit her lip, looking like she had to giggle. I don't know. Maybe she had freaking flashbacks to stupid Christmas. Or thoughts of seeing John in his weird-ass hot pants.

So, I just kept on talking, visualizing Thomas's smug face. "But what really pissed me off happened in the locker room." I positioned my fist on Gabby's desk.

Gabby sat with model posture again, offering complete eye contact. "It's safe to continue your story, Hayden."

"It sounded like Thomas threatened to try and get Mr. Porter fired or something because Mr.

Porter's been lecturing about how serious that virus is in places. Then, just a few minutes ago, while in the locker room, Sharp told me it didn't concern me, so I left. I didn't know what to do. So, I thought since you worked with the school, you could investigate to get him help."

"Hayden, I'll share your concerns. Thank you for your bravery. It's not easy to stick up for someone in the face of injustice. I appreciate that you even express concern about Lilly's well-being."

"Gabby?"

"Yes, Hayden?"

"Speaking of others, I heard you 'shouting' over the intercom this morning for Gretchen." I grinned because I used air quotes when I said shouting. Then, after dropping my hands on the desk, I added, "I know you can't say much, but please say she told you about her recent events."

Waiting for confirmation from Gabby, my legs turned to jello. After I spoke, I couldn't take back what I'd said, but I wasn't a tattletale if I found a way to offer the best for someone I loved. Finally, I puffed out a breath, flexing my fingers.

"So, now that we're in person, explain what you mean by events, Hayden."

My jaw clenched. "Gabby," I ground out her name. "I know, you know. The OCD. Did you witness her latest issue? I want her to be okay. She kept saying she had things under control." Finally, I looked Gabby in the eye for reassurance, rambling instead of waiting for it. "Should I have done something sooner? I only knew about one time until I saw her this morning. Please tell me how to help her."

"You absolutely did the right thing. Gretchen is very loved, Hayden. Keep supporting her. Unfortunately, sweetie, I can't divulge what I talk about with other students. But with her family, friends, and professional help, she should be okay. You did a great job talking to me about Mr. Porter and Gretchen. It takes a lot of courage to reach out for help on someone's behalf."

Of course, Gabby offered me a damn Kleenex from her designer box with Boston Terriers. I choked up some but managed to speak. "I knew when I texted you this morning to please find a way to check on Gretchen, you'd figure it out. You'd have my back. Thanks."

"Sometimes, sweetie, we must make tough decisions for the people we love most." Gabby patted the top of my hand.

This conversation with Gabby reminded me of my early days with Lisa. I'd forgotten how pissed I used to get at her for making me suffer all these emotions. Thank God for Gabby. Good grief, though. Women act difficult. Ma, are the women in my life always going to make life confusing?

Leaving her office, I noticed a frame on the wall. In fancy scrolling letters, G Santos Garcia screamed out at me. My brow raised as I glanced at Gabby. "You're G Santos? As in the animal grant G Santos G?"

"Guilty. Or should I say 'surprise'?" Gabby said, her hands in the air with a crooked grin.

A freaking mystery solved. So, Gretchen doesn't get suspicious of me hanging out with Gabby, I needed to keep the information on the down-low.

***

At home, Dad and I lounged in the den while Miss Spicy Boots snoozed on the back of the couch. We ordered an extra-large thin-crust pepperoni pizza before tuning in to ESPN with plans to watch for the entire night. In Oklahoma City, the Thunder were going to take on the visiting Utah Jazz.

But breaking news flashed across the screen before the tip-off. The announcer said, "Teams were sent back to the locker rooms while intended halftime recording artist Frankie J performed for the crowd at Chesapeake Energy Arena. This provided an opportunity to make decisions about what to tell the crowd." At 8:39 p.m., the stadium's announcer told everyone to leave because the game had been called off and added, "We are all safe— please drive home safely, and good night, fans."

Twenty minutes later, the NBA suspended the season until further notice because players officially had tested positive for coronavirus.

Dad raised an eyebrow, exchanging side-eyed looks of disbelief with me. And we even switched channels to prove we'd heard correctly.

Then John texted Dad.

John: Until further notice? This must be serious. What's next?

The pings on Dad's phone kept arriving. Dad ran his hands down his face. He'd pick up his phone, skimming the messages before putting it face down on the couch between us. I caught glimpses of Cole and Drew's names.

Instead of answering texts or talking to me, Dad stared at the TV in a trance. It disturbed me that the adults around me were freaking out. But the stress was hitting me too. I needed to make Dad consider something.

I turned to face him. "Hey, Dad, if pro NBA players can't play ball, what makes high school sports safe?"

"Good question. From my limited understanding, it might be based on your age and virus exposure. Bigger cities and whatnot. But if you ever feel sick or unsafe—"

"Okay," I interrupted Dad.

Gretchen must've been on the same wavelength because she texted:

Gretchen: WTFDD! NBA? So, what's going to happen next? I love you.

Hayden: I know. Weird AF. I love you, too.

Even though Gretchen and I don't share the same Mr. Porter class, she made me love social studies after studying together. Mr. Porter's United States map flashed in my mind's eye. There were so many what-ifs to consider. Would every state get infected? Could this virus reach our weird little town? Not out here—in the middle of nowhere, right? Again, something didn't make sense. Why did a twenty-something pro player who contracted this disease shut down an entire sport? But could I still safely attend school and shoot hoops? Is this logical, Mom?

Dad's phone rang, jolting him out of his TV stupor. But unfortunately, I heard only his side of the convo with Lisa. At first, his voice sounded tired. He communicated like someone with chronic insomnia, yawning at the end of every sentence. Lisa should've hung up on him. But after a few minutes, he beamed in my direction as if I were a coconspirator to something I knew nothing about.

He repeated to Lisa a word that sounded like kimchi and said, "Great idea, Lisa." Dad got animated, cough-chuckling. Gross. Because then came the scratching of his whiskers. Now I wanted to hang up on both of them. Dad's enthusiasm made my eyes twitch.

PS Ma, I wish you were here because I'm uneasy about the world. Sadly, the sports news isn't getting better. Like dominos, the dots on our Cozi app keep falling off the calendar. For a sports fan, this confusing disease has turned eerie.

March 12—NHL suspended the season. As a result, the PGA will not play the Masters. In addition, the NCAA will no longer have any basketball tournaments. MLB will not hold spring training for baseball players.

March 13—The Boston Marathon has been postponed.

Weird. Now, I wonder what's in store from **March 23–27** for my Summerfort High School Spring Break.

PSS Grandma invited me to fly to Florida anytime since we've talked a bit more, even if only in quick conversations. I still need to find a way to tell Gretchen I broke the ice with Grandma, but I'm figuring out a plan. Unfortunately, the timing gets in the way, but then the secrets keep adding up. . . .

Now the whole Gabby issue with Gretchen lingers. For now, Gretchen may remain jealous of Lisa. To me, Gabby acted pretty cool about everything. I, for one, think Gretchen's lucky. Gabby's got game. Soon, instead of seeing two separate playing fields, as in Gabby versus Lisa, maybe Gretchen will see we are more than even. She will also learn that Gabby and Lisa operate together as a team.

Loving someone gets messy, I realized. You don't mean to keep secrets. You don't mean to tattle on them. But I hope in both cases, it's understood my level of love for Gretchen comes from a place of protection. Over and over, I kept reminding myself that reaching out to Gabby was in Gretchen's best interest. At night, I bullied myself for being an ass-jerk for not getting John the first time I witnessed an incident at the vet clinic. But I "trusted" her. I listened to my girlfriend, who told me she had everything under control. I hope she's not lying. I hope we are going to make it. Nothing feels very stable when everything in our world continues to fall away. But I know one thing: my love for Gretchen is stronger than my fear and pain. And yet, I'd take having her walk away from me angry if it meant she chose her health. My brain keeps firing "help" signals to my heart. Ma, I don't know what else to do. Two overly used and horrible expressions that sum up my love life right now: I'm just hurrying up and waiting for the shit to hit the fan.

Other Spring Break News: Miles and Kelsey discussed double-dating with Gretchen and me in Branson to ride the Ferris wheel and coasters.

God forbid I'll eat kimchi with the canoodle-doodle Kumbaya duo.

Chapter Thirty-One

Dear Mom,
Freaky Friday, March 13

The whole wide world is in disarray, along with my calendar. I can't keep up with the cancellations. Hayden invited me to watch some sporting events at his house. But now they've ended entire seasons due to the coronavirus.

Then, I overheard Gabby's conversation with Dad from the top of the staircase. "Principal Marshall told me to begin packing my essential papers today. He said, 'Start gathering items to work from home. I think it's just a matter of time.'"

Dad whispered something soothing back to her.

I ran to my room to FaceTime Hayden.

He answered. When I didn't speak, he asked, "Gretch, are you okay? Why are you crying? Do you need me to call for help?" Hayden paced in his room. "Gretchen, what the hell is going on? Please sit down. Take a deep breath. Look at me and talk. Do you need me to call for help?"

I shook my head. Finally, I flopped down on my bed. I managed a breath. "No, I don't need help. It's nothing too bad like that. I've just had a couple of awful days lately. I should've told you before now. But I heard Gabby say something I needed to share with someone before turning it into something ugly. But it's probably a secret that I shouldn't tell."

Hayden propped himself against the pillows on his bed. "That's what I'm here for. I'm glad you called me. What did Gabby say?" Hayden rubbed his forehead. He cleared his throat and repeated, "Now, what did Gabby say?"

I wiped my tears on my hoodie.

Then, Hayden cut in with humor. "Wait." He squinted as close as possible to the phone. "Did you just put tears and boogies on the Summerfort Eagles football hoodie you stole from me?"

We both giggled for a solid minute. And it felt so good.

"I needed a good laugh, Hayden."

He smiled. "Okay, now, please tell me what Gabby said."

After clearing my throat, I said, "I'll paraphrase, but Principal Marshall told her to gather her stuff because she will probably work from home soon."

"As in, our school will close?"

I shrugged but added, "I think so."

"That's so weird. I don't know how to react or feel about this. Do you?"

I shook my head. "It's complicated. With OCD, I like stability in life. I like to know what's happening. My calendar stays planned. So, please be patient with me."

"Angel, of course. What can I do?"

I bit my lip so hard. "Listen, I suppose. You've always been a good listener."

Hayden smiled that smile showing me his dimple.

It made me tell more. "So, I confessed to Gabby about my nails the other day when she summoned me into her office." I cupped my hand, playfully giving a demo. "Do-to-ta-doo."

We chuckled.

"I'm the worst at making a drumroll sound."

"I meant to ask you about that day with Gabby, but we got sidetracked with everything. Life is so freaking weird." Hayden readjusted his pillows. "Do you want to share more about what you talked about, or is it too private?"

"No, I'll give you some fun facts and the short version." I smiled. "She had me come in to get grant paperwork."

"For what?"

I leaned close to the phone, blinking. "Hayden, she's G. Santos G as in Garcia—a combo of her parent's names. Her trust helps animals. How cool is that?"

"Oh my God, that's freaking amazing, Gretch. I'm glad you solved the mystery."

"What else did she chat about, *sweetie*?" Hayden asked, with a teasing undertone, but his eyebrows and mouth soon narrowed as he focused on me. I knew he cared most of all about this part.

"Yeah, she noticed my hands when I couldn't hide them. So, I told her. I described my guilt a little bit about the Color Street nails. She suggested I have Dad show me some pictures of Mom's hands, so I can see her nails and polish colors to remember her. By the end of our conversation, she used the example of her relationship with her aunt and how she wasn't trying to take her mom's place. But they were good friends, and maybe we could be too."

"That sounds promising, Gretchen," Hayden said as his eyes widened. That look of lightness he gave me made me realize how much he loved me. He wanted me to be happy and healthy.

"No. More like a traumatizing mom lecture, Hayden. But it ended well." I twirled my hair, smiling. "But now I get what you mean about having your personal life invaded by Lisa. So, when I heard Gabby announce my name, I wanted to jump out of Mr. Porter's classroom window."

"See, it's what they call both doom and blessing or whatever." Before I understood what Hayden was trying to say, he snapped his finger, correcting himself. "We have a situation that's both a blessing and a curse."

"Yes," I said. "Lisa and Gabby have similarities. They sometimes annoy us, but overall they care a lot about us."

Hayden threw his phone up in the air and shouted, "BOOM."

I laughed.

"You used to get so aggravated when I'd say that word."

He grabbed the phone, chuckling. "But the situation fit. Here's another BOOM. Meanwhile, as John and Gabby date, I recently overheard Dad and Lisa flirt-talking about kimchi. So, you're invited for dinner that night."

We died laughing.

Hayden can barely get out the words through his laughter. "They're so weird."

"BOOM," I said.

As we talked, we got a group text from Lisa for all the adults and kids from the Summerfort Grief Center.

Dear Teens,

I cordially invite you to the Summerfort Grief Center's first Teen Open House to experience a place to heal, hope, and belong. Friday, March 27, 2020. 6–9 p.m.

Gene popped his head into Hayden's room. "What-the-flippity-doodle are you two doing on a Friday night?"

"Nothing. Our event got canceled."

"That's lame. Shortcake put the phone down. We're coming to get you soon." Gene said, jokingly, in his most resounding southern-accented voice.

Playing along, I said, "Kumbaya, Hayden," blowing him a kiss, which he pretended to catch with his hand over his heart like Lisa.

We giggled.

Gene said, "That's it. I'll take you tonight. But afterward, you're both grounded."

We laughed even more.

Chapter Thirty-Two

Dear Ma
March Madness

What could go wrong on Friday the thirteenth? It's a bit maddening that "March Madness" used to be about basketball, but that's all been canceled due to a virus people seem to understand so little about.

Everywhere I turned, things around me weren't in place. So, tonight, Gretchen and I planned to order Chinese takeout and watch sports. She's not the level of sports fan I am, but she plays with Miss Spicy Boots and makes out with me during commercials. I'm not complaining. But I'm lost as to how to rearrange life right now.

Spontaneity doesn't come easy to me. Or to Gretchen with her OCD. The awkwardness left us sitting at home, confused about what we wanted to do. She freaked me out so much when she called.

For sure, I thought Gabby had blabbed somehow about my text. But, from what Gretchen said about their conversation, I gathered Gabby treated her like she wanted to be friends. She will make sure Gretchen stays healthy. I had to smile when Gretchen compared the incident to a lecture with a mother. I want that for her, for both of us.

"So, Mr. Don't Keep Secrets From Me. . . ." Dad said, waving a sizable golden package as I made my way downstairs before we went to pick Gretchen up that night.

I grabbed the envelope from Dad. "What is it?"

"Looks like it's from Florida, U.S.A. So, I'm guessing Grandma Suzi sent something out of the blue. Do you know anything about that, Hayden?"

"I didn't want to make you mad, Dad, but I've been contacting Grandma behind the scenes for a while now. She's helping me with Gretchen."

Dad motioned me to sit by him on the last step at the bottom of the staircase. "Buddy, I never meant to keep your grandparents from you. I'm so sorry if that's the attitude I'm giving you. There's so much confusing history. I lost a wife, versus they lost a child. But why should grief be a competition? But the emotional battles continue. What stays the same through it all is that we loved you and your mom. Because we share those things in common." Dad slung his arm around me. "Can I see what Grandma sent you?"

"Sure. It might just be for Gretchen, though."

After I tore into the oversize envelope, I dug inside. "Interesting. This part is actually for you, Dad." I passed him the extra-small note that's rare for Grandma. "Let's prepare for something funny. Read it aloud."

Dad flicked his fingers against a thick pale blue cardstock. On the outside, she'd simply written *Gene* with a thick black marker. After opening the envelope, Dad cleared his throat before he read:

Dear Gene,

After reading the two winning essays by Hayden, I know why you are considered a hero. Thank you for taking good care of my daughter. Please consider visiting Florida while Bill and I are still living.

Love, your mother-in-law always, Suzi

"Whew. Good God, she's no-nonsense to the core," Dad said, blinking up at the ceiling. I leaned into Dad to soak up the moment.

"Maybe we should get crazy enough to go. What do you think?"

"All right. Maybe a long weekend or an early summer trip." He smiled. "What else got stuffed into that envelope Grandma sent?"

"It's for Gretchen."

"Oh?"

"It makes Gretchen sad she doesn't have a grandma, so Grandma Suzi sent her a gift."

"Well, Sly Suzi and Huckleberry Hayden working together. Who would've ever guessed?" Dad asked, elbowing me, with a chuckle.

"Dad, you're so weird sometimes."

"Son, you're suddenly looking like you might use the envelope as a barf bag. Tell me why." Dad patted my back.

"Gretchen wanted me to call Grandma Suzi about one of Mom's recipe cards, but I refused. So, then, I kept it a secret from her that I got in touch with Grandma on Gretchen's behalf. So, now, I have this surprise." My hand held the golden lie of omission. "How do I fix this?"

"So, you have a *surprise* gift? If Gretchen loves the gesture as much as I think she will, she'll forgive you. She'll understand. Not all surprises need telling. You went out of your way to do something kind, to help her. You're not hurting her—"

"Thanks, Dad," I said. But then, dropping my head. I still had to convince myself about the hidden Gabby text. So, with Dad's logic, you're not hurting her. I allowed myself to breathe, knowing what I did had led to helping Gretchen.

We made our way to Branson.

"Fun idea, Gene. Thanks for driving us to the Branson Ferris Wheel," Gretchen said, craning her neck to look up at the neon lights.

"While you guys ride"—Gene hitched a thumb to another spinning neon sign boasting a red-outlined

462

ice cream cone—"I'll go stand in that incredibly long line. So, what will it be, Shortcake?"

"I believe it's chocolate-covered nuts over-loaded with peanut butter." Gretchen giggled. Dad looked at Gretchen and shook his head, grinning.

"Dad, I want that fudgy mint condition."

"You two make my guts and teeth hurt," Dad said, walking away.

Our line shifted. As we neared the Ferris wheel gondolas, a voice called out, "Heard it might've been you playing hide-and-seek in Garcia's office after practice the other night. So, I hope you listened and stayed the fuck out of the Porter situation. No need to involve the little prude beside you either. Hope you got all that, Tucker."

At that moment, hearing Thomas Sharp's mouth as we loaded the ride made us disoriented, like caged animals, unable to respond.

Beside me, Gretchen turned to stone.

In a rush, I captured a photo of Sharp waltzing away with some bodybuilder-type dude wearing a Branson letterman's jacket from a couple of years ago. So, he ran with the rivals in the older crowd. Should we ever need this information in the future, I wondered if Miles or Kelsey could help us identify him.

I bit my lip, listening to Gretchen beside me.

"What in the eff is Thomas talking about with you in Gabby's office? Is there any truth to it?"

Stuffing my phone in my pocket, I said, "During practice the other day, Thomas and some guys were bashing Mr. Porter and his teaching methods over this virus stuff. Then, in the locker room, Sharp sounded like he planned to try to cause Porter trouble. So, I saw Gabby sitting in her office after school and told her about it. I wanted to protect our teacher."

Gretchen stared at me.

I swear I could almost hear her brain linking secrets together in a timeline. *Damn.* Even though it was cool outside, and we wore jackets, sweat flowed. The enclosure created cagey emotions, but I knew I had to keep my shit together. Thankful I could still breathe, I leaned over, skimming Gretchen's lips. "It's a rule for this ride to be romantic," I whispered.

She only half-smiled and turned her face, offering her cheek. "Why didn't you tell me about any of this? You gave me nothing about Thomas, Mr. Porter, or Gabby?"

My hands were sweaty with remorse. After quickly swiping my palm across my knee, I reached out, wanting to touch Gretchen. Instead, she shied away from me, allowing me only a brush with her pinky. At this point, I knew I sucked at romantic confrontations. My heart squeezed. Already I felt like it might break if Gretch misunderstood me. But I managed to be honest, choking out, "I didn't want to overload you with anything else on the day Gabby called you into her office."

"Just include me in whatever happens. I'm supposed to be your girlfriend. I thought we supported each other when it came to Thomas. Plus, I also like Mr. Porter. And I'm starting to really like Gabby."

"I'm sorry, Gretchen. I thought I was doing the right thing by protecting you from unnecessary stress. I thought you had a lot going on with your nails. I planned on telling you, but I wanted to wait for better timing."

Gretchen shook her head. "Maybe you deserve a better girlfriend—one who doesn't have OCD or stupid thoughts. I think I stress you out too much."

"I want you to be my girlfriend."

Silent tears flowed from Gretchen as she leaned into me. Those few tears dried quickly. Gretchen reared up, glaring into my soul. "It's still very unclear to me whether or not you hung out in Gabby's office more than once the 'other day,'" Gretchen said, throwing rather violent air quotes around the "other day."

At the highest peak, the gondola stopped, allowing a couple of sets of passengers at the bottom to get on and off the ride. For a split second, I closed my eyes and sighed. Then, when I opened them, I said, "Wow. Look how pretty everything is from up here." I pointed out the twinkling blue-and-green lights. Again, I stretched out my hand for Gretchen. This time she caved. She even allowed me to kiss her.

"Well—?" she asked just as soon as the ride began rotating again.

"I promise you, I went to Gabby's office only once the other day. Besides, what are you trying to get at, Gretchen?"

She stared out at the gondola away from me as we sat in awkward silence.

"If you don't want to talk to me anymore—" I sighed. My heart hammered, and my lip quivered, but I had to go there. "If you don't want a boyfriend because you need time to heal, I'll back off. It will suck, but I'll return to being just your friend. But please talk to me. Tell me what to do. Say something. What do you need?"

She spun her head around. "You want to talk. Fine. Let's talk about how Gabby found out about my nails," Gretchen said, raising an octave.

"Duh, you told her when she gave you those grant papers." My tone of voice matched hers.

"That's all starting to seem odd. Gabby acted flustered," Gretchen said, glaring.

I shrugged.

"Hayden, did you say something to her to make her worry about me?"

As I answered, I focused on my Converse tennis shoe. My freaking shoelaces, like my life, were untied. "Now, that's possible. Yeah. Do you know why?" I glanced at Gretchen, whose face crumpled. "Because I've felt guilty and worried since you told me you had things under control with your nails. You lied. Because you didn't, Gretch."

I paused, shifting toward her, so I could pull her into me. Teary-eyed and confused, Gretchen's body went rigid. So, I added, "I should've gotten your dad the first time something happened at the vet clinic. Ever since it happened, I've regretted it. Because I love you. I should look out for you." I used my fist to swipe at my own angry, silent tear. "Gretch, I just believe people shouldn't throw those they love in the ditch to die alone. Discreetly, you find professional help when you have to. So, yes, I texted Gabby one day. 'Hey, will you check on Gretchen if you get a chance?' I had no idea you were going to get summoned via intercom. Nor did I think you would give Gabby a tell-all. That's all on you. I only wanted you to have an outlet. Sorry if it sounds like I'm gaslighting you. I sure don't mean it to. I wanted to help you. So, yes, I reached out to Gabby."

"Fine," Gretchen said with a deadpan expression.

"Fine? That's it?" I asked, shrugging.

"This ride's about over. It's ice cream time. We need to compartmentalize. Be brave in front of your dad."

"Be brave? What the fuck? You're making it sound like you're breaking up with me. Do you still want to at least be my friend? Please don't let an ass-jerk like Thomas Sharp come between us and win. Or the Gabby situation. That turned out to help you. Don't let it ruin a great relationship. I'm so confused. I didn't mean for any of it to be a secret. I only wanted the timing to work out better and for you to be okay. I love you that much."

Chapter Thirty-Three

Dear Mom,
March

What would you say if you could tell me about the most unexpected days of your life? Would it include the day you fell in love with Dad? The day I was born? Or did you know the moment you were dying?

Which life events made you laugh? Which ones made you cry? Which of them involved me in our short time together? Mother, I want to listen to your stories. I need to learn not to be so afraid. With my mother, I believe I'd laugh more, understand the world, and put myself out there to have more friends. Or at least be a better friend.

The calendar reminds me of our short times together, month after month, with each holiday spent from a little girl's perspective. My body and mind are growing up. But I just don't know about my heart.

Sometimes the concept of secrets and surprises evolved into a blur. For example, my heart shattered and mended at the same time recently.

Lisa called, saying Mia's grandma dropped off information at the Summerfort Grief Center. She left a note from Mia to give to me. The idea that Mia chose me seemed strange. I thought that girl despised me.

So, I asked Lisa, "How is Mia doing?"

"I can share that Mia's still in treatment and doing okay, according to Grandma. However, her letter may give you more information. I didn't read the note but opened and peeked inside to ensure it contained nothing harmful. I'll give you some privacy to read," Lisa said before leaving the room.

Hey Red,

Whenever you chitchatted about an animal clinic in your backyard, I wanted to believe in that kind of future for myself. I guess I never bothered to tell you how much I enjoy animals, especially dogs. Who knows? Maybe one day I can own a dog boarding and grooming place. Anyway, I wanted you to know that I'm willing to volunteerarly scoop turds with you. My volunteerarly doesn't look right, but whatevs. Also, I have Grandma, while you have a dad. Just think about it. If two people were looking to share what's missing in their lives . . . then us being friends sounds like it might just be legit.

~Mia~

PS Say hi to everyone and show them this copy of my pic.

Standing in awe, I grasped Mia's letter next to my chest. So perfectly Mia—like a freshly baked strawberry rhubarb pie. Still a tad flaky, with layers of bitterness gone, replaced with fruity sweetness. No one has ever come out and said to me, "Let's make a grief deal; let's share." Yet we all wished and thought about it. Like me. I want a mom. I want a grandma. Then Mia, with her attitude, does with a dose of "what's the big deal?" added in. Life can suck sometimes, so why aren't we all just hanging out and sharing? *I have Grandma, while you have a dad.* That line will always touch me.

Her approach worked so much better than mine with Hayden and his grandmother. Of course, it's best not to hoard the emotions of anger and jealousy. But I guess Mia and I aren't so different in that aspect—choosing to hide behind some of our hurts by self-easing the stress or pain. Each of us had some vice at some point. Gene was a workaholic, Hayden lived in silence, and Dad chose women and booze.

But Mia's the one who held the answer all along. She's the courageous one who asked for what she wanted and needed. I respected Mia's honesty in doing so. And for the way she looked at grief. And for the way she pushed me to view grief in a fresh new light—as a shared concept—with pinpoint precision.

When I first pulled Mia's picture from the envelope, I stared into the faces of ordinary people. Or the appearance of a young Mia and her mom before addiction. A thought invaded my mind. Maybe this is why Mia cherished this photo best. My knowledge of drug abuse and the opioid crisis emerging in the Ozarks because of them is limited. But because I have witnessed what it has done to Mia's life by taking both her parents, I'm willing to research, ask questions, and learn.

Judging by the frayed corners of the snapshot, my hands touched the same places Mia must've held onto a million times. I envisioned young Mia at Ha Ha Tonka State Park with her parents. In the photo, Mia's mother stood behind her, arms draping over Mia's eight-year-old shoulders. They both smiled, wearing matching sunglasses and fancy flip-flops with a poufy flower on their big toes as they leaned against the castle ruins of a window. The emptiness of the window acted as a faux picture frame. Yet the photo painted a world of happiness even in the black-and-white photo as their long summertime hair twirled in a breeze.

Knowing how the story turned out, I studied the photo repeatedly, trying to make sense of what had happened. But, Mom, I don't remember ever rooting for a little girl more in my life to own a castle all her own one day.

Hayden's words now haunted me. "Gretch, I just believe people shouldn't throw those they love in the ditch to die alone. Discreetly, you find professional help when you have to. So, yes, I texted Gabby one day. 'Hey, will you check on Gretchen if you get a chance?'"

The more I analyze this situation, the more I realize it took a lot of guts for him to execute a plan and still try to honor my ridiculous wishes. So, now I am standing in Mia's shoes, reliving the Mardi Gras party. And the moment Mia glared at me from the bathroom floor in her worst state of mind. *"I'm not worth saving, Red. Why didn't you let me die? You're a narc."* But I'd pleaded with Mia, "I only want to help you, Mia. One day, I hope you understand and forgive me."

Our stories might be slightly different, but they collide.

Over the holiday season, I thought I could color my way out of every situation with patterns and designs. Still, I didn't outrun the con man. Finally, the jealousy and guilt caught up to me. Hayden listened and was vigilant and worried. And thankfully, with Hayden's sneaky ways, Gabby cracked the code. Even though Hayden acted in a way I detested initially, I wanted to apologize.

I'll make you proud someday.

When Dad said, "Gabby gets grief," I didn't pay enough attention. But she just had to go and gift me some Color Street nails. So, now, I have to get "nail appointments" with Dr. Han (yes, pun intended). It's more than a bit of Happenstance, but Dad's *girlfriend*, Gabby, wants to be my friend. Throw a few sweeties, Poco the dog, hair flips, and edginess in, and she's a Lisa 2.0.

Like you, Mom, Gabby loves animals. I know I've talked about Gabby's Boston Terrier, Poco, matching clothes, and looney dog-related gadgets. You actually applied for her first G. Santos G. grant before you died. What are the chances? Maybe Dad fell for Gabby based on her charitable heart? The more I learn about her, the more tolerable I find her. Even my teeth don't grind at the word sweetie anymore. In fact, I owe her a thank you for listening to me, Mom. I want to give her a gift, but I'm at a loss.

At first, I rolled my eyes when Dad made me rehash everything. "GG, please come to me with anything. I'm your dad. I hate that you were hurting. You wore work gloves or winter mittens so often I overlooked the problem. Again. I feel like I failed you. We can find solutions together." He hugged me tightly, then pulled away, studying my puffy, red-tipped cuticles. "Gab said you wanted to know something about your mom."

Gab, I thought with a Happenstance ew, but then I quickly let it go. "Yeah, can you show me some pictures of Mom?" I asked, choking up. "Because it's hard to remember her hands." I slid my hands off the table, hiding them. But Dad reached for them, lightly cupping his hands over mine.

"What else, GG?" he asked, his kind eyes shining behind his black Clark Kent glasses. We sat face-to-face while he wore those Superman sleep pants I ordered during my Valentine's Day spree.

"How did Mom like to do her nails? Did she have a favorite color she wore?" Now sobbing, I blubbered, "Oh my God, I feel like a stupid little girl. Kids at school talked about going to salons all the time, Dad. But I never got to go. Gabby's gift made me want to experience those things with Mom. I felt guilty. Everything just felt so right and so wrong. I'd put the nails on. Think of Mom and scrub them off. I'm sorry I took my anger out on Gabby, but I didn't know how to cope."

Dad grabbed me into another hug. "GG, I'm so sorry. You were only six years old. Sometimes I forget I need to share more details I might not think to talk about. But, Gretchen, you're not stupid. You have a right to know your mom. And I know that Gabby's understanding." Dad's chin wobbled some. "Please try to experience those things that can bring you joy. I'll do my best to help you."

I nodded.

Dad used his thumb to wipe away the tears streaming down my face.

"I'm so ashamed that I can't get my life together," I said, stuttering and catching my breath.

"Gretchen, you're intelligent, hardworking, brave, and you offer so much love to those you let in your life. I know it's hard. But a lot of people go through tough times. You're not alone. Remember how I went through my secretive drinking phase?"

I nodded, thinking of those words. "Be brave." They must've devastated Hayden when followed up with near radio silence on my end.

"Be kind to yourself. I love you. And I'm proud of your willingness to fight for help. And as soon as we're done talking, I'll look for a photo of Mom. Since she worked with animals, she had to keep her nails trimmed, but she liked classic pink and red shades. In daily life, Mom was practical, but she enjoyed getting glamorous. Gwen would have loved those aqua ones you wore. So, when you feel better, wear them with confidence. Mom would've gotten a kick out of the colors, designs, and names. She'd probably tell you to sparkle on."

I giggled, wiping away the final tears.

"So, if there's any question, please come to me, Gabby, Lisa, Dr. Han, Hayden, Gene, or anybody."

"Okay. I will. I have a change of subject. Do you remember that Vietnam veteran, Mr. Carson, from the heroes' ceremony?"

Dad tilted his head. "Sure, I do."

"Well, I'm working on ways to better understand my jealousy. Like Mr. Carson, I make wreaths for the cemetery and put them on Rosie and Mom's graves. Do you think the veterans would allow me to volunteer for one of their wreath-decorating programs, so I could be around senior citizens—like grandparent figures?"

"It would be easy for us to find out."

"If I clock enough hours, I can use it as a practical art credit in volunteer community service if someone will be my independent adviser from school. Maybe Gabby or Mr. Porter since they just have to verify my work."

"That's a great idea and a good match for your creativity. I liked Mr. Carson too. I could relate somewhat to his story of overcoming depression and alcohol. I know I don't often talk about your grandparents. I'm sorry. It's my job to give you more of our family's history. As a son, it's hard sometimes to talk about losing both of my parents. But before I send you on your way, I want to share a little bit of wisdom I used to get from my dad. He taught me a lot in parables. So, this one might guide us. Your grandpa said the author is unknown." Dad swallowed. He stared at me with droopy-dog-eyed intensity. Then, after gazing up at the ceiling as if pulling the words from his memory bank, he shared a ghost of a smile before telling the story.

An old Cherokee told his grandson, "My son, there is a battle between two wolves inside us all. One is Evil. It is anger, jealousy, greed, resentment, inferiority, lies, and ego. The other is Good. It is joy, peace, love, hope, humanity, kindness, empathy, and truth."

The boy thought about it and asked, "Grandfather, which wolf wins?"

The old man quietly replied, "The one you feed."

Chapter Thirty-Four

Dear Ma,

Be brave. I feel like that's all I have ever known. So, in the face of listening to others call me Hayden Queer as Fuck and Hardly Speaks Hayden, I tried to act brave with my shield of silence. For example, my six-year-old self bravely brought cinnamon toast to my sick mother on her deathbed. After you died, maybe I wasn't so brave? I hid in the kitchen pantry, dosing myself with cinnamon—hoping to make a reconnection. And now, I wanted to revert to being a little boy and take my heart back. Eff bravery—standing up to Gretchen with some painful truths might cost us our relationship. Screw it. My heart might be cracked in two, but asking Gabby for help took balls on my part.

I wish I could ask Miss Gretchen if bravery means hiding a broken heart, sweat, torn cuticles, and tears. Screw her dancing dots on the phone that disappear. What's so brave about those? And her unanswered phone calls? Those keep pissing me off too. But I know I did the right thing. But unfortunately, this misunderstanding of the semantics of words got twisted, and we didn't know how to communicate what we needed to help one another.

Ma, I miss her.

After Gretchen said, "Be brave," why did I feel weak? I think it's the not knowing. Because I don't know where we stand. Her three or four-word texts trickled in to tell me she was hurt by my actions. **Gretchen: So, why did you tell on me?** And **Do you have to keep secrets?** Which I understood. Now, she's ghosting me. Maybe she'll forgive me soon. Fingers and toes crossed—be brave. Go for gold, Hayden (he said to himself, sarcastically). And I planned to go for gold.

Grandma mailed Gretchen a present. Yes, here I go again with secrets versus surprises. At this point, Grandma may gain a victory. Since Gretchen doesn't seem to want to "chat" much with me, the US snail mail will have to do. Thank goodness Dr. John owns a large mailbox for his combination house and vet clinic. When Dad and I dropped Gretchen off last night from Branson, I decided the timing for a present would not land well. So, I stuffed the goldenrod envelope bubble mailer measuring approximately 12" by 14" with TO: GRETCHEN GARDENER on the front.

Dad had consoled me. "Buddy, I bet she'll come around. I think it will just take a day or two for her to understand you meant to help her, not tattle on her. That's a lot for her to deal with too. I know her saying 'Be brave' sounded weird. I think she said it, so she didn't have to break up if you want to know my two cents. But I'm old and say things like 'Kumbaya,'" Dad had said in the driveway as soon as we got home from dropping Gretchen off from our trip to Branson. He'd pressed me for what happened. Finally, I broke down, spilling out everything, showing Dad the photo of Sharp. Then, I told him about Mr. Porter getting bullied. And I'd shared the text I had sent Gabby regarding Gretchen, hoping she might get help.

Sometimes fear and bravery blur, as do secrets and surprises.

In the morning, I rolled over to find my phone lost on the floor. It still seemed way too early for Dad to yell up the stairs, "Hayden, you have a visitor." Miss Spicy Boots acted none too pleased when I cradled her to move her from my chest.

Somehow, I threw together an outfit of yesterday's jeans and hoodie, finger-combed my hair, ran to the bathroom, and brushed my teeth.

As I jogged down the stairs, Gretchen met me halfway, trotting up the stairs, clutching Grandma's gift. But she carried something else with her. "I brought a peace offering." She showed me a platter of snickerdoodle cookies. They looked like the ones we'd baked together. "First, let me make a confession," she said, leaning against the wall.

480

"The day we baked these cookies, I almost stole your mother's recipe card because I wanted your life. I liked the idea of a mom who baked. And the story of a grandma who made it possible." A silent tear fell, but Gretchen kept talking.

"I felt lost or disconnected, needing some family history. So, instead of stealing, I took a photo of the recipe," she said, attempting a teary smile. "And Dad and I talked more about my nails stemming from guilt and longing. For so long, my mind has tricked me into thinking negatively. I'm sorry I put you in an awkward situation with Gabby. I should've been the one who asked for help. I know my secretive issues. Thank you for being brave and acting on my behalf. You're the kindest, sexiest, and hopefully, the most forgiving boy—" Gretchen rambled, so I barged in, bravely snagging items from her hand and placing them on the staircase. Afterward, I embraced Gretchen before we tumbled to the steps, giggling. That's where I kissed her senselessly without giving her a chance to speak another word.

When we slipped apart, she reached for the envelope.

"I'm sorry I didn't tell you I called her"—Gretchen held up a hand in protest—"No, I wanted to include you, but I needed to figure out how. I'm new at connecting to a long-distance grandma. That can get pretty overwhelming and interesting," I said, chuckling.

"I know you worked your quiet magic behind the scenes. Sometimes, I worry that no one cares or that I'm unworthy, but then you prove me wrong. Your words about getting people help discreetly and not throwing them in a ditch to die alone have played over in my mind since Friday night."

"Well, it feels like forever since I saw you, and it's only Sunday. So, I'm glad you've forgiven me. But you made me realize my grandma may not be so bad if I got to know her, and you're so right, Gretch."

"Can I show you what she sent me?"

I nodded, putting my arm around her. She opened the envelope. Together, we read over Grandma Suzi's words:

Dear Gretchen,

Hayden tells me so much about you. It's a pleasure hearing that you enjoy baking Rose's cookies. Gene said you've designed beautiful handmade wreaths to take to my daughter's grave. Then he shared the website www. findagrave.com so I could see them. I want to thank you for looking out for my boys and for my daughter. When I saw your pictures, I couldn't believe how much you looked like your lovely mother. She used to come in to pay her insurance bill—that's how we conducted business in Summerfort years ago. We also gave out calendars. So I made you one for the new year. With help from the salespeople, I learned how to include photos.

Sincerely,

Grandma Emerson

We flipped through the months, grinning at the photos. Dad and I sent them to her. Some of our favorites included us at my football, baseball, and basketball practices or games. Or the two of us playing with Miss Spicy Boots. Grandma managed to fit in the silly Rudolph Christmas photo. And then came the fancy attire from the heroes' banquet. In August, she chose a shot of us in a back-to-school look Dad took on the front porch of us after school, arm in arm. Next, she picked a photo of us celebrating my birthday in late September. Gretchen and I held up some #41 football cookies, grinning. At the time, our relationship was very new. Then when we got to October, Gretchen's eyes filled with tears. At first, I only saw the funny Halloween Party photo of us at the Summerfort Grief Center with her dressed as Madonna. Next to her, I tried looking like an eighties Johnny Depp from 21 Jump Street.

Finally, I saw Grandma Suzi's handwritten note in the tiny square. OCTOBER 16, just three days after Gretchen's mom died. **HAPPY BIRTHDAY, GRETCHEN.** Grandma had also drawn balloons. I pressed my forehead to Gretchen's before pulling her in tightly and kissing her.

"So, after I looked at that tiny square, my heart exploded, Hayden. I mattered. She included *me* in the special events. Until now, I've never remembered having a grandparent. No one has ever written my name in celebration on a calendar. After I saw what it said and experienced what it must be like to have a grandparent, I knew I needed to show you."

"Gretchen, you—"

Dad interrupted. "Sorry to barge in on you two. Shortcake, Dr. John wants you to come home. But he said, please don't panic. He's okay. Your Aunt Jolene's fine too."

"I'm glad he clarified that because that's where my mind went, Gene. Do you know what's wrong?" Gretchen squeezed my hand.

Dad shrugged unconvincingly. "Maybe later you can come back over. We can give you a ride. I'll throw your bicycle in the back of the truck."

"Gene, I asked your permission to come over. I cleared it with Dad. Am I in trouble or something?"

"No, I don't think it's that."

GRETCHEN

Chapter Thirty-Five

Dear Mom,
Mid-March

"Thank you for coming to this impromptu gathering. Unfortunately, we each received the rumored phone call earlier explaining spring break has arrived earlier than anticipated for Summerfort due to the COVID-19 shutdown. None of us completely understands everything at this point. However, many businesses and schools will lock down for two weeks to help flatten the curve. Let's hope the virus numbers go down across the nation. We know that we have each other to lean on moving forward." Lisa said, smiling with her hand in her signature stance. "It puts life on hold for some events. The school will be held online. Plans may be canceled, on hold, or up in the air. Life may feel at a standstill for some of us. People you have seen daily may switch to a new format or routine. Let's focus on the positives and gear up to be patient through this virus. Again, we have one another."

Lisa had sat us in the lounge area. And already, my eyes were glued to the white sheet Lisa had tacked to the community room wall. The one with the sectional couches forming a semi-circle. This couch looked like a happy smile or, ironically, a macaroni noodle when the pieces connected. Kids use this area for their activities and playroom. It's convenient because it's near the bathroom and kitchen.

Of course, I plopped down beside Hayden, still in disbelief about our school closing. Before Lisa started talking, Hayden asked, "What do you think about this?"

"I'll miss seeing you at school first thing every morning. But I'm happy I'll not have to deal with Thomas Sharp or look at Lilly's perky boobs in person for a couple of weeks. UGH. I'll still see them on a computer screen."

Hayden kind of snorted. "Good points. Flatten the curve they talk about on the news—I'll miss your curves every morning." Hayden winked at me. "I'll not miss everyone either. But I'll miss my ball practice, just not listening to the guys bully Mr. Porter. I can't believe he's their new target."

"I'm sad for Mr. Porter. I hope the school puts a stop to it. Is it just me, or do you feel a lackluster oddness to the school closure? I feel like there are too many loose ends floating in the universe. Maybe I'm in such shock it hasn't hit me yet. I don't know how to react to a pandemic. *Is this really happening?" Be brave.*

"I know." Hayden shrugged. "We postponed our spring break double date with Miles and Kelsey and our trip to see Jolene. And, Gretch, I wanna dang do-over on the Ferris wheel, and now it's closed."

"Do-over for sure when they reopen." I rested my head on Hayden's shoulder, sad about missing those two opportunities.

My eyes and mind bounced around the room. Finally, I spotted Dad with his arm around Gabby. It reminded me of something. Leaning close to Hayden's ear, I whispered, "I have a strange question for you. Do we know anyone that's adopted from Summerfort High?"

"Maybe Jun?" he answered, raising an eyebrow in confusion. "Why?"

"Gabby had a blank adoption paper accidentally in with the grant papers. I think this shutdown made her pack in a hurry, so she put one in the wrong pile or something. Now, I'm just curious. Maybe Jun wants to know her birth parents? For some, adoption could be like grief—a missing piece, ugh? Wait. I can see that way. Or it's a special gift. I think it takes the most courageous person to offer love to someone else."

"I agree. It's complicated. Ask Gabby or Jun," Hayden said.

"I don't have that level of relationship with Jun at this point," I said, adding, "maybe someday soon."

Hayden brushed my lips. "Besides, Gabby can't give away student secrets."

I shrugged, moving on. "Tell me about driving here."

"Hey, yeah. I wanted to tell you all about that—" Hayden got interrupted.

Looking around the room, I assessed that it would be a couples' event. Dad had brought me tonight. Gabby met us after a late-night school meeting. Hayden practiced driving Gene's truck, and Lisa got to be a backseat driver. I can't wait to hear more details about this adventure. Sadly, Mia's grandmother couldn't make it on short notice. And the Branson schools were having a school-wide meeting about the shutdown, so Miles and Kelsey missed out.

Lisa pointed out the sheet. "Before I unveil why I hauled you here tonight, I want to tell you about a technique known as kintsugi."

Under his breath, Hayden asked, "Kintsugi, not kimchi?"

"Do what?" Gene leaned over, asking.

"You and Lisa had a conversation a few days ago about eating kimchi," Hayden said wide-eyed, shrugging.

Lisa covered her mouth, stifling a laugh. She walked to Hayden, giving him a side-hug. "No, I told your dad about kintsugi."

The room chuckled.

"So, kintsugi is pronounced like Ken Sue Ghee, not kimchi," Lisa continued with a grin, "and it's about taking something broken and mending the seams with a material such as gold. So, I'd like to share an item created using broken pieces from one of the activities Hayden and Gretchen did with others."

Knowing his cue, Gene jumped up, pulling the left side of the covering down, while at the same time, Lisa commanded the right side until the word **LOVE** stood out. This came from our broken plates. When pieced together, they appeared more like polished white marble with swirls of gold.

"It's just like your little song, Gretchen," Hayden said, pulling on the sleeve of my hoodie. His mouth went so wide I saw his dimple and the minor gap in his front tooth. My eyes hopped from Hayden to the **LOVE** and back again as they brimmed with tears. But I also smiled. Another happy-sad grief-filled moment.

Lisa nodded at Hayden's comment as she motioned for us to join her next to her photo and **LOVE** plaque display. After a sweet group hug, Lisa pulled away to speak. "Look. Hidden inside the 'O' of **LOVE** are the words from our very own Gretchen.

Standing alone, feeling broken.
Our lives and dreams were shattered.
So, to the world, we shouted words left unspoken.

And love pieced back together what mattered . . . most."

Lisa choked, "When Gretchen first shared her words with me, they reminded me how much the Summerfort Grief Center operates more as an extended family than a business. Our mission is to help those who come to us when they're shattered and broken. And we do our best to piece lives back together. So, I couldn't have written a better statement."

Everyone clapped again. Lisa waved everyone to stand.

Dad sprang off the couch, headed to me, and hugged me tightly. "I'm so proud of you." My heart pounded with new hope.

In the background, Lisa said, "Let's mingle, eat snacks, and enjoy the other new photos."

Above the LOVE plates, two photos hung. Each was meant as a centerpiece in an eight-by-ten gold frame. Lisa had captured Miles and Hayden jumping midair in a victorious high five from the plate smashing. I liked that Lisa chose to sneak a group photo at the beginning of the Mardi party of everyone wearing their masks, so Mia was included in one. And since the gold framed the picture, it made the colors stand out.

And two other photos were anchored below. Lisa had selected a group shot of the two couples arm in arm in their safety goggles, smiling— Hayden, me, Miles, and Kelsey. In the other photo,

Lisa demonstrated the concept of kintsugi by painting three words on three dishes. Afterward, she smashed the china, piecing them together, and photographed the result. It looked stunning. It read **HEAL, HOPE, BELONG** from top to bottom in the cracked message weaved with gold.

Gene had taken the guys on an architectural tour of the center while Lisa needed to return to her office for a phone call. That left Gabby and me alone. Out of the corner of my eye, I watched Gabby roaming into the Blue Room. If I followed her, maybe I could finally tell her. But did I have the courage to go through with it?

My pulse quickened. I threw my handbag over my shoulder in a crossbody style. Instantly, I found comfort when I squeezed the handle of my purse. "Gabby?"

She turned. "Sweetie, I wanted to look at your favorite room and the photos from the early years." Gabby gestured to the photo that started everything—the lopsided tree of hearts made by six-year-old grieving hearts missing their moms. "It's no wonder you love Lisa." So, why did I feel like Gabby had these unspoken words "more than me" lingering in the room, punching my gut and piercing my heart?

"She's made such a difference in your life," Gabby went on, staring at the walls.

"Gabby, you've helped me so much too. I don't know if I ever said a heartfelt thank you. Some things are so hard to talk about. But you stepped up and filled in when I went through my first period. I felt so awkward and alone. You're all I had that day at school. But I also resented you for it because I wanted my mom."

"Oh, sweetie. I understand." Gabby motioned me to sit on the abstract chairs across from each other.

First, I untangled myself from my crossbody bag, which didn't mix with a cowl neck sweater. Then, a moment later, I regained my composure. "And the same thing happened with the Color Street nails. But I'll work on getting better," I said, puffing out a breath to hold back tears.

"I agree with you, Gretchen. I believe in you. Each of us can be both broken and beautiful pieces."

"Do you remember having the conversation about visualizing grief from different points of view with me? Kind of like the saying about walking a mile in someone else's shoes?"

"Of course."

"Then, I want to gift something to you." I leaned over the arm of the chair, fumbling inside my purse on the floor until I found the envelope. **GABBY** was written in aqua bubble letters and underlined with a scroll design.

Without shaking too much, I handed it to Gabby. She slid the envelope open, reading the title **"Motherless Child**."

"Do you want me to read it aloud or silently?"

"I'll let you decide."

So, Gabby took off reading my words. She stumbled in places, choking up with emotion and getting teary-eyed.

"Motherless Child"
"Why are you all alone, sitting in the dark?"
"Lady, turn off the light. Let me hide.
I'm a motherless child."

"Other children go outside to play and wear
    smiles."
"Lady, I try, but my frown just won't bend.
Turn off the light. Let me hide.
I'm a motherless child."

"Maybe other mothers will let you tuck near
    their side?"
"Lady, I try, but no one likes sharing a mother.
Not a single friend's willing.
Turn off the light. Let me hide.
I'm a motherless child."

"Maybe God or your mother sent someone like
    me?
May I try to shed some comfort, light, or hope
    in your life?"

"Go away, Lady! Let me be! Can't you see my
    heart breaking?

Besides, there's no hope for someone like me.
You can't stop this ache. So, let me cry in peace.
I stopped mattering to a world that doesn't see
>   *me.*
Inside dark spaces, no one hears, and no one sees.
Most of the time, I'm not sure God cares that I'm
>   *aching.*
Now, turn off the light! Let me hide.
I'm a motherless child."

"May I join you in silence?
Or just hold your hand?
When you're ready to talk, I'll gladly listen.
For now, I'll turn off the light.
But I believe I might understand.
Because, *sweetie*, just like you,
I, too, am a motherless child."

"Lady, you can stay. Please, sit by me.
Here, in the dark, will you squeeze my hand tight?
Lady, I know you can't promise me any
>   *guarantees.*
But, still, do you wish to stay and help me?
If so, please, try to answer one big question for
>   *me:*
Am I ever again going to feel all right?"

"I know you're sad.
As a motherless child, you have every right to
>   be.

Grief is complicated with all those ups and
    downs.
Sometimes the feeling is so scary fast.
It's loopy, as if going backward or dangling
    upside down.
It's like being on a rollercoaster journey,
    spinning around.
Give yourself time. Again, you will believe—
in yourself—in your willingness to live life.
And, even in this thing called the 'new normal'
    life.
One day, you'll think you're just a heartbeat
    away
from getting out a great big ole breath.
You will see it's inside the same
spaces as your same old life.
And, again, you'll look around,
starting to feel less empty and numb.
You might even say:

Oh, I get it.
I'm still breathing and living inside my own life.
Only now, without my mom,
everything seems a tad different.
I guess I'm learning healthy new ways to cope.
I'm getting a different set of established routines.
Unexpected things begin falling into place.
I'm starting to seem okay.
Somehow, I'm getting by from day to day.

Even good days begin adding up and up.
My 'new normal' works, bringing some hope.

A lot of darkness begins to disappear.
And your heart adjusts as you flip on *your* light
    from within.
Life takes on feelings a bit brand-new.
Maybe you're even ready to join others
    grieving like you.
Sharing your story may encourage someone
    who's motherless too.

Your once-broken heart flutters and
    pirouettes—
As if dancing a dance on the mend.
Perhaps a hand clutches over your chest.
As you feel changes happening inside of you.
The fading frown upon your face
performs a bit of tug and twitch.
In the brighter light, you take a peek.
More and more, you look, and you look.
You ask yourself what's all tangled up
among a hint of hope?

Go ahead, don't give up.
Believe in what you see.
Appearing once and then again.
Look!
What's spreading across your face?
What does that little thing seem to be?

Perhaps it's still just a little mixed up?
Maybe on the verge or on the mend?
Wanting, willing, waiting to be freed—
Ready to curve right up and bend.

"To quote you—what-the-flippity-do-da have you done to me, Gretchen?" Gabby asked, dabbing at her eyes.

We smiled.

She stood up and reached for me in a quick side-hug. It reminded me so much of the hugs Lisa gave Hayden that I cracked up. "Thank you. Thank you so much. That's the kindest gift."

"You're welcome." I managed a grin, but my emotions were all over the place. My mouth wanted to do that happy, sad, ugly twitch. "I'm glad you like it."

We heard the guys socializing in the kitchen, so Gabby left to join them. For a minute, I stood alone in the Blue Room, absorbing years of memories. Uncertainty lies ahead. But today, the calendar outwitted me in unexpected ways. Before tonight an empty box on the calendar glared back at me. But now, a golden heart commemorated the date. Lisa taught me that sometimes people make things happen under pressure, even if they must go against the calendar to juggle or bend time. An event may not be exactly what you planned. But if you show up for the people you care about, even with your heart broken, just let the golden parts shine the most—before you know it—others will join in noticing the best details.

I thought I needed another minute alone to reflect on everything happening in the world before joining everyone. So, I took a stroll down the back hallway near Lisa's office when I heard voices that stopped me.

"Lisa, let's dance. They're playing our song." Gene's phone clunked to the desktop as he must've pushed play. Then I assumed I listened to shuffling feet.

"Ah, Gene, will you ever forgive yourself for saying all I'd do here is make macaroni necklaces and sing 'Kumbaya'?"

Gene hummed, quietly singing out "Kumbaya," which we knew represented "I love you, Lisa." He'd admitted as much to Hayden. This old spiritual song often gets a cheesy rap. But, after paying attention to two people who constructed an eight-year love story around the lyrics, my heart shifted. It delivered goosebumps down my arm. And what might be described as an electrical charge filled my soul.

As the lyrics "someone's crying Lord" played, my cheeks grew wet. Down the hall, Hayden veered toward me. I held a finger over my lips for him to sneak through our make-out hallway quietly. After he reached me, he kissed my temple. We slid undetected down the wall to the floor. Hayden pressed me to his chest.

He whispered, "Historians believed 'Kumbaya' stood for 'O, Lord come by here.'"

His heart beat next to my body as he spoke, deliberate and enduring, thumping in time with the music. Instead of hiding my hands, still mending, I laced my fingers with his as a declaration of love and hope.

"Someone's praying Lord, Kumbaya" lulled in the background. Hayden lifted my hand until his lips grazed the tips of my fingers. His eyes greeted mine. Then he devoured me with smiling kisses. Who knew "Kumbaya" welcomed neck and ear nibbling too? This song offered sizzling prayer elements. "Kumbaya" earned a five-star review initially, but it lacked staying power. It's because the hymn drifted away too soon. So, I assigned it four stars. Until I reversed my decision, giving back the five stars.

But in the end, Gene broke the silence in the office with "I love you, Lisa. I thought it was finally time you should know."

"Aww, Kumbaya, dumbass, I love you too."

My hands covered my mouth in disbelief, holding in excited laughter. But I had tears falling down my face. See, five stars.

Hayden pointed to the nameplate "Lisa Marks" before mouthing, "By the way, in a stupid argument, I accidentally slipped and almost called her Mom while driving on the way over here today."

WTFDD? I stayed silent, but my breathing quickened as one hand fell over my heart. Inside,

I shouted, screamed, and danced. I'd have been much too loud if I had spoken. My hand kept wanting to beat the floor. So, I grabbed Hayden's wrist, squeezing. I couldn't wait to hear his story. And soon.

Hayden delivered a crooked grin, pointing over his shoulder, plotting our getaway. He helped me to my feet. Once on our feet, he whispered, "I finally get to tell you another special secret. Ariana is pregnant, and I'm going to be an uncle."

As quietly as possible, I gasped before we tiptoed out of range, so I could hug Hayden in celebration. He lifted and spun me in circles at the end of the hall. It felt right to acknowledge and celebrate all these love stories with my best friend. Because our own love story also started here.

We found Dad and Gabby browsing Lisa's photography in the classrooms.

While we visited, I reflected on the history of the Summerfort Grief Center, a repurposed church on the outskirts of town. It's my second home because the builder and owner filled it with love. Then they even fell in love. And I got a front-row seat to watch it all. Lisa's parents would be proud. As part of her grieving family, I'm proud. My roots are buried deep at Summerfort Grief Center. So, perhaps I should begin seeing myself as a founding member. Because when I widened my acceptance of my painted family tree on the walls of this place, my jealousy lessened—it opened my heart and closed more of the pain. Our lives unfolded on the walls. It was whispered in the hallways or rooms. And written in the pages of journals.

Hayden may have mistaken kintsugi for "eating kimchi." Still, I thought about kintsugi as the moments with people who wanted to help me piece myself together. They allowed me to learn. Or to grow from the tarnishing jealous loser I presumed myself to be. They refined me. And with their help, I discovered I even carried inside myself fragments of gold. I had written it once myself. Now, I could believe its truth. Love pieced back together what mattered most.

Grief changed our universe. Individually, sorrow rippled into our lives with far-reaching effects. Fears seeped in. Hearts shattered. In time, beyond some of the grief, our hearts found enough rhythm to dance. And I realized we danced and spoke our shared secrets aloud, believing in the power of love. Together we tackled fears and jealousy until we cheered for one another with the courage to forgive and win. In the end, love remained the only ingredient capable of healing us.

At dusk, we agreed to gather outside. The mid-March air awakened to the coming spring. Yet a hint of wind nipped at my bare hands until Hayden circled me. Arms looped, anchoring me. More links worked together like tree roots until we were one. As a group, we posed near the marquee sign. My memories unfolded like upcoming chapters in *Love at the Center of Grief*, the book we continually work to create. After all, as a founding member of the center, I'm slowly building history with roots buried so deeply. Such an unexpected event like this would never fit inside a calendar box.

Guilty, we stood. Some days we still tried to outcon the con man. And, as a group, we might always be faulty. Maybe it's because we sometimes loved too much in the face of our losses. But it's because, after death, we learn even more about the value of life, friendship, and love. We know there is no chance to get back what's lost, but we can love the similar qualities that live on within us.

I looked around at the smiles in plain sight. Before me, the big, bold, black-and-white letters were illuminated as a spotlight holding a lot of truths. I mattered, standing on the renovated church steps—a fact never kept secret. Still, after all these years, it seized my heart by surprise. Once broken, I felt more whole.

No matter what we faced moving ahead, I remembered I had family to lean on. A family to help me create the pages of my life. Finally, I believe I found an answer. We learned most when we stepped inside each other's shoes until we saw reflections of ourselves. Every jagged edge of grief created us. Elements so imperfectly perfect they shined like gold once polished. Beyond the center of grief, I tucked this recipe inside my heart and carried it home:

Welcome to the Summerfort Grief Center
A Place to Heal
A Place to Hope
A Place to Belong

About the Book

*C*AN MEMORIES HOLD THE key to unlocking hearts and finding uncommon heroes?

After losing their mothers at six, Gretchen Gardener and Hayden Tucker grew up to find *Love at the Center of Grief.*

Welcome back to Summerfort, Missouri, where the holiday season is underway. Gretchen and Hayden share something in common with their widowed dads—the dating scene. But did their dads have to choose the counselors from school and the grief center?

Can this small town on the outskirts of Branson deal with this much romance in the midst of grief?

Gretchen writes Dear Mom entries in her grief journal. She tells her mom she's dealing well with her OCD. But is she keeping secrets too deep to tell anyone—even her loving boyfriend, Hayden? Gretchen obsessively compares herself to others while reliving hurts. The lovingly creative and overthinking Gretchen cannot always get out of her own head. Gretchen's on a collision course with jealousy, desiring what others take for granted. Can she find the recipe she needs to fight against envy? Or will she risk cutting off everyone she loves?

Inside his grief journal, Hayden writes his mom. He hopes to rebuild the broken family bonds, removing fear and guilt. And he's concerned his Summerfort Grief Center world might stumble into his home life since his dad now dates the founder. Hayden also wishes to understand the meaning between a secret and a surprise since his family might be keeping things from him. Will he jump to conclusions, unraveling family secrets and memories? And if secrets involve Gretchen, when is he obligated to tell?

Beyond the Center of Grief offers an unapologetic perspective of grief, complete with every emotion. No exact recipe exists to fix grief, but some ingredients are healthier coping skills than others. In *Beyond the Center of Grief*, inspiration emerges from unlikely characters, narrated by Gretchen and Hayden with empathy and humor. It delivers a message of friendship, forgiveness, family, and fun. Ultimately, it's taking a walk with another through grief to find hope.

Beyond the Center of Grief will appeal to fans of Julie Buxbaum's *Hope and Other Punchlines*, Val Emmich's *Dear Evan Hansen*, and Kathleen Glasgow. It's like a teen version of *This is Us*.

About the Author

*C*INDY MCINTYRE IS THE IPPY-award-winning author of *Love at the Center of Grief*, as well as *Eulogies Unspoken: Stories of Worth* and *Caring for Dad: With Love and Tomatoes*. She taught in at-risk education for twenty-five years. After the loss of her parents, Miss McIntyre set out assisting others, volunteering as a group facilitator at the Lost and Found Grief Center. In addition, she serves as Secretary for the Ozarks Writers League. She is originally from Earlville, Illinois, but now calls Missouri home.

Acknowledgments

RITING A BOOK WOULD not be possible without the support of several family members, friends, and former coworkers. Thanks to my siblings—John Jay, Theresa, and Sandi. I also want to thank my numerous cousins, nieces, and nephews in Illinois and Kentucky who support me from afar.

Mom: I love and miss you every day. You are the reason I write. I wish I could celebrate life more often without you. Because I still need a daily phone call, a mother's prayer, and a hug. So, I will use my words instead and hope they inspire others.

Dad: I love and miss you every day. Thank you for trusting me to care for you. You'd be proud to know I volunteer in a caregiving group. God does work in crazy ways. For a while, I didn't feel like I had any purpose. Now, I get to share little tidbits about you. Helping others helps me to smile.

Lost & Found: For providing a place that allows memories to be created. I have watched people laugh as much as I have watched them cry. I am so inspired by every story.

Shirley Rash: Thank you for standing by a newcomer to the writing world. You've helped me take every character to the depth they deserve. You've made my fictional world come alive.

HEC Students: I'd like to shout out to students who lost their mothers and read small sections for me. I appreciate the tiny elements of "Hayden" they brought to light. Aaron and Dale, thank you for inspiring me.

Angie Smith-Twenter: We've been friends for so long. Plus, you have such a possum-loving heart. Because I bought Color Street nails from you and a storyline was born, you had to be acknowledged.

Mattie Pollreisz: My sweet former student, I enjoyed our conversations about your grandmother. We chatted about recipes and memories. Your grandmother's memory inspired a whole chapter in my book.

Stephanie Releford: Thank you for all your support with the Parentless Podcast shoutouts. You are creating a whole grief community for so many.

Acknowledgments

Lerose Flowers-Morales: We bonded because of grief. But I love that friendship can be the result of a loss. Thank you so much for your support.

Jim Tucker: Thanks for loving me. I appreciate you sharing your Grandma Eula. Unfortunately, like Gretchen, I lack grandparents. And Eula wrote my name on her calendar. So, mark your calendar for a bit of Happenstance and #Geneissketchy. May the 4th be with you always.

Author's Note:

*I*T TOOK ME LONGER to finish this novel than I had hoped. At times, I wanted to give up. But I fought my way back. And I will continue to write the Summerfort Grief Series, as Hayden and Gretchen have so much more to tell! Oh, Dear Mom. . . .

Please don't hesitate to reach out to someone if you are suffering through grief. The new mental health crisis hotline: Dial or Text 988.

Or consider finding ways to honor your loved one. How might you get involved? If you can't afford to give money, can you donate time? Did they like animals? Do you have a local food bank? How about a veteran's program? Or a local nursing home or hospital?

Also, who is the hero of your grief?

I would also love to hear your stories.

Missouri Author Cindy McIntyre
PO BOX 356
Richland, MO, 65556.

Unsung
You are an unsung hero
Of someone's life,
Finish your story for them.
Don't give up.

~Helen Iouna